ROYAL COCONUT BEACH
LUNCH CLUB

DIANE BERGNER

ROYAL COCONUT BEACH
LUNCH CLUB

MERIDIAN EDITIONS

MERIDIAN | EDITIONS

ISBN: 978-1-959170-03-7 Paperback
ISBN: 978-1-959170-04-4 eBook

Cover and book design by John Lotte
Author photo by CAPEHART

Manufactured in the U.S.A.

With gratitude to my family for the riches of the heart

you provide each day

ROYAL COCONUT BEACH
LUNCH CLUB

Chapter 1

BELOW THE DECK

THREE MONTHS INTO A NEW CAREER, and here I was aboard one of the most opulent yachts in the world. It was January, and the Royal Coconut Beach social season was in full swing. Docked at the end of the pier, the Lady Sweet Savannah IV towered over all the other vessels. Illuminated by underwater and deck lighting, the buoyant palace seemed to float above the water. Tangerine hues from the sunlight only added to its splendor—and something that happened below deck made it a night to remember.

I didn't tell my husband, Mark, about it until Saturday, when I finally had his undivided attention. We were enjoying a peaceful afternoon in our backyard.

"About the party the other night on Savannah's yacht. I thought I was dreaming," I said, as Mark reclined on a chaise lounge, sipping iced tea. His dark wavy hair had a bit of gray around his temples which added to his distinguished appearance, along with fine lines around his warm brown eyes.

"Another good story? They seem to be getting better and better," he said.

"Yes, they do. Look at the clear periwinkle sky. And the billowy clouds; they look like cotton candy." I pointed to the palm trees swaying in the breeze. "We're lucky to live here. South Florida is so under-rated."

"The story, please." Mark reached over and nudged my arm.

"Okay. So Savannah saw me standing around and, in her sweet drawl told me, 'Julia, dear. Before I pitch a hissy-fit, would you be a sweetheart and go to the galley below the deck? The servers are slow as molasses, and we need more caviar and champagne passed. They're about as useful as a screen door on a submarine. Light a fire under them, please.' It wasn't so much a question as an order." Mark laughed at my awful imitation of the Southern matriarch.

"I mean, where was her crew? Wasn't that their job?" I added.

"Calm down. This falls under 'other duties as assigned'." His fingers made quotation marks, referencing all the extraneous assignments that fell under the umbrella of my new job as Fundraising Coordinator at the Addison Performing Arts Center.

"Yes, but she made me feel like I was the hired help. I wasn't really offended, though, since she was oozing charm."

"Go on." He gestured with his iced tea.

"Well, I managed to find a narrow staircase leading downward, even with my poor sense of direction."

"That's for sure." Mark rolled his eyes upward.

"No expense was spared upstairs, but the downstairs was unfinished and poorly lit. The doors were all locked until I made my way to the end of the corridor, where I heard soft music playing from the last room. Since the door was slightly ajar, I opened it slowly, thinking it was the galley."

"Yes?"

I squared my shoulders and took a deep breath. "There they were!"

"Who?" Mark asked, sitting up straight in his lounger.

"Chrissy was stark naked on a bed—unless you count several strands of diamonds draped around her neck. Chrissy. My b-o-s-s."

Mark shot up from his chaise, swinging his legs around and planting them firmly on the pavers. His mouth gaped open, as he stared at me.

"Chrissy's long hair was spread out on the silk sheets— I think they looked burgundy, what with the candles. She was spread-eagled, and not just any eagle. Full Kama Sutra position, long legs high in the air, knees slightly bent."

Mark's face had a blank expression, but he motioned for me to continue.

"The man was kneeling between her legs, holding onto her ankles as he had his way with her. And get this: her hands were tied above her head with an orange Hermes tie."

"Are you serious?"

"Yes. Definitely Hermes."

"Very funny, Jools," he said, twirling his finger by his temple. "I have to admit, this tops them all."

I'd only been working at the Addison Center a few months, but had already regaled him with a few choice tales. "Here's the thing, though. It was hard to see who Chrissy was with, because all I could see was his back. But then he turned his head. It was Chandler, Georgina's husband of at least fifty years! You know, the past chairman of Addison's board. He heads the development committee now. Never mind her spread legs; think about the age spread. Twenty-five years at least!"

Mark took a gulp of his tea. "Well, thank god for Viagra. Did they see you?"

"I'm pretty sure they didn't. They were too busy."

"Sounds like it."

"One more thing," I added.

"There's more?" Mark lips formed a sexy half-smile.

"The song that was playing was 'Reasons' by Earth, Wind and Fire." Not being able to carry a tune didn't stop me from belting out some lyrics. Mark chimed in on the chorus.

"Okay, enough with the seventies," I said. "Do you think they're in love? Or is it just one big sex-fest? And for how long?"

"All night?" Mark asked, cocking an eyebrow.

I frowned. "Not how long were they going at it! How long has this been going on?"

"I have no idea, but did you ever find the head server?"

"All you can do is crack jokes, when I've been traumatized."

"Okay, calm down. So a rich, older, successful married man is having a fling with a younger, very pretty woman who happens to be your boss. It's probably Chandler's last hoorah. He's around 75, right?"

"Yup."

"It has to be a thrill for him. You keep telling me what an enigma Chrissy has been since day one."

I thought about how Chrissy passed by me in the hall several times this week and ignored me when I said hello. I was paranoid I'd done something wrong. "She is. When she's around donors, she knows how to act charming. Everyone's enamored with her. But she's so patronizing to me. On top of that, she makes me feel like I'm incompetent."

"Don't worry about Chrissy. Just ignore her." He put his iced tea on the table.

"You're right. Despite her, I'm really happy. I feel like I'm doing something meaningful, raising money for the arts."

"Chrissy and Chandler were just having a good time. It's probably a passing fling." He waved his hand dismissively. "Maybe his wife Georgina knows, and looks the other way."

"You sure perked up when I told you about it," I said.

"Hey, it's good to know there's something to look forward to in life." He winked.

I gave his shoulder a playful shove. "Ha, ha. Don't worry, you have a long way to go." I thought for a minute. "I guess I should keep this to myself, right?"

"Duh. Of course, let it go. Or, as your friend Savannah might say 'Go rest the mule'."

"For the record, she isn't my friend. I happened to be on her yacht because of my job."

"That's true." Mark reclined in the lounger, and shut his eyes.

"I'm going to make dinner. Thanks for listening." I stood and bent to kiss the top of his head.

It was a relief to get the story off my chest, since Mark had been out of town earlier that week. Once inside the house, the air conditioning was refreshing. I took a deep breath and exhaled slowly, looking around at the open floor plan. The house was a bargain when we moved from New York City to West Coconut Beach five years ago. Mark was a corporate lawyer specializing in mergers and acquisitions. His partners had charged him with managing a satellite office in Royal Coconut Beach, and we agreed it was a great opportunity. Our home's large windows allowed ample sun to stream in, and hardwood flooring flowed throughout the first floor. Compared to our small viewless apartment in New York, it felt like a mansion.

As I took the chicken and mushrooms out of the refrigerator and began to prepare dinner, my mind drifted to when Mark and I first met. He was in my dorm at Dartmouth, and was visiting some girls down the hall. I instantly judged his maturity level from his tee-shirt—*How About a Nice St. Pauli Girl*—and assumed he was just a player. From the flirty way he told me he loved my tennis shorts, I knew he was checking me out. He was much taller than me, and had dark hair and sparkling eyes, sported a glowing tan, and possessed a driving energy that was contagious. Even "Wild," his last name, had a certain dangerous allure.

Despite my initial impression, we became good friends when I realized that the body came with a brain. Our relationship blossomed into much more later on. Since we'd been friends first, lust was never at the forefront. Needless to say, we'd never had forbidden sex, much less on a yacht.

Mark was a few years ahead of me in college. He always knew he wanted to be a lawyer, and his self-assurance was a big part of my attraction to him. He majored in foreign languages, and then headed to NYU Law School right after Dartmouth. By his third year, he was elected Editor-in-Chief of its Law Review. I was captivated by his sharp mind, quick wit, self-confidence, and perhaps most of all, his unwavering attentiveness to me.

Back in college, we went out for dinner to celebrate Mark's birthday. He caught me eyeing his plate, and reached over to switch our entrees.

"You don't need to do that," I protested. "Besides, it's *your* birthday. You should eat what *you* want."

He leaned forward. "What I want is for *you* to be happy. Your happiness matters more than anything else."

His words sent shivers down my spine, since he wasn't usually that effusive. It made me feel safe and whole. Later that night, in the middle of our lovemaking, he gently whispered that he wanted to be with me forever. Seduced by his words, along with the tender kisses he planted on my neck, I knew I wanted the same thing.

I sorely missed him when he graduated, and looked forward to weekends and holidays together. Over the summer, when I worked in New York City mainly to be near Mark, we had our first serious discussion about our future. I was thinking about law school, or possibly graduate school.

We were sitting on a Central Park bench on a perfect summer day, wearing shorts and sneakers, after walking several miles.

"There's so much you can do with a law degree," Mark said. "You're smart and driven; it'll take you places. Trust me."

"What if I don't like law school?" I asked, not convinced that I should go. Facing graduation, pressure was mounting to decide on a career path.

"No one likes law school. Besides, I want you close by me. I'm sure you'll get into NYU." He reached into his pocket and pulled out a sparkling engagement ring. "I want us to be together. Marry me."

His authoritative tone sent shivers down my spine. It felt great to be with someone who knew exactly what he wanted—and that included me. I put my hand out, and he placed the ring on my finger. Ecstatic, I wrapped my arms around him. I felt secure, enveloped in his warm embrace. Bound by love, the idea of a future together with Mark immediately outweighed any other plans I was considering.

We lived together in his tiny bachelor apartment while I attended law school. Afterwards, we married and I went to work at a law firm in the city, specializing in trusts and estates; the least confrontational practice area.

Jolted out of my reverie when the boiling water overflowed, I wiped it up and added the penne. I was looking forward to the evening, just the two of us. I made a mental note to have lots of candlelight later. I'd been focused on my new position and trying to prove myself at work. As usual, Mark was intent on finishing negotiations for a client. We were equally busy, and both of us worked long hours, so it was great to finally have a relaxed evening to ourselves. There was a chilled bottle of Sancerre; a delicious dinner of Chicken Marsala with whole-wheat pasta; and glowing candles all around to set the mood.

Later that night, I rummaged through my pajama drawer as it overflowed with tee-shirts and boxer shorts, and snatched up the sexy white silk negligee buried at the bottom. I slipped into it, and noticed how the cool smooth fabric draped my bare skin, suggestively outlining my figure. I lit the unused lavender candle on my night table, inhaling its sweet, intoxicating scent. Mark looked up for a second and went right back to his book. *Couldn't he have at least said something about how I look?* Regardless, I slithered into bed, and snuggled against his warm body.

Our love-making was filled with fervor and excitement; much more satisfying than the usual status quo. After we cuddled for a while, Mark fell asleep. Seeing Chrissy and Chandler must have stirred my desire for more passion, which made me feel slightly guilty. I should be more grateful for all that Mark and I did have. I reassured myself that craving more intimacy in my twenty-two-year old marriage was completely normal. It wasn't as if I was thinking of having an illicit affair.

Tonight was a good start toward a second honeymoon. Not only in the bedroom, but perhaps in other dimensions of our relationship. I drifted off to sleep.

The next morning we lingered in bed, a welcome change from our rushed routine. I stayed beneath the fluffy duvet a while longer, grateful that it was Sunday and I had no work obligations. But the rest of the day, as I went about my chores, I couldn't stop thinking about what I'd witnessed on Savannah's yacht, and all that had transpired in the past months—beginning when I accepted a position at the Addison Center.

Chapter 2

SECOND ACT

"YOU JUST LANDED A JOB a million women would die for!" Nina shouted into the phone. "You have to put your wardrobe in order. You'll need cocktail dresses, gowns, everyday outfits. Clothes for dining with the society ladies who lunch. Designer shoes, like those Jimmy Choos Mark bought you."

I swiveled my desk chair to face the window. "Calm down," I said. "It's not like I've joined a Royal Coconut Beach country club. I won't be catapulted into a glamorous social scene, not that I'd want that anyway. I'm simply switching careers. For the first time ever, I'm relying on gut instinct. I based this move on a leap of faith."

"I'm surprised, since you over-analyze everything. But it's great news. I couldn't be happier for you. I'm coming down now to give you a hug," Nina said.

I hung up and gazed out the window, at the stunning panorama of the inland waterway and bridge that led to Royal Coconut Beach, the barrier island two hours north of Miami, on Florida's east coast. Aside from my swanky view, I wouldn't miss much else at Reid, Bennett except Nina, but I felt sure that our friendship wouldn't wane.

A fierce attorney, Nina had risen through the firm's ranks to head its matrimonial and family law practice. Her reputation as a rainmaker allowed her entry into the all-boys club of senior partners. She dated sporadically, but claimed she enjoyed being single, devoting herself to her practice. Nina was also my only close friend at the firm—which was why I needed to share the news with her before the company-wide email landed in her in-box.

A few minutes later, she stood in the doorway of my office in her dark gray suit. At six feet, her head almost hit the top of the door frame. I stood up and we embraced.

"Wow, the Addison Center!" Nina said. "It's the jewel of this town. I guess all of your volunteering there really paid off."

"I just wanted to try something different while I was studying for the Florida bar after we moved here. I got lucky with this offer."

"Lucky? Don't underestimate yourself," Nina said. "Luck is for those types who have good things magically fall in their laps. For the rest of us, it's about working hard. So when a rare chance converges with luck—voila!" She snapped her fingers. "Your whole career trajectory changes."

I laughed at her dramatics. "I guess. But I'll be starting all over again."

"Stop. It's a great move for you," Nina said, cutting me off.

"You really think so?"

"Yes, I do," Nina said. "I always tell you the truth. You'd do the same for me. It sounds like a perfect opportunity."

I smiled. "I'm so lucky I was assigned to you as my mentor when I first joined the firm."

"It was meant to be. Since you just told me your plans, I'll tell you mine. I'm also thinking about my next move, what with all the infighting between partners and morale so low. Although I love what I do, so I won't be switching careers."

I was glad to hear that Nina was considering other options, given the firm's recent turmoil. It also further validated my own decision. "That's exciting, Nina. I'm so happy for you."

"We'll see how it goes. In the meantime, let's talk about your new career. Addison is magnificent," Nina said. "The theater is stunning; I took my mom to hear Paul Anka and Tony Bennett there. I bet you'll get to see all the great shows and meet the stars."

"Um . . . maybe." This was the furthest thing from my mind. Excited about the professional opportunity, yes; starstruck, no.

"I took my nieces to the Nutcracker there. Real snow was coming down on the stage. You'd better invite me," Nina said.

Did she say *real* snow? Lawyers had a habit of stretching the truth.

"I will," I said, assuming that was an option.

"We'll have to have lunch and celebrate. Speaking of, don't forget our plans to start a Prosecco lunch club. It'll have to wait, now that you're leaving, but let's do it when you get settled."

"It feels like yesterday that we first talked about launching the club. We were commiserating about the lack of camaraderie."

"I remember. Anyway, back to the chain gang. My next client's going through a bitter divorce."

"Thanks again for listening," I said.

"Of course. You go, girl!" We high-fived, which turned into a hug before she headed back upstairs.

It was just sinking in that I was actually leaving the firm, and giving up law. Telling Nina had made it real for me. I leaned my head back against my chair and soaked in the moment.

When the firm emailed the announcement about my resignation, statements like "I didn't know you had an arts background" (I don't), and "Will you be able to get me tickets?" (Don't count on it) followed me through the halls. But a comment from one of the senior partners won the prize.

"So, now you'll be hobknobbing with the rich and famous," he said with a smirk as he passed me in the corridor. Suddenly he pivoted on his wingtip shoes and shouted, "Don't turn into one of them!"

His comment rubbed me the wrong way, and I told Mark about it while we were on the couch watching television that evening. A few buttons on his form-fitting gray Henley shirt were opened, making him look sexy.

"He made me feel as if I was a shallow wannabe, just because I'm going to be raising money for Addison. He acted like I'm going to turn into some kind of poser. Which I'm not." I grabbed the remote by his leg and turned the volume down.

"C'mon, he was just messing with you. He's probably

jealous. Working at Addison sounds like fun, compared to legal drudgery."

"I guess I'm just a little nervous."

"Don't worry, you'll be terrific. Besides, you've had loads of experience dealing with high-society types." He took a sip of iced tea.

"I sure have. Wingate's campus was good training." Located in Porter Valley, an affluent suburb half an hour from New York City, my dad had been Wingate Academy's headmaster, and my mom taught math there. Thanks to their livelihood, their only child got to attend a high-caliber prep school for free. But my mother always reminded me that it didn't make a lick of difference whether you were raised in a barn, or an impeccably decorated estate. "It's what goes on inside those walls that's important," she'd cautioned me.

Considering that our small cottage was the most popular stomping-ground, she made a good point. Even as a kid, I was aware that my easygoing, liberal folks were a dream compared to my friends' uptight, mostly-absent parents who were caught up in their frenzied, materialistic lives. Thinking about all this made me miss my parents; both had passed away several years ago.

"Hello, are you there?" Mark said, waving his glass in front of my face.

"Sorry, I was thinking about Wingate, and my parents. I suppose that's why that partner's comment irritated me. Why would I *ever* want to turn into one of *them?*" I shrugged my shoulders. "Anyway, do you think 'Fundraising Coordinator' sounds like a demotion compared to 'Attorney-at-Law'?"

He casually raked his hands through his tousled hair. "Since when do titles mean anything? I'm sure you'll enjoy this new job; that's what matters, not a dumb title. We've already discussed this, and your pay cut, and I don't care; I just want you to be happy. You'll be good at it, too."

"Thanks for putting things in perspective. I'm going to get ready for bed." I kissed him on the cheek as he grabbed the remote, switched the channel and raised the volume.

Mark always was confident of his professional decisions. He had nimbly climbed the law firm ladder years ago, while I'd yanked myself off the firm's partnership track. I had yet to tap my full potential, but making it to partner didn't interest me. I didn't share Mark's passion for law.

Growing up on a preparatory school campus, I enjoyed being around kids. I always thought we'd have them. Try as we might, it wasn't meant to be. As the years passed, being at the heart of each other's lives, and work that was satisfying felt like enough.

The opportunity at the Addison Center came at a good time, giving me the perfect motivation to get cracking on a new career—one that was filled with possibilities.

Absorbed in my thoughts, I finished washing up and looked at my reflection in the mirror. I was still blessed with a youthful face and shiny wavy brown hair, despite the couple of gray strands that I hid by parting my hair differently. Expression lines around my lips and mouth were barely visible; crow's feet that formed near the corners of my eyes added a touch of personality to my face. I was ready to embrace a second act.

Chapter 3

BACKSTAGE PASS

"I'M SO THRILLED YOU'RE ON BOARD," Poppy Adams had said, flashing a mega-watt smile when she met me at the entrance on my first day. The summer humidity lingered, typical for October in Florida, and it felt good to be in the air-conditioned lobby.

"Great to see you again," I said, shaking Poppy's hand. I hoped she didn't notice that my palm was sweaty from being nervous. I had chatted with her in that area when I interviewed with Chrissy Hathaway, executive vice president of Development at the Addison Center. Poppy was the event coordinator and worked for Chrissy.

"I told Chrissy that you were a diamond in the rough, and she should hire you." Petite and pretty, Poppy had silky blonde hair and huge blue eyes spaced just far enough apart.

"I can't thank you enough. I'm so excited to be here in the fundraising department."

"Development. That's what we call it now," she said.

"Right. I need to remember that."

"And keep in mind, we're the ones who have the fun. Parties galore—at least people think that's what we do all day long. I have to admit, along with the hard work, we manage to have a good time, even though it's so intense in season."

"When exactly is that?" I asked.

"January, February and March are the height of season, but right now—the end of October—is when it begins. It'll taper off again by April. Once we hit January, you'll need to fasten your seat belt and take plenty of vitamins!"

"Thanks for the heads-up," I said. "It's a big change. We had steady work all year at Reid, Bennett."

"I hardly even go out on dates during that time, but make up for it during the summer months," Poppy said.

She walked me upstairs to our offices and introduced me to Maya, also on the development team. She was strikingly beautiful, with olive skin, long dark curly hair that framed her angular face, and almond-shaped, almost-black eyes heavily defined by thick eyeliner. I noticed how tall she was when she stood up to shake my hand.

"Welcome aboard," she said. "I was thrilled when Chrissy told me she hired you. Perfect timing, too, with season almost here. I'll come by your office shortly. In the meantime, give me a holler if you need anything."

"Thanks. It's nice to meet you."

Poppy told me later that before coming to the states, Maya did a mandatory stint in the Israeli army. Now she was a workout queen, which explained her exceptionally fit body. The fact that both women were in their mid-twenties made me feel old. I'd hit forty a few years ago, yet here I was starting over.

I settled in to my tiny windowless office, and soon Poppy appeared in my doorway.

"Going through this will help you get acclimated," she said, handing me a stack of brochures and a list of donors. Aside from being kind, Poppy was a whirlwind of energy, and I liked her immediately.

Maya also stopped by a little later.

"Don't get overwhelmed, there's a lot to grasp. You must be smart. I hear you were a lawyer," she said.

"Yes, I was. Still am, I guess. I'm just not working as one anymore," I said. Saying that out loud, and in my new office, felt a bit surreal. I tried to ignore the knot that formed in my stomach.

"Addison is a great place to work. You'll love it here," Maya said, making me feel more at ease. "Again, let me know if you need anything. You know where my cubicle is."

"I appreciate it." I put my hands together in a prayer-like position.

"Sure thing." Her broad smile showed off her white teeth, and created a dimple on her cheek.

I pored over the materials, recognizing a few names because they were former clients at Reid, Bennett. Familiarizing myself with the categories of giving, along with meeting co-workers who stopped by my office, made my first day very busy. Everyone seemed friendly and interested in getting to know me. A refreshing change from dealing with mostly distant, grumpy lawyers.

Before I knew it, it was five o'clock, and Chrissy was hovering in my doorway. It was the first I'd seen of her all day.

Dressed to the nines, Chrissy was even more attractive than I recalled. Rich chestnut-brown hair cascaded down to her slim waist. Her body-hugging oatmeal cashmere sweater accentuated her curves. Long legs and beige Manolo Blahnik heels made her even taller. Perfect posture and matching diction added up to the ideal fundraising package. It was hard to believe she was a mother of two teenage children.

My black Ann Taylor pencil skirt and jacket, ivory silk blouse, pearls and black two-inch pumps had seemed professional this morning, but now gave off a dull vibe. I felt dowdy compared to this stunning, perfectly-put-together fashionista.

"Julia, hello. Welcome. Reading our materials, I see. You're familiar with the Addison Center anyway." Her voice was honeyed, just like at the interview.

"Yes, I am." I smiled.

"Okay then. Let's go help ourselves to the buffet in the Green Room."

"That sounds great." Fueled by nervous energy, food was the last thing I was interested in. But spending quality time with Chrissy was worth it.

"This room is reserved for the artists and their entourages," Chrissy said, as we parked ourselves at a small table. Up close, I noticed subtle signs of Botox and filler. "All theaters have a Green Room. Historically, they were painted green, so the name stuck, even though ours is a cool shade of blue." She gestured at the walls. "Feel free to help yourself to dinner here when you're working at night."

"Good to know," I said wondering how many late nights I'd be keeping. I'd thought the hours might be better than lawyering, but maybe not so much.

"The drill is basically what you'll see tonight. Sponsors

love to meet the performers. Randall Perkins, a professional freelance photographer, will be here. He'll take photos, and later they get sent to the sponsor; that's your responsibility. In the future, you'll need to schedule Randall so he can snap their pictures. We put our donor photos in *Curtain Call*, Addison's magazine. They think *they're* the stars, and we make them feel special because they write big checks. If it's an unusually dull week in Royal Coconut Beach, with no major charity events, gossip or scandals, sometimes the *Society Script* runs our pictures," Chrissy explained.

"Okay," I said, wishing I'd brought a notepad.

"The artist isn't always willing to meet with the donors. Then it gets tricky, breaking the news to them. Sometimes they're really upset, but you have to stay cool."

"Prima donnas and divas. I handled a few of those in my previous profession," I said, to remind her I wasn't a total novice.

"Are you referring to the artists or the donors?" she asked, her mouth turning up in a smile. But her expression quickly hardened. "The goal is to keep the donors happy. That's key, first and foremost. Remember, they're giving us a lot of money. Things need to run smoothly."

"Got it," I said softly. We headed backstage to find the stage manager.

"Always check in with the manager of the evening and make sure everything's all set for the meet-and-greet after the performance," she warned me. "If our backstage crew gives you a hard time or says no to the meet-and-greet, remind them that the development department pays their salary."

I had no idea whether she was joking or serious, as her tone seemed to shift with chameleon-like ease. We weaved through several corridors, and eventually landed in the Parker Pavilion, where a number of sophisticatedly dressed people were gathered before the Pinchas Zukerman concert. The antique furnishings were in a restrained palette of black, brown, burgundy, green and bronze. The soft lighting and warm ambiance were inviting.

"Welcome to our world," Chrissy said, standing upright with outstretched arms at the entrance, as if she owned the place. "This is the donor's lounge, named for Sara and Richard Parker, R.I.P. They paid a fortune to have their names on this room."

"How much is it to get access?" I asked, biting my bottom lip.

"You have to be a member of the Maestro Society, which takes a contribution of $250,000 or more. Then you can come in here, and meet people before and after performances. It's open at intermissions, too. Talking with our donors as much as possible is really important, so you get to know them. They'll introduce you to other donors, who you can ask for contributions. This year's goal has been raised to $3.2 million." Frowning, she massaged the back of her neck.

The crazy hours, temperamental stars and sponsors, and huge monetary asks suddenly sounded overwhelming. What the heck had I signed up for? Would I ever see Mark? Having just eaten, fretting about all this made me queasy, while my damp armpits were probably ruining my new silk blouse.

As I glanced at the complimentary bar, the bartender handed me a glass of champagne; he must have read my mind.

"Time to mingle," Chrissy said. Gliding around the room,

she flowed seamlessly in and out of conversations. I had no idea how I'd ever fit in, or what I was even doing there. At the law firm, I'd dealt with many well-to-do clients, but I was advising them on estate planning. Here, I'd have to come up with social chit-chat. I thought of Mark, and how he could work a room like nobody's business; one of his unique gifts. I'd have to get my game on.

The women wore silk or chiffon long-sleeved dresses with clean lines and nipped waists. Some were dressed in bouclé suits, and apparently the puffy bouffant hairstyle had made a comeback. Shiny Kelly bags reflected the lights. The men were equally debonair in bespoke suits and ties. Everyone looked exactly right, which made me feel totally wrong in this sea of posh humanity. To my relief the lights dimmed, indicating it was showtime.

Chrissy came over to me. "Let's head to the balcony. We'll sit in our special box; it's reserved for us." I followed her upstairs, and we sat together for the duration of the energetic concert. I tried to sit back and enjoy the jubilant show, but an undercurrent of anxiety prevented me from relaxing.

After the encore, Elise and David Miller, the sponsors, assembled with their guests in the Parker Pavilion. They would get to meet Pinchas Zukerman, whom I went to fetch. Excited to see him, I found the stage manager, who took me to his dressing room. A few minutes later, Zukerman appeared holding the neck of his violin and bow. I was struck by how handsome he was. He had changed into a black shirt and pants which hugged his muscular physique. His blue eyes, a Roman nose, and a full head of gray hair added to his appeal.

"That was magnificent," I said, after introducing myself.

"Lively, wasn't it?" Zukerman said.

"Yes, it was. Elise and David Miller, the sponsors, loved it. They're very excited to meet you."

Buzzing from adrenaline, I escorted the master violinist to the Pavilion, making small talk. When we reached our destination, I was relieved to hand him off to Chrissy, who graciously made introductions.

"Would you mind if I played something for you?" Zukerman asked the group.

"We'd be delighted," David said. Up close, Zukerman's prodigious technique was even more remarkable than from the stage.

After a few photos, the evening was over. I got into my car, kicked off my heels and drove home barefoot, overtired and on a high from meeting Zukerman. Maybe I was a little star-struck, after all. Then I reviewed Chrissy's litany of responsibilities, which brought me down to earth. But none of those tasks were impossible.

Mark must have heard me as I crept into bed, even though I tried to be quiet. He reached over and took my hand.

"How'd it go?" he asked.

"I survived, but I'm exhausted."

"I bet." Our hands were still touching as I fell into a deep sleep.

Tired and hungover, I woke the next morning later than usual and skipped my daily run. Already dressed, Mark came into the bedroom. I rubbed my eyes and sat up when I saw him.

"Be careful, use the handle," he said as he handed me a mug of piping hot coffee. "Tell me about your night." I watched as he straightened his tie in the mirror. He looked handsome, his hair short from a new haircut. His crisp white oxford shirt contrasting with his dark complexion and suit. I put my mug on the night table and tried to smooth my bed-head hair.

"I kind of followed Chrissy around the Parker Pavilion like a puppy. She knows everyone. I had to escort Pinchas Zukerman to meet the sponsors all by myself. I wasn't sure what to say to him; I probably babbled, but it was all very exciting. Honestly, though, from what Chrissy said, I'm going to have to be at the Center many more evenings than I'd ever imagined."

"You'll do fine." He turned to me and smiled.

"Whenever you want to join me in the evenings, feel free. We have our own box in the balcony. I just don't know how I'm going to do all of this." I shook my head. "It's so different from pushing papers all day. I'll have to be 'on' all the time."

"I promise I'll come with you. Just get comfortable first."

"You're right, it *is* my time, and I have this great opportunity. I'll do it."

"Atta girl. One step at a time. Just don't overthink it." He stood up and bent over, kissing me goodbye on the lips.

"Me? Overthink?" I said. He chuckled and left.

I lingered in bed drinking my coffee. Then I got dressed and headed to the office.

Chapter 4

CHARM SCHOOL

I WAS SHOCKED to see an enormous arrangement of white roses on my desk. I doubted they were from Mark; he had his own style of romance, but it didn't usually involve flowers. Instead, he sent me texts during the day, telling me he was thinking of me; or if I got dressed for work before he left, he'd tell me I looked pretty. I snatched the card from the arrangement:

> Thank you for making our evening so special.
> It was nice to meet you. Our very best, Elise and
> David Miller.

"I put those there for you," Poppy said as she appeared in my doorway.

"Thanks," I said. "That was sweet of the Millers." I handed her the card to read.

"How lovely," she said. "Chrissy got some too."

"Considering I didn't do much except trail Chrissy, and introduce the Millers to Pinchas Zukerman, I'm touched that they thought of me. The little we spoke, they seemed nice," I added.

"Did you know that Elise is a well-known decorator?" Poppy asked.

"No, but her outfit was gorgeous. That woman looked like she's got it going on."

"Enjoy the flowers." Poppy gave a little wave and left my office.

The Millers' gesture was indeed lovely, but I had my work cut out for me and I dug in. After scribbling some notes based on Chrissy's explanation the previous night, Nina's good luck gift caught my eye. It was a plaque that said *You Make Things Happen*, resting on a tiny easel. Its message offered reassurance; a good counterbalance to my overwhelmed state. I went back to my notes, trying to get a grip on what I was supposed to be doing at my new job.

Mark called at eleven. "How's your day going?"

"So far, so good. I got flowers!"

"From *who*?" Mark asked.

"Are you jealous? They're from Elise and David Miller, as a thank you for last evening."

"Flowers and schmoozing with famous folks. Can you handle it?"

"I think so. How's your day so far?"

"I have to interview a few attorneys. First, I wanted to check and make sure you're doing okay."

"Thanks. Will you be home at a normal hour tonight?"

"Yes, I should be."

"Great. I'm going to bed early; I'm tired from working last night."

"I'll find you," he said in a near-whisper.

"You do that, please," I said. As I hung up, Chrissy came into my office. Today she was wearing a purple form-fitting dress, and short matching jacket with a diamond heart-shaped brooch on her shoulder. Her elegant and sophisticated style contrasted with my lackluster wardrobe.

"Nice flowers," she said, and took a seat. "The Millers had such a good time sponsoring, maybe they'll want to increase their donation and become Maestro members. I've invited them for a full backstage tour of Addison. You'll join me."

"Great, I'd love to." I welcomed the chance to see how she coaxed more money from donors.

"Right now, I need to talk with you about our welcome back luncheon," she continued. "We hold this event every year for our donors, whoever is in town, before season picks up in January. Poppy's put the details in place, but we need a program done; it's next week, so we need it immediately. Maya will lay it out and prepare it to be printed. She's good with that sort of thing."

"I'll get working on it," I said.

"Please do," Chrissy said, and left.

I had no idea where to begin, figuring Maya could help. I went to find her and gently tapped her on her shoulder. She swiveled in her chair as I explained the assignment.

"No problem. I'll email you last year's program as a guide, along with our current list of donors. Once you've finished, email it back to me. I'll format it so that Poppy can get it off to be printed."

When I finished the program, I proofed it carefully and

emailed it to Maya, who sent the formatted document back to me. I proofed it again, and off it went to Poppy to be printed.

The rest of the week flew by. The following Tuesday, I placed programs at each person's seat, and handled the check-in with Poppy and Maya. Most of the table cards had been picked up when a woman with a funny looking hat approached the table. She crossed her arms and locked me in a stare. I froze, unable to speak.

"Don't you know who I am?" she finally said with a raised voice.

"Um . . . I'm sorry, I'm new here. What's your name?"

"Mrs. Bronwyn Fenwick." She pursed her lips. "You should be ashamed of yourself for not knowing."

My eyes zoomed to the F's, and I grabbed her card. She snatched it from my hand and walked away, leaving me shaking my head in disbelief.

"You're welcome," I said, once she was out of earshot.

I heard Poppy and Maya giggle, and turned to them. "Geez! Please say this stuff doesn't happen often."

"There's one in every crowd," Maya said. "It's part of your initiation."

"Did I pass?"

Poppy clapped me on the back. "Yup. Welcome to our world!"

We finished up, and joined the luncheon that was in progress, but I still couldn't get over that donor's haughtiness. From what I observed from the back of the room, it went smoothly. Afterwards Chrissy came into my office and slammed the door, but remained standing, both hands on her hips. *Had I done something wrong?*

"There's a problem," Chrissy said. "Chandler Fairbanks—
he's our development committee chair—was reading through
the names of our donors on the program, and pointed out
that it says 'Mr. and Mrs. Matthew Snob'. Their last name is
Stob—not Snob. That's a huge mistake!" She pounded her
fist on the edge of my desk. "Didn't you proof it?"

"Yes, several times." I knew I'd been tired when I worked
on the program, but that wasn't an excuse. I had a sinking
feeling in the pit of my stomach.

"It's a good thing Mr. and Mrs. Stob are still in Capri,
otherwise they'd have been at the luncheon. We work hard
to develop relationships with donors. Keeping them happy
is key, which includes getting their names right." She stared
down at me with piercing eyes.

"I'm so sorry, Chrissy." I couldn't believe I'd mess up
something so easy.

She shook her head. "Let's hope they don't find out."

As the former *Notes and Comments* editor of NYU's Law
Review, I was a fail-proof spell checker. How did I miss
this? I was bummed to have screwed up my first real assignment; a simple one, too. But did she have to talk down to
me, too? Maybe Maya would make me feel better. I headed
to her cubicle.

She was on her computer, but must have heard me because she turned her head and looked up at me.

"What's up?" she asked.

"Apparently, there was a typo that I missed in today's
program. I have no idea how this happened, but Chrissy's
upset and I feel awful. I had to tell someone."

"Don't feel bad. I'm making sure names are correct on
our listings right now. It's tedious, so it can happen. Check

with Poppy. Maybe something went wrong on the printer's end."

"Okay, I will. Thanks for listening," I said.

"Of course." She turned back to the screen.

I headed to Poppy's office, and barged in.

"I'm really upset," I said. "Chrissy found a typo in the program. I know I proofed it carefully. Is it possible something went wrong at the printer?"

"I doubt it. We've been using the same company for a while. They've been reliable. Don't worry about it; it's no big deal. It's bound to happen, with all the proofing we do."

Too bad Chrissy didn't have the same nonchalant attitude.

Over the next few weeks, I followed Chrissy's direction and spent as much time as possible in the Parker Pavilion. I got to know some of the donors, which eased my comfort level. Chrissy was there the evening Cirque du Soliel performed, maneuvering around the room. When the bells sounded, indicating the second act was going to start, I saw her at the bar sipping wine, along with Georgina and Chandler, and another couple.

Later that evening, I headed back to my office to gather my things. Floria, the cleaning lady, was pushing her cart of supplies in the lobby. She was in her uniform, and as usual her hair and make-up were perfect. The other night she'd told me she was a cosmetics saleswoman on the side.

"Another late night, Julia," Floria said.

"Yes. I have something for you." I dug through my purse and handed her a new lipstick. "I picked up this new color at the drugstore. It's waterproof and supposed to stay on longer."

Her face lit up. "How nice of you."

"Have a nice evening." I gathered my things, and on the way out, saw Chrissy walking towards me, a bounce in her step.

"Chandler introduced me to several of his guests, and I have their contact information. They'll become new donors. This is how you fundraise," she said, pointing her index finger at me.

"I've been meeting more people since I've started," I said, wanting to stand up for myself. She simply walked away, failing to recognize my efforts. Annoyed and frustrated, I got in my car and headed home to a quiet house, since Mark was away on business.

The following week, he and I sat in the box and listened to Kristin Chenoweth radiate energy. There was a crowd of people in the Parker Pavilion at intermission. Turned out Mark knew a few of the people in the room, and was the one making introductions to me. He looked elegant in his gray pinstriped suit and purple tie. He possessed an air of confidence and was socially engaging as we moved around the room together. I felt proud that he was my husband.

"Thanks for being there tonight," I said to him in the car as we drove home together. "I hope it adds perspective."

"Your descriptions were right on," he said.

"You're a good talker," I said. "Charming as always, too. I need to step that up. Chrissy was in the Pavilion with me last week. She's great at playing the schmooze game, and introduced me to a few people. But in the office, she's so different. Her charm totally disappears."

"Quit worrying about what Chrissy does, and focus on yourself," Mark said. "And remember, it's easy to make small talk; ask how the family is; tell them you like their outfits."

"Okay. I used to talk with clients about things like how IRS loopholes can help save on estate taxes. It's all small talk now."

"True, but that doesn't mean you don't have a great personality. Your clients loved you. Use your charm to your advantage."

Mark's encouragement made me feel more relaxed. Back home, I changed into a silky nightgown, and snuggled in bed. After we made love, I fell asleep securely in his arms.

Chapter 5

THE MAZE

A WEEK LATER, Maya came into my office, her hands supporting her weight on the edge of my desk while I remained seated. Her form-fitting black sleeveless dress showed off her well-defined arms and sexy body.

"Elise and David Miller will be coming by at 4:45 today," Maya said. "Chrissy had a late dinner with a donor, and is taking the day off. She wants you to show them around, and to try to get them to become Maestro members."

"Okay," I said. "That should be fine. I met them already when they sponsored on my first night here."

"You'll be all right; don't worry. You have a nice dress on, too."

I stood up and stepped away from my desk so she could

look me up and down. She gave me an okay sign with her fingers.

"I'll freshen up my make-up later," I said. "I'll be here late."

"Just let me know if you need anything."

Never mind that late evenings had become my new norm, and I wouldn't be taking the next day off like Chrissy did. Nor was the extra cup of coffee helping. Knowing that the Millers were a lovely couple, I hoped that touring them around would give me a chance to prove myself to Chrissy— and get them to up their gift.

Carefully tracing my lips with liner and applying a neutral lipstick, then adding a layer of CVS eye cream, I checked my vanity mirror and felt pleased with my new look that included black patent high heels. I headed to the stage door entrance to greet them.

Elise's brown shoulder-length hair was perfectly coiffed, and complemented her tanned complexion and sparkling dark eyes. Like the first time we met, her outfit was classy, yet current and chic. Her blush pink bouclé Chanel jacket, complete with fringes and big silver buttons sporting the CC logo, was paired with tapered ivory slacks. Ballet flats in ivory and pink, bearing the same logo; silver jewelry, and an edgy Chanel bag with a thick chain completed her ensemble.

"So nice to see you again. I'm Julia Wild," I said, shaking their hands. "We met the evening of the Pinchas Zukerman performance. Thank you again for those gorgeous roses. It was quite unnecessary, but much appreciated."

"I thought we were meeting Chrissy," David said, his voice laced with disappointment.

"Oh David, it's fine," Elise said. "Julia, it's so nice to see you again, and we're glad you enjoyed the flowers."

"Yes, it's nice to see you," David added, shooting a look at his wife.

Feeling uneasy about this exchange, I said, "Chrissy couldn't make it today, but I'm delighted to show you around. Shall we?" I asked, leading the way.

I led them through Addison's stunning lobby entrance, with gleaming marble floors and full glass walls. The twin set of stairs descended from both sides of the loge levels, and were joined at a huge landing before cascading down as one unit to the floor of the lobby. Small talk revealed that David had been a professional cellist at one time; but he'd quit to make money, and went into the pharmaceutical business.

"How many seats are in here?" David asked, once inside the theater.

"2,800," I said, glad that I knew the answer. We went backstage and walked down a corridor past dressing rooms, then walked onstage.

"What other classical programming does the Center offer during the season?" David asked.

"World-class orchestras and soloists, such as Yo-Yo Ma, the Kalichstein-Laredo-Robinson Trio, and, as you know, Pinchas Zukerman," I said.

"This place is quite remarkable," David said. "Having moved from New York, you understand our concern about there not being enough cultural stimulation here."

We stood on the stage where so many famous artists had performed, taking it all in. Glancing outward toward the seats, David pointed to a box.

"Tell me about the sight lines," he said.

"To be honest, I'll have to find out. I'm not quite sure," I replied.

"In many of the more modern theaters, walls have special acoustics. Is this the case here?" David asked.

"Good question for our technical director. I'll find out." Did we even have a technical director? Realizing I was out of my league, a tour of the basement might score points. The one time I was there to fetch something with Poppy, we saw a barbershop a cappella quartet practicing scales, and got to chat with them.

Leading the way as we exited the elevator, we headed down a corridor, where there were more dressing rooms. As we passed the open door to one of them, we came upon several ballerinas in their underwear. The door slammed immediately as we passed by.

"Gee, how embarrassing! I don't know whether to apologize to them, or to you. Oh well, that's show business!" I threw my hands in the air.

"Don't be silly," Elise said. "Do you think David minded?"

"Didn't bother me in the least." He grinned.

Relieved that they weren't offended, I turned a corner, and we passed two chorus rooms. Next, came laundry facilities and locker rooms. The multiple twists and turns, coupled with my poor sense of direction, made it confusing. I'd now have to fake it through the labyrinth. My heart started racing, and my calves ached from walking in my heels.

With a nervous smile, I said "Mr. and Mrs. Miller, I have to let you in on a secret. I'm new here. In fact, the night of your sponsorship was my first day at the Addison Center. Today, I wanted to make sure that you were in great hands and that you enjoyed your tour. . . ." I took a deep breath. "But I think I'm a bit lost."

Elise looked at me wide-eyed for a moment, and then broke into laughter. David joined in as she gave me a hug, making me feel at ease. Fortunately, a staff member came by wearing a badge.

"Excuse me," I said. "I'm Julia Wild, and I'm pretty new in development, so we haven't had a chance to meet. I'm giving a tour. This is Mr. and Mrs. Miller. . . . Um, we're a little lost."

"No problem. Nice to meet y'all," he said. "I'm Tim, with the technical crew. Follow me." He led the way, escorting us through more twists and turns. "It can get confusing down here."

"No kidding. And I wanted to give these lovely folks a cook's tour," I said, smiling at the Millers.

"You're doing just fine," Elise said, making me feel even more comfortable.

We arrived at the elevators, and I thanked Tim. Once upstairs, I was relieved to be in familiar territory, and we walked over to the Parker Pavilion.

"I noticed how magnificent this room was the night of our sponsorship," Elise said, as her eyes darted around the space. "Who's the decorator?"

"I don't know, but I'll find out." I led the way to the plush couches, where we sat.

"How much would it cost to join?" Elise asked.

"$250,000, but you can pay it in multi-year installments. There are many other benefits, other than access to this room."

Halfway through my explanation, she turned to her husband. "David, we should do this, don't you think?"

"Absolutely. You did well, Julia. We enjoyed getting lost with you," he said, with a chuckle. Taking a check out of her bag, Elise filled it out for the full $250,000. I looked at David, who was smiling at his wife.

Although I managed to maintain my composure, I felt like jumping up and down on the couch. We chatted for a bit more, and discovered that Mark's law firm in New York had represented David's company on several matters. Having that in common, we planned to have dinner together as a foursome.

By the time they left and I headed back to the office, it was well after six. Everyone had gone for the day. After placing the check in the top drawer of my desk for safekeeping, I gathered my things and headed back to the theater. On the way, I saw Floria pushing her cart of cleaning supplies in the lobby.

"Hi, Julia," Floria said. "Another late night?"

"Yup. I'll be here to the bitter end. *Swan Lake* is here, and we'll be doing a meet-and-greet after the performance."

"Enjoy," she said.

The performance was outstanding, and the principal ballerinas came into the Parker Pavilion to meet the sponsors. By the time I got home, Mark was already asleep.

What attorney in her right mind would leave a large check sitting in a desk drawer? Blame it on exhaustion. Blame it on excitement. Whatever it was, I sorely regretted it the next day.

Chapter 6

MISSTEPS

"HELLO, SLEEPYHEAD," Mark said, when I entered the kitchen the next morning. He retrieved my coffee from the microwave, and handed it to me. He looked handsome in his navy pinstripe suit and pink oxford. A blue tie was casually draped over his shirt. I put the mug down, sat at the table and stretched my arms. The bright sun beamed through the window, helping me wake up.

"How'd it go last night?" he asked, joining me.

"Dancers in tutus; the perfect photo op. Everyone loved the performance. Boy, I'm tired. Sorry, I know I've been saying that a lot lately."

"Yes, you have. Drink your coffee."

I chugged down some more caffeine. "I toured these nice people around yesterday who I want you to meet. They became Maestro members. I was trying to make the tour interesting, so I took them to the basement, but we got lost. The best part was when we passed by a room and saw some ballerinas almost naked."

Mark cocked an eyebrow. "Is that what closed the deal?"

"No, it was my charm."

"Way to go. Take a look at this." He pointed to his laptop screen. "It's about Reid, Bennett. Looks like the troubles among the partners have escalated. Now the firm's involved in several major disputes, including the value of some key partners' equity interests."

I skimmed the article. "I'll give Nina a call and see how she's doing. I'm glad I'm not there anymore; their problems were starting to push me over the edge."

"It sounds like a mess," he agreed. "By the way, I just hired a new associate. Her name is Olivia Woods." His eyes lit up when he mentioned her name. "She went to Harvard Law, and she's incredibly smart; I think she's really going to work out well."

"That's terrific," I said, although I wasn't thrilled about his delighted expression.

"I'm off to a meeting." He gave me a kiss on the lips. I heard him get into his car and drive off. After I finished my coffee, I forced myself to go for a run.

The first thing I did at the office was browse through the *Society Script*. I was disappointed that none of the photos I'd sent had made it into the *Knowing Society* column.

Putting down the paper, I opened my desk drawer to retrieve the Millers' check. Not seeing it on top of my files, I took everything out of the drawers. Still no check. I reached all the way in back of the drawer, hoping it might have gotten stuck—*nada*. Calm down, I told myself. It isn't the end of the world. The check was made out to the Addison Center, so no one could cash it. But getting lost in the theater's basement was child's play compared to my losing a two-hundred-fifty thousand dollar check! Elise and David would think I was a total flake—or worse.

Mentally retracing my steps from the evening before, I was sure I'd put it in the top left-hand drawer so I could give it to the finance people in the morning. I'd headed off to the Green Room for a quick bite; I'd stopped by backstage, then the Parker Pavilion. Next, I'd tucked myself away in our box, and had dozed off while ballerinas leaped across the stage.

Meeting and greeting the principal and several corps de ballet dancers had been followed by steady conversation, with everyone finally wrapping up at eleven-thirty. This morning I'd taken it slowly for the first time, getting to the office at 10:00. If the check had been stolen, it must have happened last night, or early this morning.

Frustrated and upset, I went to find Poppy. The last thing I wanted was for Chrissy to hear about this.

"Are you sure you didn't put it in your bag?" Poppy asked calmly.

"No. I looked three times," I whined, and instantly regretted my tone. I apologized; she was way too nice to tick off.

"Okay, let's go speak with Maya. Maybe she saw it somewhere." Relieved Poppy was taking over, I followed her to Maya's cubicle.

"Julia put a check in her drawer late yesterday—a huge one—and now it isn't there. You didn't happen to see it, did you?" Poppy's voice was very composed.

"No, I haven't. Don't fret, Julia. I'm sure it'll turn up,"

Maya said. "I'll keep my eyes out in case I see it. Who was the donor?"

"Elise and David Miller. Thanks," I said, and sighed.

"Don't worry," Poppy said, as we headed back to our offices. "Go about your work, and maybe it'll turn up later." Luckily, Chrissy was out visiting donors all day.

Following Poppy's lead, I tried to relax and put everything in perspective. It wasn't like I'd stolen money, so a missing check couldn't jeopardize my position. Who knew, though, the way Chrissy was. Tackling my to-do list was a good distraction. But one thing was certain: the sheer joy of securing a major gift was completely overshadowed by its disappearance.

Later that evening, sleep eluded me. I scolded myself for not locking the check in my drawer. *I could lose my job over this.* Mark began snoring lightly, so I cradled my head in the pillow to muffle the sound, and eventually drifted off to sleep.

Chapter 7

SOIRÉE SAVVY

THE CONFERENCE ROOM TABLE was large enough to hold twelve people. Chrissy and Maya were seated at one end when Poppy and I got there. The check still hadn't turned up, and I was worried that Chrissy might finally ask about the tour. I had no idea what I'd say, and my heart started to race. *Stay calm.*

"Hi ladies," Chrissy said as we took our seats for the meeting. "It's December, and we're about to hit the ground running. Poppy will first review the gala kick-off party which is coming up right after New Year's. That's the pre-party event that's held before the main event—the gala—which is in February. She nodded at Poppy.

"As you know, Savannah and Winston Colbertson are hosting the gala kick-off party on their yacht," Poppy said.

"The Lady Sweet Savannah IV. Last year's kick-off was on the Savannah III."

"Hopefully it'll get us publicity for the actual gala, and we'll sell more tickets," Chrissy said. "Let's aim for a sell-out. Talk this up in the Parker Pavilion, would you, Julia?"

"Yes, of course," I said. *Good, no mention of the check.*

Poppy continued. "Erin from the *Society Script* will be there, so Julia and I can work together to make sure she snaps the right photos. Maya, will you handle the check-in table?"

"Sure," she said, and smiled.

"Hold it," Chrissy said. "Let's be clear: the donors need to see their photos in the paper. Savannah and Winston must be front and center. They're the hosts, and she's chair of this year's gala. Make sure we get multiple shots of them." I used to handle some pretty complicated tax strategies, but now Chrissy was ordering me around about party photos. Had I made the right career move? At times like this, I wasn't sure.

"Oh, that reminds me," Poppy said. "Randall Perkins will be there too, taking pictures. We'll tell him to just aim and shoot, since he knows everyone; he's a permanent fixture in Royal Coconut Beach society."

I looked closer at the invitation. "M/Y?" I asked.

"The Motor Yacht," Maya said. "Did you see it says 'shoe check—socks provided'? The crew actually stands there making sure you take your shoes off, so the teak doesn't get scuffed. And wear pants to avoid unexpected breezes. That's what most women do. We don't need a Marilyn Monroe moment."

After Poppy finished discussing the kick-off party, she shifted to the gala. Timeline, décor, photography, public relations, and other elements were rattled off with Marine Corps efficiency.

Chrissy chimed in. "Addison's lavish fundraising event is logged on to the *Society Script* social calendar a year in advance, Julia. Galas are a big deal for Royal Coconut Beach residents, as well as for all the charities they serve. They're held in the peak of season." Her voice was laced with authority.

"That's good to know," I replied, even though Poppy had already told me this.

Once the meeting wrapped up, Maya and Chrissy remained to review some things, while Poppy and I left.

"Did you know that Sweet Savannah's started out unintentionally?" Poppy asked as we chatted on the way back to our offices.

"No, I didn't," I said.

"It's a good story. Savannah was baking cakes in her home in Greensboro, North Carolina, for her family, church, friends, whoever. Winston, her husband, turned her talent into a business. Before long, they had a bunch of bakery shops, and then over a hundred franchises. They recently sold it for a fortune."

"Lucky them," I said.

"Yeah. She's really nice, too. Wait until you meet her; she's a hoot."

The upcoming yacht party made me think of my former office view, and when I got back to my desk, I called Nina.

"Remember when we looked out the window and saw the Sweet Lady Savannah III?" I asked.

"Yeah, with your binoculars," Nina said dryly.

"Well, get this. The Addison Center is having a kick-off party on it, so guess where I'll be going? It's now the IV."

"Lucky you! It sure beats the horrendous week I've been

having. The divorces and prenups are ridiculously complex. I'm up to my eyeballs in documents. On top of that,
the firm's a royal mess, as you know. This place is on the
verge of imploding in spectacular fashion. There's just been
a mass exodus of attorneys, in case you haven't read the
papers."

"Yes, I saw the latest," I said. "It must be tough. I have
no doubt you'll land on your feet."

"I've formulated a game plan, but I'm too buried neck-
deep in clients to move forward. Oh ... excuse me ...
you're going to a party on *that* yacht? You definitely have the
best job. I'd trade places with you right now."

"I'm not so sure about that these days," I told her.
"Chrissy is so critical. She's bossy and annoying, but then
of course she turns on the charm with the donors. On top
of that, I'm working my tail off night after night, trying to
meet people, handle sponsors and get new donors. I'll explain when I see you."

"That good, huh?"

"I'm just venting. Despite everything, I like what I'm
doing. And I'm sorry if it came across like I was bragging;
it's not like I'm a guest of Savannah's. I'll be working.
Although to be honest, other than getting the right pictures
snapped, I'm not sure what I'm supposed to do."

"Well, you won't be passing out the hors d'oeuvres, will
you?"

I laughed. "No, at least I don't think so. Who knows,
though."

"I'm teasing. I know it won't be the same as hanging out
with your Winchester Academy buddies."

"It's Wingate. And I never went on a yacht with any of
them."

"Well, enjoy the soiree, if you can. You're no wallflower; just be your lovely self.

And don't forget to wear something really cute. I hate to cut you off, but I have to prepare for trial. These people are all nuts. Hang in there, and say hi to Mark."

"He's out of town, in California on business. I miss you."

"I miss you too. Have a Prosecco for me. Although it's more likely you'll be indulging in some high-end champagne on the yacht."

"Yeah, right," I said, and we both laughed. "The event isn't until January. Speaking of Prosecco, when are we going to get our lunch group going? I know we're both too busy. . . ."

"We are, but no more excuses," Nina said, cutting me off. "Let's set a lunch date now, so we can talk about who to include. It'll be our official first meeting, just the two of us. Otherwise, we'll never get it going."

Before hanging up, we coordinated our schedules.

Chapter 8

MOTOR YACHTS AND CAVIAR DREAMS

THE NEXT DAY, right before five, I was startled when Maya stormed into my office waving something.

"I found the check!" she shouted, waving it to show me.

I shot up and grabbed it, giving her a mammoth hug.

"It was face-down on the floor in the women's lounge. I thought it was scrap paper sticking out from under the chair and almost threw it away."

We barged into Poppy's office proudly waving the prize and explained what had just happened.

I handed it over to the finance people right away, but by the time I was back in my office, I realized something seemed off. Why was the check in the women's lounge? I was in there *before* the Millers' visit, and *before* I received Elise's check. So how could it possibly be in there? Had someone taken it from my desk and dropped it on the lounge floor? Floria had access to my office since she cleaned it every night, but I couldn't believe she'd taken it.

I took a few deep yoga breaths. Paranoid? Probably. But just because I was paranoid didn't mean I shouldn't trust my instincts. Someone had moved that check.

Poppy stood in my doorway moments later. "I bet you're relieved," she said.

I smiled. "I am, but I've been thinking; remember that incident with the "Stob" spelling error? I'm positive I proofed the program very carefully. I don't understand how I screwed up. Both things are just weird."

"Hmmm . . . maybe you're being too hard on yourself," Poppy said.

I chuckled. "Probably."

"Well I wouldn't worry too much," she said. "I forgot to tell you before, but I missed some typos last year, which Chrissy pointed out. We do a lot of proofing; it's easy to mess up."

"Maya told me the same thing. I guess I'm not alone. This check business has thrown me, though."

"Forget about it. It's time to call it a night. We need our rest for the kick-off party tomorrow night."

"Have a good one," I said.

"Same. Hey, I really like working with you, by the way."

I gave a quick smile. We had good rapport, but I couldn't get over how easily she brushed off my suspicions. Come to think of it, the program was in her hands before it got printed.

I doubted she was behind my missteps, and hated that this idea even crossed my mind, although I couldn't rule it out altogether.

———

POPPY AND I GREETED PEOPLE as they arrived aboard the Lady Savannah IV. It was hard to believe it was January already, with the much-anticipated high season here. As directed, guests removed their shoes and donned socks from the big baskets. The crew was dressed in crisp white nautical uniforms. Everyone seemed familiar with the drill. Butlers in white gloves flanked the entrance, holding silver trays of Dom Perignon. When most of the guests were there, I headed inside.

Chrissy showed up soon after, spotted Savannah, and made a beeline for her. "Savannah, it's so good to see you," she said. Kisses were planted on both of each other's cheeks, Euro-style. I was standing nearby, and Chrissy introduced me.

"Well, aren't you just an adorable thing," Savannah said in a strong Southern accent. Her comment made me feel pretty. Savannah was groomed to perfection, with a white eyelet lace jumpsuit elegantly outlining her thin, tall frame, and blonde shoulder-length hair topped with a pink bow. Anyone else would have looked ridiculous, but she looked sophisticated and elegant. No way could she possibly consume her own decadently sweet creations.

Following Randall and Erin, the photographers, I learned who was who by listening to them set up each photo. After they finished photographing a few groups inside, Erin and Poppy headed outside to the deck where many more people congregated, and Randall and I followed.

"You really know everyone here," I said to him.

He lifted his shoulder in a half-shrug. "If you'd been

snapping photos of high society as long as I have, you would too."

"I'm just trying to get to know everyone," I said.

"Give it time; it'll happen."

When we finished outside, together, we made our way to the upper deck, as the majestic view of the skyline appeared. Rows of skyscrapers, not as tall as New York, but still impressive, had many windows still alight from within. The Addison Center was perched on the other side of the water at the foot of the Royal Coconut Bridge, illuminated to the hilt, even though there was no performance that evening. I felt a rush of joy, thrilled to be a part of what went on behind its stunning façade. The pristine blue water was a far cry from New York City's East River.

More photos were taken, and Randall and Erin wandered off. Poppy and I leaned on the railing.

"Everything about tonight is stunning," Poppy said.

"Yes, it's a little over-the-top, isn't it?"

"It sure is. One day, when I have my own event business, I'll do high-end parties like this."

"Go for it," I said. We both laughed.

"I'm going to check on Maya at the registration table, and see who hasn't showed up yet," Poppy said.

"Okay. I'll find someone to schmooze with." We made our way back downstairs, and I noticed the steady stream of champagne and hors d'oeuvres being passed. Poppy got lost in the crowd. Feeling hungry, I took a piece of toast with caviar, when Chrissy appeared out of nowhere.

"Julia, I'd like you to meet Mrs. Chandler Fairbanks. Georgina, meet Julia."

Gulping down my caviar, I stretched out my hand.

Georgina had a formidable handshake, and her gargantuan diamond ring dug into my palm.

She looked directly into my eyes. "Nice to meet you, Julia," she said, her voice robust. Swallowing, I shook my head, finally able to respond. "I'm thrilled to be part of the team.

It's very nice to meet you, Mrs. Fairbanks. Chrissy has told me about you."

"Please call me Georgina," she said.

We chatted about the beautiful yacht, the sun setting and the delicious caviar. Then Georgina saw people she knew and took off to say hello. Chrissy had disappeared, probably to schmooze on another deck. Taking my cue from her, I introduced myself to people, not daring to eat another morsel. A feeling of loneliness swept over me; I wished Mark was there. I felt awkward, but went ahead and made feeble attempts at intruding on conversations to try to say hello to guests.

That's when Savannah saw me, and asked me to go below-decks to get the servers to pass more food. Below-decks, where I stumbled on Chrissy and Chandler, engaged in passionate love-making, music playing and candles ablaze.

I ran back upstairs, and bumped into Poppy.

"This is some party," she said. "Hey, are you okay? You look like a deer caught in the headlights."

"Oh. . . ." Images of the Hermes tie filled my mind. "I'm just a little tired, I guess. Is there anything else that needs to be done?"

"No, I think we've covered all the bases," she said.

"Great. I'm going to head home, if you're okay," I said.

"I'm good. Maya's here, just in case. Thanks for asking. You're the one who's usually working late, anyway. I don't know how you do it. You should get some rest."

"I appreciate it. I'll see you in the morning." I shouted goodbye to Maya as I left, and hurried to my car. Once inside, I sat there for a while. Still in a state of shock, I wasn't quite sure what to make of what I'd seen. Chrissy was my boss, and while I knew little about her, I never would have expected she'd have an affair with a member of Addison's board, let alone literally right under his wife's nose. Was this how she went about getting donations? And was Chandler the only one? The very idea made me cringe. Seeing what Chrissy was really like made me think I might have made a mistake in taking the job.

The house was empty, and I was sorry Mark was at a partners' retreat. I stayed awake for a long time, staring into the darkness.

I spoke with Mark on the phone the next morning, although I did most of the talking. "There was a huge master stateroom, a Jacuzzi for at least ten on the fourth level sun deck, a sauna and a sprawling outdoor dining area. They even had a helicopter pad," I told him.

"No kidding," he said.

"Are you shaving?" I asked.

"How did you guess?"

"I hear water running. Anyway, that's just some of it. It was fun watching everyone indulge in fine caviar and champagne. Then later all the stuffed shirts loosened up, having chugged enough alcohol."

"Sounds *dee-vine*," he said.

"I missed you, though. Too bad you couldn't be there.

I have lots more to tell, but I'll wait until the weekend when you're back."

"Can't wait to hear about it. I'm going to get dressed now. We'll talk later." We said goodbye and hung up.

As much as I was dying to share the outrageous story of what I'd witnessed, it was worth the wait to see his expression that Saturday morning when we lounged outside, and I spilled the beans.

Chapter 9

AN AFFAIR TO REMEMBER

I ARRIVED at the office early the next morning after the kick-off party, having gotten very little sleep. I had tossed and turned all night, thinking about Chrissy and Chandler. Maya came in to see me mid-morning.

"Chrissy wants to see you when she gets in." She gave me a frosty look, which was odd.

"Okay," I said, although Maya was gone before I got the word out. I sat there on edge, worried that my boss might have known I'd seen her and Chandler in action. What would I say? It was as if *I* was the one having an affair and had something to hide.

Thirty minutes later, Maya alerted me that Chrissy had arrived. Nerves humming, I headed next door to her office.

"Maya told me to come see you," I said.

"Have a seat," she said, motioning to the chair. "What did you think of the party last night?"

She could be testing me. "Umm . . . the yacht was stunning. I met some new people, and got all the right photos." All I could think of was Chrissy's legs pointing toward the ceiling.

"Good. How's everything else going? Tell me about the evenings you've spent here."

"Well, I've been getting to know donors in the Parker Pavilion," I said. "Elise Miller is there a lot, and she's been introducing me to her friends. I really like her. Meet and greets with sponsors have gone smoothly."

Chrissy didn't say anything, so I continued. "You were so right about what you said on my first night—donors really like to meet the performers."

"That they do. Speaking of sponsorships, Chandler just made a gift of fifty thousand dollars." She waved a check. "That's why I wanted to see you. He and Georgina want to sponsor something. I need the list of sponsorships that are available; highlight the good ones for me."

"I'll get it to you right away. His gift will help a lot with the annual campaign goal," I said. Of course my mind immediately went to the scene on the yacht. Now I was convinced *that* was how Chrissy solicited donations. *Geez, I hope she doesn't expect me to be that devoted to the job,* I thought.

"Chandler's a great guy," Chrissy continued. "His great-grandfather was an important Revolutionary War figure, and his grandfather was a well-known representative in Congress. But you'll never hear him brag about his background or money," she added. "Choate Rosemary Hall, then Princeton. Memberships at the most elite gentlemen-only clubs, exclusive country club memberships, and a listing in the Social Register."

"Wow, that's impressive." I thought about how nefarious it was for Chrissy to be sleeping with Georgina's husband, and then talking up Chandler with me now.

"Georgina's lineage doesn't match his thoroughbred ancestry, but it's not too shabby. Her job was to prepare their children to follow in their upper-crust footsteps. She organized prep school educations—two as Choate legacies—and one who went on to Princeton like granddad. Just like a dutiful wife." Chrissy's voice was tinged with sarcasm.

"Sounds like a traditional marriage," I said lightly.

Chrissy frowned, but her Botoxed brows hardly moved. "You can call it that. Chandler's ancestors amassed an obscene amount of wealth, and grew it exponentially so it could pass through the generations."

"He did this all from Florida?" Chrissy was on a roll, and I was playing along.

"No. His offices are headquartered in Boston, but he maintains an office in Royal Coconut Beach."

"Interesting," I replied.

"Yes. He now manages things from here, except in the summer when they're in Martha's Vineyard."

The way Chrissy went on about Chandler wasn't surprising. It reminded me of when I was in high school, and I chatted with my girlfriends incessantly about our latest crushes. Chrissy started to say something else, but Maya barged in to tell her that Chandler was on the phone. Chrissy put out her hand, signaling for me to stay put, while she took the call. She loudly chatted about an upcoming lunch appointment with a potential donor, while I watched her fiddle with her gorgeous hair. Behind her desk was a picture of her with her two adorable children, standing by a swimming pool. I knew Chrissy was divorced, but did she think she had to sleep with potential donors to excel at her job? What else could she be getting out of an affair with a married man who was decades older—was he buying her stuff, or paying her mortgage?

Surveying her office instead of staring at her on the phone, my eyes landed on her desk, which held a second check on top of a folder. Curious to see who this latest contributor was, I snuck a peek, then froze. It wasn't a donation, but a check made out to Maya Raffa, in the sum of twenty-five thousand dollars—signed by Chandler A. Fairbanks. Could it be that Maya knew about Chrissy and Chandler's affair, and she was being paid off to keep mum? Or was Maya also sleeping with Chandler, and the check was a payoff for sex? I liked Maya, and didn't really want to believe this.

Chrissy said good-bye to Chandler, and looked at me with a blank expression. "I can't remember what I was saying."

"You were telling me about Chandler's background."

"Oh, that's right. I think I finished. Please get me the list of sponsorships."

"Will do."

A few minutes later, I returned and handed the list to Chrissy.

AFTER ALL THAT, I kept my head down, my mouth shut, and continued to get my work done. Poppy was right about the pace of the season's activities escalating in January. There were a million things to get done, and I needed to stay focused. The weeks in between the kick-off party on the yacht and the gala were busy with lunches, late evenings in the Parker Pavilion, and many assignments for the big fundraising event.

I managed to squeeze in time one day during lunch to shop for a gown for the gala, and got lucky when I found something perfect right away.

"Nice legs, or should I say 'leg'," Mark commented that evening as I showed off my new Donna Karan dress. He looked me up and down, and I flashed a teasing smile.

The dress had a slit going up the right leg, stopping at my upper thigh. Keeping Mark on his toes wasn't a bad idea after all these years, so I paraded around the room, knowing how fabulous the dress looked.

"What do you think?" I asked, and twirled.

"Very pretty and stylish. I like the stretchy fabric, too. Fits like a glove."

"Thank goodness for my daily runs," I said.

"Yes. Where did you get it?"

"Second Chances, a consignment store. I heard some ladies talking about it in the Parker Pavilion. That's where they dump their couture at the end of season. Some of the clothes still had tags on them."

"Sounds like you had a very productive lunch break," Mark said.

"I did. Combing through the racks reminded me of when Mom and I used to shop at Loehmann's; a bargain would always jump out, so I felt right at home at Second Chances. Someone's size 4 couture sheath is now mine for a fraction of the price."

Mark gave me a thumb's up.

"The shoes are a different story. Remember these?"

I said, pointing to the old but still- dazzling Jimmy Choo stilettos. Despite our common belief in frugality, Mark had splurged on these beauties for my 30th birthday. I loved the shoes, mainly because Mark took the time to select them, managing to get the right size, too.

"I sure do," he said, as I strutted towards him. "I had just made partner when I bought them. I knew they'd show off your great legs. Pretty things should be enjoyed. Like you." His eyes were filled with desire, his comment a total turn-on.

I parked myself sideways on his lap, my bare leg showing and the shoe sticking out. I gave him a quick peck on the lips, which was returned with an electrifying and intense kiss. I went with the flow. Just when it was going great, I pulled back for a second and our eyes locked with a blend of passion and curiosity. I had fun teasing and titillating. Then he began kissing me all over.

"The dress is pretty, but you look better without it," he said, as he slowly unzipped it. I stood up and it fell to the floor. Next thing I knew, he got up, took my hand, and led me to the bedroom. I followed, wearing nothing but the stilettos.

Mark left for New York early the next morning before I awoke. He'd been gone for a few days, to handle the closing for a private equity deal. When I got to the office, Chrissy called me from home, skipping any pleasantries.

"I need you to fill in for me tomorrow evening. I'm supposed to attend the Society of Ambassadors gala tomorrow night. It's a big event in town. Chandler's friend, Ambassador Blair Carleton, invited me, but I'm sick." She sneezed into the phone. "Blair's the former ambassador to Finland. I told him you'd attend in my place. Get his assistant's number from Maya and call for the details."

"I'd be delighted to go. Thanks, Chrissy," I said.

"Make sure you maximize this opportunity and network." She started to cough.

"Yes ma'am," I said into the phone, but she'd already hung up.

I speed-dialed Mark. "You're not going to believe it, but I'm going to the Society of Ambassadors gala.

Chrissy asked me to go in her place!"

"I'm impressed, Jools," he said. "Don't pick up any handsome ambassadors."

"Might you be worried?" I asked, as I twisted the phone cord round and round my finger.

"Always."

"Gotta keep you on your toes! I'm surprised Chrissy is sending me to this affair. She could've just cancelled."

"Perhaps she trusts you more than you think. Good thing you got that dress yesterday."

I put the dress on the next evening, and did a once-over in front of the full-length mirror, turning around to see how I looked from the side. *"It's showtime,"* I said out loud.

I arrived at the Oceanfront Hotel, where I was directed down the stunning hallway to the ballroom where the event was being held. "Step this way, ladies." A staff member directed guests as she pointed to the step-and-repeat line for photos. Protocol required that all guests make their way through the long receiving line of ambassadors, dignitaries, and philanthropists from around the world. My photo was snapped by Erin, who I recognized right away from Savannah's yacht. I knew the chances that I'd actually be pictured were nil, with all these rich and famous people present.

"Pleased to meet you," I said, shaking the Danish

ambassador's hand, admiring his slew of medals. I shook the former Japanese ambassador's hand, more medals covering his chest. A few more diplomats were lined up, and I shook hands like clockwork. Ambassador Carleton, my host, was on the line. I shook his hand, intending to thank him for having me as his guest, but his eyes were already focused on greeting the guest behind me. I kept moving to prevent a bottle-neck.

At the end of the line was the former ambassador to Argentina. But instead of looking at his medal, our eyes locked. His platinum name tag read "Honorable Julian Jorge Mendoza."

"Nice to meet you," I said. Breaking the stare, I moved on to Singapore, then Ireland and France. Exquisite jewelry had come out of safe-deposit boxes. In the mix were royalty from Scotland, England, and other European monarchs. It was a Who's Who of international society, and I recognized many faces from the *Society Script*. The room was flush with cachet, everyone busy kissing, gripping and grinning.

The lively music had everyone shouting over each other. I made my way to my table, and introduced myself to those standing by their chairs or already seated. They were from the professional business community; doctors, lawyers, accountants. I wondered if I was moved to that table when it was discovered I was Chrissy's replacement, but I didn't really care.

While guests were finding their seats, Ambassador Carleton stopped by to say hello to someone at my table. Gentleman that he seemed to be, he went on to introduce himself to my tablemates, ending with me. I stood and shook his hand, thanking him for having me there. Just then, Ambassador Mendoza stopped by to say something to his fellow dignitary. The two men chatted. Unsure whether to sit down again, I awkwardly stood with an uneasy smile, while I fidgeted with my hands.

Within minutes, Ambassador Carleton left, but Ambassador Mendoza remained there. He stared directly into my eyes with the same penetrating dark gaze as on the receiving line. I was immediately drawn into his intent look, unnerved by it. He had an olive-colored complexion, and his black hair was slicked back. His broad shoulders filled out his jacket, which was heavily decorated with medals. He appeared to be in his early sixties.

"I'm Julia Wild. I'm new with the Addison Center, in fundraising. Lovely event, isn't it?"

"It certainly is," he said, his accent slight but noticeable.

"I'm sure you go to a lot of these events, Ambassador Mendoza," I said.

"Call me JJ," he said, as if it was an order.

"Okay," I said.

A man tapped him on his shoulder and interrupted us. He turned his head to see who it was.

"I'll be in touch," he said, turning again towards me for a few seconds before walking away with the other man.

I went back to the safety of my table. The rest of the evening was filled with speeches, music, and social chit chat. Before dessert was served, our table disbanded and headed to the valet. Unlike most of the other guests in the room, we had to be at work early the next day.

As I drove home, I thought about how disarming JJ's intense gaze was.

Chapter 10

OH, WHAT
A NIGHT

CHRISSY RETURNED after taking a week off to recover, and in time for the Addison Center's gala. On the day of the event, Poppy asked if I'd mind picking up the engraved sterling silver picture frames for Savannah and the ladies on the gala committee. I welcomed the chance to get away from the office craziness. We'd been dealing with cancellations, seat request changes, and other last-minute details all day.

Barreling down the majestic palm tree-lined Laguna Drive, I was hell-bent on finding a spot outside Tiffany's. A white Bentley had just started its engine in front of the store's art deco doors. Slowing down so I could edge my small Acura into its spot, under my breath I muttered "C'mon, c'mon," willing it to pull out. The Bentley that had been tailgating me finally shifted into the other lane as the

woman behind the wheel cast me a dirty look. Fifteen minutes later, with the frames loaded in my car, I took off. The
rear-view mirror now showed a black Bentley pulling into
the vacant space. You'd swear this was the Bentley capital of
the world.

The bridge had just gone up. To quell my edginess about
getting back to the Addison Center, I took a deep breath,
put the car in park and zoned out.

I thought about what Savannah and all the other ladies
on her gala committee must be doing at the moment. I was
sure they were getting gussied up; not rushing to Tiffany's
to lug gifts to a pressure-cooker office. By the time evening rolled around, these pampered ladies would be fully
relaxed, ready to unwind with friends and dance the night
away in stunning first-hand couture. I was already tired and
stressed before the evening even began.

I was startled by the blaring horn of a red Ferrari behind
me, having tuned out the sound of bells emanating from the
bridge, indicating that it had come down again. I pressed
the pedal, and my trusty Acura sped forward.

After the gifts were unloaded onto a cart with help from
a security officer, and placed in a closet for later, I headed
upstairs. There, I found Chrissy, Poppy, and Maya huddled
over the table in the conference room, shuffling table cards.

"Last-minute additions and subtractions. It never fails,"
Poppy said, looking up.

"Oh, Julia. You're *finally* back," Chrissy said. What, did
she think I was out enjoying myself? "First get dressed, and
then head over to the ballroom to check on the tables," she
ordered.

I put my sheath on, quickly ran a brush through my
messy hair, and then spritzed it. Adding black eyeliner and

eye cream, I was already looking better. Blush and a light red lipstick completed the three-minute beautifying session.

The ballroom was in a separate building on the Addison Center's campus. I opened its doors, and the combination of beautiful sapphire and green jewel tones created a rich, satiny effect that was breathtaking. Feathers were everywhere, with blue and green lighting to match. Since peacocks were in vogue this season, Savannah, the gala chair, had decided that this would be the theme. Ziggy, a brilliant Royal Coconut Beach decorator, had magically transformed the space.

Ziggy and I had first bonded when his team staged some events at Reid, Bennett that I helped plan, as part of the firm's recruiting committee. I spotted him in tight white skinny jeans, with a turquoise fitted shirt and matching cashmere sweater flung over his back. Ziggy looked like he was headed to brunch at a tony LA restaurant. Known to stand in as a date or "walker" for wealthy ladies, I imagined he had some interesting stories locked away.

I summoned Mr. Très Chic with a shout from across the dance floor, and he swaggered toward me. After a quick round of Euro-kisses, I shoved the floor plan in his face.

"This whole row of tables needs to be pushed up to the stage area. Tables 5, 7 and 9 are way too far back, and not close enough to the center. Major donors are sitting there, and they'll pitch a hissy-fit. Chrissy, will, too." Ziggy started to say something, but I kept going. "C'mon, Ziggy, help make me look good. She trusted me to check on things. I've been trying to impress her since day one."

"No need to get your panties in a wad; I just got here. Ziggy will fix." At his signal, his people sprang into action, making the necessary adjustments. "Dim the chandeliers, and turn up the blue and green lights for more contrast. Now that the tables are moved, realign the pin lights. Chop, chop!" He clapped his hands. "Have you forgotten we're having a gala here in just a few?" To my relief, he instantly took command of the room.

I was counting seats at Table 23 when Ziggy came up behind me, waving a small fan of peacock feathers.

"I have an idea that these feathers would add the perfect touch to your gown. Let's turn it into a Givenchy. I just love feathers; they make everything sexy." Carefully he pinned the makeshift brooch to my gown. I went to look in the mirror, and barely recognized the chic woman in the reflection. Gala guests would be arriving any minute, and now I was dressed to kill.

There was a standing ovation after the performance, and a happy crowd danced out of the theater to "Oh, What A Night," sung by Frankie Valli and his suave-looking Four Seasons. The concert paved the way for the dinner dance in the Addison Center's ballroom. People poured in, causing a bottleneck at the entrance. Once inside, the fourteen-piece band that was selected by Savannah was pumping out six-ties songs to echo what guests had just seen in the theater. Men strutted around in their tuxes, while women in glittering gowns with matching jewels shared air-kisses. Some ladies even sported tiaras.

Savannah had her own crowning glory of gorgeous blonde hair, in an elegant partial up-do. Her teal gown was slit all the way to her thigh like mine, and iridescent sequins hugged her lithe size-zero body. The leggy blonde beauty was a standout among the other socialites, many of whom possessed Botoxed blank expressions and icy smiles. Floating on air as she walked around the room schmoozing with guests, Savannah played her role with finesse.

Chrissy was also flitting around before landing in her seat at Georgina and Chandler's table. Because of the Fairbanks' hefty donation to the event and his status, their table was front and center. I thought that it was odd that Chrissy fraternized with Georgina while carrying on an affair with her husband. Did it even bother Chrissy that she was being so deceitful? I noticed Maya greeting Chandler and Georgina, which made me wonder again about the $25,000 check made out to her. I watched as Maya headed towards her seat in the back of the room. Chrissy wanted me seated at a table near the dance floor, so I could get to know more donors.

Once everyone settled in, a voice commanded silence.

"Ladies and gentlemen, please welcome the chairman of the board of directors of the Addison Center for the Performing Arts, Mr. Webster Ashton," the wizard behind the curtain boomed. In actuality, it was one of the technical crew.

Flanked by two teleprompter monitors, Webster went to the podium and began to read some notes he held in his hands.

"The Addison Center is grateful to all of you for. . . ."

Webster stopped speaking and shuffled through the notes. What was going on? A chill went through me as my stomach dropped. Was I supposed to make a beeline in front of everyone and help him out? Fear said no, but logic dictated yes, since I was Webster's handler for the evening. I looked over to Chrissy, who sat there motionless.

To get to the podium, I'd have to cross the mammoth

white dance floor. Gathering my courage, I took a deep breath. I pushed off my chair and stepped onto the floor. But the back of my left heel—the precious stiletto—got caught on the rubber border separating the carpet from the dance floor. A split second later I was flying in the air, landing face-down on the floor. A gasp arose from nearby tables. I struggled up on to my elbows, my knee throbbing and my wrist numb. At least I wasn't bleeding. I willed the faux parquet to swallow me up.

A few of the men seated nearby leaped up to my aid and helped me to my feet. My right arm was firmly in someone's grasp, and I looked to see who it was. The man gazed into my eyes, and the commotion around me became distant background noise. I was drawn into his dark stare. It was hard to tell who he was with the lights dimmed, and all I cared much more about was escaping from this awful and embarrassing moment. I managed to become semi-steady, getting my footing back. Minus a stiletto, I balanced on the toes of my shoeless foot.

Prince Charming reached down and plucked the shoe from the rubber border where it was lodged. Carefully, he placed it on my foot while taking my arm again.

"Are you okay?" he gently whispered with what sounded like a slight accent. His voice was familiar, but from where?

"Yes, I'm fine. Thank you."

"Okay, then. I'll lead the way." Again, that accent. My Cinderella moment continued as he escorted me to the podium. The man vanished into the dark ballroom space.

"You made it," Webster whispered. "Now would you be so kind as to read the remarks for me?"

"*What?*" I whispered back.

"The teleprompter malfunctioned. I can't see a thing up

here, so I can barely make out my notes," he said, holding out the pages. "You're young, and your eyes are better than mine."

"Um . . . okay."

Webster put his typed notes on the podium, and with my voice an octave higher than normal, I began to read them. Savannah stood, the spotlight beaming down on her as I thanked her for serving as the Chair. Everyone applauded and the cameras flashed like fireflies in a summer meadow. Because she was beautiful, had brought her friends to the gala, had hosted a party on her yacht, and had written a big check, she was recognized as the star of the evening. As I worked my way through the speech, my voice normalized, although my legs wouldn't stop trembling, and my knee was throbbing. Thankfully they were blocked from view by the podium.

Once the ordeal was over, I headed to the ladies' room. A minute later, Poppy came in. She saw me sitting on the lounge chair with a pack of ice on my elevated leg, given to me by the caterer.

"Are you okay? I was outside the ballroom dealing with guests who arrived late, and heard what happened! I had a feeling I'd find you here."

"My knee still hurts, but I'm all right."

"If it's any consolation, I heard you rebounded," Poppy said.

"I don't understand what happened," I said, shaking my head. "You checked on the teleprompter earlier, and said the speech was loaded."

"I did. Hold on." She put out her hand to stop me. "You're not accusing me of. . . ."

"No, of course not. Was anyone in the ballroom, other than Ziggy and his crew?"

"Hmm . . . no, I don't think so. Just Maya and I were checking on tables. I don't know what went wrong."

"I'll be in shortly," I said, and she turned around and headed to the door. "Hey Poppy, I didn't mean to imply. . . ." But she walked out in the middle of my sentence.

I was still soothing my knee when Floria came in. Dressed in a plain but elegant black dress, her hair in a bun, she was making sure the facilities were properly stocked.

"What happened to you?" She put her hands up to her face.

"Clumsy me, I tripped."

"Are you okay?"

"Yes. Nothing's broken, as far as I can tell," I said.

"At least you still look beautiful in your dress. Need more ice?"

"No thanks," I said. She was such a nice lady. After using the ice for a few more minutes, I fixed my hair and headed into the ballroom. Saying hello to guests helped push away the prior events of the evening, easing my humiliation. I bumped into Maya while limping around from table to table.

"How are you doing? That was an awful fall you took," Maya said. "I saw it from the back of the room. I would've come running over, except those men instantly came to your rescue."

"I'm fine, thanks," I replied. "I can't believe I did that. How embarrassing!"

"As long as you're alright," Maya said, as she gave my shoulder a quick rub.

I was glad she'd returned to her normal friendly self, after she seemed a little cold the other day.

The rest of the evening flew by. Chrissy didn't bother to come over to me, probably adding my ungraceful fall to her all-around inept view of me. I wanted to thank Prince Charming for his chivalrous act, but he was nowhere to be seen. Then I remembered. I was pretty sure he was the suave ambassador I met at the Society of Ambassadors event. I didn't see his name on the guest list, though—unless he was a last-minute addition.

Feeling slightly guilty about being disappointed not to see him in the room, I told myself that being a happily married woman didn't mean I couldn't look at other men. Besides, my real Prince Charming, Mark, was in New York at a senior partners' meeting. Otherwise, he would've been at the gala retrieving the shoe and placing it on my foot.

It was late, and the party was beginning to break up. Within an hour's time, the entire ballroom would be dismantled: five hours, and a million dollars raised. It was just past midnight, and I was thrilled to head home, wondering how I'd managed to survive the evening.

Chapter 11

STRAIGHT FROM THE HEART

THE NEXT MORNING, I told Mark what happened when he called from New York.

"How's your knee now?" he asked.

It was sore and stiff, but I was able to move it. "Just bruised, along with my ego. I was mortified!"

"I'm sure it was mortifying, but I'm glad you're alright. No one will remember."

"You're right; they have other more important things to think about. I probably shouldn't wear those stilettos anymore."

"Don't be ridiculous. You look great in them. More so with nothing else on."

"Thanks. I miss you."

"Same."

"How are all your meetings going?" I asked. He'd been uptight before he left.

"Not so good. We didn't come up for air yesterday. The DC office is losing money, and the firm might shut it down."

"What a shame. At least your office here is doing well. They must be happy about that."

"I think so. Good thing I hired Olivia. She's getting a lot done while I'm away. What a fast learner, and super smart."

I wondered if his eyes lit up when he said that. "Great that you found the right help."

"Gotta go; early morning meeting. Have a good day; watch your step." Lately, Mark was always in a rush.

"Will do." I downed my java, and headed to the office. Going for a run was out of the question.

Despite being at Addison until midnight, I got to the office by ten only to find Poppy and Maya there already.

"There's Miss Twinkle Toes," Poppy said when she saw me in the hallway. Good; she wasn't upset with me. Maya was standing near her. Her curly hair was in a messy French twist, a few stragglers framing her beautiful face.

"How are you doing this morning?" Maya asked.

"Other than my knee being sore and bruised, I'm okay. Except I'm exhausted. Both of you must be, too."

"Beyond. I'm in overdrive," Poppy said.

"Ditto," Maya said. "Did you hear about the Brogans? They just showed up decked out

wearing black-tie. They never bought tickets but had the audacity to demand they be seated with Chandler. 'Otherwise, you'll never see another dime from us.' That's what she said."

"Such nerve," I said. "What'd you do?" When I heard

things like this I wondered what gave people the right to feel so entitled.

"Maya acted quickly and figured it out," Poppy said.

Maya rolled her eyes. "I had no choice. Oh, Julia, before I forget, Chrissy wanted me to speak with you about drafting letters."

I yawned. "Okay, let's go to my office."

"With all the hoopla with the gala, we've fallen behind in writing acknowledgment letters," Maya said on the way. "They need to be special, not a form letter. They're for larger donations. It's all in here." Maya handed me a folder when we reached the doorway.

"I've got this," I said. Eager to dive in, I whipped off a few in no time.

MAYA HANDED THEM BACK to me the next day. "Sorry, but Chrissy said you need to make these letters more friendly. She'll speak with you about them when she gets in."

"More friendly?" I asked.

"Yes." She shrugged.

What was up with her lately? It was hard to tell what mood she'd be in. I was also nervous that I'd messed up another assignment. I told myself to stay calm and carry on, and reread some of the letters. They were excellent. Professionally written, and very business-like. Lawyerly, even. I might not be up to par in other areas, but business writing came naturally.

By the time I made several phone calls, Maya told me Chrissy was ready to see me. With a knot in my stomach, I went to her office.

"Ah, there you are," Chrissy said. She motioned for me to sit.

"You wanted to see me?" I asked.

"Apparently you need a lesson in how to write letters."

Writing letters was what I did best. *What the heck is she talking about?*

"Make them warm and fuzzy. Yours are very business-like, instead of being in a development-like voice. They need to sound fluffy."

I tapped my fingers furiously on my thigh, while she continued berating me. My normally low blood pressure must have skyrocketed.

"I'll be signing these, but when you write your own letters, you need to change your style, too," she continued.

"I'll fix them right away." I rose, pivoted on my shoes and strutted out of her office.

Completely deflated, I revaluated my job situation. "Losing" a check, taking the brunt for screwing up a donor's name in print, falling on my face on the dance floor—not to mention dealing with demanding donors, witnessing my boss having crazy sex with a board member, sheer exhaustion, and plenty of criticism—were in the debit column.

The plus side was that each day was different, and never boring. So far, I met some very interesting people. I was exposed to the unique lifestyles of people with extraordinary amounts of money, and it made me feel like I was on the inside track. There was also the backstage buzz and excitement when an artist was in the house. Most of all, raising money was a good challenge, and much better than law. I knew I *had* to get it right.

Once again, I reread some of the letters. Chrissy was right: they lacked a personal touch and were devoid of

warmth—just like her, except when she was around donors. But since when were business letters supposed to be
touchy-feely?

With a few strokes of the keyboard, *How to Write
Fundraising Letters* appeared along with sample templates.
Phrases like *Giving hearts deserve giving hearts*, *Speak straight
from the heart*, and *Heart Matters* leaped off the screen.

Copies of donor acknowledgment letters from our files
revealed letters replete with fluffy, heartfelt sentiments.
Please send my regards to Helen and your beautiful family; or *We
had a splendid time at your dinner party last week*. And over and
over: *grateful, generous, generosity, commitment, loyal, devoted
friends* were repeated like broken records.

Soulfully written warm notes were reserved for personal
occasions, or so I thought. Like the thank you notes I'd
written for our wedding gifts; a skill that had lain dormant
for years. But fundraising was a whole new ballgame.

From a practical viewpoint, people were generously
emptying the contents of their wallets, giving away their
money out of their own free will. Our job was to thank
them for these acts of kindness. What Chrissy was basically saying, although spiked with attitude, was that donors needed more than a practical, efficient thank you to
match their level of generosity. In my "aha" moment, I realized this.

Furiously, I scribbled notes on my legal pad. All of the letters closed with Warm Regards, or in some cases Warmest
Regards; not the more standard Sincerely or Yours Truly.
"Thanks a million" was handwritten by Chrissy often on
the bottom of the pages.

When I finished the new version, I gave them to Maya
who was in her cubicle.

"Here's Chrissy's letters, revised. I sure hope they meet her approval this time around," I said.

"Great." She gave me a quick smile, although she appeared to be preoccupied.

They must have hit the mark, since none were handed back. My crash course had paid off. In the weeks that followed, I became Chrissy's go-to person to write her letters. Maybe I was proving myself, after all.

Then out of the blue, Ambassador Mendoza called.

"I told you I'd be in touch," JJ said. His voice was breathy. "How's everything going?"

"All's well at work," I said, in my best business-like voice.

"Good to know," he said, his accent a little heavier than I recalled. "Have lunch with me; we can talk about the Addison Center."

"Perhaps some other time," I said. "But thanks for calling. It's nice to hear from you, and I appreciate your interest."

I was flattered by his invitation, but I was positive he didn't want to have lunch with me to discuss business. Instead, meeting with Nina for our first Prosecco lunch club get-together was on my calendar. Without a doubt, it was a much safer date.

Chapter 12

EATING CAKE

"WHATEVER HAPPENED to plain coffee and tap water?" I said to Nina as we sipped soy lattes at Cake, a new hot spot.

"Oh, please," she said. "Their fancy bottled water probably contains H_2O from the faucet." Dressed to kill in a stunning red power dress, the red lacquer soles of her black Louboutin heels picked up the dress's color as Nina crossed her legs. "Anyway, the latest scuttlebutt is that even more attorneys have left Reid, Bennett. I just finished a big trial, and I've finally had time to weigh all my options, before I ink a new deal for myself."

"I knew it was a matter of time before you'd figure out what to do." I reached out to touch her hand. "I'm so excited for you. I can't wait to hear about it."

"I promise to keep you posted."

We both sipped our drinks.

"I have some work drama to share," I said."

"Oh?" Her eyebrows shot up. "I'm always up for a good story. Shoot."

"Remember I told you I went to a party on the Savannah IV?" I asked.

"Sure do," Nina said.

"Well, I didn't tell you the whole story. I told Mark about it, but I still feel like I'm walking around with this big secret."

Leaning forward, hand on her chin, she listened intently as I detailed what happened below the deck.

"Geez, it must be awkward for you at work," Nina said sympathetically. "I can only imagine what you must be thinking when you see Chrissy in the office. Knowing what's going on and not being able to say anything must be hard."

"It's uncomfortable, to say the least. And it's not like I'm naïve; I know people have affairs all the time. It also crossed my mind that Chrissy could very well be sleeping with Chandler in order to get big donations. Who knows? It's possible she's slept with other potential donors, too."

"It's not so far-fetched." Versed in all of the inner workings of marital discord, Nina had cred.

"It sounds sleazy, although Chrissy seems classy when 'on', and she's good at leveraging Chandler's social contacts to raise money. But what about Georgina? How does Chrissy look his wife in the eye?"

"It may not bother Georgina. Ever heard the saying about keeping your friends close and your enemies even closer? It's an age-old tactic. Befriending the other woman. At least Georgina can keep tabs on what's going on."

"Georgina gives the feeling that she's made of steel. I'll bet in her heyday she was pretty. She has nice blue eyes and high cheekbones."

"She and Chandler may have worked out an arrangement," Nina said. "Women like her are often willing to put up with a lot to get a lot. Georgina's used to his philandering, and has made her peace. I guarantee she's still in love with being Mrs. Chandler Fairbanks IV, and will never give that up. She might not be in love with him, per se. But definitely his money, which equates to their money."

"You mean throwing parties, running their homes, her charmed lifestyle. *Their* lifestyle, *their* being the operative word," I said.

"Yes, exactly," Nina said.

"Well get this. Chrissy just told our team yesterday that since it's April, with summer not far off, it'll be soon time to recharge our batteries. Only she'll be off to Martha's Vineyard. Excuse me: 'The Vineyard'. Georgina and Chandler have a summer home there. She talks as if she's part of their family," I said. "It gets better. Chrissy will be staying in their cottage, only thirty feet from their main house. Georgina calls it the 'Angel Cottage'."

"How convenient for them," Nina said, her eyebrows raised.

"Uh-huh. The Fairbanks are planning a huge party for Addison Center donors and prospects there, and Chrissy is organizing it, so it's legit that she's going. Lots of the same people from here are headed there."

"Birds of a feather. They play in the same social sandbox, only it moves up north for the summer," Nina said.

"Can you picture Georgina, Chandler and Chrissy enjoying breakfast on the patio in the Vineyard, smiling over coffee and biscuits as they review party details?" I asked. "Sounds so utterly civil."

"It certainly does," Nina said.

"Sorry, but this leading a double-life bit is still hard for me to wrap my head around. Chrissy being with Chandler when he's married to Georgina. Chrissy being there with Chandler, while Georgina might know about them."

"Georgina and Chandler have been together, what, a gazillion years?"

"Yes. Probably like 55," I said.

"Sounds like it's one of those 'until death do us part' deals. I can almost guarantee that he's not willing to lose half his fortune. C'mon, you're an attorney. All their assets are intricately tied together."

"I know, I get it. The tax breaks, the businesses, loads of trusts," I said. "They're way better off to stay married. It just sounds so shallow to be stuck with someone because you have to. It's like making a deal with the devil."

"That's one way to look at it. Don't kid yourself, though. Some men, like Chandler, think they've got it made. They keep up their image as a good family man, and have someone on the side."

"So he has his cake and eats it too." We laughed, and ordered two slices of lemon cake, along with Proseccos.

Getting Nina's reaction to my boss's secret was a relief to me.

"I don't know how you do it," I said. "Dealing with all these bitter, cynical spouses. You're amazing at it, and never get upset or frazzled. I always admired you for that."

"Oh, please. These relationships are second nature to me. I'm immune from living and breathing this stuff. I approach each client like a business deal. The same way you worked on transactions when you were at Reid, Bennett. I omit the emotions and listen, be sympathetic. Then when I'm in court, I go for the jugular."

"You're tough stuff. I say that with great affection."

"So are you. You just don't realize it. Anyway, here's to our first Prosecco club lunch date." She raised her glass and clinked it with mine.

Without lowering my glass I added, "And here's to the *Royal Coconut Beach Lunch Club* and many more fabulous lunches to come."

"Perfect name for our club. Who else should be invited?" Nina asked.

"What about the Reid, Bennett attorneys that we talked about when I was still there?"

"Nah, I'd like to get far away from there." Nina scratched her head. "I have an idea. There's this attorney named Valerie Caine. We're friendly adversaries. We sit on the matrimonial and family law committee at the bar association; we pick each other's brains often. She's a real powerhouse. You'd love her. She handles some pretty high-profile divorces; you may have heard of her, now that you're in high society." Nina gave me a tight smile.

"Very funny. She sounds fantastic," I said. The idea about getting the club going was exciting.

"I'll speak with her. Anyone you can think of?"

I thought about Elise Miller, but I hardly knew her. Nor would it seem appropriate to invite a major donor to our personal social club, although she was someone who I really wanted to get to know better.

"Let me give it some thought. Getting back to my situation at work, should I just ignore that I saw Chrissy and Chandler? Pretend I know nothing?"

"Well, you're not under any obligation, legal or other-wise. Witnessing them doesn't make you an accessory to a crime; nobody stole money. . . ."

"Actually, someone did."

"Someone stole money?" Nina squared her shoulders and leaned forward.

"Not exactly. It's a story for another time." Nina's brows shot up to her hairline.

"Please tell me. Make my day. As if you haven't already." She finished her drink, and I took another bite of cake.

"Okay. Here goes. I placed a huge check from a donor in my drawer, and it wasn't there the next day. Thankfully, Maya found it in the ladies' lounge. As if that wasn't enough, I've messed up a few assignments already, and Chrissy doesn't cut me any slack. She's condescending, nitpicks, and is impossible to please. At least I've finally figured out how to write development letters."

"How frustrating. She should only know how smart you are."

"Wait, there's more," I said. "There was another check."

"Another stolen check?"

"Not stolen. I saw a check made out to Maya from Chandler, sitting on Chrissy's desk. For twenty-five thou-sand dollars. I think Chandler might be paying off Maya not to tattle about his and Chrissy's affair." I licked the gooey, tart cake off my lips.

"This is getting better and better," Nina said. "Forget the drama on stage. Sounds like a soap opera behind the scenes. Could Maya be sleeping with Chandler, too, and he's paying her?" Nina asked, tapping her fingers against her lips.

"Yes, of course it occurred to me. Except I get the feeling

Chrissy wouldn't want to share Chandler, other than with Georgina, which she has no choice."

"Well, whatever the reason, the check business sounds fishy. Stay away and don't get involved. Unless Chrissy's telling you that you have to sleep with donors to get gifts, don't go there. Just do your job, and see what unfolds," Nina said. "In the meantime, cheers to Georgina, Chandler and Chrissy." She raised her glass, and I clinked it with mine for the second time. We drank, finished our cake and headed outside.

"I'm going to go home tonight and start a new novel. Or better yet, focus on Mark. He's been super busy since he got back from New York; maybe he'll appreciate some attention," I said as we waited at the valet.

"Oh, I bet he won't mind," Nina said, laughing. "Have fun, recharge your batteries. I'll keep you posted as soon as I sign the deal." We said goodbye, and I realized how much I missed seeing her every day.

I got home that evening after Mark. He hung up the phone when I walked into his office in our house. He was taking deep breaths, a sign he was stressed.

"Who was that?" I asked.

"Olivia. She's done a lot of research, and unfortunately our latest deal is even more challenging than usual." Mark often worked with female attorneys, which never bothered me. After all, I'd worked with a lot of men at Reid, Bennett and in New York. But Mark was spending a lot of time on the phone with Olivia in the evenings. It seemed she'd wound him up about their latest case.

"I'm going to fix us something for dinner," I said.

I went into the kitchen and looked on my laptop, pulling

up his firm's website. Olivia Woods was a total knock-out; huge brown eyes, long straight dark hair, and full lips. From her bio, she was in her early thirties. If being the Editor of Harvard Law Review, and a former clerk to a top federal judge was an accurate measurement, Mark was right about her being really smart. No wonder he had plenty of time to review issues with her.

I made a quinoa salad and called Mark in.

"I saw Nina for lunch today," I said, in between bites. "She says hi. We've started our Prosecco lunch club. Remember we were going to do that when I was at the firm?"

"Sort of," Mark said.

"We ate at Cake, and I got you a slice of New York cheesecake, your favorite. It's in the. . . ." His phone rang again, its piercing noise interrupting me. I wanted to slam it against the wall.

"I need to finish up with Olivia." He retreated into his office, leaving half of the food on his plate. I waited for about ten minutes, ate alone, and refrigerated the rest of his dinner. By the time I got into bed, I could still hear his voice from the other room. I put a pillow over my head and fell into a deep sleep.

Chapter 13

DOUBLING DOWN

THE NEXT MORNING, I found Mark in his office and on the phone. I waved, and went for a run. By the time I returned, he had left. No note. I checked my phone. No text goodbye. I knew he was so busy, but it was still disappointing.

When I got to the office, I went into the kitchen where there was usually a fresh pot of coffee. Poppy and Maya were there, already. We all agreed how thrilled we were that finally it was the end of April. Season was over, and it was quieter.

But I knew that sponsors for performances and events for the following season needed to be secured, so there wasn't much time for a breather. I headed to Chrissy's office to discuss enlisting the rest of the team with sponsorships.

It looked like she was signing letters, and I knocked on the door, which was open.

She looked up, a little startled. "C'mon in. What do you have for me?"

"Would it be okay if I ask Poppy and Maya to help?"

"I don't have a problem with that," she said, and went back to scribbling her name.

I asked Maya and Poppy to join me in the conference room.

"As you know, the season brochure will be printed in a month, and when donors return in the fall, they'll want to see their names next to a performance. You know how it works. But we can easily double-down on getting sponsors if the three of us do the work; divide and conquer," I said. "We'll raise much more money."

"*We're* going to be making the calls?" Maya said. "But you're so good at that, Julia." As she'd been doing lately, she shrugged a shoulder. I felt like smacking her.

"Chrissy thought it was important that you should be involved."

Maya toyed with a lock of her curly hair. "I just have so much on my plate right now." She struck a pitiful pose.

"Like I said, Chrissy wanted you to help." It was a stretch, but so be it. "The three of us have been speaking with donors during the year. All we need to do now is to contact those who already sponsored, and invite them to do it again. It was a great year, and they had a fantastic time."

"Just like that, they'll write another check?" Maya asked.

It wasn't an unfair question. "No reason for them not to. Review their ticket history, and make some suggestions about what you think they'd like. If they like going to Broadway shows, suggest *Miss Saigon*, for example. The line-up that programming put together is great for the up-coming season."

"It's like matchmaking," Poppy said.

"Exactly. Good analogy," I said.

"Hey, I'm just putting my skills from the dating world to good use."

Maya rolled her eyes, but Poppy wasn't facing her.

"Benefits are important, so tell them about how they'll get to meet the artists backstage, and get great seats," I said. "Their names will be in lights, too. Literally, on the marquee out front. I put together a cheat sheet with all this information." I handed copies to them.

Poring over the list of sponsors this past season, Poppy and Maya seemed pleasantly surprised at how many people they already knew.

"After we're done with renewing these folks, we'll regroup and take a crack at some of our lower-level donors. See if they'll increase to the sponsorship level. One donor at a time," I said.

"You think they'll really do this?" Maya asked.

"Definitely. That's how we'll get donors to contribute more." Armed with scripts, dialing for dollars began.

I made a few calls, then realized we hadn't selected a gala performance from the list. That was important, and I headed back to Chrissy's office. This time around she was standing at her desk. Her form-fitting sleeveless pale pink dress, perfect for the warm and increasingly humid late spring weather, outlined her svelte body.

"Sit, Julia," she motioned with her hand. But she remained standing, allowing her to look down at me.

"I wanted to speak with you about the gala; I meant to do this before," I said.

"Which performance on the list are you thinking about?" Chrissy asked.

"Sarah Brightman."

"I was thinking the same thing," she said. "Any ideas who should be the gala chair? I don't think Savannah wants to do it again this coming year." Finally, she sat down and crossed her arms.

"Um . . . I'm not sure."

"Well have you given it any thought?"

"No." There was so much to think about with sponsors and performances; I'd assumed Chrissy would choose the chair. I didn't have an answer, and felt unprepared.

She sat down, and tapped her fingers on the desk making an annoying clicking sound. There was perhaps fifteen seconds of stony silence.

"How about Artie Brass from our board, and his wife? Penny Brass, what a name. They know everyone at the Waterfront Club. He's referred to as 'Big Artie'. He acts like the mayor at the club, so he's a good choice. He'll get his friends involved. Go ahead and call him. See what he says."

I knew he had a reputation for being mean and nasty. "He doesn't know me. It's probably better if you ask."

"No, Julia," Chrissy said sternly, writing down a phone number. "This is a good opportunity to introduce yourself. Tell him we talked, and that we think it's a great idea. Fluff him up. Tell him it's so important to have their name as the chairs."

I resented Chrissy pushing this off on me, but I had no choice. "Okay." I got up, not realizing Chrissy was still talking, so I sat again.

"Besides, he and Penny just made a gift of fifty million

dollars to Lincoln Center. I assumed you saw the headline in *Society Script*?"

I nodded, and was about to say something but she put her hand out to stop me.

"I know, New York is where they have roots," she said. "But that shouldn't stop them from eking out $100,000 for our gala. He's a huge publicity hound. Whether he has a permanent scowl on his jowly face is irrelevant."

"I get it. He's the right guy," I said.

"He is. First of all, he's on our board. Despite being notoriously grumpy, like I said, Artie is very popular at the Waterfront Club. He still goes to work every day, not only to manage Top Brass, his investment company, but to oversee a group that he'd assembled called the Knights of the Golden Circle." Chrissy clasped her hands behind her neck.

"What does that group do?" I was intrigued.

"It's no different from an ordinary investment club, except that it's on steroids in terms of the amounts invested."

"What does this have to do with our gala?" I asked.

"It's about his elite network. All Artie has to say to his Knights is 'Write a check to Addison,' and they'll do it. Our gala is guaranteed to be a huge success."

"It's that easy?"

She gave me a tight smile. "No one will say no to Artie. He cherry-picked a group of successful investors, former captains of industry and other titans, amassing even more of a fortune for his cronies. Rumor has it that there's a waiting list to become a Knight. A few Addison board members made a boatload of money with him, by the way."

Immediately I thought of Chandler; was he also a Knight? The two men travelled in different social circles, but when it came to an opportunity to accumulate more wealth, they could overlap. I frowned. "It's a shame his acute financial skills can't negate his offensive persona. That's what I've heard." Then I realized I shouldn't have made the snide remark to Chrissy.

"To his credit, he earned every dime toiling on Wall Street," Chrissy said. "First with a big brokerage firm, where the poor boy from the Bronx made it big. Then he created Top Brass Investments, making more of a killing. Depending on the year and the day, he's worth somewhere in the vicinity of 10 wads."

"What's a wad?" When it came to the players in Royal Coconut Beach, Chrissy liked to talk.

"In Royal Coconut Beach lingo, a billion dollars. Year after year, Artie makes the *Forbes* list of the world's wealthiest. He isn't shy about flaunting his wealth around town, so asking for $100,000 is nothing."

I agreed to call him, and left her office. I wrote some bullet points, took a deep breath, and dialed.

"Brass residence," said a man with a British accent.

"Uh, hello, this is Julia Wild from the Addison Center. Is Mr. Brass available?"

"No, but Mrs. Brass is. Would you like to speak with her?"

"Yes, please."

A woman's voice said hello.

"Hi, Mrs. Brass. I'm Julia Wild with the Addison Center. Chrissy Hathaway suggested that I call. We wanted to invite you and Mr. Brass to be next year's Gala Chairs. Your names mean so much in the community, and we very much hope you will consider it. Sarah Brightman will be performing—it will be wonderful, and. . . ."

"I love the idea." Penny interrupted me in a New York accent. "Call me at four. Artie should be back from golf. I need to ask him."

Shoot. I had a meeting at four with marketing, but I'd move it.

"Artie wants to know what the expected contribution would be," Penny said, when I called back.

"$100,000." I was relieved she'd asked. There was a long pause. "We'd be delighted to call you the gala hosts," I added to sweeten the pot.

"Let me see what Artie says. Hold on." After I waited a few long minutes, she returned. "Hello, Jennifer?"

"Actually, it's Julia."

"Right. Artie said fine."

"That's terrific! Thank you so much! Please thank Mr. Brass, too. We're so grateful for your outstanding support." I hung up and smiled. Chrissy had done me a favor by asking me to make the call. Having had success, my confidence skyrocketed. I knocked on her door, excited to share the good news.

"Good," Chrissy said, nonchalantly. "Listen, I'm leaving for the day and won't be in the rest of the week, now that the season is over."

Seriously? Here I was under enormous pressure to line up sponsors; I'd just put the gala chairs in place, added $100,000 to Addison's coffers, and that was her response? But I just nodded and told her to have a good weekend.

That evening, I told Mark about Chrissy's attitude. Then I complained about Maya's initial push-back with sponsorships.

"What do you expect? It's a job, and you get paid to do it," he said.

I was taken aback by his less-than-supportive comment, but continued anyway. "I was so thrilled to get the Brasses on board, yet Chrissy's reaction was ho-hum. I just wish she'd show a little appreciation, and that we could be a team. Instead, she's taking the week off because 'season's over'. Doesn't she realize that we have our work cut out for us, raising money for next season?"

"Apparently not. But you take everything so personally. You want a more sympathetic boss. Guess what? We all do. Just do your job, and stop complaining." He looked at his watch and gave me a dismissive blink.

"I'm not complaining. I'm just telling you what happened," I said. "Geez." *What was up with him?* His phone rang; it was Olivia. Again. He went into his office, and I cleaned up the kitchen.

I remembered when he was a busy fourth-year associate in New York, climbing the ladder. I had just had a miscarriage.

"You're still awake," he said, seeing me propped up in our bed late one night. He sat down sideways beside me, and sweetly brushed the hair out of my face. I hugged him and cried, raging hormones and disappointment to blame.

"It's okay, let it all out, Jools," Mark said, tenderly. "We'll get through this." He kissed me on my head and held me for what seemed a long time. I stopped sobbing. Then he said, "I'm going to take my clothes off, wash up, and get into bed. Are you okay now?"

"Yes," I said, and snorted. He grabbed a tissue from my night table and handed it to me.

"Here you go."

I blew my nose loudly.

"How was your day, by the way?" I asked.

"Pretty crappy. Goes with the territory, I suppose."

Despite the little time we spent together back then, he could be compassionate even after a bad day. That part of him was missing in action now. And his constant talking to Olivia—the woman who now sucked up all his time and attention—was starting to really bother me. The thought that something romantic might have developed between them crossed my mind. I went into the bedroom and lay there for a while, wondering what was going on, before falling asleep watching television alone.

The next several weeks, Poppy, Maya and I continued to line up sponsors. You could feel the buzz of energy, and despite Maya's initial reluctance, she was willingly participating. By the time we finished, we were thrilled that the number of sponsors had tripled from last season. We'd come up with a record-breaking million dollars committed for the upcoming season, and all the names got included in the brochure. Everyone would be happy.

Except Chrissy. She came by my office, waving the catalogue as if it was a fan. She remained standing, peering down at me.

"Chandler said that an acquaintance of his tried to reach you several times when I was out, but you never returned the call. He was interested in becoming the title sponsor for our Broadway series. According to Chandler, he's a billionaire with a pretty new wife, and wanted to impress her with a large donation that would put their name in lights. It's too late, now that the brochure is printed. Why didn't you return his call?" she asked, her jaw clenched.

"Honestly, I never received a message. You said he called

me in your absence? Maybe he called on your line, and Poppy or Maya took the message?" A chill ran through me. Chrissy buzzed Poppy.

"Did a Howell Jackson call recently on my line for Julia?" Chrissy asked.

"Nope."

Maya had the same response.

"Chrissy, I would have definitely returned the call. C'mon," I said. Somehow, I remained calm, despite my frustration and strong urge to lunge at her throat with my hands. "You know I stay on top of things. Always. For once, can't you give me the benefit of the doubt?" Chrissy looked at me with wide eyes, and her eyebrows raised a notch.

"It looks like we left a lot of money on the table," she said. "I'll get Chandler involved to do damage control. Hopefully Mr. Jackson will still donate." She shook her head.

At that moment, I realized that no matter what I said or did, Chrissy was never going to be happy with the job I was doing. Disheartened and feeling defeated, I needed a break—but then the next big assignment landed in my lap.

Chapter 14

ON A WING AND A PRAYER

MAYA HOVERED in my doorway the next morning, wearing a black pantsuit with a black lace camisole underneath that added a touch of femininity.

"Hi there," I said. "You look pretty."

"Thanks. Just wanted to let you know that Chrissy will be out and about today, but she's calling in at three. She'd like to speak with you."

That sounded dire. "I'll be here. Any ideas about what?"

"Sorry, I have no clue." She threw her arms in the air.

Maya started to leave. "Wait a sec, Maya," I said. "About Mr. Jackson's phone call. Are you *sure* he didn't leave me a message? It seems odd that he'd claim he left me several messages on Chrissy's line, yet I never received them. He wanted to donate a lot of money."

"You know these people," She flicked her hand. "They like to sound like a big shot to their friends, so they claim they tried to call someone. Folks like that don't intend to give a dime."

"Got it. Thanks." She probably was right.

As scheduled, Chrissy called at three. "I'd like you to do some research and apply for a grant," she said.

Could this new assignment be punishment for having allegedly not returned the call?

"Meeting an annual fundraising goal is paramount to our fiscal success," Chrissy continued. "Only the private and corporate sectors support us. Addison's founders agreed not to dip their hands in the government cookie jar. But with artists' fees escalating, and major growth in the community, it's time for us to get a fair slice of the pie."

"Okay," I said.

"There's a Florida grant that offers the opportunity to get a million dollars. Go on-line. I'd like you to take a stab at it. And let me know how long it's going to take you."

"No problem," I replied, and hung up.

I went to the website, reviewed the questions, and estimated that it would take a week. I told this to Chrissy. But compiling information in an orderly, methodical way proved more time-consuming than I'd anticipated.

"You need to work on your time-management skills," Chrissy said, when I gave her the new time frame, while seated in her office. She was signing letters while she spoke.

"It's not a problem. I assure you, I'll meet the deadline."

She looked up at me. "Make sure you do. I don't want us to miss this opportunity."

"No worries," I said firmly. What nerve she had to lecture me on time management! I thought as I returned to my office. I should have told her how I kept meticulous hours as a lawyer, met every client deadline, handed in work to senior partners in a timely manner, and found time to manage a home and a husband.

Instead, I put my ignorers on and began writing. Over the next two weeks, I crafted a good case for support, just like a legal brief. It was a welcome break from being "on" all the time during season.

Standing at Kinko's, all of the state-mandated copies were made, and the product was worthy of our executive director's signature. But since I was a virgin grant writer cutting my teeth on a notoriously difficult grant, self-doubt kicked in.

"Well, you got it done," Chrissy said, holding up a copy of my masterpiece in my doorway.

"Yup. Told you I would," I said, and gave a smug smile.

"We'll head to Tallahassee to appear before the Florida grant panel. Maya will make the arrangements; we'll take Webster's plane. It's in a few weeks."

Did she just say *we?* I was looking forward to spending quality time with her, only for the chance to win her over. Even better, I'd try to find out what the real scoop was regarding Maya and the check that I saw on her desk. I still couldn't let that go, and wanted to get to the bottom of it. If I was lucky, Chrissy would be in one of her rare talkative moods.

That evening, Mark and I were scheduled to have dinner at Hibiscus with Brad, one of his partners from his firm who was in town from New York, and his wife Susie. I arrived before they did and was seated promptly. The hip place was packed, mostly with younger people who lived in town all year round.

Mark, Brad and Susie showed up at the same time ten

minutes later. I stood up and we all exchanged kisses. Mark put his phone on the table and sat down, loosened his tie, and ordered a drink. There was some business talk, and we spoke about what living and working in Florida was like. Halfway through dinner, Mark's phone rang.

"Excuse me," he said. "I need to take this."

Couldn't he just turn his damn phone off for a few hours? I disguised my aggravation, not wanting them to think I wasn't a supportive wife. He returned perhaps ten minutes later.

"Sorry," he said, picking up right where he left off with us. "It was Olivia from the office; it was important." He looked at Brad. "She had a question about the Quinzy merger."

"Wow, she's really turned out to be fantastic," Brad said. I caught Susie rolling her eyes, and wondered why. Did she know something?

"She is," Mark said, smiling broadly. I didn't like it one bit.

Later that night, as I put on my nightgown, I asked, "What did Olivia want that was so urgent?"

"Seriously, Julia? Olivia's been such a help with this merger. You won't complain when I get a big bonus, so don't complain now."

"I'm not. What's wrong with you? I'm just asking why you needed to speak with her when we were having dinner."

"Nothing's wrong. I'm just under a lot of pressure, and you're now questioning me?"

"I'm sorry. It's just that . . . oh, forget it." I wasn't sure why I just apologized.

We got into bed, and Mark fell asleep immediately. I stayed awake for a long time. Mark became so bad-tempered and defensive just because I mentioned Olivia. Could they really be up to something?

After Mark left the next morning, I called Nina and told her about Olivia.

"It's not as if he talks about her all the time, right?" Nina asked.

"Not really."

"Associates are at the beck and call of senior partners. You remember, they need to prove themselves. C'mon, Mark's probably enjoying it. He's a guy."

"I might be overreacting."

"Don't worry so much. Catch you later, I'm off to court."

I understood what Nina said, but I still wasn't happy about it.

THE FOLLOWING WEEK, Chrissy and I were off to Tallahassee to present the grant to the panelists. Looking pale compared to her usual rosy color, Chrissy slid into the seat next to me on Webster's plane. She had no make-up on, and wore a dark pantsuit. She leaned over, practically whispering.

"I woke up with terrible laryngitis. You'll need to present our case to the panel," she said. "Introduce me, so they know Addison's vice president of Development took the time to be present." An uncontrollable coughing fit seized her.

The plane took off. Chrissy was resting, her eyes closed. I was bummed that her cough would put a damper on our conversation; I'd hoped to get to know her better on this trip.

After landing, a car whisked us to the building where the interviews were being held. Once inside the conference room, we were astonished that panelists had already whizzed through the docket, and we were next.

With no time to gain my composure, I made my way

to the podium. The silence in the room accentuated my pounding heart. Taking a deep breath, I began.

"My name is Julia Wild, and I am the Grants director at the Addison Center. Chrissy Hathaway, the executive vice president of Development, is here today." I pointed in her direction, "but she's lost her voice." Chrissy stood up and gave a queen-like wave.

After I recited the bullet points with what I thought was a surprising amount of authority, the firing squad went at it.

"How many brochures get distributed?"

"Fifty thousand," I said, fairly certain it wasn't a criminal offense to commit perjury before a state grant panel.

"How many students do you serve?"

Easy. "30,000."

"Will you be expanding the program?"

"Yes . . . if we get funding." Even the grumpy-looking woman with a perpetual frown broke into a half-smile. Ten minutes later, it was over. Returning to my seat, Chrissy smiled, and tried to say something. But this only instigated another coughing fit, and she made a quick exit.

As we boarded the plane, I said to Chrissy, "A girl sure could get used to traveling like this." Then I realized who I was talking to: Chrissy, who'd soon be heading to Martha's Vineyard on Chandler's private plane. It also occurred to me that it was likely she'd faked her illness today so she wouldn't have to speak before the panel. Anything was possible with her.

Once we landed, Chrissy went straight home, and stayed there for a few days to recover from her alleged illness.

I returned to my empty house and fell asleep reading. I didn't wake up when Mark got in.

Chapter 15

LUNCH DATES

MARK WAS IN HIS OFFICE at home when I got up the next morning. The paper was lying on the counter. On the cover was an article about Reid, Bennett. It described how there had been a recent mass exodus of attorneys, as other prominent firms were looking to expand and enticed them away with money. I was in the middle of reading it when Mark came in.

"Good morning," I said. I could smell his sweet and musky cologne.

"Morning," he mumbled. No kiss. He was still in his underwear, but clean-shaven, his hair neatly combed. He grabbed an apple from the refrigerator and took a bite.

"Did you read the latest on Reid, Bennett?" I asked.

"Yes."

"I can't imagine what will happen to them."

"Why do you care? Can't you just move forward?"

I was stunned by his answer. "I have. I like where I am, but I still like to know what's going on there. How can I not be curious? Nina's still there, and she's my friend."

He shook his head and left. Lately it seemed like our casual conversations erupted into arguments. All I'd done was comment on the status of my former employer, yet he'd criticized me for that. I took a shower, got dressed and shouted goodbye from the other room, slamming the door.

On the way to the office, I fantasized about going to lunch with JJ, and how his dark, intelligent eyes would look right into mine as we dined on lobster rolls by the beach. Maybe we'd meet at the Oceanfront Hotel, the place where the Society of Ambassadors event was held. By the time I parked my car in Addison's garage, the fantasy had escalated into a passionate kiss in the hotel's elevator. When the doors opened, we'd head to a luxurious room overlooking the ocean.

I snapped myself out it. In the past, straying from Mark had never been a possibility. Once, back in New York, a partner at the law firm I worked at actively pursued me. The minor flirtation was fun, but I wouldn't have let it go anywhere, nor did I have outrageous fantasies. Somehow I was in a different place now.

When I reached the office, my thoughts shifted to today's luncheon at the Coconut Garden Club with Elise. Although it was June, and even though many residents had left for the summer, the room was filled with ladies in colorful flowered dresses when I arrived. Elise and I sipped lemonade and strolled the beautiful gardens after the event.

"What did you think about the presentation today?" Elise asked.

"I enjoyed it, eco-friendly gardening is new to me. How'd you get involved here?"

"Clients suggested it. I'm on the board, only because it helps with my interior design business." She finished her lemonade and threw the cup in the trash.

"We had a great table. The guy next to me talked art, politics, the latest books. He was smart."

"That's why I sat him next to you. I have pull."

We walked around the lush gardens, stopping every now and then to admire flowers and plants. The scent from the creamy white flowers on the large magnolia trees was intoxicating, the rows of tropical flowers bursting with color. It was days like these that I loved my job.

A week later, she called. I was happy to hear from her.

"What a touching, adorable little card you sent," Elise said. "Nobody takes the time anymore to handwrite anything. Everyone's way too busy on their iPad and laptops. Our grandchildren especially. They're so young, but that doesn't stop them from having their phones superglued to their little hands."

"Well, call me old-fashioned, but I enjoy writing notes. I had such a good time. The best part was the quality time we spent walking through the magnificent gardens."

"Don't you just love that old banyan tree? When my clients mention they'd like a family photograph for their living room, I suggest it as a backdrop."

"How's your new project going?" I asked. "Your work and what you've done is so inspirational." I hoped my kissing-up wasn't too transparent, but the Millers were major donors.

"You know the phrase 'carpenters, painters, and curtain-makers'? David and I just cancelled our trip to Monte

Carlo. We're staying put so I can finish a job. *Architectural Digest* is interested in doing a feature story on this soon-to-be beauty I'm working on. Rumor has it that it's going to be nominated for a major award. That is, if I get it done."

"That's fantastic, Elise. Congrats!"

"Fingers crossed. Anyway, while I'm in town I'd like to set up lunch with you and my friend Valerie Caine. You may have heard of her," Elise added.

"Yes, I have. She's an attorney who handles some pretty high-profile divorces. I know about her because my friend Nina is friendly with her."

"That's Valerie. Top-notch in her field. Before going to law school, she had a thriving practice as a therapist. She's a fantastic woman. She and Teddy Stevens, her husband, would like to join us for performances at the Addison Center. I told her they need to become donors."

Now, that was great news. "Thank you for thinking of us."

"You bet. My assistant will set up a lunch at the Waterfront Club. Valerie's a member there, too. Hey, why don't you get your friend Nina to join us? You've said such nice things about her, and I'd love to meet her. It would be perfect, since they know each other already."

"Great idea."

As soon as I hung up, I called Nina.

"You're in the big league now," she said. "Plus, I know the point of the lunch is to get you a new donor. But you, me, Valerie, and Elise having lunch together—we couldn't have planned our Royal Coconut Beach Lunch Club any better!"

"I know! It really worked out well," I said.

"Since you'll be pitching the Addison Center to Valerie,

you should know that she founded Valerie's House, in addition to her practice. It's a shelter for abused women and their children. She's quite the raconteur, too."

"I'm looking forward to it," I said.

"Okay. Back to work!"

As soon as I hung up, the phone rang.

"Julia?" I recognized his voice immediately.

"Yes?" I played dumb.

"It's JJ. How are you?"

My stomach fluttered. "I'm good."

"It's been awhile. I hope you'll reconsider having lunch with me," he said.

"I can't right now. Perhaps another time. I'd really like that." I would've said yes, but because of my attraction to him, I was afraid.

"Sure. I hope so." He hung up without waiting for a reply.

I whispered into the phone, "I hope so too."

Chapter 16

ROYAL COCONUT BEACH LUNCH CLUB

THE FOLLOWING WEEK, I pulled up to the Waterfront Club for lunch, parking my white Acura next to the Mercedes-Benzes and Bentleys in the circular driveway. The lobby smelled of fresh paint, with plush mint-green carpet and bright wallpaper sporting whimsical motifs like monkeys and colorful butterflies.

Elise hugged me tightly and introduced me to Valerie. Her perfectly tapered black pantsuit with gold buttons, gold necklace and colorful scarf screamed "high-class professional". Her hair was brown with caramel highlights and styled in an asymmetrical long pixie cut that complemented her soft, round face. I guessed she was in her forties. We were seated by the window, overlooking the lush golf course dotted with royal palms.

"I understand you're an attorney, Julia," Valerie said.

"Yes, but I don't practice now. I'm sure Elise has shared with you that I work at the Addison Center as a development officer," I said, upgrading my title a bit.

"Good for you for following your dream," Valerie said. Which dream she was referring to, I had no idea.

"Yes, I'm so fortunate," I replied.

"I love what I do, so it doesn't feel like work. I know Elise told you I'm a matrimonial attorney in town. Oh, Nina just walked in," she said, pointing. "That woman's in a league of her own."

"She said the same exact thing about you," I said.

Nina gave Valerie and me a hug, and I introduced her to Elise.

As Nina took her seat, she asked, "Have I missed anything? Is Valerie in the middle of one of her wild stories?"

"Not yet," Valerie said. "Want to know why I love what I do?" We all bobbed our heads.

"This morning I met with my client, a very fine gentleman. Attorney-client privilege, so no names. He told me he'd been having a candlelit dinner with his fiancé. He told her he loved and trusted her, and wanted to spend his whole life with her. He just turned 92! I mean, how much longer does this stud muffin thinks he has? I tell you, with Viagra, it's a whole new world." We all laughed.

"Next, he asked her to sign the prenup," Valerie continued. "The one that I prepared. She stood up and proceeded to splash her glass of wine in his face before storming out."

"Talk about a Hollywood moment," Elise said.

"No shock that he's worth a fortune," Valerie continued. "I'm talking billions. She's a divorced 55-year-old. They met while he was shopping in Bloomingdales's in New

York, where she was a salesperson in the men's clothing department. Beautiful, sexy, and a great bod, by the way. He showed me pictures of her in her bikini on his yacht. No amount of diet and exercise ever paid off like that for me."

"Ditto," I said, although Valerie looked pretty fit.

"What's wrong with her? She'd be getting a huge windfall," Elise said.

"People sometimes don't think things through," Nina said.

"No kidding. You know how the saying goes: a man gets a nurse, the woman gets a purse," Valerie said.

"Except that in instances like these, the catch is, the nurse is rarely the younger wife. It's the young wife who *hires* the nurse and runs off with the purse," Elise said, and we all laughed. She summoned the waiter with a wave of her manicured hand.

"Please bring us some Prosecco, will you dear?"

Nina met my eyes when she asked for Prosecco. I gave her a wink.

"You know, lately I've been seeing a huge uptick in prenups," said Valerie. "Have you, Nina?"

"Yes, I have, as a matter of fact."

"All these older men and younger women. Drafting these documents has been keeping me in business these days. I'm also involved with Valerie's House, what little time I have left."

"That's wonderful that you created the shelter," I chimed in. "We're focused on kids at the Addison Center, too. Our education program is an important part of our mission."

"Tell me about it," Valerie said.

"We bring in 90,000 students from local schools each year. They get to see live performances. Most of them are extremely poor, so chances are they'd never experience the magic of the performing arts. While we might not be feeding them, we're providing food for the soul. It can have a huge impact on a child's life."

Elise smiled. "David and I support Addison because of the performances we attend. We get great seats and meet artists, but now I'm learning it's more than that."

"Well, my heart is all about helping the kids," Valerie said. "Let me speak with Teddy. We'll do something. At the least we'll become Maestro Society members, so we don't have to freeload off of Elise and David to get into that beautiful room." She smiled at Elise.

"The Parker Pavilion," I said.

"Yes, that's it. Send me the information, will you please." She handed me her card.

"Absolutely. Thanks for considering it."

"Of course. Teddy will love the idea. When I was launching Valerie's House, he was supportive. He was absorbed in his own practice, but listened to me ramble about it."

"He's a lawyer too?" I asked.

"Nope, a neurosurgeon," Valerie said. "We've been happily married for ten years. I was married before, when I was young and immature. I was absorbed with my career, which didn't help. Not that I'm not now, but my priorities have shifted."

"Well, ladies," Nina said, and clinked her fork on her glass. "Since we're on the topic, I've met someone. His name is Girard Bissett. He's a lawyer, white-collar crime." She looked at Valerie. "Val, you probably know him."

"I sure do," she said, nodding. "Handsome devil, and smart. Best in his field."

"That's great, Nina," I said. "I'm happy for you."

"It's too soon to really know, but I'm crazy about him."

"Sounds wonderful," Elise said, and clapped her hands.

Nina looked at me, and I motioned for her to speak.

Nina cleared her throat to get everyone's attention. "Since we're all here together, I want to throw out an idea. Julia and I had always wanted to start a Prosecco lunch club."

"Sounds like fun," Elise said.

"We decided that we have to get it going, once and for all," Nina continued. "So, how would you ladies like to be part of the Royal Coconut Beach Lunch Club? We can get together every few weeks, share bubbly, lunch, advice and gossip."

"That's a great idea," Valerie said.

"Count me in," Elise said. She raised her glass and we all clinked. "To the Royal Coconut Beach Lunch Club! I insist on hosting next time."

Elise, Valerie, Nina and I continued to bond over Proseccos. Slightly tipsy, I made a mental note to let Mark know how I'd lightened up at lunch today.

Along with the roses I sent to Elise later that day to thank her for lunch, I ordered a bottle of Prosecco for the middle of the arrangement, with a note saying, *Hats off to you! Here's to a great season ahead, and to the Royal Coconut Beach Lunch Club! Cheers.*

I left Chrissy a message that I'd met Valerie, and that she and her husband were going to become Maestro Society members. At least she'd know I was getting results.

Shortly after, Nina texted me:

> Loved meeting Elise, and isn't Valerie terrific? I'm thrilled we finally have our Prosecco lunch club!
>
> XO Nina

I wrote back right away:

> You're so right. I'm excited, too. And what
> great news about Girard! You were glowing
> today—Now I know why!
>
> XO Cheers, Julia

Afterwards, I handwrote some notes, made some phone calls, and left for the day.

On the way out, I spotted Floria in the lobby.

"It's so nice to see you again," I said.

"I've missed seeing you, now that season's over and there are no shows at night," Floria said. "What a colorful dress," referring to my bright orange frock. "And you're wearing pretty lipstick, as usual. I should sell that shade."

"Thanks. It's my favorite." I dug through my purse to show her what it was, then I headed home. Mark was working late, which was an everyday occurrence lately. I took a warm bubble bath, and went to sleep.

I was at my desk the next morning, deeply absorbed in composing a letter, when the phone rang.

"Thank you for the beautiful flowers," Elise said. "The Prosecco was a lovely touch."

I laughed. "I had such a good time, and am thrilled to have met Valerie. Not just because she'll be a donor at Addison, but she's such an interesting, fun person."

"Yes, she is. Nina's also terrific, too" Elise said. "I'm excited about our lunch group." Her assistant had a lunch date coordinated with the four of us an hour later.

The next thing I knew Maya came in. She shut the door behind her.

"What's up?" I asked.

"I hate gossip." She sat in the chair, and drew in her lips. "I've wanted to tell you about something, but wasn't sure if I should."

I figured she knew about Chrissy's affair. I'd play dumb.

"You've piqued my interest," I said, nervous to hear what was next.

"Okay. Someone in programming told me that Poppy had applied for your job, and was really upset that Chrissy hired you. But Chrissy had doubts about whether Poppy would be able to solicit donations. Just because she's a good event planner doesn't mean she'd be good at fundraising."

"That's interesting." I put my finger on my chin. "Meanwhile, Chrissy thinks I don't do anything right. Like the spelling error. . . ."

Maya cut me off. "Did you ever think Poppy might have had something to do with that? She could have changed it right before it went to the printer, after you proofed it."

"You think Poppy was jealous, and tried to make me look bad?"

"Uh-huh. To show how competent she was, and how careless you were. Then there's the teleprompter disaster." She smirked. "Mr. Ashton's remarks were *your* responsibility. I bet she tinkered with it."

I thought about it. "I did ask Poppy to double-check on that while we were working in the ballroom. I didn't think twice about it at the time." After a pause, I said "What about the check that you found?"

"No idea why it would be in the ladies' lounge. Maybe Poppy had something to do with that as well."

I leaned back, and put my hands behind my head. "It's all

making sense. How could I have been so blindsided? Anyway, please say you didn't want my job, too." I smiled.

"Nope, I hate asking people for money. I'll do something bigger and better one day. For now, this place pays the bills, and I'm learning."

"Good to know," I said.

"You should confront Poppy," Maya said.

"Nah, I don't usually like confrontation," I said. "But I'll think about it."

She nodded and left.

Disturbed by this news, I called Nina and told her everything. "Stay away," Nina said. "Chrissy is so strange, she may not believe you. You're too new to go around accusing co-workers. Besides, you have zero evidence."

"What if I talked to Paul Hess? Addison's executive director."

I heard Nina sigh. "So you're now going to go over your boss's head? Does he even know who you are?"

"Um . . . I don't think so. I've rarely seen him. Okay, dumb idea."

"You said it, not me. Looks like your hands are tied, for now. Try not to worry."

I felt even more uptight after speaking with Nina, and decided to discuss it with Mark over dinner. I ordered pizza and salad, but it was cold by the time he got home so I reheated it. He took his tie and jacket off, and sat down at the kitchen table. I filled our glasses with wine and told him what Maya had said.

"C'mon, don't invent a problem." His wine glass made a ping sound when he put it down.

"I'm just telling you what Maya said. Geez." I used to

tell him about work problems all the time, and he'd help me solve them. *Why not now?*

"You're being ridiculous," he said. "First, you're freaked out about Chrissy and Chandler, for no reason."

No reason? Seriously?

"Now someone's trying to sabotage you. Stuff happens in an office. Can't you let it go?" He took a bite of salad.

"Sure." I snapped my fingers. "Easy as that. So how was *your* day?" I was so frustrated I wanted to scream.

"Stressful. I'm working with an awful client to negotiate a huge transaction. The firm's depending on me to finish."

"Sounds like a lot of pressure."

My issues sounded petty next to his, but his sharp reaction was uncalled for. When dinner was over, he went to his office. After loading the dishwasher, I went to see him, unsure what I'd say. The door was closed, his voice loud and snappy.

I changed my mind and retreated to the bedroom.

Chapter 17

LIKE A MILLION BUCKS

TWO DAYS LATER, I had just gotten home from work, and overheard Mark on the phone saying that his partners in New York wanted him to finish up another important merger quickly. He came into the kitchen, still dressed but without a jacket and tie. He looked tired, his eyes bloodshot and slightly drooping. In between bites of salad, I told him about our lunch group, intentionally keeping the conversation light. I also mentioned I needed some new makeup, but I doubted he was listening.

On Saturday, though, Mark suggested we head to Royal Coconut Beach for a shopping excursion.

"You said you needed makeup," he said.

Ah, so he *was* listening. Why Les Saisons though? I usually got my makeup at the drugstore.

Black Opium's intoxicating scent bombarded us as we opened the door of Les Saisons.

"Let's take a look on the women's floor," Mark said. Cutting through the cosmetics area, we headed up the escalator to women's apparel. I turned around to show Mark a pretty white blouse with ruffles, but he was missing in action. A few minutes later, I heard him chatting with someone. Standing next to him was a distinguished woman in a white blazer, navy and white striped palazzo pants, Chanel ballet flats, and tons of gold jewelry.

"Julia, come meet Vianora Vanella," he said as I walked in their direction.

"*Bonjour.* Your husband asked me to help you find some things. He tells me you are a big deal at the Addison Center."

Mark had found me a personal stylist at Les Saisons! On top of that, he'd told her that I was a "big deal." He was rarely effusive; now he was bragging about me. I wondered about the sudden change of mood, given that he'd been so grouchy lately, but I was happy to go with it.

"I'm not such a big deal. I just started working there last fall."

"I've been to the Addison Center. It's so elegant, in a class by itself. Let me see, a size 2, I'm guessing?" I motioned with my thumb heading upwards. She walked around picking up items, flinging them over her arm until she could no longer hold them. Mark was already seated on a large silver pouf, on his phone again. Just because it was Saturday didn't mean his business came to a grinding halt.

Following Vianora into the dressing room, I began trying on clothes.

"Keep, keep. Out! Definitely a keeper. I like your

husband, by the way," she said. "He's a keeper, too." I knew he was, which made me even more concerned about how distant he'd been acting lately.

"No, take it off," Vianora continued.

The "keep" pile was getting bigger. Among several items was a red power dress, and a dressy black pantsuit.

"Perfect to wear all day and into the night. So long as you put heels on and change your jewelry, maybe add a scarf for the evening." Looking me up, down and sideways, she said, "I'll be right back."

I actually was enjoying her scrutiny. Graduating to the big league, I desperately needed all the help I could get. Vianora returned in a few minutes with some brightly colored scarves, and draped them over the black suit.

For fun, I put the red dress back on to show Mark. He broke into a broad smile, giving me the "OK" sign, then returned to his call.

Vianora then brought in an elegant black cocktail gown with a matching flower on the shoulder.

"It's a new designer. What size shoe are you?"

"Seven."

"I'll be right back." She liked saying that. A few minutes later, she returned with a pair of black silk closed-toe Valentino four-inch beauties. On the side of each was a large rhinestone arrow embedded in the fabric. The store's seamstress pinned the dress so the hem was perfect with the shoes; insurance against trip-and-falls at next season gala.

Looking in the mirror, Vianora was right on the money. My money, in fact. Thrilled to have someone helping me, I'd ignored the prices, but now I snuck a glance at the gown's tag. Vianora noticed my shocked expression.

"It's worth spending a little more on your clothes. Your image is important. You're in a high-end business. The key is to remember that you wear the clothes; the clothes don't wear you. Own the look. Anyway, don't worry. Your adorable husband is taking care of your purchases today."

"He is?" Usually I paid for my clothes with my own earnings.

"I told you I liked him," she said.

"I have to pick up some foundation and blush. Is there a brand you recommend?"

"Go see Ameline, our makeup consultant; she's a genius," Vianora said, as we rode down the escalator with Mark tagging along, still on his phone.

By the time we left, I was the proud owner of new clothes and shoes, as well as the perfect foundation, blush, mascara, liner, brow pencil and everything else under the Royal Coconut Beach sun.

"Now you'll be dressed to kill, and look like a million bucks," Mark said on the way home.

"I was wondering why you wanted to go with me to buy makeup. I hadn't expected to walk away with beautiful clothes."

"You needed some new things. I want you to enjoy them," he said. Then his phone rang again.

"Thank you, sweetheart," I managed to get in before he answered the call. I meant it, too. I could walk into the store and buy beautiful clothes without Mark, but it had been his idea. Owning the clothes didn't matter all that much. The act of thinking of it and taking me there had made me feel special. It didn't even bother me that he'd been on the phone in the store.

Having thought something might be going on romantically between Mark and Olivia now seemed far-fetched. And in a few weeks, the two of us would be heading for vacation in the Galapagos Islands. Things may have been wobbly between us lately, but nothing all that unusual. As we drove home, I chalked Mark's distance up to work pressure on both of our parts.

Chapter 18

WAR PAINT

THE FOLLOWING WEEK, I headed to The Upper Crust Café to meet the group for lunch. The restaurant was known for its quiches, kale avocado salads, and warm French baguettes. Translated, this meant that lettuce, bread and cheese were served up for seventy-five dollars. It wasn't the food that was the attraction, though. In existence for four decades, it was famous in town for its A-listers, a robust happy hour, and impossible-to-get dinner reservations; a place to see and be seen. Artists who performed at the Addison Center were known to grab a nightcap there after the final curtain went down.

With brightly painted toucans and palm trees adorning the walls, and white embossed fans swirling, it was an indoor tropical oasis. The female waitstaff were in crisp Lilly Pulitzer neon-colored dresses, their male counterparts equally colorful in Lilly ties and bright green slacks. The hostess, also in Lilly, escorted me to a table in the back.

Elise stood, and we hugged. On the table was a large white box secured with a bright pink gigantic bow. "I got a little something for you, Julia. To congratulate you on all the new sponsors you brought in. David and I are proud of you," she said. "Valerie loved you, by the way. She'll be here in a few minutes; she just texted me."

"She's so impressive," I said.

"I'll say. First, to have been a psychologist, and then go back to law school, and become top-notch in her field."

"I was looking forward to today and I'm glad the four of us are going to get together regularly."

"Me too." Elise smiled.

"Oh, Nina texted me, too. She's running a little late." I looked at the box in front of me. "Thank you for this gift. You always make me feel special. May I open it?" I asked.

"Please, go right ahead," Elise said.

"Bonne Vie Gifts! My favorite store on Laguna," I said when I untied the bow to reveal the store's sticker. I opened the box, and uncrumpled the hot pink tissue paper. Inside was a sparkling silver makeup mirror and lipstick holder, followed by a compact mirror adorned with vintage *Vogue* artwork. There was also a lipstick with coordinating lip liner and gloss, in Chanel's latest color.

"I thought it would look great on you. The Chanel's reddish plum shade would go nicely with your fair complexion."

"This is so kind of you," I said. Given her incredible sense of style, anything she'd select would be perfect. But it was the thought behind it that mattered the most.

"It's time to look your best. You're in the front row. People are watching, and they care how you look. My mother always told me, you never get a second chance to make a first impression. It takes only seconds for people to size you up."

My own mother never would have said something like that, comfy in her glamour-free academic world. But the world that I was part of now required having the right image.

"Yes. Always be 'development-like'," I said, agreeing with Elise.

"If you ask me, it's all about confidence in a tube. Or beauty in a bottle. The rest is up to you."

The last part made me nervous. Only so much insecurity could be masked by beautiful make-up.

"Oh, before I forget, do you and David want to change things up next season? Hubbard Street Dance Chicago is coming. I know David loves classical music, but you both love dance. I'll reserve it for you, if you'd like."

"Pencil us in. I'm sure he'll be happy to take a break from classical music. Besides, I want to see Hubbard, and I always get my way. I say that with affection," she said.

"Thanks, Elise. David too. May we get an additional sponsor? You know how popular it will be."

"Get as many as you can; the more the merrier. Pair us with another nice couple.

Maybe we'll co-host cocktails or a dinner. That reminds me, I wanted to tell you that there's lot of cocktail chatter in the Hamptons about the Addison Center. Hold on," she said, looking towards the front of the restaurant. "There's Valerie and Nina." Elise's arm shot up and she waved. When they reached our table, everyone exchanged hugs.

"Sorry we're a little late," Valerie said, as they took their seats.

Nina nodded. "We both got detained with clients. What've we missed?"

"I was just about to tell Julia that her hard work with sponsorships has created quite the buzz."

"I'm shocked to hear it," I said.

"They're also saying how wonderful Chrissy is, but I know you're the one who has made it happen."

"I should've known. It's always about Chrissy," I said, my mood now deflated.

Elise continued. "To tell you the truth, I spoke with Artie Brass when I called Penny about some antiques; he picked up her phone. Knowing David and I are involved at the Addison Center, he made sure to brag about how he and Penny are the gala chairs, but he also mentioned 'the new girl' and said 'she's riding on Chrissy's coattails. She's too young, and green behind the ears', was what he said."

"Too young? I'm approaching mid-life! Who knew 'looking young' would be professionally detrimental? I didn't even think he knew I existed. I dealt with Penny." I put my hands to my cheeks and they felt warm. "Is my face red?"

Elise smiled. "It matches the new lipstick, actually. I'm only telling you this because I want you to have your guard up."

I was furious. I knew I was doing a great job—but with Artie's comment, Chandler only having eyes for Chrissy, and who knows what their other board cronies thought, proving myself was more than just an uphill battle. The perception of riding on someone else's coattails was far from the truth, but the board wasn't going to rally around and provide support; worst case, they wanted me to fail. In addition, Poppy was probably determined to make me look bad, and gaining Chrissy's confidence despite my successes seemed impossible.

"I appreciate your telling me this," I said. "But it's so disturbing." I sighed, feeling tears well in my eyes, and was a little embarrassed.

"Oh, dear. You're really upset." Elise reached over and put her hand over mine and gave it a gentle squeeze. "I'm so sorry; that wasn't my intention. On the contrary, I wanted you to be careful and know who you were dealing with. Artie is an awful guy with lots of power."

I simply nodded, trying to calm down.

"Let's order some Prosecco," Nina said. "Look, Julia. You can't control what other people say."

"Listen to your friend," Valerie said. "She's right. I say the same thing to my clients, especially if they're in the middle of a divorce."

A minute later, the server brought our drinks. I took a sip. "No matter what, I can't seem to get it right." I shook my head.

"What do you mean?" Elise asked.

I drew a deep breath. "I'll start from the beginning."

They leaned in, and I told them about Chrissy, Maya, Poppy, and all that transpired. I also shared with them Chrissy and Chandler's relationship. Although Nina was my close friend, divulging confidential information about Addison to Valerie and Elise was risky. As new donors, they could have second thoughts about donating. But I felt comfortable with them and took my chances. It was good to get it off my chest.

"Julia, now that you've shared the whole picture, I certainly understand why you're upset," Elise said. "I'm still not sorry I told you about Artie's comments. With what you're dealing with, it's important you know."

Elise reached over again and touched my hand. "I'm sure you'll succeed, despite all of them. I have every confidence in you; cream always rises to the top."

"My mother used to say that," I said, with a slight smile. "Just keep moving forward and don't worry about them, right?" This would be my new mantra.

Elise smiled. "Exactly. Your day to shine will come."

"I know Artie Brass, and I agree with Elise, you need to watch your back," Valerie said. "It's best to be forewarned, not that you can do anything about what he says, to Nina's point. You seem like you're mighty disciplined. Stay focused on results, and pay no attention to this nonsense. Trust me, it'll serve you well."

"Thanks for your encouragement; all of you. It's difficult to believe when you're in the thick of it, though. I can't believe they're talking about *me*. It's pathetic."

"Some people have nothing better to do than gossip. The men win the award in that category," Nina said. "Don't fret, they'll be on to the next topic by next month."

Their support helped. Still, it felt like the odds were stacked against me. I feared another ambush, but was determined to carry on. We finished lunch, and I grabbed the check.

"I insist," I said. "We talked business, so it's Addison's treat." I gathered my Bonne Vie goodies and we went outside.

Now that we were in the warm, tropical-scented air, the smell of gardenias filling my nostrils, I felt better. I'd keep my nose to the grindstone, but it was comforting to know these women had my back.

Chapter 19

FANTASYLAND

"NICE DRESS," Nina said when she saw me enter The Upper Crust Café. It was only a week later from when our group met. This time it was just the two of us; we were trying to make the effort to get together consistently now.

"Thank you. Mark took me shopping, a few weekends ago. Les Saisons. I now have a personal stylist—Vianora— who helped me pick some beautiful clothes. You'd approve of them."

"You're lucky. How many husbands would actually be interested in what you wear?"

"Not many, I suppose," I answered, and gave a half-shrug.

"C'mon, he wants you to succeed. It's showtime, and he knows how important playing the part is. I think it's great."

I nodded, weary from hearing about how looks mattered.

"Anyway, too bad Elise is in New York with a client picking out artwork," Nina said. "As you know, Valerie's unable to make it today, unless by some miracle the judge dismisses her case."

"Either way, it's still a Club lunch, right?" I pointed to the split of Prosecco that she'd ordered.

"Yes, but it's also a celebration lunch. I'm able to share my news with you, finally. It involves Valerie. . . ."

"Don't tell me," I said, cutting her off. "You went over to Remsen and Clearwater? And Valerie's heading there too?" I asked.

"No, no. I'm done with big firm practice. Forever. But you're not far off. Valerie and I have formed our own partnership. Say hello to one half of Fields and Caine."

"Wow, that's fantastic! I assumed you'd take your clients and go to another big firm. Congratulations!" We clinked glasses and sipped.

"I want to be on my own, and work with good people. Valerie's the best. We clicked in the past, even when we were opposing counsel. I admire how she advocates for victims. By the way, have you been reading about Reid, Bennett?" She quirked an eyebrow and smiled.

"Sure have. Different firm factions are being gobbled up. That's why I thought you might have gone with Remsen. Want to know something, though? Whether the firm is thriving or disintegrating, I'm not looking back."

"I bet you aren't, despite all the drama," she said. "Look at the people you've met."

"I know. You know how sometimes you have to look for your moment in life?"

"I sure do. Look at me, becoming partners with Valerie, after all these years. I couldn't have anticipated this."

"Exactly. In spite of everything, getting this job is my moment, and the last thing I want to do is blow it. But between Chrissy, someone throwing me under the bus at work, and now Artie, it's so difficult. Yet, for the first time, I'm actually doing something meaningful, instead of just making law firm partners richer." Nina gave me a sharp look.

"Sorry, I left my filter at home," tapping my head. "I'm so comfortable with you that words fly out of my mouth. I didn't mean you specifically."

"I know. Besides, look who you're married to—a partner in a law firm!"

"Right. Now that I'm raising money for the greater good, it's a different feeling, that's what I meant."

"Relax. If you recall, I was the one who was super excited when you got the job. Of course, since then I've had no time to go to the theater. I totally get the rewarding part of what you're talking about, though. That's why Valerie and I are going to be partners."

"This is such great news, Nina."

"Don't get me wrong, we're still about making *beaucoup* bucks, but we've vowed to take on pro bono cases and help those in need. Women, especially. Like those at Valerie's House."

"I'm so happy for you." I reached over and touched her hand.

"I'm very excited. In the meantime, it sounds like you're ready for your vacation."

"Am I ever!"

Later that day, I sent flowers to Nina. My note read:

You make things happen. So happy for you, and forever proud.

XO Julia

MARK AND I HEADED to the Galapagos Islands the following week. Correction: Mark, Mark's cellphone, and I went on vacation. The five-star trip to South America that reeked of postcard envy was enabled by his law firm practice; not my Addison Center salary. But by day two, his constant need to be attached to civilization was beginning to get under my skin.

"Mark, maybe you should consider giving the phone a rest?" I finally said as we were drinking coffee and waiting to be served breakfast inside the hotel's restaurant. "Try to relax a little. I know you're under pressure, but can't you just enjoy yourself for once?"

He scowled. "Sometimes I think you're in a fantasyland."

Ouch. Did he really think I was checked out from reality? He knew how grounded I was. Tossing his phone in the glistening blue Pacific was the only fantasy I'd had lately.

"No, I'm not. It's just that we both work so hard, and we're finally on vacation. Glancing at your phone every two seconds won't help you unwind." I'd been looking forward to having him all to myself.

He went into the shower, and closed the door with a loud noise. In his haste, he left his phone in plain view on the bed. Out of curiosity, I peeked at it. There were some emails from Olivia relating to work. There was a text from her as well. I knew I shouldn't, but I couldn't stop myself. I picked up the phone and read the text:

We'll get through this.

The message was benign enough, but the emoji kiss and the winking cat that came after was not. The pretty, young, smart woman who seemed to consume my husband's attention was now sending him flirtatious messages. Maybe he'd taken her shopping at Les Saisons, too. Worry snaked through me.

"Mark," I yelled through the bathroom door. "I'm going to the gym. Be back soon."

As I ran on the hotel's treadmill at a ridiculously fast speed, different scenarios flipped through my mind. Should I ask him about Olivia? What if her text was just a show of support about the case they were working on? But what about those emoji's? Running three miles helped to calm me down. Determined not to ruin our time together, I resolved instead to make it special; something he wouldn't forget.

I returned to the room, and pretended I hadn't seen the messages. We spent the rest of the day outdoors in the wilderness; lucky for me, there wasn't any cell service. We saw sea lions on the beach, and had close encounters with iguanas, dolphins, and tropical birds. Our favorites were the blue-footed boobies.

Captivated by these almost comical birds, I picked up a book about them in the bookstore at our resort. Thumbing through it, the caption Blue-Footed Boobies' Mating Dance caught my attention.

"These birds pull out ALL the stops when asking a lady to mate," it read. Underneath it was an explanation about their mating rituals. I learned that the male birds show off their feet to prospective mates. The bluer the feet, the more attractive the mate.

It must have been the combination of the fresh air, and sheer beauty of seeing wildlife in action, followed up with reading details of the sex lives of these splendid birds. Or maybe the idea of hotel sex with my husband was thrilling.

One thing was certain: I knew I wanted to be wanted. What woman wouldn't? Especially when some younger woman was toying with my husband. He wasn't a blue-footed boobie, but the seduction game was on.

We were off to a good start with a romantic candlelit dinner in the hotel's outdoor patio restaurant, complete with a bottle of Pouilly-Fuisse and the stunning Galapagos sunset that made Mark's face glow with the last orange rays. All this, along with the splendid hotel, the soft balmy air and sparkling water, and stunning view of the enchanting surrounding islands, made it the most beautiful place in the world.

"I hope you're having a good time," I said, looking directly into his eyes.

"I am. I love going away and seeing new places," he replied, taking a bite of his swordfish.

"Me too," I said. "With you, especially."

"I agree," Mark said. "I love it here. It's beautiful where we live, but this is heaven. I don't think I've ever seen a sunset like that." He pointed to the horizon.

I had tried to pave the way for him to say something meaningful. In return, he talked about the scenery.

Back in our room, I took my time freshening up. I shaved my legs for the second time that day, spritzed a little perfume on, and brushed my teeth. My pajamas that were leaning on the bathtub stayed there. I donned the fluffy hotel robe, with nothing underneath, and left the bathroom.

The light by Mark's night table was still on, but he was fast asleep. So much for the seductive entrance I'd orchestrated. I went to turn the light off, and he rolled over. Disappointed, I let him sleep.

The next morning, a guide took us on a walk on the beach filled with sea lions sunbathing. We trailed behind her, holding hands.

"Nice to see you enjoying yourself," I said.

"You too. You've been working like crazy. You've turned into one of those ladies who lunch," Mark said.

My back was up. "Oh, stop it! You know how hard I work."

"Julia, I'm just joking. Quit taking everything so seriously," he said, shaking his head.

"You're right. Sorry." I realized I was being ridiculous, and that he was teasing.

We continued to walk, listening to our guide describe the life of a sea lion. Some were practically lying on top of one another. It made me think about how Mark and I slept together. We should try to make more of an effort to snuggle at night; we used to do that all the time.

Sharing this incredible experience—being outdoors, hiking, breathing fresh air, and witnessing nature up close and personal—finally translated to the bedroom. After our sunset dinner, we made passionate love that night. We lay awake afterwards. Mark moved closer to me, and wrapped his muscular arm and leg around me. Enveloped by his warm body made me feel safe. He pressed the button on the wall that opened the shades.

"Look at how the moon is glowing, Jools," he said, lifting his arm to point to it. "Just like you." He kissed me tenderly on the cheek.

We must have fallen asleep, because next, the sunlight was beaming into our room. It was seven o'clock, very late for us. This became our pattern the rest of the trip. Mark's phone was eventually forgotten.

A beautiful tan from the Ecuadorian sun had me glowing. Re-engaging with each other and enjoying uninterrupted time together was priceless. While things might not have been perfect, I was sorry when our trip ended.

Chapter 20

LUCKY VAGINA CLUB

MAYA KNOCKED ON MY DOOR. It was my first day back in the office, and I needed to tackle the work that had piled up.

"C'mon in," I said.

"How was your vacation—did you have a chance to relax?"

"I did. It was wonderful. It's hard to be back."

"That's why we call it work," she said. She gave an uneven smile and half-shrug; I couldn't tell whether she was being funny or snide. "Anyway, Chrissy left this list of prospects for you to follow up with. Some of them she met while in Martha's Vineyard. She said the networking was amazing." Handing me the papers, she said, "Here. She'll be in later if you have questions."

"Okay, no problem." *So much for easing back in.*

A few days later, I was excited to be heading to the Waterfront Club to meet the Royal Coconut Beach Lunch Club ladies. Seated in the dining room, Elise, Nina and I chatted while we waited for Valerie, who was detained in court. Fifteen minutes later she joined us.

"My apologies. I had a crazy morning," Valerie said. Elise ordered a bottle of Prosecco.

"I can use a drink," Valerie said. She sat back in her chair. "I'm worn out from listening to everyone's problems. Kids, second wives, step-children. It always boils down to money. Everyone thinks they're entitled."

"I see you've had a fun morning," I said.

"Yeah, well, today I dealt with folks you know, Julia. They're major donors at Addison." She looked at me as if I had ownership of them.

"Who are you talking about?" I asked.

"No names. Suffice it to say that when my client remarried years ago, his daughters were awful to him. They were only after one thing." Valerie crossed her arms.

"Money," the rest of us chimed in.

"They must be members of the Lucky Sperm Club," Nina said.

"Wrong. It's the LVC. Not the Louis Vuitton Club, either, but the Lucky Vagina Club," I said.

"Touché," Elise said, and we all broke into laughter.

"Girard has a son from his first marriage," Nina said. "I have to consider these kinds of things."

"Sounds like your relationship has heated up," Elise said.

"Yup," Nina said. Her eyes sparkled and she smiled broadly. "I'm so happy, for the first time."

"Nothing like being in love," Elise said. "After 42 years

I still love David. Even if it's much different when we first met."

"You're lucky. He's always been supportive of your career, and proud of you too," Valerie said.

"Yeah, he is. Being creative brings me joy."

"As you all know, it took me the second time around to get it right," Valerie said.

"At least you did," Nina said.

"What makes a happy marriage, anyway?" I asked. For many years, Mark and I couldn't wait to see each other at home in the evenings, and on weekends. But even after we reconnected in the Galapagos, things still felt a little amiss.

"What makes an *unhappy* marriage is the real question," Elise said.

"I can answer that, without having been married," Nina said. "I've heard all the stories. Barring scandal, abuse, and other extreme situations, there's the usual: money, in-laws, kid problems. Couples get stuck and settle for low-level dissatisfaction, feeling unfulfilled. Sometimes, that's when something gives."

"You mean an affair?" I asked.

"Yes, exactly. People look elsewhere for what they're not getting at home," Valerie said.

"Girard felt like he settled the first time. He says I challenge him, unlike his ex-wife."

"Oh hush," Valerie answered. "You're still in the honeymoon stage."

"Who said anything about a honeymoon?" Nina asked.

The newness of Nina's relationship sounded fresh and exciting. Our conversation was interrupted by a small commotion coming from a few tables away. Turning our attention to the noise, we saw that it was Big Artie Brass barking for a waiter.

"Man with the badge, man with the badge. Come over here now," he ordered, while chomping on an unlit cigar.

"What ever happened to 'sir' or 'excuse me'? Who does he think he is, being so condescending?" Nina said.

"Seeing how people treat waitstaff is good proof of moral character. That's what my mother used to say," I commented. Mom had a good frame of reference, from all those years interacting with Wingate parents.

"So true," said Valerie. "And Artie's a prime example. How Penny tolerates all his crap is beyond me. She's nice, if a bit flaky."

"Money has nothing at all to do with why she stays with him," Elise added.

"Yeah, right," Valerie said. "Speaking of money, has Nina told you that we're going to represent women who can't afford to hire an attorney?"

"She told me you'll be doing some pro bono work," I said.

"That's great," Elise said.

"This calls for a toast!" I held up my glass of Prosecco. We toasted Nina and Valerie's new firm. They wanted the firm's name in lights at the Addison Center. As we were discussing what performance might give them maximum exposure, another raucous noise came from Artie's table.

A couple of men had been standing over him, speaking very loudly. Artie's round face was getting redder by the second, until he resembled a giant tomato. The men left, and a few minutes later Artie stormed out, leaving Penny by herself. After asking our permission, Elise went over and invited her to join our group. We moved seats and shifted our lunches to make room for Penny and her Cobb salad.

"Hi ladies, what's up? Thanks for letting me join you." Penny took her seat, seeming unfazed that her husband had just behaved like a two-year-old having a tantrum.

"We're talking about Nina and Valerie's new firm; they've just formed a partnership," Elise said. "You must know Julia, from the Addison Center?"

"We spoke on the phone about our gala," I said to Penny. "We cannot thank you and Mr. Brass enough for chairing the event, and for your generosity."

Penny smiled. "It's our pleasure. Call me Penny."

"How's Kevin doing in Alaska?" Elise asked, referring to Penny's son.

"He's doing great. He met a nice woman. He drives a tour bus, and she quilts. They care for sled dogs on the weekends. He's finally gotten his act together."

Despite all the money at her disposal, navigating Artie's antics and guiding a troubled son must not be an easy feat. I didn't envy her. Seeing Artie making a scene made me feel grateful to have Mark. In comparison, I had it good.

We finished our lunch, drained our Proseccos in a final toast, and I headed back to the office.

Chapter 21

WHITE HOT NIGHT

"SAVANNAH COLBERTSON called for you," Poppy said, intercepting me when I returned from lunch.

"For me? Are you sure?" Savannah usually dealt directly with Chrissy. She must have called looking for her, and resorted to me.

"Yes. She called me because she has my number. I told her you were at lunch. She asked if you'd call her right away when you returned."

I went to my office, closed the door and called her.

"Julia, darling. I hear you're goin' to town at that place."

"Excuse me?" I was at a loss.

"Sponsorships. Raising money. I hear what's going on at Addison."

I was floored. "Really? I'm not sure. . . ."

"Aw, bless your heart. We should give praise where praise

is due. Anyhow, I'm chair of the Blossom Ball this year. It's the first major event of the season, even though it's way early. People fly in from all over for it. It's tomorrow night. I know it's last minute, but I have an extra seat. I'd love it if you'd join my table. There'll be networking galore."

"I'd be honored—thank you!"

"My assistant will drop off the invitation later. Don't forget, you'll need to get all gussied up in white. It's all for the good of the cause."

"What does the Blossom Ball support?"

"Darling, all the money that's raised goes to support basic needs for underprivileged children—mainly food and clothing—so they can blossom."

"That's fantastic. Good for you to be involved in such a big way."

"Growing up poor myself, I have a soft spot. I was one of the lucky ones who still had a magical childhood. It warms my heart knowing we're doing something to help those less fortunate."

Behind Savannah's fancy dresses, yacht, caviar, and private jets was an admirable woman who used her resources to help those in need. On top of all that, Savannah was just plain likable. I felt shallow for having judged her as a society lady who only cared about material things.

A while later, Poppy handed me the invitation. She watched me open it.

"Savannah's invited me to the Blossom Ball," I said, then read aloud the pink heart-shaped post-it:

> Thank you for being my guest. Don't forget to
> wear white. XO Sweet Savannah.

"Wow, how exciting!" Poppy exclaimed. "I bet you'll pick up some great pointers for this year's gala. Do you have a white dress?"

"Not other than my wedding dress. But it's not very traditional, so it might work. That is, if I can squeeze my body into it."

"Good luck, I hope it fits."

I was finding it difficult to believe that sweet Poppy was out to get me. Acting normal around her was probably the best thing for me to do.

Excited, I went to see Chrissy to tell her about the Blossom Ball. I stood in her doorway, and gave a subtle cough.

"What is it?" she asked, lifting her head. It looked like she had been signing letters.

"Savannah's invited me to the Blossom Ball," I said. "I'm so thrilled."

"She did? You're joking!"

Was it that shocking to her?

"No, I'm not." I contained my irritation.

"Well, it's about time you traveled in the right social circles," she said. "Savannah probably had a last-minute invitation and plunked you in." She gave me a patronizing smile and returned to scribbling her name.

Receiving a coveted invitation from the quintessential socialite was a mammoth professional milestone, and *that* was what she had to say? Savannah wanted *me* to network for the Addison Center. I'd bet Chrissy was jealous that Savannah asked me instead of her to mix and mingle with the hoity-toitys. Unlike Chrissy, I hadn't slept with anyone to get results!

I threw my clothes on the floor that evening and retrieved my wedding gown from our spare closet. It was an elegant long white dress with a dotted Swiss overlay. It was a miracle that I was able to zip it; sucking in my stomach helped. The Jimmy Choos would be perfect. I looked in the mirror and twirled around, while I heard the front door open.

"Hello?" Mark said.

"Hi. I'm in the guest bedroom," I yelled.

Mark stood at the doorway. "What on earth are you doing?" he asked. For some unascertainable reason he looked annoyed. Not exactly the expression you want your husband to have when he sees you for the second time in your wedding gown.

He loosened his tie as I told him that Savannah had invited me to the Blossom Ball, and I needed to wear white.

"How virginal." He got distracted by the buzz of his phone in his hand.

"One sec," he said. "I need to read this."

I posed in the mirror while waiting.

"I've got to go back to the office," he said a minute later. "There's a problem. One of the companies we represent might file for bankruptcy before the merger." He rushed out of the house.

The last time I wore the dress, Mark couldn't take his eyes off of me. Our wedding was outdoors, under a tent on the Wingate campus. It could have been anywhere. Mom and Dad were the ones who thrived on all the wedding hoopla, their only child getting married. Other than seeing them happy, all we cared about was that we'd be together for life.

I lay face down on the bed, trying to manipulate the zipper downward. Able to shimmy out of it, I hung it up.

I skipped dinner, chugged a glass of wine, got into bed and called Nina.

After catching up I told her I was going to the Blossom Ball tomorrow night.

"Now we're talking. Who invited you?"

"Savannah Colbertson; she's the chair. She promises there'll be good networking."

"Maybe you'll meet your next million-dollar donor. That'll impress Chrissy."

"Don't even go there. I think Chrissy's jealous I was invited."

"Too bad on her. By the way, how's Mark?"

"He's in the office for a change." I told her about his attitude when he saw me in the dress, and opened up to her about my concerns.

"Hmm . . . why don't you plan a date night? That's what Girard and I do."

"Might not be a bad idea."

We chatted a little more and discussed scheduling our next lunch. Before I fell asleep, Mark texted me. He was getting on a plane early the next morning and going to California for an emergency meeting. Could it be possible that Olivia was joining him? I cringed at the idea that this meant they also would be staying in the same hotel.

Later the next day, Maya came into my office to retrieve the letters I was working on.

"Poppy told me you're going to the Blossom Ball," she said.

"Yup. I've got to head home and get dolled up. I can't believe I've been invited."

"It's nice that you get to do something fun," Maya said with a broad smile.

"I'll be networking." I gave a wink.

"Yeah, right," she said. "Tonight, you'll just be like one of them."

"What do you mean?" I asked. "Socializing is the way I get my job done."

Maya's smile disappeared, and she crossed her arms. "Don't be so defensive," she said, short and snippy, before she left.

What was up with her? She was the one who was being defensive. I left and headed home. The event was an hour away, so I got dressed and headed to the Oceanfront Hotel. When I arrived, I was directed down a stunning hallway to the cocktail reception.

"Step this way, ladies," I heard a staff member direct guests as she pointed to the step-and-repeat line for pictures. Erin snapped my photo and a staff member directed me to where the cocktail reception was held. There was lots of kissing, hugging, gripping and grinning. The tiaras and fine jewelry had come out of vaults. I headed to the bar and got a club soda with a lime. I sipped my drink and networked until the chimes rang, a signal that it was time to enter the ballroom.

I made my way to my table. Finding my name on the hand-engraved place card, I saw that to my left was The Honorable Julian Jorge Mendoza, the former Ambassador to Argentina. I felt a tightness in my stomach as Savannah strolled over to me.

"Please take care of Julian Jorge," she said pointing to his place card. "JJ's good people. Oh, here he comes," she said as he strode over to our table. His hair was slicked back, just like it was when I met him at the Society of Ambassadors event, only he was even more handsome. He looked suave in his tuxedo, his broad shoulders filling it out. His white shirt was tight around his neck, and his bronze skin tone was more noticeable than before. My heart started to race.

"JJ, please meet Julia Wild, from the Addison Center," Savannah said.

"I believe we've met," he said, staring into my eyes.

"Nice to see you again," I said.

He pulled out my chair.

"Please, sit young lady."

Young lady? I obeyed, and he sat next to me. There were around twenty years between us, but he seemed so energetic and youthful.

"We finally get to dine together," he said, and smiled. "I love your dress."

My cheeks felt flushed. "It's my wedding dress, actually."

"Oh my, the blushing bride." Even though we were sitting, he was still looking me up and down. "You look stunning." He let out a small exhale.

"Thank you."

"So, what is it you do at Addison?" he asked, with a trace of South American accent. The band was playing soft dinner music as we chatted away. His eyes stared into mine, all of his attention fixed on me.

"I'm sorry, I talk way too much," I said after describing my job.

A sexy half-smile tugged at his mouth. "No, you have a very interesting story. I'm enjoying it."

"Now tell me about you." But we were interrupted by a staff member. It was time to present the ladies. Savannah and her cadre of event co-chairmen were each formally escorted into the ballroom by a dignitary. JJ's assignment was to escort Dame Merry Lawford. Tonight, Savannah was announced as Mrs. Winston R. Colbertson IV, when she was presented by the Ambassador to Ireland.

"That was a really tough assignment," JJ joked, returning to his seat after the presentation. Various people came over to shake his hand. He was skilled at this game, standing up, making small talk.

The grandiose ballroom was filled to the brim with royalty, high society, and every sort of VIP under the Royal Coconut Beach sun. Yet JJ made me feel as if I was the only person in the room, and I reciprocated his attention. After all, Savannah had given me explicit instructions to take good care of him. He had an aura of reserve, especially compared with the red-faced alpha-male billionaires that packed the room.

"Now that you've done your job for the evening, let's talk about you. Did you grow up here?" I asked.

"No. I was born and raised in Argentina. Generations of my family owned the Mendoza vineyards in the Uca Valley region. I wanted to spread my wings, and came to the United States. That's where I began in the wine business. Eventually I started a franchise of wine stores."

His dark eyes blazed as he spoke perfect English with that sexy accent. The rest of the evening flew by. JJ escorted me to the valet, and kissed me on the cheek. I breathed in his lemony scent.

"It was a pleasure having dinner with you. Thank you for making the evening special. I'll be in touch," he said.

"It was nice to be with you too." Our eyes locked again before we parted. Next thing I knew, I was in my car. I thought about him the entire way home, rewinding our conversation over and over. I'd thoroughly enjoyed flirting with him, but knew it wouldn't go anywhere.

I had googled him when he had called me for lunch previously, and I did it again now. My new friend had created the World of Wines, known as WOW, the international wine franchise. No surprise that he and Savannah were friendly, both being international franchisors. He owned most of the real estate through Uca Industries, Ltd., one of Argentina's leading investment holding companies focusing on high-growth, internationally-oriented Argentinian companies. He was 63, and married to Catalina, his wife of 42 years. They had a daughter Natalia, a son Augusto, and two grandchildren. Net worth: $4.6 billion, or 4.6 "wads," as Chrissy would have put it.

More research showed Catalina dressed to kill at the many society soirees in Washington, DC. She was usually front and center, either as a chair, or recipient of some distinguished award. Appearing to be in her early sixties, she was attractive, and clearly she'd had lots of cosmetic work done.

It was midnight when a text came in from Mark. Three hours earlier on the west coast, he was heading into dinner after meetings all day.

"Are you up?" he asked in a text. At least I was on his radar.

Yes, I had a great time at the Blossom Ball.

"Sweet dreams," he wrote back.
I was sure I would.

Chapter 22

DOLLARS TO DONUTS

A RUSH OF LIGHT-HEARTEDNESS swept over me when I awoke, something I hadn't felt in a while. Thinking about the charming ambassador made my arms tingle, but realizing that Mark didn't make me feel this way was a let-down. Guilt for feeling so ecstatic about last evening kicked in. I never knew that all these emotions could happen at once.

By the time I got settled in at my desk, there was an email from JJ.

> Thank you for a perfect evening. I'll be in touch. JJ

My heart skipped a beat. I was interrupted when Poppy hurried into my office.

"Tell me all about it," she said. "Flowers, décor, music. The ladies, the gowns, the food. I want to hear it all." I shared some details, but as I spoke, my mind was distracted by thoughts of the handsome Argentinian.

"Maybe one day the Blossom Ball committee will hire me to plan the event," she said. "Oh, before I forget, Tracy from Andy McCormack's office called. She wants you to call her back right away."

I was glad that Poppy was being so helpful. Maybe she'd gotten past any issues she'd had about not getting my job.

Andy was president of Evergreen Florida, one of the many private wealth management companies that were rapidly dotting the landscape in Royal Coconut Beach. We'd met a while ago in the Parker Pavilion. He was friendly, and we clicked instantly. In addition to banking, Evergreen and others advised wealthy clients on sophisticated investment strategies, tax planning, and most of all, tax avoidance— all in the name of wealth preservation.

Given Andy's exceptional sales ability, Evergreen had relocated him from New York to Florida, its newest expansion market. He'd assembled a crackerjack investment team, and Evergreen gave a donation to the Addison Center. Andy recently was asked to join the board at Addison.

When Poppy left, I called Tracy back.

"Are you available on Friday morning, at 8:00 a.m.?" she asked.

I looked at my calendar. I had to be at Addison Thursday evening, but that wasn't an excuse to avoid an early morning meeting. "Yes, I am."

"Good. You'll be meeting Tripp Reid, the president of Royal Swiss Bank. Hopefully, you'll get a donation. Andy will meet you there. He asked that you bring an Addison Center package."

"Great. Please thank Andy. I'll be there."

"Oh, he also wants you to stop by Dunkin' Donuts and pick up a dozen assorted."

"Really?" I wasn't offended by the request, and I hope she didn't think so; I was just surprised.

"Yup. He likes to bring goodies on sales calls. I'll let him know that you're confirmed."

Next, I arranged the Lunch Club ladies' upcoming lunch. Just knowing I'd soon see them lifted my spirits.

I met Andy at the Royal Swiss Bank lobby a few days later. I wore a short-sleeved ivory dress with kick pleats. It was sophisticated and classy, so I could make a good impression for the meeting. Tall and fit, with high cheekbones and a square jaw, Andy exuded confidence. He captured a smidgeon of the Royal Coconut Beach look by going sockless.

"Thanks for getting the donuts," Andy said when we met in Royal Swiss's lobby. He took the box from me, and headed into the elevator.

"Sure thing," I said. "I bring the dough, and we get the dough."

He gave a wide grin. "Funny. We'll be rolling in dough!"

Tripp's assistant greeted us, and he handed the donuts to her. She escorted us into a modern conference room.

"It's no secret that Tripp is a trust fund baby," Andy said. "He comes from an old English line of bankers. Bank owners, actually. But despite his blue-blooded roots, he got even wealthier by earning it. In our industry, he's known as a dual passport advisor."

"I worked with several attorneys at Reid, Bennett in that category. They practiced trusts and estates, mainly because they could relate to wealthy clients."

"Oh, that's right. I forgot you worked there," Andy said.

A few moments later, Tripp came in and greeted us, followed by his assistant, who carried a tray of coffee, water, and the donuts neatly assembled on a doily.

"So nice to see you, Tripp. Meet Julia Wild from the Addison Center," Andy said.

"Pleased to meet you," I said as we shook hands. He was well over six feet tall, and had sandy blonde wavy hair, stunning blue eyes, and a square jaw. Up close, his aftershave smelled enticing. Seated in the spacious room at one end of the table, the two men chatted about industry trends before Andy launched into an Addison Center pitch.

"Tripp, you really should think about getting involved in the Addison Center. It'd be a big bang for your buck if Royal Swiss joined as a corporate member. It's helped Evergreen; I've already met new clients in the Parker Pavilion. Julia can show you around when you have time."

"I'd be happy to," I added.

"Look, you can't buy an ad for the amount of publicity Addison provides with a donation," Andy continued. "The Royal Swiss name will be listed everywhere. Julia can explain."

"The bank's name will go on our donor wall of honor," I said. "As well as in *Playbill*, our magazines that are sent out to many people. Then there's sponsorship. Royal Swiss Bank will be the star that evening, and you'll get to entertain clients in a first-class manner."

Andy nodded. "Simply put, you can't beat the return on

investment," he said. "After all, the ROI is what we're all about."

"I understand; it makes good business sense."

Tripp grabbed a jelly donut. Andy followed, opting for a Boston crème. I settled on water. How these guys stayed so trim was beyond me.

In between bites, Andy said, "Your clients will be quite impressed with Addison when you bring them. It's a great way to score points. Trust me."

Tripp chugged some water. "Well, a few of my clients have been nudging me to contribute," he said. "They skim through *Playbill* when they go to the theater, and ask why Royal Swiss Bank isn't included. We've been given marketing dollars from headquarters in Geneva, so the timing is perfect. By the way, I've been in that room." He looked at me.

"Parker Pavilion," I said. "As a member, you can get great seats to the theater, and bring your guests into that beautiful space. It's a perfect way to entertain clients, as Andy explained."

Andy was on his second donut. Taking a sip of his coffee, he said to Tripp, "We might be in competition for clients, but when it comes to the community, we all need to play together in the same sandbox. There's room for all of us at the Addison Center."

Andy's eloquent delivery didn't smack of the slick sales pitch I'd expected. A few minutes later, he and Tripp shook hands. Tripp told me to follow up with the paperwork so he could sign a commitment on behalf of Royal Swiss Bank. After that, Andy walked out with me to the parking lot.

I turned to face him, shielding my eyes from the sun.

"Thank you so much, Andy. Really. I enjoyed meeting Tripp. He's a nice man."

"I've known him for years. He and his new wife just bought a gorgeous house on Sand Dollar Way." Gliding into his black Mercedes sedan, he said, "My assistant will call you again. I have some ideas for more appointments. I want to make sure I'm doing my job as a board member; we're supposed to help with fundraising. We're a good team. It'll be the same routine; you just bring the Addison package. And don't forget the donuts." He waved and drove off.

It was 9:00 as I slid into my Acura and headed off to start the day at the Addison Center. Andy's compliment boosted my confidence, and I was grateful to have an ally. Approaching the bridge, the bells rang and the gates had gone up. Two mega-yachts and a sailboat were lined up to pass through. Putting the car in park, I took the pad and pen out that was in the side door, which came in handy for times like this. I started jotting notes about what I needed to get done that day. As I finished, the bridge gates went up. I pressed the pedal, and drove on.

Chapter 23

WARM COOKIES, HOT LIPS

MAYA INTERCEPTED ME on the way to my office.

"Julia, you're back. I just picked up a call from someone named Claudia on Chrissy's line. She said she's from Ambassador Mendoza's office. Very impressive!" she said, with a smile, her moods still unpredictable.

I called right away, expecting to talk with him. "Mr. Mendoza's office, Claudia speaking," said the voice on the other end. In my excitement, I forgot that billionaires had other people answering their phones.

"Um ... hello. This is Julia Wild from the Addison Center. Is Mr., uh, Ambassador Mendoza available?

"He won't be back in the office until much later. I was expecting your call, though.

He asked me to arrange lunch with you right away."

She made it out to be a request, not an invitation. I looked at my calendar as Claudia continued.

"The Ambassador and Mrs. Mendoza would like to contribute to the Addison Center, and he'd like to discuss this with you in person."

"That's terrific. I look forward to it." He and his wife wanted to donate money; it was perfectly legit. We arranged a lunch date at the Sealine Club in a few days. I didn't know that he and wife were members. Notoriously reserved for the old guard, a South American on the club's snooty roster was unusual. Maybe it was becoming fashionable for bluebloods to step beyond their insular, segregated world. Or it could be that JJ and Cat were so important, they couldn't say no to them.

That evening, I arrived home before Mark, who was coming back from California.

"How was your flight?" I asked when I greeted him by the door, and kissed his cheek. He was in a dark suit, his tie half-undone and top button open. He had dark shadows under his eyes, and the lines in his face were more pronounced.

"Uneventful."

I smiled. We both went into the bedroom to change.

He was in his underwear as he hung his suit up in the closet. "How would you like a back rub? I bet you can use one after the long flight," I said.

"Not right now," he said, focused on getting his pants to fold neatly on the hanger.

"You're welcome," I said, with a laugh.

"What?" he snapped.

"Nothing." I pulled on my sweats. "Eggs okay?" I rarely had the energy to cook anything complicated after a long day.

"Sure," he said, and followed me into the kitchen. He was also in sweats. He sat at the table with a folder and phone while I cooked. He turned the dimmer up on the overhead light.

"How was your day? Do anything special?" Mark asked, moving his paperwork aside as I sat.

"I had a meeting at Royal Swiss Bank, set up by Andy McCormack. He's on our board, and a banker himself. He was smooth and engaging. He reminds me of you a little. How about you? How did everything go?"

"Fine."

"Are you stressed?" I asked.

"Sort of," Mark said, sounding annoyed.

"Sorry. I just want to make sure you're okay," I said, unsure why I apologized.

"Things are a mess at work." Mark frowned. "I don't want to talk about it."

"Since when *don't* you want to talk about it?" If Mark was hurting, why *wouldn't* he want to talk about it?

"Julia, please." He closed his eyes and shook his head for a few seconds.

I wanted to do more, but given the situation, I'd be hovering. I changed the subject and told him about my upcoming week. I tried to act normal, but I wasn't sure when I was supposed to be quiet or when I should keep chatting.

"I need to make a call," he said, interrupting me. "Sorry." He went into his office, while I cleared the table and banged the silverware into the dishwasher. I went to bed, unaware what time Mark joined me.

———

COMFORT BE DAMNED, the stilettos came out. Not exactly lunch shoes, but the elevated heels translated into elevated status; just what I needed for lunch with JJ. I couldn't walk much in them, but as soon as I pulled up to the club's valet, on they went. A bright red dress, baroque pearls, and Hot Lips lipstick selected by Ameline at Les Saisons added the right amount of sophistication.

JJ was waiting for me in the lobby. He saw me and came right over, planting kisses on both cheeks, as I breathed in his refreshing lemony scent. He looked impeccable in a white button-down shirt, perfectly pressed beige linen slacks, a navy sport jacket with gold buttons, and dark suede loafers with brass hardware. We headed toward a table in the back, passing a donor I knew was dining with her friends, their noses literally in the air. I said hello to show JJ that I knew some people in his circles.

I delved right into talk about the Addison Center's development goals. Talking about what I knew relaxed me.

"Tell me, how did you get out of practicing law?" he asked. I gathered he wasn't too interested in the Addison Center; in fact, he seemed more interested in me.

"While I was studying for the Florida Bar Exam, I volunteered at the Addison Center. I was at Reid, Bennett, the law firm, when Chrissy—now my boss—heard good things about me and asked me if I'd be interested in working at Addison. I was ready to make a change, and jumped at it."

"Addison sounds like a great place; what you do is worthwhile," JJ said.

Just like at the Blossom Ball, he made me feel like I was

the only person in the room. Nothing else existed as he looked at me with those dark eyes and unfettered interest.

I asked about his background; how he'd gotten into the wine business.

"I always knew I wanted much more than living on the vineyards. It was a magical life growing up—don't get me wrong. And hard work, physically. Cat's father—Catalina, my wife—was in real estate, building instead of tending to the land. I had an idea: instead of servicing just South America with the Mendoza label, go outside."

"That was very forward-thinking." I was fixated on him.

"There was so much money in Miami, especially South American money. Some of my relatives were there. So I opened my first franchise of World of Wines with a loan from my father-in-law, and began importing wine from the family vineyards."

"What a great idea." That was an understatement. JJ had been focused on making his business work, fiercely determined to make it happen. I had deep admiration for him. Mark also possessed these qualities, along with a strong work ethic. I had no business comparing them.

"Well, I was in the right place at the right time. It became a gold mine, and soon I bought the real estate that the first WOW store was on. It was in a terrible neighborhood; got held up at gunpoint a few times."

"Must've been scary, but that didn't stop you." I was captivated by his ambitiousness.

He nodded. "I took the money I made, invested in another store, then another. It had a domino effect, with investors soon knocking at my door for a piece of the action. We began opening stores on the eastern seaboard and mid-Atlantic states. Then globally. The rest is history."

And this guy thinks I have an interesting story? Suddenly I felt very small. Interacting with some of the brightest and wealthiest captains of industry, so many people were extraordinary, which in turn made everyone else seem ordinary.

Finally, towards the end of lunch, he asked me what contribution he needed to make so that he'd do the right thing by Savannah. I told him to become a Maestro Society member.

"Claudia will call you and take care of it." It was as simple as that. The server brought over a plate of freshly baked chocolate chip cookies. He passed the plate to me first. "Tempting, aren't they?" he said in a soft voice, holding the plate as I breathed in the rich, buttery scent of melting chocolate.

"You look fantastic; you can have a cookie," he added. While I didn't need permission to eat one cookie, my stomach fluttered. I wasn't sure if it was the compliment, or the in-control way in which he said it, that frayed my nerves and excited me.

JJ walked me to the valet, and waited while they brought my car. He kissed me on both cheeks, while our eyes held for a few extra seconds. Feeling wobbly, I almost twisted my stiletto-ed ankle getting in the car. A few blocks away, I pulled over and threw off the shoes, driving back to the office barefoot. As I sat in the parking garage for a moment, my heart pounded. I kept rewinding our conversation over and over, just as I had done the night of the Blossom Ball. And his face. And his voice, and lemony scent, and . . . everything.

"Oh, so they let you in there?" Mark said that night, referring to the Sealine Club when I told him where I'd been that afternoon.

"Yes, I'm becoming a regular." Mark got interrupted with a phone call: Olivia, again.

"What's up with you and Olivia?" I asked, after he hung up, without thinking before I spoke.

"Very funny," he said, and started typing on his laptop.

At least he didn't get defensive. But while Mark tapped out messages, I wanted to say, "Guess who I had lunch with today? Oh, did I mention he locked eyes with me? It wasn't the first time, either." I wanted him to feel jealous, a little threatened. I yearned for Mark to look at me with the same intensity that JJ had, but he was too busy looking at his screen. Unlike Mark, JJ made me feel so special. And I thought so highly of JJ that his opinion carried a lot of weight. Then again, I admired Mark too, but he didn't make me feel appreciated. I had a discouraging sense that I wasn't that special to him anymore.

I went to bed alone, leaving Mark tapping away.

Chapter 24

TROPICAL ATTITUDE

"JULIA, C'MON IN," Poppy shouted as I walked by her office. She and Maya were laughing.

"You gotta hear this. Mr. Lack just called. He wanted to know why his friends got better seats. 'It was an embarrassment,' he told me, 'considering I give more money than they ever will.'"

"Poppy was lucky to get her hands on those seats for Mr. Lack. He called last minute," Maya said.

"You snooze, you lose," I said.

"You go tell that to him." Poppy frowned.

"I'm sorry you had to deal with this," I said. "We must add him to our list of demanding donors."

"He was already on it," she said with a smirk.

"Then move him up on that list," I said. "Like his seats."

She smiled. "Good idea."

When I got to my office, my phone was ringing. Caller ID showed it was Chrissy calling from home. I knew I better pick up.

"I hear Penny and Artie Brass are back in town," she said, skipping pleasantries. She hadn't been in the office all week. "Warming up to them would go a long way, given their social circles. Now that they're our gala chairs, we need to kiss up, so they get their friends on board. Get an appointment to go see them."

"You mean at their home?" I asked.

"Absolutely. Make sure Penny's there. Even though Artie controls the purse strings, she needs to feel important too. Take Maya with you."

It was off-putting that Chrissy was dictating orders from home, while she was probably relaxing and enjoying herself. I was also pretty sure that the reason she wanted Maya to come along was because of her sex appeal. But whatever it took, I was determined to win the Brasses over. As soon as I hung up with Chrissy, I called Penny and set up a meeting with them at their home.

Two days later, Maya and I got in my car to head to the Brass residence. Maya was in her usual black attire, a form-fitting pants suit today. Her hair was tied in a sleek high ponytail.

"I do miss the quieter time we had over the summer," I said, as I pulled out of the parking garage. "I was able to hear myself think. When I first started at Addison, Poppy told me how intense the season was. She wasn't kidding."

"Whatever," Maya said. "Poppy knows everything."

Lately, Maya was difficult to read. One minute she'd be friendly, and snippy the next.

I pulled up to the pale yellow Colonial mansion on a side street off of Laguna. Its grass green shutters framed the windows, which was also used on the front door. Geraniums filled planters and ornamental bougainvillea hung over other plants. A plaque next to the front door told us we'd arrived at The Gardenia House. Their butler welcomed us with a British accent, escorting us into an area adjacent to the living room.

"Please make yourself at home in the family parlor," he said. I glanced at Maya to see her reaction when he said 'parlor', but she didn't crack a smile. Returning a minute later with a silver tray, he said, "Some apple cider and warm cinnamon donuts for the ladies."

"I thought cupcakes were the latest fad," I whispered to Maya as soon as he left. "But it seems donuts are."

"Huh?" Maya stared at me.

"Never mind."

Having Maya there felt like a security blanket, despite her being considerably younger, let alone her rudeness. Having someone else with me would help me maintain my composure, in case Artie hurled obnoxious comments my way. We each ate a donut and drank cider, so as not to offend the butler.

Given their reputation, I'd expected the Brass's home to be gaudy. Instead, it was a refined blend of classic and modern decor. The walls held lithographs of palm trees and other foliage. A massive steamer trunk served as a coffee table, with a pair of zebra-pattern footstools. Framed photos gave a personal feel, and the sophisticated space had the right amount of comfort.

Gazing into the living room, the floor-to-ceiling windows allowed a view of the outdoors.

Elise had told me that a few years ago, Penny and Artie had received the prestigious Coconut Palm Award for their lush garden. I noticed that palm trees were strategically placed around a turquoise infinity pool.

Startled when Artie entered the room, Maya and I simultaneously rose, as if court were in session.

"Sit, sit," he bellowed, his hands gesturing downwards. His broad forehead was furrowed above his bushy eyebrows, and sagging jowls made his face appear longer. Brown hair was gelled, and he wore a canary-yellow golf shirt and cobalt shorts. Yellow and gold wasps were embroidered on his velvet Stubbs and Wooten loafers.

"Thank you for meeting with us, Mr. Brass. Your home is lovely." He looked at me, then at Maya, saying nothing and still standing. "We cannot thank you and Mrs. Brass enough for chairing our gala. Will she be joining us today?" I asked.

"No," he growled. "She's filling in at canasta."

I began babbling about what a splendid evening the gala would be, and how grateful we were to him.

"What'd you have for me?" He interrupted my spiel. Dutifully, Maya took out the list, including different levels of support and their accompanying naming opportunities. He snatched it from her hand.

"We created these levels and accompanying benefits. We're hoping that you would ask your friends to donate to the gala. Red Carpet sponsors give $100,000, like you and Mrs. Brass. Showstoppers are at $75,000, and. . . ."

"I know the drill," he interrupted me. A flush spread up my neck. He folded the paper and stuck it in his shorts pocket.

"I'll take care of this." He bellowed for the butler to show us out. I hoped the poor man was getting paid a fortune to work there. While harsh manners could conceal good intentions, in Artie's case, it was all bark *and* all bite.

But staying focused on the goal was the important thing. His offer to "take care of this" was a consolation. To expect to win over everyone was unrealistic, and leveraging Artie's impressive social connections would be worth putting up with rudeness.

Maya and I got in my car and headed back in silence for about a minute before simultaneously breaking into laughter from pent-up nerves.

"Well, it was a step in the right direction," she said.

"Yeah. A cook's tour of that gorgeous house would have been fun. Maybe the butler will invite us one day," I said.

"That would be nice. Penny's got her priorities straight choosing canasta over us," Poppy said with a wry chuckle.

Back at the Addison Center, I made a stop at the box office to pick up tickets I'd promised to hand-deliver to a donor. A staff member gestured for me to wait a minute while she finished a phone call.

"We can find something better for you, probably in Row A. Just hang in there," she was saying, as if good seats were a matter of life and death.

"Hi Julia," she said, when she hung up. "That was a big donor."

"Well, you handled him, or her, with finesse."

"You know how it goes. The word 'no' isn't an option for someone who contributed lots of money," she said, her voice upbeat.

"I've heard that you deliver bad news so well, it actually

sounds good. That's a great talent." Sometimes I couldn't understand how they did their jobs so pleasantly. I took the tickets and headed to my office, and ran into Poppy.

"I bet you're coming from the box office." She pointed to the tickets I was holding. "That's where I'm heading. Maya said your appointment with Artie went well."

"She thought it went *well*?"

"Yes. She just got off the phone with Artie. He called her."

"Are you serious?"

"Yes. Why?" Poppy asked.

"Because all he did was growl and say, 'I'll take care of this' as he grabbed the list. Maya and I laughed about it in the car."

"Well, don't say anything to her. It would seem weird that I told you they spoke. I don't want to get on Maya's bad side; she's been acting weird lately."

I didn't want to gossip with Poppy about this. "Mum's the word." I put my index fingers on my lips.

As I walked back to my office, I wondered why Artie would call Maya, and not me. The only reason she went along with me was because Chrissy told her to. Now Artie was talking directly to Maya. Maybe he'd called looking for me, and she took the call since I wasn't there. Maya didn't say a word about it when she saw me later.

I wanted to tell Mark about my day, but as soon as we sat down to dinner, his phone rang yet again. It was one of his partners from New York. I knew he'd be on for a while, so I ate by myself while he was in his office with the door closed. After he hung up, he came back to the table to finish, and then Olivia called. Once more, he headed back to his office.

"What does she want?" I asked when he finally returned to the table. "It seems like she calls you every night."

"She's identified some crucial issues that will help our client in this big merger. What's up with your attitude? Oh, just forget it." he said. He went back to his office, and slammed the door.

My attitude? Mark had been so edgy lately, anything set him off. After being married all these years, it was easy to detect nuances in his moods, but never had he been consistently bad-tempered. And his addiction to his phone was out of control.

I sat at the table alone. We used to chat about our day, bouncing ideas off each other. I recalled when Mark was the lead attorney for the first time on a merger of two corporations many years ago. At the time, I could recite all the major details. If all went well, he most likely would make partner—the youngest ever at his firm. While the case was going on, one night I had dozed off. When I heard the door open, I perked up. He tiptoed into the bedroom, and saw that I was up.

"How's it going?" I asked.

"Ah, you're still up." He took his tie off, and unbuttoned his shirt. "I've got to put in the extra time just to keep my head above water. I've got so much riding on this. Correction: we have everything to gain if it goes smoothly."

"You're so smart. I know you'll do it," I said.

"Thanks. I'm sorry I'm not around much." We talked a little more in bed, and he shared how he felt about making partner.

But all I got from him now was comments about his schedule. And it was the little things that he wasn't doing that really upset me. Recently, he'd stopped handing me my coffee in the morning. In fact, he was usually gone before I awoke. He rarely called or texted during the day, and when I texted him, I got back a one-word answer, hours later. I missed our light banter, and being able to tell him anything. I felt shut out of his world, so I'd stopped sharing what was happening in mine. The growing chasm between us weighed heavily. I thought of Olivia. Was it possible that she was my replacement for such heartfelt conversations?

When he left for work the next morning, I looked in his suit pockets, not sure what I expected to find. They were empty. I checked on his desk, but all I discovered were work papers. I flipped through them and froze when I saw hot pink heart-shaped post-it notes slapped on some pages. In a neat, loopy handwriting were notes. They referred to documents and exhibits. Good thing they were harmless, but I would've preferred they were on square yellow post-its.

Later that day, he texted to say he'd be at a working dinner with a few attorneys at The Upper Crust Café. Paranoid about Olivia, I wasn't sure if he was telling the truth. Eager to find out, I hatched a plan to spy on Mark.

At 7:30, I parked my car down the block instead of at the valet. The folder I took provided an alibi in case Mark happened to see me in the restaurant: I'd say that a donor asked me to drop something off for her at the café.

I told the hostess I was just looking for someone, and scanned the restaurant, its interior much darker than at lunch time. That was when I saw Mark and Olivia huddled at a corner table covered in stacks of paper. *Where were the other attorneys?*

Mark took a sip of wine and smiled; something I hadn't seen in a while. I watched them talk, and then he handed her some papers. She looked through them, leaned in and said something, putting her hand on his arm. Since I couldn't get too close, it was hard to see her face, but I noticed her hair. It was very dark, long and straight, and she flipped it to the right side in a suggestive maneuver. Her ivory silk blouse was cut low, but she still looked professional.

"Ma'am, are you okay?" the hostess asked, interrupting me as I tried to process what I was seeing.

"Fine," I whispered. I left and headed to my car. How dare Mark lie to me! I was shocked that he would do this. Never before were we dishonest with each other, or at least I wasn't aware that he'd ever lied in the past. I felt jealous of Olivia, the beautiful woman that Mark seemed captivated with. I pulled out a tissue and wiped the sweat on my forehead.

Fixated on spying, I hadn't noticed the sign that required a permit. Frustrated, I plucked the ticket off the windshield. To cover my tracks, I'd pay it with cash at the city office. Ironically, now I was the one sneaking around. I drove home, thinking it was possible I was losing my mind. I changed into my pajamas and ate vanilla bean ice cream straight from the carton.

I waited up for Mark, aware of the slow passage of time. I heard the bedroom door open around eleven. I took a deep breath and exhaled so that I'd remain calm.

"You're up," he said. There was no kiss hello.

"Yup. I'm reading a good book and can't put it down. How was dinner? Productive?" "Very. Josh, Andrea and Beth wound up staying in the office, so it was just Olivia, and we got a lot done. The others joined us later."

Mark fell asleep, and I lay awake, my thoughts spinning.

What if he saw me spying on him, and was now covering up? I doubted he'd be that devious. I assumed he was telling the truth, although it didn't negate that he seemed to be having way too much fun with Olivia. Then again, with JJ preying on my mind often enough, and having thoroughly enjoyed flirting with him at lunch, who was I to judge? Only with JJ, it was just business. Supposedly, it was just business between Mark and Olivia too. . . .

For the time being, I'd keep my mouth shut and my eyes wide open.

Chapter 25

WHITE KID GLOVES

THAT NIGHT, I dreamed that Olivia and Mark were in the south of France, sitting outside and overlooking the beautiful turquoise Mediterranean. Olivia had on a red bikini, her matching coverup resting on the back of her chair. There was a pot of coffee on their table, which Mark picked up and poured into Olivia's cup. Next to that was a basket of large croissants. I awoke covered in sweat, despite the air conditioning. It took a few long seconds to realize I'd had a very vivid dream. Still dazed, I got out of bed to look for Mark, but he had already left.

An early morning run perked me up. I texted Mark to say good morning and make sure I was on his radar. The dream had really thrown me.

Chrissy was in the office by the time I got there, which was unusual. Maya told me she was looking for me, so I went in to see her.

"I'd like you to draft a solicitation letter to these folks," Chrissy said, handing me a list of names from across her desk. She buzzed Maya. "I'm giving Julia a list of prospects. She'll give you a copy. Will you please find out their addresses?" Chrissy hung up. "Maya's a wiz at all this stuff," she added.

"She sure is," I mumbled, keenly aware that Chrissy never praised my work.

I scanned the list and emailed it to Maya, who sent it back with the addresses soon after. I went to her cubicle to thank her.

When I approached her desk, I saw a screen about the Nasdaq.

"Is that what's keeping you busy these days?" I blurted out. With a quick click, donor listings replaced the stock market.

"Checking names gives me eyestrain," Maya said.

So would picking stocks and doing trades, I thought. Could it be that Maya was still getting checks from Chandler and investing the money? I doubted it was her salary alone that she was using.

After that, Poppy and I met in the conference room and worked on details for the upcoming season. We set up décor meetings, hired photographers, and handled other logistics. Halfway through, Poppy said, "I keep overhearing Maya on the phone. She's not talking about work. She's been on with Artie. I think something's up between those two."

"Oh, c'mon. Beautiful Maya with Artie?" I asked. "I can't imagine it."

"It's hard to picture, I know. But I think it's possible they're having an affair."

At that moment, Maya came by and said Chrissy wanted to see me again. What could she want now? I excused myself and headed to her office.

"Chandler just told me he doesn't want to chair the development committee, although he'll remain on it."

"Oh, too bad." *Not really.* "Good he'll stay on, though."

"Yes, he's loyal. Do you have any suggestions about who might replace him? We're behind on this. I'll cancel the first meeting, but we need to get going."

I would've assumed it was her job to initiate this. I sat there for a few seconds. "Andy would be an excellent choice," I said. "He socializes with his clients, many whom are our donors."

"Hmmm...." Chrissy crinkled her brows. "He represents the corporate community, but he himself isn't wealthy, as far as I know. Typically, it's a rich person who get their rich friends on board; birds of a feather flocking together. But this could work. It's out of the box." She tapped her pen on her desk. "I like it. I'll talk to him."

I hoped he'd say yes.

Andy called me a few hours later. "Hi, Julia. How have you been?" he asked.

"Good. Season's upon us and I'm ready for the action," I said.

"I know what you mean. I've been visiting clients and reviewing their portfolios at their summer homes. Now they've almost all headed back here. So tell me about the committee. Chrissy said she thought I'd be a good chair." No doubt, she'd taken the credit for my idea.

"Yes, actually I suggested you. They sit around and

review lists of names, and committee members volunteer to call people."

"What are the results?" he asked.

"By the end of the season, perhaps there are a few new donors at the lower levels. One-on-one in-person meetings are what's effective. Like our morning donut . . . I mean donor meetings."

"Ha! Good one. So they hide behind those lists, instead of actually getting out there?"

"That's pretty much it. It's a waste of time, if you ask me."

"My salespeople at Evergreen used to do that. Each manager now reports to me on how many lunches they and their teams have had the past month with clients and prospects."

"Yes, but your bankers get bonuses," I said. "They're incentivized. Our committee is made up of volunteers like you—but you're different. You're a working guy. Our committee isn't made up of people whose livelihoods are contingent on hooking big fishes."

"I do get it," Andy said. "They're donating their time. But scrapping the committee and starting from scratch after years of involvement sends the wrong message. They'd feel unappreciated and offended. Plus, I'd be accused of being the one who fired them."

"You're right. I'm just anxious. The Addison Center can be truly great if we set this up the right way."

"We will, in due time. For now, get out your white kid gloves. And let's deal with what we have. I have several people in mind that may want to contribute large gifts. Let's focus on raising money, and not the committee right now."

"Sounds like a plan. Thanks." I was glad we got to team up.

Later that day, I looked at my phone. Mark hadn't responded to my text from early that morning. He came home again late that night, when I was already asleep: our new pattern.

I'd begun receiving texts from JJ while he was abroad. Most of his messages were about his business, and I was glad to be on his mind while he was globe-trotting. But the last one thrilled me:

Thinking about you. Miss you.

It was followed by three emoji hearts. I immediately wrote back:

I miss you too. Hope to see you soon.

. . . and added a heart. *Why the heck not?*

Chapter 26

ROOMMATES

IT WAS EARLY DECEMBER when members of the development committee sauntered into the large conference room for the first meeting. I stood tall in my new high heels. The bright red power dress that Vianora had selected was doing its job, masking my anxiety. The edge of confidence it gave me made it worth its price. Artie could say whatever he wanted about being young and riding on Chrissy's coattails, but I knew that I could win people over.

I observed an outpouring of warm greetings and hugging. Chandler took a seat at the other side of the conference room. Hunched over slightly, his hair was gray, but he still had a full head of it, along with a lanky body. Savannah was at the meeting having been added to the committee by

Andy. A few extra chairs behind the conference table, reserved for staff, other than Chrissy; she'd be seated next to
Andy.

"Thank you all for being on this important committee,"
Andy said, bringing the meeting to order. "I'd like to thank
Chandler Fairbanks for his leadership as the past committee chair. Chandler, our sincere thanks for your willingness
to remain on the committee and help us with our fundraising efforts." Andy applauded and everyone else joined in.
Once the clapping stopped, Chandler cleared his throat and
spoke.

"Everyone here has made it happen. But—and there's a
big but—if it wasn't for Christine Hathaway, none of this
would have been possible. She's done all the heavy lifting,"
Chandler's face was beaming. Seriously? Was he expecting
someone to make a toast? You could hear a pin drop.

A few seconds letter, one of Chandler's buddies picked
up his glass of water and said, "Cheers to Chrissy." Everyone
raised their glasses.

"Thank you for your comments, Chandler. Everyone
has been *so* important, and we are most grateful," Andy
said. He called on Chrissy to provide a report on monies
raised to date.

"We're way ahead of schedule for the first time," Chrissy
said in her familiar honey- smooth voice. "More money
has been raised than ever before in Addison's history," she
added with a smile. "As you can see, many of our performances are sponsored, accounting for the sharp increase
in dollars raised. We also got awarded a big grant from the
state." Maya elbowed me.

This was the first I'd heard that we got money from the

state for the grant I'd written and defended at the panel interview. I was sure Chrissy didn't want me to tell anyone that I was responsible.

"Penny and Artie Brass will be this year's gala chairs," Chrissy continued. "They agreed to be the gala hosts, too. Sarah Brightman is the performer."

"Hold on," piped up Dori Wilkinson, a leader in the philanthropic community. "I've never seen so many names on sponsorships. This is impressive." She scanned the room.

"Julia, there you are." Dori's voice was robust despite appearing elderly and frail. "Don't you line up all the sponsors?"

Chrissy's back was to me, but now she turned halfway around.

I nodded. "Yes, and these ladies to my right, Maya and Poppy, helped." Maya stopped taking notes, while Poppy smiled.

"See me after the meeting," Dori ordered.

Dori was good friends with Chandler and Georgina, but she was also a former major in the Marines, with a rep for being fiercely independent. Her comment felt like a small victory, in light of Chrissy having stolen all the glory.

Next, Maya passed around the lists of prospect names. Most of the members pulled the papers close to their faces to read, and I made a note to use a larger font next time. Andy let them bandy people's names around. Like ordering Chinese takeout, they picked off names of people they'd approach; one from Column A, two from Column C, and so on.

At the end of the meeting, I went over to Dori.

"Let's get together next week," she said. "Meet me at the

Sealine Club." She dug through her purse and retrieved a calendar. "Two Tuesdays from today at noon."

"Sure," I said, clueless as to what my schedule was on that date. But lunch with Major Dori would supplant anything.

Later that day, Poppy stopped by.

"Thank you for mentioning Maya and me at the meeting. I really appreciate it."

"Of course. You both did a lot of the heavy lifting to get all those sponsors."

"I can't believe Chrissy didn't say a word about us today, especially you."

I just shrugged. I doubted Poppy wanted me to bad-mouth Chrissy so that she could report it to her, but I played it safe.

Mark's breath reeked of alcohol when he snuck into bed that night. I peered at the clock; it was almost midnight. I went back to sleep. The next morning, he was typing furiously on his laptop in his home office.

"I had to let go of several attorneys for not producing enough billable hours," he said when he looked up and saw me in the doorway. "Fortunately, not Olivia or Josh."

I wrinkled my nose when I heard her name.

"This means I have more work to do, at least until I can replace them. And there's another M & A coming up."

"Can't the New York office help?" I asked.

"Nope," he said, without looking up.

I started to head out. "Bye," I yelled from the other room.

"I probably won't be home until much later tonight!" I heard him shout.

"Okay," I answered. We sounded like roommates, or

business partners who filled each other in on our schedules. I wanted to tell him how excited I was that I had a lunch date with Dori, but didn't. We reported facts to each other, but they were no longer colored with emotion. No more goodbye kisses or little jokes.

I headed to the Waterfront Club at lunchtime. Although I scheduled it, Elise and Valerie insisted it be at their club. Fields and Caine had become corporate sponsors at Addison, and Elise was already a major donor. Lunch with these women qualified as legitimate business, since we also discussed ways to expand Addison's programs and sponsorships.

After we were all seated, Valerie asked, "Did you hear the latest gossip? Artie was seen swinging a golf club at a duck on the links."

"Yup." Elise said. "He claimed the duck was going to attack him, and he was just defending himself. The duck was minding his own business, according to bystanders."

"And rumor has it that there's video implicating him," Valerie said.

"Oh dear, I hope this doesn't affect our gala. Penny and Artie are the event chairs," I said.

"It won't. He'll probably get a slap on the wrist," Elise said. "He's too powerful. He has a group called the Knights of the Golden Circle. Artie's made a fortune for its members."

"Chrissy told me about the Knights. I guess no one will care what he did on the golf course, as long as they're making money."

"You're right," Valerie said. "Artie can get away with murder. In this case, attempted murder of a duck. Why Penny puts up with him . . . well, we all know why."

"I would never put up with anyone," Nina said. "That's why I've stayed single."

"What about Girard?" I asked.

"It's different. I *want* to be with him. I look forward to our date nights."

"Need I remind you for the millionth time that this is because you're in the honeymoon stage?" Elise asked.

"True," Nina replied. "But c'mon. None of us would put up with someone like Artie."

"Of course we wouldn't," Elise said. "But don't go into your relationship blind, thinking it's all wine and roses."

I raised my eyebrows. "All kidding aside, what happens when there aren't any more wine and roses?"

"I can speak to that," Valerie said. "I was young and in a state of bliss when I was first married. Then reality set in, and I was miserable. My ex didn't respect me."

"Was that when you were a therapist?" I asked.

"Yes. There's a lot more to it." Valerie took a deep breath. "You might as well know. My husband was abusive. I counseled people all day, but had no idea how to help myself. Later, I realized that dealing with other people's problems was my way to forget my own."

"I'm so sorry to hear that," I said. "Is that why you created Valerie's House?" I asked.

"Don't be sorry. Everything happens for a reason. Now I get to use my money to help others."

"It must have been difficult at the time," Elise said.

"It was, but I pulled myself together for our son and daughter's sake. I feared for our safety. After ten years, I left with them, went to law school at night, while keeping my therapy practice during the day."

"You should give yourself a lot of credit for having the

strength to do what you did," Elise said. She reached over and touched her hand, and Nina joined them. Since I was seated across from Valerie I reached over the bread-basket, and we all clenched hands in the center of the table.

After more conversation, lunch ended sooner than I wanted it to. I got in my car, and slowly drove back to the office. I had always believed in Mark and our marriage, but I wasn't sure anymore. Feeling a dangerous attraction to JJ, and worried about Olivia, going back to wine and roses didn't seem realistic. That realization scared me. I couldn't understand what happened to us.

Chapter 27

PRESENCE OF YOUR COMPANY

LATER THAT DAY, the caller ID on my office phone showed that it was WOW. My heart dropped. I took a deep breath and let it ring a few times before I picked up. Most likely it was Claudia.

JJ cleared his throat. "I'm back in town, and wanted to say hello."

Holy crap, it's him.

"I'm glad. How've you been?" I asked.

"It's been nonstop. Since I returned from Europe I've been back and forth between Potomac and New York City."

"Busy man."

"How are you?" he asked. "Personally?"

Personally? As opposed to what? "I'm fine."

Actually, I'm not. My husband who I adore has a thing for his young, beautiful associate; my boss is having an affair and steals all the accolades; and my co-workers can't be trusted. Oh, and did I mention you keep entering my mind?

"I'd like to invite you to Cariblanco. I'll show you around and introduce you to some potential donors."

"Cariblanco?" I asked.

"The equestrian stables," he said, as if it was common knowledge. "Please give Claudia a call."

It was fun to fantasize about JJ and send flirty texts. Now that he'd invited me to lunch again, I was a little nervous. But I called Claudia right away.

"I was expecting your call," she said. "JJ wants to know if you're available tomorrow for lunch."

The guy wasted no time. "Um . . . let me check." I knew I was free, but waited a good fifteen seconds before I responded. "Okay, it works."

Mark didn't come home that night until really late, and I was sleeping. He left for work the next day before I was awake. I was so preoccupied about my lunch date, I was relieved that we didn't have to interact.

I pulled out casual chic skinny black pants and a white-form fitting long-sleeve blouse. It was the next best thing in my closet to jodhpurs; perfect for my excursion to Cariblanco. The black suede boots that I bought in the fall finally came in handy in South Florida. Soft eighties music helped calm my nerves as I drove to the stable. The half-hour ride west went by unnoticed.

Claudia had given me explicit directions. The under-the-radar equestrian and polo center curiously did not exist, according to google. Later, JJ told me he he'd had it blocked from search engines to maintain its exclusivity. Its green fields stretched out farther than I could see, elegantly framed by mammoth black iron gates with gold letters spelling out its name.

I was instructed by Claudia to go to the main house. Upon entering, it smelled of freshly painted wood. JJ appeared from an office and headed my way. With a confident air, he hugged me. I reciprocated his tight embrace as I took in that familiar delicious lemony scent, as well as his waistline. He was slightly thick in the stomach, but still chiseled. It felt good to be embraced by someone so strong. He wore a collared white shirt and tight jeans with woven loafers and a belt to match.

"Julia, good to see you. Thank you for coming out here. I'll show you around." He led the way to his SUV, and gave me a tour of the grounds.

"My goal was to replicate the pastures of Argentina. The facilities had to be superb, but most important to me was to have spacious stables and paddocks for the horses, and large riding rings. Of course, there is a field, too. I used to play polo years ago, back home. My love of the sport and the animals never left me," he reminisced.

"Sounds like you had a magical childhood, working on the vineyards and playing polo."

JJ was anything but boastful, never mentioning that he was an elite polo player way back, and the car was an understated Land Rover. He was able to afford absolutely anything, but that was what he chose to drive, if only in equestrian territory.

We headed back to the main house and into a spacious dining room. The room's picturesque windows allowed the space to flood with natural light, and offered unobstructed views of the paddocks. To the left was a pool, tennis court, and quarters for the staff. We headed into the dining room, where he led me to a table by the window, allowing us to admire the serene view.

"I'll be very honest with you: I just wanted to have lunch with you. No worries; we will meet some members here, who would be potential donors. Truth is, I enjoy talking to you." He drew a breath. "Just being in your company."

Caught completely off-guard, those five simple words—just being in your company—penetrated my soul. I felt the same way. A feather was tickling me inside, a sensation that I barely recognized. Yet all we were doing was talking. *Just talking.*

I tried to process his words before I spoke. I couldn't remain silent; I had to let him know.

"I enjoy your company, too," I finally said, and let out a deep breath.

"That makes me happy. So tell me, Julia. What are you working on these days?"

"Managing sponsorships, mostly. I'm there in the evenings to do meet and greets, and during the day I'm on the phone often, trying to raise money.

"You work hard," he said.

"Yes," I said softly. There was so much more to it, but I didn't feel like talking. I gazed outside, watching the horses enjoy their hay. "It's so peaceful here. I wish I could stay." I didn't intend for that to sound like I was leading him on.

"That's exactly the ambiance I wanted to create. Being here feels like an escape."

"Do you still play polo?" I asked.

"Not that much, really. I come out here and ride, though. My grandkids like it, too. We may start a new polo team. I've been walking and riding my bike a lot lately to get in shape."

"I try to do something every day, too. I ran track in high school and college. I still go out jogging in the morning, just to get outside before the day begins. Claudia seems nice, by the way. How long has she been with you?"

"Not very long, but she's terrific. I'm lucky to have found her. She's nonstop; manages all of my Washington and Royal Coconut Beach operations. She's my right and left arms. She went to Wharton, worked for a while, then went on to get her MBA. Stanford Business."

His eyes brightened when he spoke about Claudia, the same way Mark's did when he mentioned Olivia. Claudia's credentials were impressive, too. Like some of the other wealthy, powerful guys in town, JJ had hired a uniquely talented and bright woman to run the show.

"So, tell me how you got the privilege of serving your homeland?" I asked, batting my eyes a little. JJ laughed.

"Well, because my business is so linked to Argentina, it made perfect sense for me to be an ambassador. Cat's father was political back home. He needed to be to do his real estate deals. VIPs from Washington were always around Cat's family."

He leaned back in his chair. "Historically, Argentina was the States' closest Latin American partner in the '90s. Then it fell apart with the Kirchner government. The focus was to rebuild the relationship. Given my business, which straddles both countries, I was a good choice."

"It sure sounds like it," I said. I was in awe in him, hanging on his words.

"Our home is in Potomac, Maryland. Cat is very involved in DC society, and knows everyone. The appointment was the right fit at the right time. Sorry, I didn't mean to give you a history lesson."

I wasn't sorry at all. He had such steadiness of character, masculinity, and a strong sense of self. There was something wildly attractive about him. His large world made me feel small. It wasn't his wealth that overwhelmed me; it was his drive, his sheer determination, his success story that was astonishing. He knew what he wanted and went right after it. And got it.

Needing air, I was grateful when our server came over and cleared our plates. We left the dining room.

"Thank you for having lunch with me today," JJ said as he walked me to my car. "I had a nice time. I'm off to Europe tomorrow for a week, but I'll be in touch. I know where to find you," he said as he sweetly brushed a stray hair from my face. My cheeks were blushing, my sleeves hiding goosebumps. His powerful words coupled with the gesture were like kryptonite, both scary and exhilarating.

As he opened my car door, he gave me a quick, unexpected soft kiss. Not on the cheek, but on my lips. It was warm outside, but I was burning inside. Stunned, I got in my car and blasted the air conditioning. I was aware that men kissed women on the lips from time to time, although usually it was made to seem accidental. Today's kiss was no accident. For sanity's sake, I allowed myself to believe it was.

Exposure to wealthy, powerful men was an experience I often enjoyed from my position at Addison. The difference between being extremely comfortable, like Mark and I were, versus having a superabundance of money, was rarely given a thought. It was different with JJ, though. I felt as if I'd been asked into a special club; one that he held the keys to. Being invited to Cariblanco under the false pretense of meeting donors, I was welcomed into his private world. It was enthralling to feel close to such power.

Yanking myself from these thoughts, I realized that nothing had really happened. We'd toured an equestrian center and had a delightful lunch. No lines were crossed. Lighten up, let it go. Isn't that what Mark was always urging me to do? Before I knew it, I was back at the office. With plenty to do, I compartmentalized the lunch date.

Mark came home early that evening, which was unusual. I was sitting at the dining room table responding to emails. I hadn't thought about dinner, but when I saw him, I ordered Chinese food. I called him into the kitchen when it arrived. He had changed into sweatpants and a tee shirt.

"How was your day? What did you do—did you go anywhere?" Mark asked as he opened a bottle of wine. How ironic that he finally asked me questions like he used to, and now I didn't want to share.

"I went to meet a donor for lunch."

"Oh, where'd you go?"

"We met at an equestrian club. Different from the Waterfront, the Sealine, and my other usual haunts," I said, making light of the lunch. I was thankful he didn't ask who the person was.

"How was your day?" I asked, almost obligatorily.

"Fine."

But nothing felt fine.

Chapter 28

MAJOR BONDING

L UNCH WITH D ORI W ILKINSON at the Sealine Club was on my calendar a few days later. Changing outfits a few times, I settled on a black sheath, hoping Dori would look favorably on a business-like look. With perky morning energy I headed to the Addison Center. Ten minutes later, beautiful white roses arrived from Ziggy's. There was no note inside, so I called him right away.

"A Miss Claudia placed the order," Ziggy said. "She specifically said not to include any note. Who is this Miss Claudia? Now, now, don't tell me you have a secret admirer named Claudia."

"Stop it, Ziggy." I was shocked by JJ's gesture. The first thing I thought of was, what if Mark happened to stop by my office? Surely he would ask who sent them. I knew I was being paranoid since he seldom dropped by.

Clueless as to how deep JJ's interest in me was, there was no denying I was being courted. It was also hard to believe that I was developing feelings for someone other than Mark, further compounded by JJ's attraction to me. Did he really see something in me? I convinced myself that it was perfectly natural to feel this way. It made complete sense: the fact that Mark and I were not as connected recently made another man seem attractive. For now, I was grateful that JJ was thousands of miles away.

At noon, I headed to the Sealine Club. When I'd met JJ there, I ignored details about the club's interior, fixated only on him. Today I noticed large oak tables in the lobby, white-washed Adirondack chairs, and floral wallpaper. The fireplace was blazing, despite the eighty-something weather. I knew that its membership initiation fee wasn't made public; if you had to ask how much it cost, you didn't belong.

Dori was already there, waving at me from the back of the dining room, even though I'd arrived a few minutes early; military punctuality must have been heavily ingrained in her. She extended her bony hand while remaining seated. Despite her frailness, her grip was strong. She wore a navy suit that had gold buttons, and heavily sprayed white hair. It could have been the lighting at the club, but it had a slight bluish tint.

"Hello, dear," she said. "Sit down." She pointed to the chair. Her eyes widened. "Tell me about yourself. How did you wind up working at the Addison Center?"

Face to face with Dori, I was intimidated by her mere presence, let alone her directness. I crossed my legs, as if they would steady me. Donors typically chose to talk about themselves, while I dutifully listened.

"Mark and I—Mark's my husband—moved here from New York. I didn't know anyone, and Mark was so busy."

"Go on, dear." Dori was making direct eye contact. I looked away, breaking the intensity for a few seconds, before meeting her eyes again.

"Well, I was taking the Florida Bar exam in the ballroom of a hotel. During a break, I noticed a bunch of *Playbills* near the concierge counter, and picked one up. An ad seeking volunteers grabbed my attention, and I jotted down the information. Trying to adjust from our recent move was much more difficult than I'd imagined. I missed my job, my friends, and my life in New York. Although I'd been all right with the move—Mark's firm offered him a great opportunity—I grappled with my misgivings. I called the volunteer coordinator the next day." Dori nodded, encouraging me to continue.

"No task is beneath me, but when he returned my call and said he needed help stuffing envelopes, I went into my elevator pitch. I told him I was an attorney from New York City, and that I had submitted many briefs and published articles. You'd think I was applying for a position on the Supreme Court."

Dori let out a laugh and said, "That's swell, dear." She leaned over toward me. "You were smart to throw yourself into something." I nodded.

"The next thing I knew, the head of the marketing department called me, and I landed an unpaid volunteer position. To tell you the truth, it was the best thing I did, despite not getting paid."

"Your empty feelings diminished, I'm sure," Dori said.

"They did. I was so busy studying the rest of the time. When I passed the bar, I got a 'real' job at Reid, Bennett. And guess what? The marketing director at Addison provided a glowing recommendation."

"So, you're an attorney. I knew there was more to you than meets the eye. You're a smart woman, and pretty, too."

"That's kind of you, thank you." I smiled, a little embarrassed. Despite the intimidating front Major Dori put on, she was all bark and no bite.

"It's great to volunteer," Dori said. "When I met Thad— Thaddeus, my late husband—we wrote big checks to causes we believed in. It wasn't just check-writing that mattered, either. I spent countless hours at the Veterans Administration Hospital, talking with vets. Still do, once a week. They named a wing after me. I was trained to serve my country. When Thad and I accumulated enough money, we gave back." Her eyes sparkled, and she beamed with pride.

Lucky for the Addison Center, along with the vets, the arts were at their forefront.

"But if you want to know the truth, our commitment to philanthropy stemmed from our deep Christian faith," Dori continued. "You're Jewish, right?"

"Yes," I said quietly, not sure where this was headed. I was fairly confident I was the only Jewish person in the dining room at the mostly all-Gentile club.

"Well, we're all one in spirit. One God. No matter what we have been given, it's not really ours. We're here simply to be good stewards of our fortune. That's what we do—serve, either with money, or by doing. How lucky for me that I get to do both. You said you were with Reid, Bennett, dear?"

"Yes."

"Well, that's swell. A first-rate firm. Used to be, anyway. Too bad they're in hot water. I recently moved my estate planning to Harry Langhorne. He was at that firm, but went into his own practice."

"I know him. He's a nice man."

"Yes." Her raised eyebrows made creases in her forehead. Before lunch ended, Dori insisted that she host the gala kick-off party at the Sealine Club.

As I headed back to the office, I tried Chrissy from my car to share the good news, but Maya picked up and said she wasn't in, so I asked to be dropped into her voice mail.

I waited for the recording to end. "Hi Chrissy," I said after the beep. "Great news. I just had lunch with Dori Wilkinson. She insists on hosting our gala kick-off at Sealine. She was so nice, too. I'm super excited!"

Knowing Chrissy, she'd probably be jealous that I bonded with Dori.

Chapter 29

HAIR HEAVEN

My stomach dropped, and I grabbed the phone when I saw "World of Wines."

"Julia, how have you been?" JJ said. I forgot how sexy his accent could be.

"I'm good. Thank you for the flowers." A week had flown by since I received them.

"How would you like to go walking with me?" There was silence from my end, so JJ said, "You said you go jogging in the mornings. I need to start training again for polo. C'mon, go walking with me. Maybe a run. I'll meet you halfway, at the middle of the Coconut Bridge. 6:00 a.m. tomorrow." His authoritative manner sent shivers down my spine.

"Uh . . . sure."

Jolted from a deep sleep, the clock read 4:12. I tried to fall back to sleep, but couldn't. Mark got up soon after, showered and left for the office. I was relieved that he'd left early. "This would look great on you." I recalled what Mark told me when I tried on the slenderizing black leggings and form-fitting top with the crisscross pattern in the back. I brushed my hair, applied a light shade of lipstick, and stared into the mirror, feeling scandalous. *"What's wrong with you?"* I said out loud.

JJ was leaning on the bridge's wall, staring into the water. I crept up behind him and tapped his shoulder, and he turned to face me.

"Ah, good morning. Nice to see you." He was in navy golf shorts and a bright yellow collared polo shirt, which worked well with his dark complexion. His hair was slicked back. He kissed both my cheeks, and led the way to the other side of the bridge. His side, which was defined by money, status and its posh residents.

"Tell me, what's going on at Addison? What is it that you like about your job?" he asked.

"Fundraising isn't about bake sales and party planning. Well, a little bit of the latter," I said with a nervous giggle. "Anyway, it's mostly about relationships. It's a very social business. I love being around people, but I'm more serious than being a social butterfly; I treat it like an important business. When you come right down to it, it's who you know, and equally important who they know. Look how we met; through Savannah's social circle."

"Lucky for me." His smile gleamed against his bronzed face.

I pretended to ignore his comment and continued.

"Come to think of it, I never actually ask for money. It's about building relationships."

"Good point. You should really look at all you've accomplished and feel good. First, with your law practice, and now all you do at the Addison Center. You have a strong sense of purpose. I felt that same instinct early on, when I decided to start WOW. We're actually very much alike. It's not just our names: Julia and Julian."

Did he just compare himself to *me*? A man of his caliber? JJ's comment was heady stuff, and I felt giddy from his compliments. While I hardly saw what I did professionally as any big achievement, he'd given me pause to reflect. Always ambitious, it was refreshing that he identified qualities in me that I knew existed many years ago, but had lay dormant; sort of like a new-yet-old part of me had resurfaced. The driven part of me that I really liked, but then got caught up being a wife and juggling a career. Up until now, I never stopped to consider what made me tick.

"I always knew I wanted to be successful," he continued. "Working for Cat's father had no appeal. I wanted to build something. Create something," he said, snapping his fingers as if he invented something out of thin air.

"That's so admirable. I wish I'd built something, too. I must've missed the entrepreneurial train."

"Well, you act like one. Look what you are doing for the community, helping the Addison Center. I bet you're always thinking of strategies to grow."

Again, he saw in me what was lurking beneath the surface.

"Now that you mention it, I am. We have fundraising goals, but the sky's the limit when it comes to raising money. It's exciting. Much different from practicing law, and more enjoyable."

"I like who you are." He moved closer to me as we walked, our arms touching. My heartbeat quickened.

There was a comfortable silence for a few minutes. JJ had approached the sweet spot in life when most men rested on their laurels, played golf, and dined at the early bird specials. But JJ's vitality and wisdom made him even more attractive. In turn, he saw something in me that made him want to be closer, and it excited me. I should have felt guilty, but I was too keyed up to feel anything except desire.

We made our way to Royal Ocean Way. The beautiful turquoise ocean and white-capped waves were soothing.

"I've spent my whole life working. Cat would host extravagant dinner parties in Potomac. Then I'd have to jump on a plane to placate WOW's investors. I'd miss my own parties. And if it was someone else's event, off went four dozen roses to the host; one dozen wasn't a good enough apology, according to my wife." He gave a partly suppressed laugh.

"How was Cat with that kind of life? It must've been difficult."

"She understood. She brought up the children. Supervised the help that brought up the children, anyway," he said with an amused smile. "Ran the homes. She was so busy. Still is, always on the hunt for more property."

"Does she enjoy that?" I was filled with curiosity about their life.

"Cat loves real estate, both as an investment and to decorate. She gets very excited when she finds something, then she becomes overwhelmed with the latest project. So she goes and hires more help, which in turn means more help for her to manage. Or, more help to help manage the help and all the stuff she buys. It's a vicious cycle," he said with a shrug.

"How about you? Do you get involved in any of that?"

"No. The homes, that's her thing. Except for the landscaping. I love that, mainly because it brings me back to the vineyards in Argentina." JJ was more multi-dimensional than I'd imagined. How he had time for everything was baffling.

"Anyway, who could blame Cat for amassing properties for us, given that her father is a real estate king? Her mother did the same thing in Argentina." I'd learned about Cat's rich, glamorous life, but he'd revealed nothing about his feelings for her. I wished I had the nerve to ask.

With the glistening water on one side of us, the right side of the street boasted one mega-mansion after another. As we passed a few more homes, he told me that the white modern masterpiece was his. It was straight out of *Architectural Digest*; I'd passed it a million times when I went running. Once when Mark and I had gone walking, we'd passed it and he said he loved that house, which gave me an eerie feeling. At least my taste in men was consistent.

"Are you there? Hello?" JJ asked.

"Just admiring the scenery. Your home is beautiful."

"Only the staff is there now. Cat's in our apartment in New York overseeing a renovation job. We just bought a triplex overlooking Central Park. She'll be there for two weeks." To my relief he kept walking past the house, much as I would've liked an invitation inside.

We walked for a little while longer before we parted to go in opposite directions. I sprinted back to my house and dashed into a hot shower, as if to cleanse myself. Not just my body, but my soul. From what? I was being ridiculous. Nothing had happened. I was terrified of my feelings, though. Compared to all of Mark's angst and stress, JJ seemed light and airy, despite the fact that he was an extremely sophisticated, complex man. Just the thought of him was intoxicating.

First on my agenda that day was to call Elise for a hair salon recommendation.

After we made small talk, I asked, "Now that I have makeup, and nice clothes, why not go for the gusto and have gorgeous hair, too? I'm sure you can make a recommendation."

"Of course I can. You absolutely must make an appointment with the master hairstylist, Christophe. He's a genius with this merciless Florida humidity. Doesn't matter that it's January. You'll love his place's glam vibe. It gave me good ideas for a new client. Use my name when you call."

"Thank you," I said.

"Remember, Julia," she said in a serious tone. "You're on the front line. It pays to look your best."

"Yes, but you'd never know it. It's all about making Chrissy look good. I'm convinced *that's* my job."

"It doesn't matter. Keep your head high, and stay classy. Things never remain the same forever."

"Now that you mention it, Dori Wilkinson pointed out what a good job I did with sponsorships in front of everyone at a meeting. Do you know her?"

"Sure do. She's still a major player on the social scene. She believes in the causes she supports."

"I had lunch with her, and she offered to host our gala kick-off reception, which is next week."

"Way to go. See, you *are* being recognized for your work," Elise said.

"Anyway, I do want to look my best, so I'll book the Bentley of hairstylists. I always listen to you."

" 'Atta girl."

What I wouldn't share with Elise was that it wasn't only for work that I wanted a good stylist. Everything felt exciting and new, including the urge to harness my feminine energy.

Christophe's receptionist squeezed me in for an appointment that week during lunch. Washing, coloring, straightening, styling, blowing, head up, head back, moving from chair to chair in between cappuccinos, made me dizzy. Once the music finally stopped, I landed at Christophe's station. Gazing around the salon in the oversized mirror, I was able to fully appreciate its ambiance. Simone, Christophe's third assistant, was using a flatiron on my hair to seal in keratin.

Catching glimpses of activity around the salon through the mirror, my gaze became fixated on the checkout counter. Artie Brass was standing there, speaking with Maya. I watched him leave, while a perky assistant with an exaggerated pop in her step escorted Maya in my direction. She wore white skinny jeans with deliberate rips in all the right places, and an off-the-shoulder sexy top. The assistant parked Maya in the station right next to me.

"Hello, Maya," I said. She looked at me quizzically. Maybe it was the smock and my straightened hair.

"It's Julia," I added.

"Oh, sorry. I didn't recognize you. Funny meeting you here!" she replied breezily.

I thought the same. I assumed Artie must be paying for her haircut.

"Nice to see you're enjoying your day off. I saw you with Artie by the checkout." My tone dripped with sarcasm.

"Oh yes, he was there. He stopped by to give belated Christmas gifts. The Brass family gets their hair done here."

Now that was a lame excuse. "I just find it a little odd that you speak with him at the office now," I said. "Especially after we visited him together at his home." *And might be having an affair with him.* Being outside of the office on a level playing field must have contributed to my boldness. The white wine that Christophe's assistant had given me helped, too.

Maya's face hardened into an expression I'd never seen before. "It's none of your business who I talk with."

I was shocked that she would speak to me this way. "Oh, but it is!" I said, surprised by my own boldness. "Let's talk about. . . ."

"Mademoiselles, bon jour." Christophe appeared and cut me off. He must have heard the ruckus, which wouldn't be good for his business. "So much commotion. Let me see your hair," he said to me, and ran his fingers gently through it. A few seconds later, Maya's hairdresser came over to blow-dry her hair. I left without saying goodbye to Maya, and practically skipped out of the place.

I got in my car, turned the air conditioning on, and laughed. It was best that Christophe had stopped my small outburst. I don't know what got into me, but Maya had become so puzzling with her attitude lately. Then there was Chandler's check, Artie, trading stocks during the day, and talking about Poppy.

As usual, I arrived home before Mark.

"Your hair looks nice," he said when he saw me in the kitchen. He was in his suit, and he put his briefcase on the floor. I was whipping together penne and salad for dinner.

"Thanks. I went to Christophe's in Royal Coconut Beach during lunch. Elise recommended him. You won't believe who I saw. . . ."

"How much did that job cost?" He pointed to my hair. Was that all he cared about?

"More than you'd like to know." I'd forgotten I needed to walk on eggshells.

"What does that mean?" His eyes narrowed and he took a small step back.

"It was expensive, and I treated myself. Why are you upset about it?"

"I just asked was how much it cost," he said. "What are *you* getting so upset about?"

I refused to answer him. "Did something bad happen at work? Is this why you're attacking me? It's like you're still in lawyer mode."

"No. It was fine." He picked up his briefcase. "Going to change."

"Fine," I said, shrugging. When he was out of earshot, I said out loud, "That's all you ever say anyway. 'Fine'. We have a *fine* relationship."

He returned to the kitchen a few minutes later in his sweats, and we sat at the table.

I didn't realize how upset I was and concentrated on downing my pasta to prevent the tears from streaming down my cheeks. Mark barely looked up from his bowl. The silence was broken by a piercing ring. For once, I was glad it was Mark's phone. He picked up.

"Hold on, Olivia. I'm going into my office." He left and shut his office door. I cleaned up the kitchen, got into bed, and cried myself to sleep.

But a few hours later, Mark's arms enveloped me. I felt his warmth through my silk nightgown, which he slipped over my head. He kissed me on the mouth, and then all over. Our lovemaking lasted a long time. Make-up sex without talking was a good way to end the disconnect of our non-conversation. I knew it wouldn't make any of our real issues disappear, but it was a welcome reprieve.

The next morning, I found coffee next to my night table. It was still pretty hot, which meant Mark might still be home. There was a text from JJ, too.

> Please meet me at the bridge this morning.
> Does 7:00 work?

"Yes," I wrote back.

Chapter 30

UNORDINARY ROUTINES

A FEW MINUTES LATER, it dawned on me that Mark might have seen JJ's text when he put my coffee mug down. I shot up, nervously put my nightgown back on, and went to find Mark. I found him seated at his desk organizing papers. He had on a charcoal gray suit, white oxford and red tie. His after-shave smelled fresh.

I stood there in my nightgown, my hair messy from our lovemaking. I cleared my throat. "Good morning," I said.

Mark picked his head up. "Good morning, Jools. Your nightgown's on backwards." He chuckled.

Phew.

"Sleep well?" he asked.

"Sure did." I smiled.

"I was just getting ready to leave. I have some important meetings today. First, I have a breakfast meeting."

"With who?" I asked.

"Brad. He's in from the New York office again."

I thought he could be lying and meeting Olivia. "I hope your day goes well."

Mark placed his papers in his briefcase, and stood. I walked him to the door, and he kissed me goodbye on the cheek. It was like old times, and for once everything seemed ordinary, except for the fact that at five to seven I headed to the bridge to meet another man.

It was a cloudy, balmy day and I hoped it wasn't going to rain. Like the last time, JJ was already there in its middle, leaning on the ledge. He was in running gear, and his face had stubble. Normally, I would think that was scruffy, but it defined his jaw line and made him appear sophisticated and masculine.

"Good morning." He kissed my cheek. "Wow, your hair looks gorgeous. You're so pretty." He gently took a strand and let it flow through his fingers.

And he didn't ask how much it cost.

We headed towards Royal Coconut Beach.

"I love starting my mornings like this," JJ said. He grabbed my hand, but I let go. He gently took it again, and brought it up to his lips, kissing the back. I felt tingly all over, yet unable to fully embrace the moment.

"I do too." At least my words were sincere. I hoped they were a consolation for not holding his hand.

He told me about his latest deal, and I told him about Dori and how I admired how passionate she was about the causes she believed in. We walked by his house again, and then passed a few new apartment buildings. He pointed to them.

"Aren't these perfect?" he said. "I recently looked at a few in this building. It's the best complex on Royal Ocean Way. I think I'm going to buy a duplex. Guests can stay there."

"Guests? How convenient." I laughed.

"You have the cutest giggle. You'd be able to stay there anytime you wish to get away." He wasn't laughing, and I realized he was serious.

I pretended to ignore his comment, knowing he could have wanted it to be a love nest. The thought of a rendez-vous with JJ at the duplex thrilled me, but no way would I let it get that far.

"I enjoy being with you," JJ said, "Walking and talking like this."

"I feel the same way." He took my hand again. It was warm and much larger than mine. I clasped it this time in-stead of letting go. He drew them to his lips and kissed the front of mine.

"We have something very special," he said.

I could feel my words bubble up, but somehow remain-ing silent made me less of an accomplice. He let go of my hand he gave me a playful grab around my torso, which sent chills down my spine. It was getting late, and I had a meet-ing at the office. He began to walk me back towards the bridge, but before we got there, he kissed me on the lips; his were velvety and smooth.

"I'll text you," he said.

"Okay." I smiled. As I made my way across the bridge, I turned around. I was thrilled to see him standing there watching me. I waved, and he blew a kiss.

When I got to the office, I went to Maya's cubicle, hoping to clear the air. The last thing I needed was her bad-mouthing me to Artie, Chrissy, or anyone else.

"Good morning, Julia," she said, swiveling on her chair so she could see me. "Wow, your hair looks fantastic. I'm glad you're here. I'm reviewing *Playbill*, and want to make sure the names are correct. I'll email it to you."

I stared at her warily. It was a bizarre reaction after what transpired yesterday at the salon.

"Oh, did you want something?" she asked.

"Um . . . no. No problem, I'll check the names."

Our interactions the rest of the week were oddly pleasant and routine. Buried in the usual assignments from Chrissy, donor lunches, and evenings in the Parker Pavilion, I pushed it aside.

Later that week, after everyone left, Floria came in to vacuum my office when I was applying lipstick before heading to the Parker Pavilion.

"Floria, it's good to see you."

"You're still here," she said. "I love your lipstick. You know I always check things like that out. Is it new?"

"No, I've had it awhile." I had gotten it at Les Saisons when I went with Mark, and used it sparingly. I handed it to her and she examined the label.

"Wow, it's Chanel's Hot Lips," she exclaimed.

"It was a gift," I said, a little embarrassed since it was costly.

She took a small notepad and pen from her cart and wrote down the name, then handed it back. My guess was she'd find a good copy to sell.

"Just between us, my cosmetic business is taking off,"

Floria said. "I only work nights here for the health benefits. Soon I'll have enough money from selling make-up and I'll quit this job. Don't tell anyone."

"You're going to be a big success one day. I know it."

I was at Addison well past eleven, so I made sure to set my alarm for 6:00 the next morning. JJ and I planned to meet on the bridge and go walking in the morning, and I didn't want to sleep through that.

This became a routine—our routine—whenever he was in town. Favorite workout clothes, hair brushed, teeth brushed. Mark had no reason to be suspicious; he knew I always went running in the morning. I reassured myself that nothing *really* happened. I was on both sides of the fence, depending on the moment. I'd tell myself that I was spending time with a new friend, that was all. Five minutes later, I'd feel completely awful. The vacillation between the two became tortuous.

Chapter 31

THE RICH MIX

THE DAY OF the gala kick-off party, I went home early so I could change into a red silk cap-sleeved dress I'd laid out that morning. Mark said he'd join me, which was a surprise. I had become so used to doing my own thing.

"Give me a few minutes to take my suit off. A sport jacket and tie are good, right?"

"Yes, perfect."

While Mark changed, I responded to some emails.

We headed to the Sealine Club, and as I drove, Mark stretched out in the passenger's seat, looking relaxed for a change. His phone was nowhere in sight. He was acting like his old self, which in a strange way I resented. Was I supposed to simply adjust to his mood swings? What about how he affected me? Knowing I'd have to be "on" in ten minutes, I ordered myself to quit thinking about it.

Sealine Club members, as well as Penny and Artie's circle from Waterfront, arrived around the same time for the party hosted by Dori. The cocktail rounds encouraged a lot of mixing and mingling. The diverse crowd represented a microcosm of ultra-extreme wealth under one roof. I could visualize the headline in the *Society Script: The Rich Mix*. I was grateful to know that JJ was away, otherwise he probably would've been there as Savannah's guest. As much as I'd love to see him at a social outing, that might be too difficult, especially with Mark here.

I saw Dori and introduced her to Mark.

"A pleasure to make your acquaintance," Dori said, extending her hand to meet Mark's.

"Nice to meet you, Mrs. Wilkinson. It's so kind of you to host this evening for the Addison Center. Thank you for including me," he said.

"Your wife is a dynamo. She's so good at what she does. You must be proud of her."

Not only was I delighted to hear someone of Dori's stature say this, but thrilled that she shared her nice compliment with Mark.

"Yes, I'm proud," Mark said. "Julia has told me so many nice things about you." I could always count on him to be charming, and say the right things. At least to others.

Mark and I mingled with the other guests. Savannah was there, and I went to say hello to her while Mark was at the bar getting us drinks.

"I heard you and JJ hit it off at the Blossom Ball," she said.

He told her that? "Yes, we had a good time. You were right about him being good people."

"Well he thinks you're a powerhouse. You sure impressed him."

I impressed *him?* A thrill ran through me. It was the other way around.

Mark returned with wine for himself, Prosecco for me. I introduced Mark to Savannah.

"Your wife has the full package, bless her heart," Savannah said to Mark. "I was just telling her she wowed folks at the Blossom Ball."

"I'm not surprised," Mark said. He cocked a dark eyebrow.

Savannah excused herself and flitted off.

The rest of the evening passed quickly. I spotted Maya standing in the corner talking to Artie, and then she resumed her station at the check-in table. Chrissy was busy working the room as usual, and looked elegant in a long, flowing cornflower blue dress.

Soon enough, Mark and I were back at home. "Thanks for coming with me tonight," I said. "I'm glad you met Dori and Savannah, too."

I thought Mark was about to say something about their praise for me, but instead he said, "You looked pretty."

Mark's words took me off-guard. Could he be warming up to me again? A few minutes later, I was stark naked except for the stilettos. Partly I was on a high from the compliments I'd received that evening, but I was also giddy that JJ had spoken about me to Savannah. Mark tenderly slipped off each shoe, and massaged my aching feet. He was a pro at that, I now remembered. Then he continued to kiss me, first on the back of the neck and then all over, effortlessly navigating my body. For a short while, everything else was cast aside as the roommates became lovers again.

But in a few days, it was back to the usual: Mark worked late, and I was consumed with details for the gala. We saw very little of each other, although we started to text each other during the day a little bit. I was occupied with drafting speeches, making photo priority lists and solicitations for additional donations. And I continued to go walking with JJ when he was in town.

That morning, we met at our usual place, the middle of the bridge. I saw him chatting with a fisherman. Whether he was in a sport jacket, or a tee-shirt and running shorts like today, he looked handsome.

"Come, see," he said, pointing into the pristine water where the rod was. We watched the fisherman's line tighten, and a spirited fish got pulled up against its will.

"A trout, sir," the fisherman said, joyfully displaying his prize.

"Nice job. Keep it up." JJ said.

I admired how well he mixed with a perfect stranger. As we walked, I told him that we were scheduled to meet Penny that day to review the seating and décor, and to select a menu.

"She's got a tough job," JJ said. "That's Cat's favorite thing. Organizing details for charity events. Mostly in Washington, but now that we'll have a place in New York, I'm sure she'll get involved in its charity scene." He shrugged.

"It sounds glamorous, but it's not something I'd ever aspire to."

"You just keep at it." I recalled Mark saying the same thing to me when I began working at Addison. Seldom did I hear that kind of encouragement anymore from him.

We sat on a bench overlooking the ocean. Aside from a few cars and an occasional jogger, it was quiet. The ocean was calm, the sun trying to peak through the clouds. He stroked my arm, and I felt a pleasurable sensation through my body.

"I've really fallen for you. What about you, Estrella? That's what I'm going to call you. Estrella, like a star. Do you feel the same way about me?"

"Yes. Very much so." *You have no idea.* "But it scares me."

"Look at me," he said. We gazed into each other's eyes. "I need you in my life. There's nothing to be afraid of."

I parted my lips, and felt my breath stop briefly. I needed to choose my words carefully. "We're both married."

His eyes squinted, tightening. "I know. But being with you is so natural."

It felt that way to me, but it also felt so good. Just then, two spoonbills walked by us near our feet, their large, flat bills comical looking. We laughed.

"Ah, that cute giggle." He gave my shoulder a playful nudge. "I enjoy the outdoors. It reminds me of my childhood."

"Where were your ancestors from before Argentina?"

"England, several generations back. My family has a crest. It was created when my family settled in Argentina. Deep blue and yellow colors signify the sky and the sun, which vineyards are so dependent on. The yellow was really gold, like the sunshine they prayed for. The panther was of European origin, representing all those who came before them in England. Then there was the chevron shape found in most crests, meaning protection. Grapes were on the shield."

"Sounds like you're very proud of your heritage."

"I am. Cat, too, had her own family crest."

"You both go so well together. On paper, that is. Your backgrounds." That part was true. Cat was a suitable wife; check. One to build a nest with and have kids with; check. Pass down good lineage; check. More than socially acceptable; check. Attractive enough; check. At least back then. JJ's family was not nearly as wealthy, but they were entrepreneurial and from good stock; check. And they must have been in love, at one time. Possible check. I wondered if Cat had ever strayed.

"Yes, we were a good match back in Argentina." Did that mean they were no longer a good match? I should have asked him if he loved her. I also wondered if he was attracted to me because we came from such different worlds.

Dark clouds started to form, and he walked me back to the foot of the bridge. He told me he'd be travelling, but that he'd be in touch. He kissed me goodbye on the cheek, and I ran, although I didn't make it home before it started to pour.

I was soaked when I got back to the house, and peeled off my clothes. I was a mixed bag of emotions. My feelings for JJ had intensified. Was that considered cheating? Regardless, I felt incredibly guilty. I started to fret about Mark's attraction to Olivia. What if he'd fallen for her, the same way l did for JJ? I had no idea what to do, which made me feel directionless and powerless. I stood in the shower, allowing the pounding water to hit my face and merge with my tears.

When I got to the office, I forced myself to snap out of it. Chrissy joined Poppy and me in the conference room.

"Penny's here," she announced. "Maya went to get her downstairs." Those two riding up in the elevator together was an amusing thought. I wondered if Penny knew that Maya saw her husband outside of work.

Chrissy gave Penny a hug when they walked in.

"Nice to see you again," Penny said to me, as we exchanged cheek kisses.

"Same. Thanks for being here today," I said.

We started with the seating. Penny pored over the list, while we waited. "Let me see. Glinda and Marcia had a big falling-out two weeks ago at canasta. Separate them. The husbands are in a big deal together, but it's best not to seat them together because of the wives." Pencil in hand, Poppy speedily moved things around.

"The Schifflers and Goldsteins need to be seated with each other. Why are Mary and Cornelius Mumford seated at one of the Waterfront tables? Do they know someone there?" She looked up at me with raised eyebrows, insinuating that I should know better, as she showed off her insider's knowledge at my expense. I shook my head "no", as guests were moved around again. "Oh, and Carly dated a couple of those men years ago," she added, pointing to some of the Waterfront tables. "Let's keep her away; she's still single. Their wives will kill me if I put her at their table."

Chrissy commented on seating for board members and prominent donors. Once the charade was done, we all headed to the ballroom where Mia, the director of catering, greeted us at the entrance. Poppy had once told me she'd earned the nickname "Gucci Lady" due to the clipboard that was permanently affixed to her arm.

"Please, come in and have a seat." She waved her free arm. "For the first course tasting, Chef Gordon, trained in Switzerland, had his culinary team prepare smoked salmon on a small pancake, surrounded with fancy greens, drizzled balsamic, heirloom tomatoes, and a shot of gazpa-cho soup," she said, reading her notes. The chef went back to the kitchen while the servers returned with a delicately prepared plate that Mia referred to as "Study of Lobster." We dug in with our fish forks, with Penny opting for the lat-ter choice, probably sold on its catchy name.

The servers proceeded to bring out three types of steaks, prepared three different ways: Filet mignon with porcini mushroom compound butter; prime sliced NY strip steak Diane; and seared steak and polenta with chimichurri. Penny selected Steak Diane. So much fuss around food de-cisions! I thought Chef Gordon was a master; did he really need us ladies to be involved? It seemed to insult his pro-fessional skills, but who was I to judge? Tasting and making decisions from a delicious array of fine cuisine prepared by a world-renowned chef was the gala chair's privilege.

None of us had room for the mouth-watering rich choco-lates, including a mousse, a ganache, and a flourless molten volcano, but that didn't stop us. The entire time, Mia took copious notes, while I took photos of the five-star dishes. Stuffed, we finished and headed next door to look at décor.

We entered to find Ziggy putting the final touches on the table. Penny and Ziggy exchanged air kisses, obviously knowing each other. Ziggy was showing off his spectacu-lar black and white Broadway décor to complement Sarah Brightman. Under anyone else's eye, the concept would scream "flashy bar mitzvah." But it was Ziggy, so it was the perfect mix of classy and cool. His décor met with Penny's approval, and we all agreed that the gala was going to be a stunning affair.

Chapter 32

WORTH EVERY PENNY

NINA AND VALERIE were reviewing the listings of education programs when I arrived at the Waterfront Club for lunch with the Lunch Club ladies. Elise was in Paris with David.

"Don't let me interrupt you," I said to them. "Let me know if you have any questions." I blew kisses and took a seat. "The program about bullying that's geared to middle schoolers," Nina said, "What do you think, Valerie? Sounds like a good sponsorship for our firm?"

"Yes, it's perfect," Valerie said. "What do you think, Julia?"

"It's an excellent choice. It's part of Addison's efforts to build a safe environment in schools."

"Teddy told me the other day that he's proud of our new

firm," Valerie said. "He'll think this sponsorship is a wise decision. He enjoys helping people, being a neurosurgeon. Sometimes, he puts his patients before me."

"Lately, work *always* comes before me with Mark," I said, not hiding my exasperation. "Do you get upset with Teddy?"

"I do. Then I remind myself that the way he cares for others was one of the wonderful qualities I loved about him when we first met."

"Funny you say that. It's what attracted me to Mark in the beginning, too. Now it's mostly all work. I despise his phone."

"Try to remember the good stuff. Maybe it'll bring you back," Valerie said.

I appreciated her comment, but Mark and I had a real disconnect going on.

"Teddy's great with my children, too," Valerie added. "He loves them madly, and treats them like his own. That means the world to me."

"Speaking of other people's kids," Nina said. "I'm supposed to meet Girard's son next week. I hear he's a spoiled brat. He's very close with his mother, too. Not so much with Girard. I'm a little uptight about it."

"Wow, I thought *nothing* fazed you," I said.

She gave me a surprised look. "Seriously?"

"C'mon. I meant it as a compliment. You're tough, and you don't let things bother you. I wish I were more like you, actually." Especially now, as I thought of JJ. "Anyway, you'll be fine with the son. How old is he?"

"In his twenties. Maybe he just needs a nice girlfriend."

"Just remember, it's his son," Valerie said.

"I know, I know."

Just then, Penny Brass walked into the dining room and headed our way. I tried to conceal my disappointment. Selfishly, I wanted my friends to myself.

"Hi Penny. How *are* you doing?" Something was up, the way Nina asked her. It couldn't be the duck incident; that had merely resulted in a hefty fine and lots of humorous club chatter.

"I'm holding up alright. Hang on, my cell's ringing. Excuse me."

She moved a few steps away. "Oh, okay. No, not Tuesday. I have lunch already that day. Are you sure? No, Thursday is ladies' golf member guest. I can't switch it. I thought we were having lunch today? Okay, later."

Penny had obviously screwed up her lunch date. I wondered if her overwhelmingly busy life served as a good diversion to Artie's craziness; exchanging one kind of craziness for another. Where was her assistant to keep all of this in order, anyway?

"Grab a seat and join us. Elise is away," Valerie said, standing and pulling the chair out for Penny. I guessed quality time with the girls was not in the cards.

"Oh, good. I have a question about that net worth statement," Penny said.

Our lunch quickly turned into a client meeting. While I was dying to know what she was talking about, I stood, about to excuse myself.

"Oh, it's fine," Penny said, looking at me. "I don't care if the whole world knows. The tongues are wagging here at Waterfront. Artie and I just decided that we're finally getting divorced," she said bluntly. "He's indulging in all kinds of shenanigans."

"I'm so sorry, Penny." Perhaps Maya fit in somehow, too.

"Don't be," she said. "Please, sit. It all boils down to the value of Artie's assets, if you really want to know."

"Do we have your permission to go ahead and talk about this?" Valerie asked.

"You might as well hear it from the horse's mouth, before the rumor mill spins it any which way. Besides, this could impact the Addison Center gala," Penny said. "I didn't want to say anything when I was at Addison going over everything."

Nina looked at Penny, who nodded. "Okay, here it goes," Nina said. "A significant part of Artie's assets were investments in privately held companies. As part of the negotiation process, Artie submitted a net worth statement in which he listed all his assets and liabilities. At that time, he indicated his total net worth as one amount, the single largest asset of which was his own investments in companies that his firm had acquired. But the estimate of the asset was way below what it was worth." Penny nodded.

"The carried interest issue," I said, dredging up the term from my lawyering days.

"Exactly," Nina answered.

While Penny would still receive a massive fortune, she deserved what she was legally entitled to. In Nina and Valerie's book, if you married someone like Artie, you'd earned every penny.

"That Maya who's been working for Artie," Penny added. "She's something else, let me tell you." She paused and looked at me. "She's at the Addison Center, right?"

"Yes, she is," I said, and swallowed.

"Did you know she's working for Artie on the side?"

"Ummm . . . no, I didn't."

I suspected they might be having an affair, but I hadn't

realized she was also working for him. Then it clicked: She was always looking at the stock market. I felt foolish for not putting this together earlier.

"Be that as it may, these gals here," Penny said, pointing at Nina and Valerie, "are the ones who have my back."

"I'm sure they do. They're the best. You're in good hands," I said, although I couldn't stop thinking about what Maya was up to.

For the rest of our lunch, we made small talk, and then I headed back to the office. To an outsider, it must seem like Penny and Artie had everything: a stunning home in Royal Coconut Beach and multiple homes elsewhere, two kids, and limitless buckets of money. Hearing the inside scoop, it was all a fancy façade. I knew Penny didn't have it easy with Artie, but now I felt downright sorry for her. *And Maya was working for Artie on the Addison Center's clock!*

Later in the day, my phone rang, indicating it was World of Wines. *It was him.* Or Claudia.

"Hello, Estrella. Glad you picked up. How are you?"

"I'm fine." *Liar.* "Been busy. Where are you?"

"Spain, then Portugal. Tell me about you."

"We had the gala tasting." *Oh god, how lame.*

"Always good to be productive. I just wanted to hear your voice."

We talked for a few minutes more, and before hanging up he said he missed me. I felt a huge surge of joy, my emotions running high.

That evening I was in the Parker Pavilion, and handled a meet and greet with some of the Les Misérables cast members. As captivating as the performance was, all I could think about was JJ's call. I was dragging the next day at work, and when I finally got home, Mark was already in the kitchen. He had put up some boiling water for pasta. I was surprised to see him cooking for a change. He had already changed into jeans and a white form-fitting tee shirt. His muscles were still very defined, and he had none of the belly fat that so many men get when approaching middle-age.

"You look good," I said. It was a worth a try to warm up to him.

He gave a quick smile while he made a salad.

I leaned on the counter. "I have a question. Do you love me?" Since we weren't on solid ground, it was bold of me.

"Who are you, Tevye asking Golda if she loves him? She responds with how she cooked and cleaned for him, gave him children, even milked his cows. Doing all those things, isn't that what love is? Why are we even talking about this?" He poured the pasta into the boiling water.

It was impossible to tell if he was being funny, or annoyed with my question. I used to be able to read him so well.

To take him literally, we had no children. Nor did we have a cow to milk, but I did buy milk at the supermarket. Cooking wasn't a fine-tuned skill, but rather my daily dinner dilemma; but I don't think that's what was on the line. Had we just become another old married couple, as I'd suspected for months now: roommates, business partners, each doing our fair share of the work? Was love a foregone conclusion? Despite an undercurrent of love, no matter what was going on with him, the "I'm madly in love with you" vibe was absent from his answer.

"What about passion?" I asked. I was now standing straight, my arms crossed.

"Passion? C'mon on, Julia. I'm stressed out and tired," Mark said. "And, I'm making dinner!"

"How come when Olivia's on the phone, you become all lively and animated? Why does she get Mr. Bubbly? All I get is 'I'm stressed and tired'."

"Stop it!" he practically shouted. "Quit being so dramatic."

He turned to me, and his eyes looked like darts were flying out of them, which frightened me. The fact that he was much taller than me and was now looking down at me didn't help. His physicality used to make me feel protected, loved.

"No, I won't. You act so different when she's on the phone," I said. "It's like you light up like a firefly. Give me a break. Is something going on between you two?" I was shocked that I'd said that, but I was riled up and there was no turning back.

"Olivia and I are working on some cases, and she's helping hold things together at the firm. You know how tough things are right now for me. I'm not even getting paid," he said with a raised voice. "And you're complaining about her? There's a temporary freeze on partners collecting income. I told you. That is, if you'd *listened* when I told you."

He did? If Mark had told me he wasn't getting paid, I would've remembered it. I didn't know how to respond, so I said nothing, while I fantasized that he'd take me in his arms and tell me how much he loved me. I could tell him that he was a great attorney; that he'd figure it out and we'd get through it. Then, he'd mention how fantastic I looked, especially since I'd lost those five nagging pounds because of the miles I ran early each morning. That I was the special woman he'd married way back, and yes, he still loved me madly. Instead, all he did was get defensive about Olivia. What was I really worth to Mark? I used to be so sure.

I went into the bedroom, closed the door and turned on the television. Our situation made me depressed, and it wasn't because of the money. A tear streamed down my face. Had we really become that disconnected? Comparing our relationship to some of the other marriages my lunch group dissected, we came out pretty well. Were my expectations too high? On the other hand, we'd had a very close marriage for many years. Except now it had morphed into something I barely recognized.

Chapter 33

DIVORCE, ROYAL COCONUT BEACH STYLE

"I'M GOING SHOPPING when the stores open," I told Mark while he was working early at home that Saturday morning. "I need to get my wardrobe organized." I was looking for an excuse to get out of the house, away from him.

"I'll go with you to the outlets," Mark said.

"Who said anything about outlets?" I snapped. "Les Saisons and a splendid array of boutiques are less than half a mile away."

"No. We're on an austerity budget," Mark sternly announced. My spirits plummeted; not because of finances, but the way he gave this edict. Whether he was getting an income from his firm at the moment or not, we had plenty of money saved. I was making a nice living, along with excellent health benefits. So what was the big deal about buying a new dress, and who was he to decide this anyway? He was the one who needed to lighten up.

"Okay, I'll be ready in ten minutes."

We drove off, not talking in the car. I weaved through the racks at Saks Off Fifth, while Mark was pacing on his phone. A few dresses caught my attention; they were perfect for working day into evening, without having to change. Stepping out of the dressing room to show him one of them, an old habit, he covered his phone and asked, "How much is it?" Not answering, I tried on a few more for fun. I headed to the register and paid for them, using my credit card.

"What's up with you?" I asked when we got in the car.

"Nothing. Everything's fine."

The deafening silence was interrupted by his phone. Olivia. He spoke to her most of the way back.

After he hung up he said, "Unfortunately, I have to go to the office. I'll drop you at home."

"How come?" I asked.

"Olivia wants me to look at some memos she drafted." He was silent for the rest of the drive home. His mouth was in a downward curve, his expression blank, appearing deep in thought. Despite his good looks, he appeared ugly. I knew my scrutiny of him at the moment was cruel, but I couldn't help it. There was no trace of my sweet, funny husband; the one who put things in perspective for me; the one who for years had lightened my spirits; the one who used to help me select nice clothes and secretly paid for them; the one that shared everything with me.

All I could see now was a gigantic emotional wall. I missed my husband. At the same time, I longed for JJ, who I felt a special connection with. I wanted to cry, but held it in. Mark dropped me off, and I got out of the car with my shopping bag, barely saying goodbye.

Mark texted me later that day and said he'd be at work a few more hours. By the time it was 8:00, I was calm. I headed to his office to surprise him and take him out to dinner. I'd try anything to help diminish our growing distance. I parked across the street, but before I got out, I spotted him with Olivia. They were standing outside talking, each holding files. I doubted they saw me, because they were deep in conversation, focused on each other.

I observed them for a few minutes, and then Olivia stepped forward and put her arms around him. Mark took her arms, removed them and took a step back. I was proud that he didn't reciprocate her hug—unless he pushed her away only because they were out in the open. I watched them talk for a few minutes. Olivia stepped forward again, only this time they embraced. They finally released each other, and Olivia kissed Mark's cheek. Then, she took his hand. My stomach dropped, and I felt queasy. I sped away and turned the wrong way on a one-way street. There was no traffic and I made a fast U-turn, my body trembling as I tried to focus on getting home safely.

I put the television on in our living room but listened for his steps, vowing to remain calm. I texted JJ, too:

> Thinking of you and miss you. Hope all's
> well.

... and included a heart emoji. Mark arrived home soon after.

"I hope you got a lot done," I said.

"We did."

"*We?*" I said, under my breath.

"Huh? Did you eat anything?"

"Not hungry, I'll grab a snack," I said. I went in the kitchen and had an apple. A few minutes later, he came in and ate leftovers. We then watched television in bed, and Mark fell asleep right away. I stared at the anchorwoman, not hearing anything she said. I was busy deciding whether to hire a private investigator. Nina and Valerie could make a recommendation. I quickly dismissed the idea, feeling overly dramatic.

Sunday was a blur. I went for a long run, wishing I could be with JJ. Mark said he'd be at the gym and then the office. When he got home, we went food shopping together, with many awkward silences. I obsessively checked my phone all day. Nada from JJ. I'm sure he had a good reason; JJ could do no wrong.

I was relieved when it was Monday. It meant freedom from all the angst at home. By the time I got to the office, JJ finally wrote: "So happy to hear from my Estrella. I hope you're taking good care. Heading back to the states, to DC. I miss you too." It was followed by a row of emoji hearts. Instantly, my mood improved.

Poppy, Maya and I met in the conference room to review the list of gala supporters.

"Artie has been writing checks to his buddies' favorite charities, and it's payback time," Maya said. She had the inside scoop on Artie, and wasn't hiding it.

Poppy shot me a quick look. "I spoke with a few of Penny's friends," she said. "One woman, I can't remember which, said that she and Penny go way back. When she joined Waterfront, Penny introduced her to a lot of people, so she's going to show her support for her friend now."

"Isn't that interesting. It looks like Penny and Artie's problems are actually working to the Addison Center's advantage," I said. "I thought for sure one of them would drop out, but each is determined to hold tight to their role as gala chair." Maya smirked at my comment.

"Yeah," Poppy said. "One of Penny's friends called to contribute and told me, 'Make sure it reads In honor of Mrs. Penny Brass. Leave Artie's name out.' I'll make a note on that page so we don't mess that up."

Nina and Valerie had also stepped up to show support for their client; their sponsorship read "In honor of Penny Brass," with no "Mrs." Over and over, the Addison Center became a mechanism to prove loyalties. One gift for Artie, one for Penny; he loves me, she loves her. Such competition made the gifts multiply exponentially.

Despite the fact that fundraising for the gala was going well I called Nina. She had her pulse on things, and could tell me what was happening with the Brasses. Besides, I felt like talking.

"What if Penny and Artie's divorce gets finalized, and one of them bails from the gala?"

I asked. "The money is flowing like Niagara Falls, but it could soon backfire. Chrissy would probably claim it was my fault."

"It's an awful mess and will be for years. You think divorce is easy when all that money's involved?" Nina said. "It's divorce, Royal Coconut Beach style."

"I forgot everything's so extreme. Lately, Maya's become full of herself, too. Bolder. I know why now. You heard at lunch that she's working on the side for Artie."

"Hey, c'mon, you survived Reid, Bennett; you could withstand anything. Besides, look at how far you've come."

"I suppose. After all, I've become a regular on the club circuit, too. Waterfront, Sealine. . . ."

"You've turned into one of those ladies who lunch!" Nina said, and laughed.

"Yeah, right," I said. "With clothes to play the part. It's just stuff, but Elise was right about having the right look in this business. Speaking of which, I bought a few new dresses at Saks Off Fifth."

"What happened to Les Saisons?" Nina asked.

"We're on an austerity budget, according to Mark."

"And you agreed?" Nina said.

"Yes. It's complicated. I know I could've gone to Les Saisons or somewhere like that, but I didn't want to push his buttons."

"Marriage," said Nina, and tsk'ed.

"How's Girard, by the way?" I asked.

"Funny you asked. We got into a tiff the other night. Remember I told you and Val that I was going to meet his son?"

"Yes."

"Well, I did, and he was less than friendly. I told Girard I didn't like his attitude. Want to know what he did?"

"What?"

"He defended him! Can you believe it?"

"It's his son. Isn't that what Valerie said? He should show you respect, though."

"That's what I said. I want to make sure the vibe between us starts out on the right foot, and that I come first."

"Absolutely."

"Speaking of vibes, are things any better with Mark?"

"Nope. It's worse. I don't feel like talking about it right now." I was afraid once I got started I would tell her everything. For sure, Nina would tell me what she thought, and I wasn't in the mood to hear it.

"Like I said, marriage. I'm here if you want to talk," she offered.

"I know, and thanks. Anyway, I've got to get back to work."

I figured things would get better. But I never would have anticipated what happened next.

Chapter 34

IN LA-LA LAND

"YOU'RE IN LA-LA LAND," Mark said, shaking his head when I walked into the kitchen. He was in his navy terry robe. It looked like he was reading something on his laptop. Next to it was a mug and a plate with a half-eaten croissant.

"Happy Saturday and good morning to you. What are you talking about?"

"The Royal Coconut Beach scene. It's la-la land."

"What do you mean by *that?*"

"Nothing," he mumbled.

"Nothing? Then don't say something like that. I don't even know what you're talking about. Who put shit in your Wheaties?" Seldom did I curse, but I was pissed.

"You don't know what's happening in the real world," he said. "The economy is sluggish, in case you didn't notice."

"How can you say that to me? I know what's going on."
I managed not to raise my voice, and stayed calm.

"No, you don't. You think everyone is made of money.
The yachts, the gowns, the spoiled women. Look at Artie
and Penny. They're too rich to even get a normal divorce."

"You forget where I came from."

"I think it's *you* who forgot where you came from," Mark
retorted, pointing his finger at me.

"Don't speak to me that way. Why are you patronizing
me?"

"Just forget it. I can't say anything to you. You're so sensitive." He threw up his hands.

I went to get dressed. Today's blowup was the last straw.
Mark's remarks were much more hurtful than the un-
gracious swipes he'd been taking lately. I dreaded the day
ahead, remembering how I used to look forward to weekends. I knew that whatever I said could provoke more nasty
comments.

"I'm going to run errands," I yelled from the other room.
On the way out, I slammed the door. Once I was around the
corner, I put the car in park beneath a large palm tree and
started sobbing, which escalated into an uncontrollable crying fit. Thankfully, I kept tissues in the glove compartment.
The sun streamed through despite its generous fronds,
making the car hot. I turned up the air-conditioning and
glanced at my puffy red face in the rear-view mirror.

Trying to comfort myself, I reassured myself that I was
far from being in la-la-land. I read the *Wall Street Journal*.
I was in the business world, and made a nice living. Blowing
my nose, the rear-view mirror showed my puffy eyes and
red face. After I regained my composure, I went to call
Nina, but before it rang, I hung up. I knew I could tell her

anything, but I also was sure she'd be matter-of-fact about my situation because she handled so many unhappy marriages. And despite her professional expertise, I was afraid she wouldn't fully understand.

Valerie would be more likely to empathize. Tough as she was, she had a soft touch, having been a therapist before becoming a lawyer. Elise was in London with clients at a home design show, so speaking with her wasn't an option.

One ring, two rings. I knew Valerie kept office hours on Saturday mornings. Not directly going into voicemail was a good sign. By the third ring, she picked up. *Thank god.*

"Hi Julia. I just finished up with a client. She's going through a miserable divorce. What's up on this sunny Saturday morning?"

"It's not so sunny for me. My apologies, but you have to hear my story. You've already gone from one story to another, problem after problem, with no break. But I need to dump mine on you." Spilling my guts, I told her what happened.

"I'm so sorry you're dealing with this. Is your job going all right?"

"Actually, no. I mean I love it. But I'll tell you what's going on at work, too."

When I finished, I sighed, relieved to get everything off my chest. The only part I left out was JJ, temporarily shoving thoughts of him away in a dark corner.

"Wow. But none of this is shocking. As far as Maya and Artie, don't worry about them. I can't really talk about that anyway, since we're representing Penny in the divorce. Let's focus on you and Mark. You need to put this into perspective. Think of all the men, those captains of industry. The old buddies who decided they needed culture, so they built a performing arts center, and sit on other prestigious boards in town."

"What does this have to do with Mark? *Please*, land the plane, Val." I had zero patience for a drawn-out analysis.

"High-octane men—and that includes Mark—feel like they are less of a man when things aren't going well in business. Success gives them strength, and feeds their ego," she said. "I know you know about the male ego, but when it's inflicted upon you, it's no picnic."

"Okay. I get it. He's scared, I think. On top of this, I'm the only one bringing in an income, since his firm has had a salary freeze, which by the way, he neglected to tell me about, then *insisted* he told me."

"Ouch. That's a major blow for Mark. You just said it yourself: he's afraid he's not being a good provider. Knowing him, it's not okay. Many men feel a sense of responsibility to protect and provide for those they love. This would include taking care of their wives financially, regardless of whether she earns plenty. That would be Mark, don't you agree?"

"Yeah. If you want to know the deep dark truth, I always thought he *would* take care of me. Not that I didn't marry for love, as I most certainly did. And I know I'm perfectly capable of supporting myself. That's not the point. Part of my attraction to Mark was how driven and ambitious he was. He always made me feel safe. I loved that about him. Am I less of a modern woman?"

"Absolutely not. Wanting the comfort of knowing you're taken care of is perfectly reasonable. Good for you for admitting it; most successful women would never. It's also not so surprising that he didn't tell you he isn't getting paid. Mark's way too proud. What you have in savings is irrelevant."

Drawing a deep breath, I asked, "What do I do?"

Valerie didn't answer right away, but I was patient, grateful to be speaking with her. "Nothing. Someone like Mark isn't going to be happy until he succeeds. It's how you react that matters."

"That's easy to say," I snapped back. "I'm busting a gut every day at work. I have a lot of pressure, too. Which I barely get recognized for, unless getting paid is considered recognition. That's what Mark said when I complained to him about work. He should be thankful that I have a steady paycheck. Oh, and health benefits: his requirement from day one. 'Make sure there are health benefits' was what he told me when I interviewed at Addison. To say I'm in 'fantasyland' is outrageous. He ought to meet some of the ladies in Royal Coconut Beach. Then he'd see what fantasyland *really* is about!" Tears welled up in my eyes again.

"Calm down." Valerie interrupted me. "You're right. There's no excuse for bad behavior; I'm not arguing. But he's feeling insecure. You need to understand his inner world."

"I suppose." I wasn't really convinced.

"Look, we all know you're the last person to be living in a fantasy world. But please . . . and don't take this the wrong way. There could be a perception that you're in a dream world because of who you deal with: the rich. The 000.1 percent. Could it be that this was the spirit in which Mark said that stuff? He does have a good sense of humor."

"No, he wasn't joking. He rarely does anymore. He sounded angry," I replied.

"Well, Mark will have to sort out his business problems on his own. Try to avoid getting sucked up in it. You won't win."

"Benign neglect?" I asked.

"Exactly."

"Okay, I'll try anything right now."

"Play the game. You do it at work, and you're good at it. Don't forget, a little compassion and flexibility might go a long way. So would shifting your expectations just a little."

"I suppose you're right. Thank you for talking me off the ledge." I wanted to also tell her about Olivia, but there wasn't enough time.

"I'm sorry, I must run—I'm meeting Teddy for lunch. Speaking of lunch, we need to gather Elise and Nina for lunch. Call me later if you need to. I'm here for you."

"Okay. Thanks so much again. You're a dear friend," I said.

"Same."

As hurtful as Mark's accusations were, in reality, we had money saved, and a roof over our heads. I gave myself a shake for feeling ungrateful. On the other hand, Mark's frustration level had hit a record high. I'd never seen him like this; this wasn't what I'd signed up for. Images of JJ were swimming around in my head, too. He treated me so differently; flattered me, made me feel special. Mark's behavior paled in comparison. For a moment I regretted that I was married to Mark, instead wanting desperately to be with JJ. But I wasn't bold enough to do anything about it. Unless I was just being wise. I wasn't sure about anything.

I headed over to browse at Les Saisons, hoping it might clear my head. Then I did some grocery shopping, and went back home in a calmer state of mind. Mark was in the same spot when I returned, and on his laptop.

"Hi Mark," I said, pretending nothing happened before.

Mark looked up from the screen. "Hey, I didn't mean anything I said earlier. I'm just stressed and worried."

Not an actual apology, but a decent concession, and it made me feel better.

"What should we do? We're in this together." Heeding Valerie's advice, I tried to show some compassion.

"Nothing. Just keep working, moving forward. The market isn't doing well, which hasn't helped the firm's business."

"Do you think this will have any impact on fundraising in la-la-land?" I smiled.

He smirked.

"Seriously, do you think with these market shifts, donors who usually give big bucks will think twice? We're stuck with an unusually higher goal, one that was based on a stronger economy. Chrissy will find a way to blame me."

"I can't tell what will happen at Addison. But when someone has a billion dollars and loses a chunk of it, they're still super wealthy."

"What about you and the firm?" I asked, going over to put my arms around his shoulders.

"I'm not sure about anything anymore," he said.

"It'll be okay." I kissed the top of his head.

In addition to compassion, I gave Mark his space. I didn't give him push back about anything, including Olivia. Most of the time he was either on his phone or silent, creating a man-cave in his own head.

Chapter 35

HUSTLERS ANONYMOUS

BREAKFASTS AND LUNCHES with donors, events and evenings in the Parker Pavilion, schmoozing and making sponsors feel special, kept me busy. Chrissy kept pouring on more assignments, too. It allowed me to forget the tension at home.

Early one Monday morning, I was jolted out of a deep sleep by noise coming from Mark's closet. I got out of bed quickly, and saw him putting suits into a garment bag.

"Morning," he mumbled.

"Going away?" I asked.

"I have to fly to California for a few days. It's urgent."

"Okay. Safe travels." I went back to bed.

That afternoon, Poppy came into my office and shut the door.

"What's up?" I asked.

"Chrissy just dumped a bunch of work on me, because Maya's 'too busy'. It's not fair! I've had it." She sat down, and crossed her arms.

I gave her a sympathetic smile. "It's not like you aren't capable. Think about how much more valuable it'll make you."

"I know you're right," she said, and leaned back in the chair, placing her arms on the armrests.

"If it makes you feel better, Chrissy gave me a bunch of easy acknowledgment letters that Maya usually does. She told me to do them in a timely manner," I added.

"None of this makes sense," Poppy said.

"What do you mean?" I could feel my eyebrows curve upward.

Poppy looked down for perhaps fifteen seconds, then made eye contact. She leaned forward.

"Maya applied for your position, but Chrissy hired you," she said. "Maya was really upset at the time. I figured she forgot it, because all seemed okay, and you both got along."

And Maya told me that YOU applied for my job!

"Except things changed," she continued. "Maya has become—I don't know, smug—and Chrissy and Maya seem tight. I don't get it, but Maya gets away with murder." She shook her head.

I shrugged my shoulders. "Honestly, Poppy, I have no idea what's up."

"Well, I've been carrying it around for a while, but I was scared to say a word."

"I'm glad you did, and thank you. Don't let it bother you. We should focus on the gala. It has crept up so fast. Between Penny and Artie, we're going to pack the ballroom. Trouble in paradise has paid off."

"It sure has. We're going to make a ton of money!" she said, and left.

Holy crap. I was sure Poppy—sweet Poppy—was telling me the truth. Maya must have been the saboteur all along, not Poppy. Maya had duped me!

I thought about it for the rest of the day, while I got my work done. Then I received a text from JJ:

> I'm back. Can we meet in the morning?
> 6:30 at the bridge?

I wrote back that I'd be there. I temporarily forgot Maya's shenanigans.

I felt less sneaky the next morning when I got dressed to meet JJ, since Mark was away. I was excited when I saw JJ. This time, he was wearing a running shorts and top, and jogged towards me. I landed in his arms, and he held on to hug me, but I squirmed out of his tight grip and took a step back. He caught his breath and inched forward, putting his hands on my shoulders. There was early morning bridge traffic. Wasn't he afraid someone would see us?

"Didn't you miss me?" he asked, his eyes penetrating mine.

"Yes, but we can't hug out here."

Furrows formed on his forehead. He extended his arm toward the ocean in a gentlemanly manner, and we began our walk.

I was holding my phone and handed it to JJ while I tied my sneaker lace. Once it was tied, I popped back up and saw he was looking at my photos. The screen showed a picture of me in the red dress, the one Mark had seduced me in after Dori's kick-off party at Sealine.

"You look amazing," JJ said, staring at it for several seconds. "I missed you."

He handed the phone back to me and we continued our walk.

"What's on your agenda today?" he asked.

"I have some meetings in the office. Lunch with a donor. What about you?"

"I've also got meetings in my office all day, and I'm heading to New York tomorrow. I'm on the board of the Argentinian Council. More meetings. I'll be back soon, I hope.

I hope so too.

He told me about some of his latest investments, and I listened with awe. From time to time, I added comments.

"You have sharp business insight," he said. "That's why I love to share things like this with you."

It made me a little depressed hearing that, since Mark didn't share business problems anymore. We strolled up a quiet street, and he wrapped his arm around my waist. I didn't try to break loose as we walked. We got to the beach and sat on a weather worn bench.

Our bodies were close enough that our arms and legs were touching. JJ rested his hand on my bare thigh. His touch on my clammy skin was electric. We gazed at the stunning turquoise ocean, admiring how the sunlight glistened on the waves and created thousands of diamonds. The saltwater smell, gentle roar of the waves, and slight breeze made me woozy. He touched my foot lightly with his foot, and I did the same. It turned into a game of footsie.

"You're something else, Estrella. When I get back, let's get drinks or dinner."

"I'd like that." The thought thrilled me.

We talked a little while longer, and he looked at his watch.

"Shall we?" He stood, then pulled me up.

Our time together was always defined by a clock, but I was so enamored of him that I willingly closed my eyes to this harsh truth. I savored the moments as we slowly walked back. We reached the middle of the bridge, and he gave me a quick kiss on the head, possibly taking a cue from when met earlier that morning. I took a shower and got dressed, completely preoccupied with thoughts of him.

I was almost ready to leave, when Mark unexpectedly arrived home, breaking my trance. His hair was disheveled, and he had prominent dark circles beneath his eyes.

"You're home," I said.

"Everything ended early, so I jumped on a plane and caught the red eye."

"How'd it go?"

"Fine." *Again, that word.*

"Sorry, but I've got to leave. With our gala coming up, there's so much to do. Oh, I won't be home until late tonight. Bernadette Peters is at Addison, and I have to handle the meet and greet after."

"Okay. I'm going to shower and then the office." He disappeared into the bedroom.

As I pulled away from the house, it became obvious how much I was actively participating in two worlds, straddling both without feeling firmly rooted in either one. I developed such strong feelings for JJ, yet Mark still meant so much—but it was getting harder to imagine us having a happy future together. Holding onto competing wishes and desires, I had no idea how such powerfully conflicting thoughts could peacefully coexist. I desperately needed to gain some footing.

I'd driven past Hustlers Anonymous a million times. It was impossible to miss its neon signs: *Sexy Lingerie, Sex Toys and Much More.* I thought that spicing things up in the bedroom might tap into Mark's romantic side. A woman had a right to dream, and that's what I was doing. Dreaming. It beat talking about milking cows. I headed to the store at lunch time.

Shockingly open and bright, the shop looked more like a pop-up candy store than a store selling erotica. The walls were stocked with a mind-blowing display of brightly colored sex toys. Sexy lingerie was hanging against the back wall. Making a beeline there, I heard Savannah's distinctive voice. It was bad enough that being in a store like this was a first for me. Savannah's presence upgraded the experience to whacky.

Fortunately, her back was turned as the woman in a leopard one-piece bodysuit rang up her merchandise. I slunk into an aisle and listened as I pretended to browse a display of handcuffs. Savannah was speaking to the woman ringing up her new merchandise.

"We'll be away for a few days on our yacht. Get away from it all. Much obliged for your help, Trisha. As always."

Examining a pair of fuzzy red handcuffs, I watched her through the window as she slid into her Bentley. A few seconds later, her driver pulled away. Now at liberty to browse, I grabbed a few sexy panties, a black velvet teddy, and a jelly-bean-colored pink gizmo for good measure, along with handcuffs. Trisha rang me up, and I left the shop with my prizes.

That evening, the sponsor wasn't feeling well and decided not to stay after the performance. It was still on the early side when I went back to my office to grab my tote bag that I left. Floria came in with her cleaning cart.

"I love your lipstick," she said when she saw me. "It's a nice coral shade, perfect for this time of year. Your friend told me she borrows it sometimes when she's here at night."

"What do you mean?" I asked, puzzled.

"You know, the beautiful one you work with. She has that dark beautiful wavy hair. She told me you don't mind that she borrows your lipstick. I see her in your office sometimes when I clean."

"Of course, that's right. Sorry, Floria, I forgot. You mean Maya. Have a nice night," I said. I grabbed my bag and left.

So Maya was snooping around in my office! With what Poppy shared about Maya wanting my job, and now Floria, I was positive she was responsible for all that had gone wrong, including the lost check way back.

Chapter 36

VELVET HAMMER

IT WASN'T MY IMAGINATION: I definitely heard "I love you" whispered in my ear in a moment of passion later that evening. Who cared that I'd initiated it?

"See, you do love me, darling," I said.

"Have you milked the cow?" Mark joked.

The trip to Hustlers Anonymous had reaped rewards. Mark was so loving during sex. As wonderful as it was, it made me think that winning over my husband had way too much to do with sex. But if this is what it took to get him to connect with me on a more intimate level, so be it. JJ's interest in me made me feel very attractive and sexy. As much as I desired him, I didn't plan on sleeping with him, so might as well seduce my husband—as warped as it sounded to me.

A business lunch was on my schedule a few days later.

Andy had secured the appointment for us with Timothy "Trey" Wethersfield, the new president of Wealth Strategies for Royal Coconut Beach, and his associate Byron "Kip" Rutherford. Wealth Strategies had just opened an office in Royal Coconut Beach, adding to the oversaturated market of wealth managers. Their names alone were confusing enough. We were hoping that they would contribute to the Addison Center. The only problem was that Andy had to be in Chicago.

"I have a great idea," Andy said when he called to tell me of his conflict. "Have Savannah Colbertson attend in my place. You're not supposed to know this, but Savannah and Winston are their clients. If anyone can charm them, she can. Let's hope she's available."

Like Andy, grass never grew under Savannah's feet. Or under her Christian Louboutins. It wasn't her enviable shoe collection that won Trey and Kip over; nor was it her perfect posture, perfect hair, perfect make-up, perfect everything. She proved to be much more than just her image. She brought new energy and vitality wherever she went. She immediately captivated Trey and Kip, too, at lunch in Addison's conference room.

I spoke about our mission. Next, I told the men about sponsoring and all the benefits associated with giving. I felt proud of myself; Andy had taught me well.

It was Savannah's turn. Taking the floor, she said in her sugary, southern but professional voice, "In my business, which you are familiar with, Winston and I entertain clients. You will find that Addison is a five-star operation. It warms my heart to know Winston and I are making a difference in the lives of kids. That's what's really important. They're our future."

It was exactly the right chord to strike with the Wealth Strategy boys. It didn't hurt that she batted her eyes, taking turns looking at each of them as if she was watching a ping-pong match. I thought of her in Hustlers Anonymous, and laughed to myself.

"We'd very much like to partner with you," said Trey. "We need to get our footprint here. We'll make it happen. Wealth Strategies' business model is different from Evergreen and the other private wealth management companies you're familiar with."

"I'm really interested in hearing about it," I said.

"We are head of the class in developing a platform to be an intermediary between the client, their money, and their existing private wealth company. A manager to manage money, adding another layer of protection," Trey said, underscoring the complexities of having an extraordinary amount of money. "Savannah can attest to this."

"Yes, Trey is correct. Witty and I sleep as snug as bugs in a rug, knowing Wealth Strategies handles our finances. It's a great partnership," Savannah said.

"Well, we consider relationships with our donors to be just that: a partnership. It's not about just writing a check. We tailor benefits to meet your corporate objectives and maximize your benefits."

"That's perfect, because corporate social responsibility is a priority," Trey said. "By supporting Addison, we can achieve this goal."

When we finished lunch, we munched on the usual mini-donuts and had warm apple cider. Saying our goodbye to the men, Savannah walked me outside, where her driver was waiting.

"You had them at hello," she said. I smiled. "No, seriously.

That was really smooth, watching you in action. It was as if you had a velvet hammer in your hands, bopping them on the head at just the right time. In a classy way and with great finesse. You impressed me."

"It was simply about showcasing. Not selling," I said.

"Yes, a soft sell. Bless your heart, you never directly asked for money," she said.

"You did the heavy lifting today."

Listening to Savannah, and hearing myself talk, I realized how far I had come in my fundraising career. A few minutes later, Savannah walked toward her Bentley, her shoes winking red at me with each step. There was something defiant about her walk, yet still graceful and soft. I finally recognized how she managed to always be in Louboutins; she must slide into them when she emerges from the car to walk short distances, to minimize discomfort. She probably would take them off as soon as she got in the car, like princesses and movie stars did. But she was much more substance than window dressing. Despite her fancy shoes, once again Savannah proved to be anything but shallow.

Back at my desk, I tapped out an email to Andy:

Dear Andy,

Thank you again for introducing us to Trey and Kip. I am delighted to tell you that Wealth Strategies made a commitment; they are our newest Maestro member. Thank you!

Based on their goals, I'm certain that they will really benefit from this partnership. They're buying the last table for our gala

this Friday! We are grateful for all you do
for the Addison Center. Having Savannah
there was a great idea.

Warmest regards,
Julia

P.S.—They loved the donuts.

A few minutes later, Maya came into my office.

"Poppy and I need to go over some details for the gala
with you," she said. Her voice was short and steely.

"Yes ma'am," I said, and saluted. I still hadn't figured out
how to deal with her.

Chapter 37

THE CRAZY ONE

I HEADED TO THE LADIES' LOUNGE to touch up my make-up and do a final once-over before going to the ball-room to check on everything, with the gala just a few hours away. I stepped back upon opening the door, seeing a cluster of women crowded into the small room. Since everyone worked all day, there was no time for anyone to go home to change. Struggling to get into a long, sparkly gowns while brushing on make-up with only one small full-length mirror was overwhelming. Members of all different Addison Center departments converged in the room to get ready, each assigned to help that night. Questions from different directions were being shouted:

"Can someone zip me?"

"Does anyone have pink lip liner?"

"How do these black sequined shoes look? No, not those. *These.*"

"What about this necklace? Does silver go with the gold dress?" Talk about a melting pot of energy, chatter, and laughter. But even in this jam-packed room, I felt lonely. I got dressed quickly in the corner, and asked someone to zip me. Then I fled, feeling claustrophobic. I headed to the ballroom to help Poppy and Maya check on the tables.

Standing near Table Six was Poppy, wearing a pastel pink gown that went well with her blonde hair done in a French twist. Maya stood nearby wearing black of course, her long wavy hair flowing down her back. The contrast between the two beauties was astonishing..

"How can I help?" I asked as I approached them. A sense of déjà vu rushed through me.

"Would you please check on ten through seventeen?" Poppy asked.

"Will do. The teleprompter's all loaded, right?" I asked.

"Absolutely. I did it myself," she said. I genuinely trusted her, too.

I was looking forward to seeing many familiar faces, including Elise and David, who'd be at our table. Mark and I would be seated with them.

I did a last-minute overall look to make sure the room was perfect. I hadn't seen Ziggy until now; he headed towards me looking dapper in a sapphire blue sweater and white tight jeans.

"Devastating. Stunning. Turn around," Ziggy commanded, as he made a motioning circle with his index finger. I swirled so he could check me out.

"Ooh, la la. Valentino?" he asked.

"Not quite," I said. "But my personal stylist at Les Saisons selected it."

"It's perfection. You've blossomed into a flower, just like the one on your dress. It's almost showtime; you're ready for the limelight."

"Thanks, Ziggy."

Sarah Brightman's performance in the main theater was magnificent. The soprano diva delighted guests by singing in several different languages. As a foreign language major, Mark was mesmerized.

After the performance, guests headed to the ballroom for the black-tie dinner dance. Artie and Penny were seated at different ends of the room, each flanked by their own entourage, although many women bounced from table to table. Most of the men stuck by Artie.

I greeted Savannah and her guests, spread among four tables. Dori's table was situated on a prime spot near the dance floor, as a thank-you for hosting the kick-off party. I gave her a hug, and she introduced me to her guests. Then I headed to Chandler's table; I stood behind Georgina and Chandler, and lightly tapped them on their backs. They both turned around.

"I hope you're having a good time," I said.

"Lovely party, Julia," Georgina said, and extended her hand. I felt the strength of her grip, and the gargantuan ring digging into my palm.

"Thank you very much," I said.

Chandler stood. "I'm impressed," he said, and shook my hand.

Chandler had actually recognized my efforts for the first time. I spotted Chrissy at the opposite end of their table in her emerald green gown, chatting with the guest next to her. I couldn't imagine what it felt like for her to be seated at her lover's table, with his wife seated next to him. I almost felt sorry for her.

I worked the room a little more. I took my seat and sipped some wine, trying to catch my breath. Mark conversed with Elise and David and others at our table. Seeing him in action was always a good reminder of how devastatingly charming he could be.

This year, Frances Ashton, Webster's wife, had insisted that she deliver the remarks on behalf of her husband. When she finished, Mark whispered, "All's well in the universe.

No slips and falls." He winked. "Go work the room again." I appreciated his encouragement.

"I'm on it." I stood up, and went off to table-hop. I headed towards the back to make sure I didn't miss seeing anyone. The band was playing loud, lively music. It was a good time to freshen up. I almost reached the ladies' room, when out of nowhere Maya smashed right into me. I lost my balance, landing on the marble floor. Maya was standing over me and offered an outstretched arm, but I got up on my own; I wasn't hurt.

"You bitch!" I lost my cool. My arm was at a right angle, my fist clinched in anger. I assumed she thought I was about to punch her, because she grabbed my wrist.

"Let go of me!" I yelped. She released her hand and I shook mine out. *"Who the hell do you think you are?"* I shouted. "You've been out to get me since day one."

"What the fuck are you talking about?" Maya shouted back. "Are you *crazy?"* The scowl on her face scared me, but I didn't lose my momentum.

"I'm not the crazy one. You go into my office at night and rummage through my stuff. I bet you stole that check from my drawer when I first started working here."

"Huh?" Maya asked. Her jaw dropped open.

"Admit it, Maya. You go in there after hours, claiming to borrow lipstick, when actually you snoop through my drawers."

Maya shook her head. "I have *no* idea what you're talking about." She put her hands on her hips.

"Don't you dare play dumb. The teleprompter malfunctioning last year; not giving me messages; the typo; the list goes on and on. C'mon, Maya. I don't care what you do with Artie, but *stay the hell away from me.*"

Her stare was part disgust, part disbelief. Just then, a woman emerged from the ladies' room, and Maya walked away shaking her head. Maybe I really was crazy. Floria's comment wasn't exactly concrete proof.

My cheeks were on fire, and I went in the room to splash cold water on my face. All it did was mess up my make-up. I spent perhaps ten minutes trying to clean it off with soap and water; time well spent since it also calmed me down. I rejoined my table, and immediately gulped down the wine that had been replenished in my glass.

Mark was talking to David, but turned to me. "Are you okay?" he asked.

"I'm okay." I gave a weak smile, and he turned his attention back to David.

As the last of the diehards straggled out of the ballroom at 1:00 a.m., Poppy, Maya, and a few staff members gathered. Chrissy had already gone home. I looked at Maya, and flashed her my best nasty look, but she seemed to look right through me. Paul Hess headed in our direction; it was important that Addison's executive director attended this major fundraising event, even if he was hardly ever in the office. His tuxedo fit snug, accentuating his muscular body, his thick, wavy white hair slicked back. I still wasn't sure Paul even knew who I was, yet he began speaking to us.

"Talk about a fluid and perfectly orchestrated event. Every segment of Royal Coconut Beach was represented, all having fun. Even with all the Brasses' troubles, too. What are you all going to do next year, now that you've raised the bar?" Paul asked.

I answered before anyone else. "I can't imagine. I think we're all happy to have gotten through this one." His compliment surprised me, and I tried to enjoy the moment. There was a lot of merit to what he said, too. Something new was always around the bend: new parties, more people to meet, and bigger goals. All the while, things needed to be kept fresh.

Mark and I were the last to leave.

"It was a nice evening," he said, as he drove home. I desperately wanted to tell him about Maya, but didn't want to spoil the evening and his good mood. He probably would think I was crazy, anyway. We undressed and got into bed. I reached out and touched him, and we held hands in the darkness.

"I'm glad you were there tonight," I said.

"I am too. I like to support your work," he said, and squeezed my hand.

For the sake of our happiness, I was willing to let him believe it was true, despite feeling completely unsupported for a while now.

"Are you tired from running all over the room in your heels?"

"I'm exhausted." My throat was scratchy from competing with the band. I thought about asking for a foot massage, but Mark let go of my hand; he had fallen asleep.

Valerie's advice was spot-on; maybe he just needed his space. Perhaps we had turned a corner.

Chapter 38

INTO THE LIMELIGHT

MARK LOOKED HANDSOME in his jeans and black tee shirt as he grabbed his sport jacket from the closet and casually flung it over his arm. I watched him as I remained in bed, stretching my arms, then wiggling my toes to get some relief from the high heels I'd worn for the gala the night before. It was way too early to hear someone beeping their horn outside.

"That must be Olivia. She's my ride. We have to go to the office," Mark said.

There's nothing's wrong with his car! He didn't bother to even tell me. I felt betrayed but antagonizing him would risk a nasty exchange, which I had no energy for. Aided by sheer exhaustion, I took a long nap. When I awoke, I thought of

JJ, and started to frame imaginary conversations with him in my head as if he was beside me.

I was sitting on our patio reading a book when Mark opened the sliding glass door to say hello. I looked at my watch; it was five o'clock.

"Did you get a lot of work done?" I asked as benignly as I could.

"Did we ever. We caught up, and at least were able to concentrate."

"Good to know," I said, with a tight smile, and returned to my book.

Monday morning, Poppy and I rehashed the gala in my office. I was going to tell her about having it out with Maya, but just then she barged in.

"Looks like we raised the most money ever for an Addison gala," Maya said. She handed me a spreadsheet. "Good thing Artie and Penny are getting divorced." She smirked.

I doubted she cared about how their divorce benefitted Addison. "Terrific," I replied.

"Chrissy wants you to give her a call on her cell," Maya said. Her lack of acknowledgment for our altercation mimicked her reaction after our previous exchange at the hair salon. Must be a strategy. Poppy got up and followed her.

I called Chrissy and started to tell her about the gala results, but she cut me off. "Hold on. I have something to share first."

"What is it?" I asked, a little concerned.

"I've resigned."

"You what?" I exclaimed.

"I've re—" Chrissy started to say.

"No, I heard you. I'm just . . . surprised, that's all."
Chrissy giving up her cushy job was shocking.

"I got my real estate license, and I'll be selling luxury
homes in Royal Coconut Beach. I was going to wait until
season was over, but decided to do it after the gala."

She probably thought it wouldn't look good if she aban-
doned ship before the big event. "Tell me about this. It's exciting!" And thrilling for me that she'd be gone.

"Chandler knows several folks from New York who are
looking for homes, and I've already lined up some clients.
I can make huge commissions; mansions on Royal Ocean
Drive are going for a fortune. Just the other day, this guy
at the Elite Agency made more than a three- million-dollar
commission from selling the Hayward estate. Never mind
the slow economy; this is Royal Coconut Beach. I'll still get
to take people out for nice lunches, but no more late evenings. The best part is, I'll make my own hours."

That pretty much summed up what she did at the
Addison Center.

"That sounds great, Chrissy. I'm happy for you, I said."
For the hundredth time, I took the high road.

"Please share my news with Poppy. I just told Maya."

"Of course." Chrissy couldn't even bother to take the
time to tell Poppy herself.

"Oh, and when I gave Paul my notice, I told him that he
should promote you," she said.

"Thank you so much." Now she was sucking up to me!
She probably wanted me to say good things about her to all
the important players I've gotten to know.

I called Mark right away, eager to share the news.

"Big game-changer," he said. "You need to speak with

Paul, before he goes and hires someone else. I'm sure there'll be a huge raise."

Was money all he cared about? Besides, what if Paul used Chrissy's departure as a chance to restructure the fundraising department?

That evening, after I got home from a Willie Nelson concert at Addison, Mark was asleep. I crept into bed and stayed awake most of the night, running through all sorts of possibilities. One thing was for sure; I wasn't going back to practicing law.

Paul beat me to the punch when his assistant summoned me to see him that morning. As I headed to his office, I felt like I was in a semi-coma from lack of sleep, but knew I'd have to put on my best can-do-anything face.

"Please, have a seat, Julia. As Chrissy might have told you, she resigned yesterday," Paul said.

"She did," I whispered.

"You look tired. Were you here last evening?"

"Yes. We had to bypass hordes of bystanders standing behind the roped stanchions. When we boarded his bus, a thick cloud of smoke with a sweet smell hit us. Beyond the haze was Willie, sitting at a table. He gave us a big 'howdy' and said, 'now you know where the song On the Road Again came from.' When I got home, my clothes reeked." I waved my hand by my nose. "This will give the cleaners something to wonder about. We sure got a dose of his Southern hospitality. A strong whiff of it, actually."

Paul chuckled. I'd barely had contact with him since I began at the Addison Center, and now I was babbling away. I didn't think I'd made a good impression.

"Do you have an interest in filling the position?" he asked, cutting to the chase.

"Unequivocally, yes. I know I can do this job," I said, feeling a tremendous sense of relief. I wouldn't have to go back to law practice after all. "I've handled many aspects of development. I've expanded the sponsorship program, written speeches. Taken great care of donors. And grants. . . ." Paul let out a small laugh. I felt embarrassed for giving a litany of accomplishments; I wanted the position more than I realized.

"I know you're qualified," he said with a smile that triggered dimples. "That's why I'm offering it to you. I've been asking around about you. I'm surprised your ears weren't ringing. Andy and Dori sang your praises. So did Savannah; she adores you. I've had my eye on you for a while."

"Thank you for your confidence in me," I said, barely suppressing the urge to jump up and down. I got up, sat down again, then gave a big exhale.

"I hate to bring it up, but there's been some issues with Maya. It could be problematic now that she'll be working directly for me." Immediately, I regretted telling him. The last thing I wanted to do was create doubt that he'd made the right decision promoting me.

"I understand," he said, and nodded. "She seems like a good worker, though. Get through season. With Chrissy's departure, it's not wise to shake things up more. Besides, you need the help and she's good at what she does, from what I've been told."

You have no idea.

"Sounds like a plan," I said with my best fake cheery voice. "We'll smile and dial!"

"Go get 'em."

Chrissy made a deal with Paul to use her remaining vacation time. There was no good-bye party, no fanfare. Exactly under what circumstances Chrissy left remained a mystery. From day one, everything about Chrissy had been an enigma. Whatever the reason, she had taken a huge leap of faith on me in the first place. Wanting her to know how grateful I was, I sat down and composed one of my best fluffy notes, thanking her and wishing her all the best. Given the company she kept, it could only work to my advantage.

Next, I called Poppy into my office and dropped the bomb. Her mouth was wide open, and she didn't say anything.

"Your job is very secure, don't worry," I said. My first words as her boss.

"It's not that. I'm thrilled," she shrieked, and clapped her hands. "I love working with you."

It was a good thing I hadn't told her about Maya. Forced comradery amongst the three of us was utterly necessary, at least for the remainder of the season.

Chapter 39

IN HER SHOES

A FEW DAYS LATER, I received a note from Chandler, with his name and address prominently embossed in navy raised letters on exquisite cream stationery:

> Dear Julia,
>
> Congratulations on your new position. It will not be easy to fill Chrissy's shoes. She is a real star, and you have your work cut out for you. The Addison Center was lucky to have had her. I wish you much luck.
>
> The Center is a great addition to our growing community. Many of us in Royal Coconut Beach appreciate it just as much as Georgina and I do.

We will see you often in the Parker Pavilion and at special events and performances.

Again, I wish you much success.

Sincerely Yours,
Chandler A. Fairbanks IV

Not easy to fill her shoes? Seriously? I wanted to be in my *own* shoes—flats, stilettos, or otherwise. I was determined to make my own mark, but I feared that I'd always be in Chrissy's shadow.

I took his note and tucked it in my purse. It was a good thing I was meeting the Lunch Club ladies for lunch. I was excited to see my friends, and waited until today, so I could share my news in person.

We all arrived at the Waterfront Club at same time, and headed to a table near the window. The waiter came over soon after.

"Prosecco, I assume?"

"Of course," Elise said.

We looked at our menus quickly and placed our orders when he returned with our drinks.

"Ladies," I said. "I have big news."

"What's up?" Nina asked.

"Chrissy resigned, and I got offered her position!"

"Congratulations!" Nina said. "That's fantastic. Even better, she'll be out of your hair now. I'm not sure how much more you could stand working for her."

"Neither could I," I said. "Only I love my job. I'm so glad she's gone."

"I knew it! I told you a while ago that cream always rises," Elise said. She raised her glass and we clinked our glasses.

"It gets better, ladies. She's going to work out of Chandler's office," I said.

"How convenient," Valerie said, and smirked.

"Yes. But I just received this obnoxious note from Chandler." I pulled it out of my purse and read it aloud.

"I hear you, except when someone is about to take over a position that a very well-liked person was in, it's common to say something like what he said," Valerie said.

"You're being overly sensitive, as usual," Nina chimed in. "Sorry."

"Ouch. I probably wouldn't even think this way, except Chandler thinks no one could hold a candle to Chrissy. She'll always be the star. He must be telling his buddies at the club this, too."

"Yes, so? Stop worrying what other people think," Elise said.

"His note rattled me. But you're right. The note was very proper, coming from a man who is all about protocol. Thanks for the perspective. Mark would also tell me to let it go. I'm not sharing the note with him; There's enough on his plate."

"I can imagine," Nina chimed in. "Since I left Reid, Bennett I'm so much happier. Big law firm practice is highly overrated. Right, Val?"

"Is it ever!" she said. "I've just heard the latest scuttlebutt on Mark's firm, by the way. How's he doing?"

"He's working through it," I said. "He spends most of his time in the office, even on weekends. When he's home, he's also working; and if he's not, being stressed takes up all his head-space." I frowned. "Things have improved between us, but he's still completely consumed with work. I wonder if things will ever return to normal."

"What can you expect?" Nina said, dryly. "We've all been in his shoes. You know how demanding law firms are." She leaned back in her chair.

I thought she seemed a bit overly sympathetic for Mark, considering she knew things were a bit rocky. "Nina, it's not that I don't understand what it's like to be up against enormous pressure. C'mon, you know me better than that. It's more than that. We've become sort of disconnected."

Nina got quiet, while Valerie glanced at me. I gave her a nod of approval.

"I suggested to Julia that Mark has to work through his issues, and to give him space," she said. "Maybe I'm partly to blame for the distance."

"Not at all, Valerie," I said. "It was great advice. In fact, like I said, things have gotten better since I backed down. I just miss the way things were." I paused. "Then there's Olivia."

"Ah, Mark's associate." Nina perked up.

"Yup. I'm convinced something romantic's going on between them."

"What makes you think that?" Nina asked.

"He changes when she's on the phone. He lights up. She's beautiful, smart and single. Did I mention she sent him emoji kisses, at least once that I'm aware of? You'll probably think I'm crazy, but I spied on them. I saw them embrace. I don't think it was harmless."

"Do you really think Mark would cross the line? He's seems awfully dedicated to you," Nina said.

"He doesn't notice me the way he used to. I hate the way he admires her." I twirled a lock of my hair, a nervous habit I'd developed.

"You feel taken for granted?" Nina asked.

"I sure do."

"I went through something like that with David many years ago," Elise said. "His secretary was smart and gorgeous. I didn't like it one bit."

I gave an incredulous stare.

"Marriages have cycles, even the best ones. Sometimes when you least expect it, things get sprung on you." Elise put her finger on her chin. "There'll always be ebbs and flows. It's not static."

"I know that. But it's never been like this between us," I said.

"Adjusting your expectations might help," Valerie said. "To Elise's point, being married is never a straight, clean line. The last thing I expected was my first marriage to be a horror show."

I let their comments sink in, which helped normalize things a bit.

"Anyway, it's your time to shine at work, Julia," Nina said.

"You deserve it, too," Valerie added. "We're all proud of you," We clinked glasses again.

"Thank you, all. And for your advice. Please don't say anything."

"Duh," Nina said.

Valerie dove into a story, and we chatted some more.

On the way back to the office, I was determined to somehow figure my marriage out. I would focus on work, too. This time I was really in charge.

Maya intercepted me when I returned. "Paul wants to see you immediately," she said, cold and clipped like she'd been before.

It was the first I'd seen him since getting promoted, but way too early for him to have second thoughts. His assistant escorted me into his office.

"We have a big problem. Sit down," he ordered, yet he remained standing. "It looks like someone might be stealing money from Addison. This includes donor checks." He started to pace.

"What do you mean?" Unable to disguise the panic in my voice, I was sure my face turned white.

"Mrs. McIntosh sent in a large donation, received an acknowledgment letter. . . ."

"Maya's been writing the acknowledgment letters," I interrupted.

"Let me finish," he said, and put his hand out. His eyebrows converged and the lines in his forehead became pronounced.

"Her wealth adviser alerted her that something was wrong. There are other things, too. Big things. Wait until the *Society Script* gets wind of this. Our reputation will be damaged. Donors only give to fiscally responsible organizations."

"I'm so sorry, I have no idea what's going on," I said in a near-whisper.

"Well, you should," he said, his voice firm. "It has to do with donors and their money. Isn't that your department?" He put his hands on his hips, and peered down at me.

I saw my whole career fly out from under me. Finally, I was exactly where I wanted to be, and poof, it would be gone. My heart was racing.

Convinced Maya must be behind whatever wrongdoing there was, I decided to tell Paul everything that transpired. He just shook his head, and barely said anything. I got up and left. I couldn't discern whether he believed me, or thought I was crazy.

I'd keep my eyes open, hopeful I'd catch Maya in the act.

DORI WILKINSON stepped out of her limo and onto the red carpet at La Palma supper club for her birthday party. She wore a gold glittery gown with a beige fur stole draped around her shoulders. She told me she wanted to make a grand entrance, and that she did, as all 90 guests, including Mark and me, paid tribute to Queen Dori for her 90th birthday. Toasts, roasts, dancing, and a magician who could have fooled David Copperfield bounced around from table to table, delighting guests.

Shortly after Dori's party, the Addison Center hosted the Maestro Society luncheon, to thank our major donors. Dori would be honored at the event for all of her past support. The beautiful invitation was exquisitely designed by Poppy.

I went to check on her. "How's it all going?" I asked. "Is Maya being helpful?"

"Yes, she is. She's finished the program. Honestly, I couldn't get it all done without her."

I wouldn't admit it to Paul but I was glad Maya was still around. He was right that we needed her to finish up season, but it also gave me a chance to keep looking for red flags to prove her guilt. Except, I couldn't find any.

Next on the to-do list was to call Dori and ask if she'd be willing to say a few words at the reception.

"It would be so wonderful for you to get up there and tell everyone why you are so dedicated and loyal to the Addison Center," I said.

"That would be swell, dear. Please write something for me."

"Of course. Would you like to invite Paige and Piper?" I asked, inquiring about her children.

"Yes, I'll do that."

I worked on several drafts, and read her the final over the phone. She was pleased, but on the morning of the luncheon, she called.

"Dear, I'm sick. I can't make it. I'm so sorry. That speech you wrote for me—well, you'll have to read it."

"Why not have Paige or Piper read it? They're still coming anyway, right?" The last thing I wanted to do was usurp her daughters' role.

"Yes, they'll be there. But you wrote it. You captured my voice, my spirit. Just read it."

There was no arguing. "Yes, ma'am."

A few hours later, looking up at the crowd of 300, I read my carefully crafted remarks, telling everyone that they were Dori's heartfelt words. Robust applause followed, and people at the front tables stood. Paige and Piper Wilkinson came over and thanked me. No harm done; at least that was what I thought at the time.

Chapter 40

TABLE TIDE

"WHAT DO YOU KNOW about Ambassador Julian Jorge Mendoza?" Andy asked, when he called me. His question took me off guard; my heart surged at the mention of JJ's name.

"He's a new donor, along with Catalina, his wife," I said, matter-of-factly.

"Savannah just added him to the development committee, and he'll be at our meeting tomorrow. I think I've seen his and his wife's photo in the *Society Script* before. Savannah said you know him."

"He's super nice. I've never met his wife."

My brain scrambled to invent excuses why JJ hadn't contacted me, now that he was back in town: Cat had him scheduled for an early dinner party; Cat needed him to focus on her renovation job in New York; Cat and he were busy entertaining important business people from Miami. I suddenly became jealous of Cat. His wife was his priority.

I kept checking my phone, and to my relief JJ finally texted me much later in the day. He told me he'd returned to Royal Coconut Beach, and would see me at the meeting tomorrow. No mention of a walk.

The red power suit was perfect for the next day. While everyone made small talk at the beginning of the meeting, I kept glancing over at the door; no sign of JJ. Andy called the meeting to order and began. Perhaps five minutes later, JJ joined the meeting already in progress, and took the empty seat directly across from me. Excited he was there, I tried not to look in his direction, but couldn't resist a quick glance at him every now and then. When I did, he was busy with his phone. *Just like Mark.*

We were discussing the report about the luncheon honoring Dori, when Savannah said, "Gosh, Julia. You were a possum, right on the stump." I was thrilled to receive her compliment; not only because I was finally getting recognition now that Chrissy was gone, but because JJ heard it.

Next, Andy called on me to report new gifts.

"First, now that Mr. Mendoza is present, we'd like to thank you and Mrs. Mendoza for your Maestro gift," I said. "We're so glad to welcome you both to our growing Addison family." *You and Cat,* I thought. *The Cat Lady.* Back when Claudia wired funds for the Mendoza gift, she said, "Always make sure Catalina is included. Otherwise you'll never see another gift from them." I wasn't able to tell whether Claudia was strutting her authority, or simply stating the truth.

Andy moved rapidly through the agenda. Chandler sat there, still on the committee, but not saying anything. Still trying to impress her, I hoped he'd report to Chrissy how well things were going. The meeting ended soon after, but JJ hung around. Some members lingered, chatting with each other, while JJ headed my way. He gave me a quick peck on the cheek. Then Savannah patted him on the shoulder, and they spoke. I got distracted by other committee members who had questions. I turned around, but to my dismay JJ was gone, but he texted me soon after:

> Great to see you today, Estrella. You looked beautiful, red's your color. Grab a drink with me tonight? Tide Table at 6?

"Okay," I wrote back. Disappointment was replaced with joy, my mood pathetically commandeered by his text.

Preoccupied with my appearance, I left work early to go home and freshen up. I changed into a black bodycon dress. Off came the panties to banish the unattractive lines. It also allowed me to indulge my newly discovered naughty side. I applied black eyeliner and mascara, but my hand was jittery, and a glob landed on my cheek. I scrubbed it away with make-up remover. I added smoky gray eyeshadow and red bold lipstick, and sprayed perfume on my neck and wrists. Black stilettos and long sparkly earrings were put on last, and I went over to the mirror. I don't recall ever trying to look so suggestive, while the anticipation of seeing JJ gave me a sexy glow.

I headed to Table Tide, feeling tremors of excitement. It was a little dark inside, but I spotted him at the bar, and slithered into the chair next to him. Noticing me, his face lit up. He looked debonair in a black suit, white shirt and bright red tie. Gold cufflinks with his initials engraved caught the light. I was flattered that he also got dressed up for our date.

JJ looked me up and down. "Wow. You look gorgeous, Estrella. Some wine?"

I nodded. "Red, please."

He summoned the bartender. "Interesting meeting today."

I gave him a playful nudge. "C'mon, you looked at your phone the entire meeting."

"Ah, you got me. But I'm good at multi-tasking. You did good, young lady."

I was gratified to hear that. "Now that you're in town, what've you been up to?"

"It's been nonstop. I've been on the phone with partners in Europe since five this morning. Meetings in my office all day, except yours, of course. Tomorrow is a state dinner in DC, and then I'll be at the embassy."

He sipped his drink, and looked at me, his eyes ablaze. "Did I mention I saw a beautiful woman today at the Addison Center?"

I put my hands to my face.

"You're blushing."

"Estrella, I've missed you. I'm so happy to see you." I rested my arm on the bar, and he gently stroked it while making prolonged eye contact. He then took my hand and slowly brushed his fingers against each of my polished nails. Nobody had ever done that before; it was incredibly sensual.

"You don't have to say anything. I know how you feel."

"You do? I asked.

"You've got goosebumps on your arm." He gently brushed my cheek. "And you're blushing. Again."

No kidding. What the hell was I doing, getting turned on by another man at a bar?

"No doubt," I said.

"No doubt about blushing? Or about me?" He raised an eyebrow.

I froze for a few seconds. "Both. I want to be with you. More than you know. I just, . . . can't. I've told you this already, but I *am* married." I became scared in the face of such intimacy. Knowing my stomach was empty, I sipped my wine slowly.

He patted my hand. "I won't push. Only when you're ready. You'll let me love you one day."

"We'll see." I teasingly smiled, crossing my legs.

"I wore a red tie in honor of you, Estrella. Your color," he said, pointing to it.

"How lovely."

"It's because I think of you. You're in my heart." He rubbed my back, causing another sensual sensation.

I was relieved when he backed off and talked about the bigwigs he'd see in DC, and his plans after that. He took my hand from time to time. Fixated on JJ, I was without any awareness of my surroundings.

After a while, he looked at his watch. "I'm sorry, Estrella. I have to meet Cat at a dinner party tonight. It's important."

My mood plummeted. If he had another appointment I might've understood, but I was filled with resentment because he was meeting Cat. But what right did I have to be jealous of his wife? We got up, and we walked to the valet.

I was quiet, thinking how naïve it was having thought he got dressed up just to meet me. He gave a quick kiss goodbye on the cheek, before we headed our separate ways,

I beat Mark home and changed quickly so I wouldn't have to lie about being gussied up. I got into bed, very frustrated with myself for wanting something that I knew I couldn't have. I was also pretty certain that JJ would tire of me if I didn't meet his expectations. *Why would anyone in her right mind submit to all of this in the first place?*

I fell into a deep sleep and dreamed of the ocean, its waves breaking on shore and receding. When I awoke, I knew the dream had complicated implications, the waves signaling the colliding push and pull in me that intensified.

The next day, out of the blue, Chrissy called. She'd barely been gone; I figured something must've been on her agenda.

"It's time that I got involved with Addison again. Let's have lunch," Chrissy said, not wasting time with small talk. We never use to break bread together, but it was in my best interest to suck it up and see her, given the company she kept. We made a date for the following week.

Chapter 41

SWEETHEART DEALS

HEADS TURNED when the following week Chrissy walked into Le Petite Pain, the new "it" place. Her chocolate-brown curls framed her face perfectly. The shorter length was noticeably more sophisticated and professional. Designer sunglasses covered her eyes, which she removed as she approached me.

With carefully applied make-up, she was even more beautiful than before. A gold camisole peeked out from her miraculously unwrinkled white linen pantsuit, and she wore an exquisite gold necklace and earrings. She took the seat across from me. "I hear fundraising is going well, even with the slow economy. I knew you'd do well. I told Paul he should promote you."

"You'd mentioned that," I said. "Again, I really appreciated it. By the way, I love your ads in the Society Script."

"I've been working on my branding. It's important to have my company's name associated with Addison. When people attend theater and flip through Playbill, they need to see that Christine Hathaway Realty contributed. It'll add to my credibility. Plus, I want to become a Maestro member, so I can be in the Parker Pavilion. I'd like to get tickets and bring clients there."

Great, now I'd still have to see her all season long, schmoozing there. I visualized her flitting around the Parker Pavilion as if she owned the room.

"Well, you've come to the right place." We both laughed.

"The arrangement working out of Chandler's office is good." She sipped her water. "Well, you do know about us, don't you?" Practically choking on my iced decaf, I looked at her, feeling awkward.

"I figured, maybe," I said.

"Really? I assumed you knew," she said. I wouldn't go there.

"It was a secret for a while," she continued. "Then Georgina found out." My nails were digging into my palms.

"Oh, wow." I didn't know what else to say.

"It almost imploded. Georgina was thinking of ending their long-term marriage. Let's just say it was a rough patch for all of us."

All of us? As in one happy family? I kept quiet, allowing Chrissy to talk. Like before, once she got on the topic of Chandler, she spewed like a faucet.

"But there's their children, and grandchildren. And of course money. Family money, and their lineage is of paramount importance. Not just to Chandler, but to Georgina too." I looked at her with not a very good poker face. "C'mon, you're in the business. You know how folks like the Fairbanks are. Chandler is fourth-generation wealth. For the sake of the family, all that money. Neither one would mess up that."

"Ah, keep a stiff upper lip and carry on," I said.

"Pretty much."

"Where does this leave you?"

"I'll tell you a funny story. It's more like an old joke, but it happens to be true in our case. Chandler and Georgina were having breakfast at the Sealine Club. Point-blank, Georgina tells him he needs to stop seeing me. Chandler tells her that some of his close friends have mistresses, mentioning Webster Ashton and his mistress. Did you know about her?" she asked.

"Of course. Everyone does."

"Well, Frances, Webster's wife, rules the roost. Don't mess with her."

"I kind of got that. Webster once referred to Frances as 'the boss'."

"She is. You know how generous they are, too. Giving to charity is the cement that binds them together. For life, in perpetuity. And she makes the decisions and has the final word when it comes to all that. Their names are plastered everywhere: art museums around the world—they are major art collectors."

"Yes, I know they've donated their artwork everywhere."

"Their names are also on a prominent building at Princeton where he's a trustee. Just plain 'Ashton' in huge letters is engraved on its façade." The often-evasive Chrissy was a fount of information today.

"Back to the story," Chrissy said. "Chandler was in the

middle of telling Georgina that he wasn't going to end our relationship. Timing was everything, because at that moment, in walked Webster with his mistress."

"Are you serious?"

Nodding her head, she continued. "You know what Georgina tells Chandler?"

"I can't imagine."

"She took a look at her and said, 'Oh, ours is *much* prettier. We should stick with her'." Chrissy let out a belly laugh, and I followed her lead.

"Chandler and I don't go to the club like Webster and his mistress. I'm well aware that Georgina doesn't want to give up her position, nor do either one of them wish to see all their money divided. It's important to keep it transferring to future generations."

"Yup. Transfer of intra-generational wealth *per stirpes,* so assets don't get divided." I was annoyed with myself; I was still trying to impress Chrissy, now with legal mumbo-jumbo. The old familiar feeling of Chrissy-envy resurfaced.

"I've made my peace. Everyone has." Listening to her made what appeared to me to be an insane arrangement sound totally normal. Chrissy had a knack for persuasion; painting a picture a certain way so you'd believe it.

"As far as the family, it makes no sense to split up all the homes, the clubs, the friends. Their social lives, religion, politics, and giving to charity. There's all their shared history, memories, heartbreaks, successes, and failures, too. You can never take that away," Chrissy said, with a touch of wistfulness. "Or compete."

"I get it. It makes up the fabric of their marriage. How are you with all this?"

"Georgina's a tough cookie. I bet now if Chandler asked her for a divorce, she'd fight tooth and nail to keep him; keep their life the way it is and finish it out together. At some level, be there for each other. They've been down that road years ago, when there was another woman in the picture. Chandler didn't leave Georgina then, nor did she kick him out. In a twisted way, Georgina has the upper hand."

"You mean she knows what she's got, and by the same token, she knows he won't leave her?"

"Yes. In fact, do you wanna laugh?"

"Sure."

"Georgina tells Chandler she's determined to outlive him so he can't get married again. 'There'll never be another Mrs. Fairbanks living in *my* home' is what she says. She's the protector of her husband—or at least their *money*. Anyway, my husband James left me several years ago, and he wants nothing to do with our kids. Chandler has made generous provisions for me and my children."

The evasive Chrissy didn't really answer my question about how she was with everything, not that she would be honest with me anyway. It sounded like Chandler got to have his cake and eat it too. I'd have to tell Nina all this.

"Well, speaking of putting names on things, let's talk," I said.

"Okay. As I told you, I want to promote my business. Not that Chandler hasn't helped. He really is a spectacular connection. I'd like to get Hathaway Realty's name out there, to help grow it more. Having its name in lights at the Addison Center will go a long way. You have that locked up more than any other charity in town."

I smiled at her compliment. "Poppy will send along the

available sponsorships. You can figure out which one you'd get the most bang for your buck. She'll send you the pledge form to become a Maestro member, too."

"That would be great," Chrissy said.

Whether Chrissy's business was thriving or not, Chandler was no doubt providing the funding. He was taking good care of her, helping to put her name on the map as a serious player in the business community. The more I listened to her, the more it sounded like a sweet deal. Then again, this was Chrissy painting a colorful scenario.

Chapter 42

IN PENNYLAND

PENNY WAS NEXT ON MY AGENDA. Following the gala, Penny's canasta ladies and Artie's Knights of the Golden Circle created factions, with loyalties all over the map. To play my cards right and in the spirit of neutrality, I needed to be nice to both of them. Artie was impossible, but at least I had a shot at developing a relationship with Penny. We had already bonded over lunch with my Lunch Club group.

She picked up right away when I called.

"I'm happy to hear from you," she said. "Believe it or not, I'm doing a huge renovation project. It'll take years. The workman are my new best friends."

"Sounds stressful," I answered.

"Yes, it is. Say, why don't we have lunch? I could use a

break from these workers. Let's go to the Waterfront Club; my treat. Are you around tomorrow?"

"Yes," I said as I glanced at my calendar.

I arrived ahead of time. The club had already started to empty out, signaling that the end of season was almost here. Penny walked in a few minutes later, finishing a phone call.

"Hello, Julia. That was Elise. She's jumped in to help with the house, as a favor. But as you probably know, she's in Monte Carlo. I love your little group—the Royal Coconut Beach Lunch Club—Elise told me that's what you call yourselves."

"They're all terrific." Did she want to be part of our club? I hoped not.

"Back to my house. The architect Maya found is fantastic, but he needs to rein everyone in, keep them on schedule. All these change orders. That means more things have been added to its construction. You know how it goes."

I did? Maya hired the architect?

"Don't think it's any better in the Hamptons. They're always behind schedule there, too. Know what I mean?"

"Yes, I do." I couldn't imagine having all of those houses. Nor did I care to have my plate overflow like hers; I had more than enough going on.

"I'll tell you, that Maya's something else. You know her from Addison." She took off her glasses with multi-colored frames. "Doesn't she work for you?"

"Well, we worked together for a while. She reports to me now."

"She's sly as a fox," Penny said.

No kidding.

"Truth is, we can't live with her, but we can't live without her."

We? What exactly she meant by that, I wasn't sure.

"Yes, she's very efficient," I replied.

"I have to say, Maya's at Artie's beck and call 24/7, but mostly at night after she finishes her Addison work. It's annoying. His phone rings non-stop with calls from her, and then off he goes trading blocks of stock for the next day. She winds him up, tells him more information than he needs. Aggravates him, actually. As if he's not stressed enough." Penny sounded like she had Artie's back; not an angry, bitter wife. Talk about an about-face.

"Anyway, I shouldn't say anything bad about Maya. She really helps us."

"Um . . . she works for both of you?"

"No, she works for Artie, but she handles everything. Oversees Artie's investment team here and his operation in New York. Also, there's his Knights of the Golden Circle. She helped find my newest EA. Executive assistant."

Thank you, Penny. She'd assumed I could relate to the renovation of her new-mega mansion, but that I had no idea what an EA was.

"When Artie and I were getting divorced, you could say Maya worked for Artie. Now that Artie and I are back together, she works for both of us, for our family. She's the trustee on some family businesses we've invested in for our son Kevin."

"You and Artie are back together?" I asked.

"Yeah sure," she answered as if it was yesterday's news.

Shocked and curious as I was, I didn't want to overstep my bounds. Unsure what to say, I asked, "How's Kevin doing?"

"Fine. We bought a seafood company and a few other businesses in his name. Also, I think Maya is on the verge of finding a new house manager for me," she said, as she zoomed from one topic to another.

It was evident that Maya was acting as the central nervous system of the Brasses' lives. Positions like running a billionaire's entire investment team were usually reserved for someone who'd earned an MBA from an Ivy League school. Now Maya had the pleasure of kowtowing to Artie and Penny, sucked into their money-fueled chaos. Definitely not a job a million women would dream of. No doubt she got paid a fortune, though. Why would she want to keep her job at Addison?

Then I recalled what Paul said: *There are other things, too. Big things . . . our reputation will be damaged. Donors only give to a fiscally responsible organization.* What the heck was Maya up to? It *had* to be connected to Paul's comments. I needed to get to the bottom of it, before either Addison got harmed or I got blamed. With my luck, probably both.

"Have you seen Nina and Valerie lately?" I asked.

"To be honest, they're disappointed in me. Artie and I decided that after all we've gone through, it didn't make any sense to divorce. For what? To tell you the truth, even before Nina and Valerie came along, I'd lie in bed having conversations with an imaginary attorney, about leaving him. Didn't really think I'd act on it, but it all happened so quickly. I poured my heart out to them over lunch, here, at the club. They went all out like warriors, taking no prisoners. You know them."

"I sure do." I smiled.

"It started to get really ugly. We're talking about Artie, so how could it not?" I gave a small laugh. "He treated the divorce like a business deal. Negotiate and win. That's why he's so successful." She sounded proud of her husband's ability to be a total prick.

"That he is," I said.

"I didn't want to go through with it. When push came to shove, neither did Artie. We talked and worked something out. Besides, there's only a handful of men who could support me in the lifestyle I've grown accustomed to. I've paid my dues; I should get the benefits. We had your friends draft . . . um . . . what do you call it?" She looked at me.

"A postnup."

"That's right. Postnup. Too much at stake. Then there's our family. And those delicious grandkids."

"They must be fun."

"Sure are. Believe it or not, Artie's great with them. He never had time for our kids, working all the time. He enjoys the little ones now."

Penny reached into her blue ostrich Birkin bag and grabbed her phone to show me pictures of their grandchildren.

After lunch, I headed back to the office and returned phone calls. I kept thinking about our conversation. Penny's decision to stay married to Artie was a well-thought-out plan, which surprised me, given how flaky she seemed.

Mark was going to be working late, and I was looking forward to a quiet evening at home alone. But Nina called, and asked if we could meet for an impromptu dinner. She tried to get Valerie and Elise to join us, but they had plans already. With our schedules the way they were, I didn't want to give up quality time with her, so I agreed to meet up later.

UNHAPPILY EVER AFTER

NINA SUGGESTED we try First Wave, a trendy restaurant that neither one of us had been to.

She was there already, sipping a Prosecco.

I took the seat across from her. "You started the party without me," I said.

"Yes. I figured we might as well make it a Lunch Club get-together, even if it's not all four of us. I ordered tapas."

"Works for me. I'm so glad to see you. I need your advice."

"Shoot."

"It's about Maya. Paul—Addison's president—said that some donor checks have gone unaccounted for. And he said there are other big things going on. So I spilled the beans about what I thought about Maya. And you know what?"

"What?"

"I got zero reaction from him. He barely knows me, he put his confidence in me, and now I think he's going to blame me."

"Whoa, slow down."

"I can't help it. I keep going in circles. I'm sure Maya's involved. Did I tell you I had it out with her at the gala? I accused her of trying to ruin my career. Floria, the cleaning lady, told me she'd been snooping around my office. And Poppy told me that Maya wanted my job. But way back, Maya told me Poppy was upset because *she* wanted my job. Which I believed, at the time."

"That's all?"

"Yes."

"First, you can't go around making accusations without solid evidence. You're a lawyer."

"Ouch. I know. Why are you always so damn truthful?"

Nina looked away for a few seconds. "Too bad you have no way to prove anything."

"No kidding." I downed my Prosecco. "Oh, and Penny told me that she and Artie are back together. She's decorating this new ginormous house. Maya's running the Brasses' show on the side, too. What's going on there?"

She gave me a steely look.

"I know, attorney-client privilege," I said.

"I can tell you a little. You know our firm was having a tough time proving Artie's real net worth. You heard the spiel at lunch. Artie is craftier than we'd imagined. So were his attorneys. The truth is, Penny didn't care so much, but we wanted to go for the jugular, zealous advocates that we are."

"I'm sure your trusty stilettos came in handy."

"Of course. In all seriousness, an outsider might think,

what's the big deal if Penny got a hundred million less than she was entitled to? On the contrary, the case would've been precedent-setting, especially for women in Penny's shoes. But Penny didn't really seem to care. She's complacent in her canasta-decorating-golf-club world."

"Yup, that's her. But to totally pull the plug on the divorce?"

"Yeah, well they have two small grandkids, and another on the way from their daughter, the New York-slash-Hamptons socialite married to the big hedge fund guy," Nina said.

"Right."

"And Artie's great with them," Nina said. "You know the type. Too busy making his fortune to remotely care about the kids when they were growing up. That all fell under Penny's umbrella. 'Ladies work', that's what she calls it. Along with the help. Tons of it."

"Of course, with the help. When Penny showed up for our gala tasting, she referred to that as 'ladies work,' too."

"It probably gives her a sense of importance," Nina said. "I doubt Artie provides that. The only ego that gets stroking is his."

"That's for sure. By the way, I was in their stunning house."

"Yeah, well, it's on the market. Do you want to buy it? $80 million. Furniture's negotiable. That's why she's so busy with the new house."

"Umm . . . I'll take a pass for now. Especially the way things are at home."

"Mark's still grumpy, huh?"

"Touchy. But it's on and off. It's better now, but I keep recalling that he told me I don't know what's going on in the real world. I can't believe he would say that. Just between us, though, I think he might be right about becoming warped. Like thinking a $80 million home is the new normal." I snorted.

"I'm sure Mark's under a lot of pressure, and didn't mean anything."

"You're always on his side," I said.

"Not true. You need to see the whole picture, that's all. Hey, you just admitted your new normal."

"You got me again."

"That's what friends are for. By the way, Penny gets all the credit for the beautiful house She has more class than her husband. Or at least she hires the right decorators," Nina said.

"Penny mentioned that Elise was trying to help her with the new house from afar."

"I'm not surprised. Penny and Artie both decided it's just not worth it to split the family apart."

"Why has the *Society Script* remained oddly quiet?" I asked.

"We made a deal with them while things are settling down," Nina said.

"I didn't know you could make deals with papers."

"Hey, it's Royal Coconut Beach. Anything goes."

"Yeah, right. So how exactly does Maya fit in?" I asked. "She must never sleep."

"She's latched on to them. There might be something going on between Maya and Artie. I wouldn't be surprised if they're sleeping together," Nina said.

"I've thought the same for a while." After a long silence, I said, "Isn't it strange how things turn out? Penny can go about her canasta games and being overwhelmed with decorating. Artie now has Maya to help manage his business."

"Yup. Assets won't get divided. The whole family and future generations will live off their inheritance."

"Don't forget that their son Kevin will probably donate his share to the Alaskan Wildlife Society," I said, and sipped my drink.

"For sure. Lucky Sperm Club," Nina said.

"I have to admit, I barely know them," I said. "But hearing about them makes me think about Mark and me. What if Mark and I had that kind of money but weren't happy. Would we stay married?"

"I'm worried about you." She put down her wine glass. "What's *really* happening at home?"

"Nothing." I shook my head.

"Stop avoiding the subject. Why else would you be dwelling on Penny and Artie's troubled marriage—are things still that frosty?" Nina asked. "And don't tell me again that Mark's got pressure. Please, we all do." She leaned forward and stared into my eyes.

"Ah, you know me too well. Sometimes I think you're my mirror." I looked the other way, then looked back at her. She hadn't broken her stare.

"So what's up?"

"You're relentless," I said, and exhaled. "I still feel like we're disconnected, as I told you at our last lunch. I know part of it is our chaotic schedules."

"I get that, but what about you?" Nina asked. "No offense, but you're always so busy running to performances and events, and feeling overwhelmed. Your time and energy are mostly spent on work, right? Could it be that you're not exactly bubbling with emotion either?"

"I never looked at it that way." I let out a sigh, knowing that much of my emotional energy was channeled toward JJ.

"I'm a self-professed workaholic," Nina said. "How else could I climb to the top at Reid, Bennett? But since Girard came along, our relationship became my priority."

"It's new for you, though," I said. "You're still in your honeymoon phase."

"Yes, but I genuinely want to be with him. I make the effort. Do you?"

"I hate your directness, even though I love you. I guess when Valerie suggested I give Mark space, she didn't mean run in the other direction." I shook my head.

"Or sulk about it and withdraw. I'm no expert on marriage, but having listened to everyone else's stories, it's seldom one-sided. When someone has an affair, it's because of something else that's happening, or for that matter, not happening."

"Like Mark and Olivia?"

"Yes. You're aware something's up."

"Well, I'm not so innocent myself." I lowered my head.

"What the hell does that mean?"

"Look, I can't talk about it." My eyes welled up, but I forced myself not to cry. "Nothing's going on. I just think about the possibility. What if I met someone?"

"I think you need to focus on Mark. Are you really that unhappy? You did meet someone, didn't you?"

"I don't know what I want," I said, avoiding her question. "I'm so confused. And I could lose my job on top of everything." With that, I exploded into tears.

She grabbed my hand, and I put my other hand on top of hers.

"It's okay. Talk to me," she said.

"I'm so sorry," I gasped. "Good thing it's dark in here. I'm embarrassed." I wiped my face with my napkin.

"Don't be embarrassed. Listen, please don't have an affair, whoever this person is. I know you. You'll regret it, not to mention the consequences. Maybe not now, but long-term. You're a mess already, and you haven't even done anything. Right?"

Without responding, I glanced uncomfortably at her.

"Okay, it doesn't matter what you've done or haven't. I just don't believe you're thinking things completely through."

There was another long silence. Finally, I said, "I wish I were more like you; you're made of steel. I could crumble at any given second," I said, in between sobs.

"You won't. You're so much tougher than you think. When things settle down, I want to introduce Girard to you and Mark."

"Maybe you guys will rub off on us."

She smiled. "Maybe so."

Nina was right: I *was* a mess already, and I hadn't even had a full-blown affair. She instilled enough fear in me to see the larger picture. It was a good wake-up call. Was I that unhappy at home? Or was it that I didn't know how to handle Mark's attitude, and had become jealous of Olivia while falling for JJ. It was a perfect storm. Somehow, I had to get a handle on this, before I did serious harm.

"GOOD MORNING, SLEEPYHEAD," Mark said the next morning. "I made you coffee. You were sound asleep when I got home."

"I had dinner with Nina. It was nice to catch up with her." I also filled Mark in on Penny and Artie's reuniting. I was in the mood to talk and share.

"Rumor has it that her new firm is doing gangbusters," Mark said. "I guess when the economy isn't good, the divorce rate goes up."

"True. Except if you're Penny and Artie. They're too rich to get divorced," I said.

"After all that drama with the gala, now they're together? They're in another world."

"Oh, and Nina met someone. An attorney named Girard Bissett. He's a criminal defense lawyer. She wants us to meet him."

"I've heard of him. Could be, she's met her match. I'm off to the office. I have a full day ahead, but I'll be home for dinner tonight."

"Good. I miss you." The words flew out of my mouth.

"I miss you too." Mark gave me a quick kiss on my cheek. It may not have been the kind of kiss I wanted, but at least it was a kiss.

Chapter 44

RICH MAN'S PROBLEMS

WHEN I GOT TO WORK, both Chrissy and Andy had left me messages. I'd get Chrissy over with first.

"Hi Julia," Chrissy said, her voice perky. "Thanks for returning the call. I'm about to close a few mega-deals, and I've been asked about the Addison Center. My clients are from New York and Boston. I'm going to have them call you. They're worth your time."

"Okay, thank you. I'll show them around," I said.

"You must. We really should collaborate. Addison's a great reason to entice people to move here."

Chrissy had a good point, although I suspected she could be hoping to make referral fees, which was out of the question. Whatever the reason, I'm sure there was a self-serving motive.

"I could see how working together might be mutually beneficial," I answered. It was best to take the high road. We agreed to talk about it at a later time.

Getting that call over with, I tried Andy.

"I hear you're rocking it, Julia. No doubt," he said. "I looked at the numbers. Despite the economy, fundraising is holding steady."

"Thanks. We have a great product; I'm just working it."

"Well, I've got news for you. Having an office right near Top Brass has its benefits. It's about Artie."

"What happened now on the other side of the bridge?" I asked.

"Top Brass is under investigation. Artie already appeared before the SEC in a private hearing. It's hush-hush."

"What's he being investigated for?"

"Insider trading. An enforcement attorney has been sniffing around for a while," Andy said. "Except now it's escalated to a full-blown investigation, subpoenas and all. You know how it is. You're an attorney." True, but that didn't qualify me for all things legal. He continued. "As a broker-dealer, Artie and his firm are held to a higher standard than the average Joe Schmoe."

"Sounds like he has his hands full," I said.

"He does. You know what they say: problems are problems; the rich just have a more expensive set."

"Could you imagine if this all happened before the gala?" I said. "We'd never raise money."

"I know. Timing was on our side," Andy said.

"Keep me posted. Thanks, you're the best."

Dying to know if Maya was involved, I raced over to her cubicle. She was typing fast and furiously. In the corner window of her screen was information on Nasdaq. She didn't look up, so I tapped her lightly on the shoulder. With a jolt she swiveled around, and her eyebrows shot up.

"Hi. I'm concentrating on some listings."

Sure you are. "I forgot what I wanted, never mind," I said, and walked away, having no idea what I'd expected to find out.

I picked up Italian take-out for dinner, changed into comfortable clothes, and set the table nicely for a change. I dimmed the lights. Half an hour later, I heard the front door. Mark found me in the kitchen. He loosened his tie and sat down. While we ate, his phone was nowhere in sight.

"I found out that Maya's been working for Artie on the side," I said. It felt good to share what was happening at work, even old news.

"Are you sure? How'd you find out?"

"Penny told me. It wasn't like she was complaining. In fact, she sounded grateful that Maya was helping with everything. She still manages to get all her work done at Addison."

"Then don't worry about it." Easy for him to say.

"Now Artie Brass is being investigated." I told him about Andy's phone call. Until things got sorted out, I hadn't told him about the issues at Addison, and how Paul might hold me accountable for the stolen donor checks. While things were better and we were talking like we used to, sort of, I wasn't sure if I'd be open to his criticism. It was one thing for Nina to question how I dealt with Maya. It wasn't worth hearing a disapproving comment from my husband. Sharing details about work, if only in dribs and drabs, was far better from barely communicating.

We talked a little more, and when we finished, he went

to his office. I heard him close the door, so I stood outside and listened. He was reviewing a memo with Olivia.

He joined me in bed later, when the ten o'clock news was on. The anchorwoman was detailing news of a securities fraud scheme that had just broken in Royal Coconut Beach.

"Big Artie's on!" I said. Mark had dozed off, but propped himself up.

"This case involves the use of sophisticated technologies by a team member, or members of Top Brass Investments. More and more caution must be taken to combat this new wave of cyber-crimes and securities fraud. We are seeing an uptick in these areas," said Malachy Mahon, the FBI assistant director who was overseeing the investigation.

"Artie Brass of Royal Coconut Beach in South Florida and his firm, Top Brass Investments, have been charged with several counts of securities fraud for hacking inside information. In this instance, members of Mr. Brasses' team are accused of obtaining a myriad of press releases from distributors including Business Line, Marketconnect and PR Newsnexus. Insiders of Top Brass obtained improperly accessed press statements well before the distributors planned to disseminate them to the public. Mr. Brasses' firm made trades based on these hacked releases. In addition to criminal charges, the SEC is bringing a civil action. Court-ordered asset freezes have been obtained."

"This will be the end of Artie's donations," I said, but Mark had fallen back asleep. I lay awake, feeling sure that Maya had something do with the scheme.

Valerie was on my calendar the next morning. She was hosting a few disadvantaged teens at the Addison Center, where they would see a performance about having manners.

I met her in the theater to make sure her seats were reserved. With the kids tucked in their seats, Valerie and
I stepped outside. She started to make a phone call, which
I took as my cue to head back to the office. I blew her a kiss
and walked away.

"Hold on, hold on," Valerie said to whoever was on the
other end. "Wait a sec, Julia. I'll be done shortly." I checked
messages on my phone while waiting.

"Okay, finished," she said. "Nina needs to talk to you
about Maya." Hearing Maya's name sent a chill through
my spine. "Artie's hired Girard Bissett, the attorney, to represent him. Nina's boyfriend. He's building a case against
Maya."

Based on what Valerie just told me, I anticipated there'd
be some sort of questioning, which I dreaded. By the time
I got back to the office, there was a message from Nina.
I called right away.

"Big trouble with Artie, as I'm sure you heard," Nina
said.

"Yes. Word's gotten around."

"Well, here's the deal. It just so happens that Girard is
Artie's attorney."

"Val told me that."

"He's convinced that Artie had nothing to do with the insider trading business. Or Artie convinced him of that. He's
a defense attorney; what can I say. Anyway, he's pointing
fingers at Maya. Your friend."

"Very funny. She's not my friend," I said, my voice raised.

"I *know* that. That's why I didn't think you'd mind one
bit. Girard is claiming that Artie had no knowledge of any
wrongdoing. He's arguing that Maya was the one hacking the sites to obtain the information—the alleged illegal

information, that is—and then she placed huge blocks of trades, based on this knowledge. I told Girard that you work with Maya, and about the incident with her 'stealing' a check, and so on. Would you be willing to be deposed about this?"

"Do I have to?" I asked.

"You know that Girard could subpoena you to testify at a hearing if you don't. It's all about attacking Maya's credibility. Obviously."

It was also obvious that Nina was using me to help Girard, who'd probably already discussed this with Artie. It would look bad to Artie, a donor and major player in town, if I refused to testify.

"I guess I have no choice," I said. "I have to go, lots of work to do," and hung up abruptly. I hoped Nina knew I was ticked off.

That evening, Mark and I had dinner plans with neighbors. With my stomach in knots, the idea of an evening unrelated to the Addison Center was a breath of fresh air. Mark arrived first, and was already seated and on his phone. I bent down to kiss him hello and he put his phone away. I quickly told him that I thought Maya had been throwing me under the bus, and about my conversation with Nina, before the other couple arrived.

"If the shoe was on the other foot, Nina would help you. Besides, she had information that you willingly gave her. She's just acting on it." Great, now Mark was on Nina's side.

"How's your case going?" I asked, wanting to change the subject.

"Really well. By the way, they lifted the salary freeze, and it will be retroactive."

By the way? This was big news, yet it was said with such

indifference. This confirmed everything that Valerie said about Mark's ego being on the line. It had to be huge for him, but he wanted to downplay that he hadn't been earning anything recently.

"I'm also being recouped for one of the big cases I worked on when I wasn't getting paid. It's a giant windfall."

Just then, our neighbors arrived. We had a pleasant dinner and laughed. On the way home, I thought about Mark's news, which made me happy. While it was good for us financially, I was hopeful that he'd now feel less pressure.

Chapter 45

INDOMITABLE SPIRITS

DORI WILKINSON took an awful fall, and had checked herself into a rehabilitative center that was the best money could buy. I called before I went to visit. Her room was at the end of the corridor, and I knocked on the door.

"C'mon in," she said. I was glad to hear that her voice still had spunk. She was propped up in a chair paying bills, a walker parked next to her bed.

"Oh, Julia. Swell that you're here. The care here is phenomenal. They have me in physical therapy three times a day, and the doctors that come visit me are top-notch." She coughed deeply. "Tell me something interesting."

"Jose Carreras performed the other evening. He still has the most beautiful tenor voice, even at his age." Other activities at the Addison Center provided light conversation. After half an hour, her fading voice indicated she was tired.

"Well, time for my nap now, dear. I'm going to call the nurse and have her put me back in this bed." Dori wasn't much on kissing, so I extended my hand. She grasped it with hers, which was near-translucent. It had lost its usual strength. Not wanting to let go, I held on for a few extra seconds before I left.

A week later, she called me.

"It's the end, Julia. The doctors told me. I'm not well."

My heart sank. "I'm so sorry."

"Don't be. It's my time. You're a strong woman, and you have a great life ahead. Go out and live it."

"I'm so grateful to have gotten to know you. I'll always cherish our time together."

"I feel the same about you," she said, her voice weak.

Her advice was valuable, and since she had such depth of character, strength and fortitude, it was especially meaningful. I recalled how eager I was to win Dori over, and was proud that I did. I vowed to emulate these qualities.

A few days later, she passed away. Piper and Paige planned a memorial service, which I attended. The pastor summed up:

Dori was indomitable. With Dori, it didn't matter whether the situation was seemingly insurmountable, or easy-peasy. The same principles applied: courage, persistence, determination, purposefulness.

Two weeks later, Harry Langhorne, who I knew from Reid, Bennett called me in his capacity as Dori's attorney and personal representative, charged with settling her mega-estate.

"Are you sitting down?" he asked, after we caught up.

"I am."

"Dori left $100 million to the Addison Center in her will."

"What about her daughters? Paige and Piper?"

"She left millions to other charities, too. I'll send over her trust document," Harry said.

"What about Paige and Piper?" I repeated.

"Ah, there's a problem. She left them each $5.00. You know what that means. Most likely, they'll sue."

"I guess we'll just have to wait to see how things unfold," I said.

Paul was traveling, so I left him a message sharing the good news about Dori's gift, and the bad news that it would probably be contested. I hoped he'd look favorably upon me because of the donation. It was eleven, and I told Poppy I'd be heading to the Savannah IV with a stack of thank-you letters for her to sign. I decided to check in on Maya, as she had been awfully quiet lately.

"How's it going, Maya?" I asked, hovering over her in her cubicle.

"Good. I was just leaving for a doctor's appointment. I'll probably be back by the time you return. I'm late." She logged out of her computer, grabbed her purse, and left.

I hadn't planned to, but I hung around for a few minutes after I was sure she was gone. A notebook was on her desk. I flipped through it, and saw notes about phone conversations with donors, mostly with notations about their tickets.

To be as quiet as possible, I slowly opened her top desk drawer, half-expecting it to be locked. In plain view were a few blank Addison checks. *What the hell could she be doing with those?* I quickly closed the drawer, hoping no one heard me.

I got in my car to head to the Lady Savannah IV, thinking

about what I should do. Do I tell Paul about the checks? When I spilled my guts to him about Maya the last time, his lack of reaction made me feel silly. Who knows, Paul might even be in cahoots with her, and possibly Artie. I needed to tread carefully.

I parked in the marina's parking lot and got out. Although quite humid, the fresh air reinvigorated me. Walking the plank brought back memories of all that had happened on her yacht the night of last year's kick-off party. So much had occurred since then. I had risen to the occasion at work, and found myself in unfamiliar territory for the first time with my husband, and became involved with another man. I told myself to knock it off; I certainly wasn't having wild sex with him below-decks on Savannah's yacht. I laughed at myself, thinking what a perfect fantasy that was. JJ probably had a yacht tucked away somewhere, or access to one.

Savannah's crew member was waiting for me, and escorted me up the stairs to the lounge area. Unlike the time I was there before, when the room bustled with people in stunning clothes, lively conversation, the sparkly skyline in the distance, it was dead silent. I waited for Savannah while the man brought me a club soda.

A few minutes later, Savannah emerged in a colorful Pucci dress. She sat down next to me, I handed her the stack of letters and a pen, and she began signing.

"By the way, thanks for introducing JJ to me. He's a nice man," I said. She looked up, stopped writing and removed her glasses.

"Well, I must tell you. He's quite taken by you." Her words made me giddy. "I've known him for years; he's a remarkable fellow. Winston learned a lot from him about franchising. JJ came a long way to make something out of himself, but never got too big for his britches, like so many other folks in this town."

"What about Cat? Would she be someone that we might want to also get involved at the Addison Center? What's she like?" I asked, trying to make it sound casual, hoping my fishing expedition was well-disguised.

"She's one tough lady. I shouldn't tell you this, but. . . ."

"What?" I asked as nonchalantly as possible.

"Well, JJ's a charmer, but Cat won't tolerate affairs. She'd never let some woman destroy her family and their good reputation; one that she's carefully curated. And all that money he made, while on her watch. He had a lady friend a long while ago, but Cat put a screeching halt to it. Cat forced JJ to end it, and made him promise he'd never speak with her again. Money was involved, to make 'the problem' go away. Trust me, Cat didn't fall off some old turnip truck."

"Sounds like she knows what she wants," I said.

"Well, things could've gone to hell in a hand basket. She was damned sure to keep their place in society. Their children went to Sidwell Friends, and were friends with the kids of celebrities, politicians, and presidents."

Savannah was leaning back in her chair. I felt like an old friend had invited me to hang out on her magnificent yacht for the day.

"Distinguished people from distinguished families, that's the Mendoza inner circle. Cat was way too invested, and will do whatever it takes to make sure her apple cart isn't upset. She'll protect the image she created for her family," Savannah explained.

"It sounds so fake," I said. I hoped she didn't think I was judgmental, and I regretted saying that.

"Oh, don't let the façade fool you. She and JJ are very

close, when it comes to business. That's what they are: business partners. Her name is on everything. Those big decisions, they're made together."

I sat back in my chair, pretending to be relaxed as I hung on her every word.

"Catalina possesses hostess skills that make an invitation from her among the most coveted in Washington's social scene. White House butlers have worked in her house, for crying out loud. She's got impeccable taste, too. Her house—'her' being the operative word—she's the boss. Heaven knows, if I were Cat, I'd poke JJ's eyes out if he played around. Then I'd kill him."

Savannah put her glasses back on and resumed letter signing, while I babbled about Dori's gift and how the Addison Center had lost a special friend when she passed away. But I was really focused on absorbing the information about Ambassador and Mrs. Mendoza.

I took the stack of letters and left. Cat was the leading lady in JJ's grandiose life, and I felt unimportant. She wasn't someone I'd want to cross, either. At least I hadn't done any real damage; Nina already warned me. I needed to seriously reconsider everything, which suddenly made me feel powerless and panicky.

When I returned to the office, I wasn't paying attention and bumped into Poppy in the hall. The folder with the letters scattered all over the floor.

"I'm so sorry."

"You look like a deer caught in the headlights. Are you alright?" she asked.

"I'm fine." *If only she knew.* She helped me pick the papers up.

"Before I forget, Nina called while you were out."

I headed to my office to return the call, anticipating what she'd say.

"Girard's going to call you about the deposition," Nina said, skipping small talk.

"I guess it beats being subpoenaed," I said.

"I'm really sorry. It just worked out this way."

"I know. You're doing your job. I'm not happy, though."

"I know you're not. And again, I'm sorry. Just get it over with, and we can be best friends again. Speaking of which, how are you doing?"

"Fine. I've gotta go," I said.

A phone conference was set up for the next day: Girard, the Addison Center attorney, and me. Girard began.

"How long have you been working with Maya?"

"Under a year," I said.

"Please explain what happened with the check."

I detailed the events.

"Did you believe that Maya stole the check from your desk?"

"Yes. I'm almost certain she did."

"What about a check from Mr. Chandler Fairbanks to Maya? Do you know what that was for?"

"No, I don't." At one time, I'd suspected it was hush money to keep Chrissy and Chandler's affair secret, but now I believed it might have had to do with Chandler placing trades via Maya. I had no proof, though, and I wasn't going there under oath.

"Is Maya trustworthy when it comes to donations?"

"I don't understand your question."

"Is Maya capable of embezzlement?"

Nina told Girard I told her I thought Maya might be stealing from Addison!

"I wouldn't put it past her," I said. "I saw blank checks in her desk drawer."

More questioning, and my sworn testimony attacking Maya's character became an official part of the record. The twisted thing was that I was dying to talk about my distrust for Maya, but when I finally did—to Paul—I feared for my job. Now I was being forced to divulge information, but I would've preferred not to. My only hope was maybe as a result, the trouble that Paul told me about at Addison might get revealed.

Nina was right about getting it over with. I was glad it was behind me, and went on with my day.

Then I received a text from JJ. He was back in town.

Does seven work? Usual place?

Sure.

So much for Nina's warning . . . where was my resolve?

That evening, Mark was home for dinner. I acted normal, trying hard to conceal my excitement about seeing JJ. I threw together a salad and fresh vegetables and poured wine, while he changed into his jeans and a white Henley. Again, he had dark circles under his eyes. His work pressures must've been getting to him. I told him about the deposition.

"I'm sure you're relieved to get it over with. You can put it all behind you. By the way, our firm closed the Colorado Springs office." He took a bite of salad. "Some of the attorneys are being moved to my office. I promoted Olivia, so she'll manage their workload; it won't be all on me."

Great. He and Olivia will probably spend more time together.

"That'll be helpful." I was upset, but wasn't going to challenge him. We had just started to get back in sync. I attributed it to the change in his situation with his firm, including his recent huge payday. It occurred to me that perhaps Olivia was just using Mark to get ahead in the firm. Would he fall for that?

Later, while lying in bed I received a text from JJ:

> Something came up, I can't meet you.
> I promise I'll make it up.

I was disappointed, but I told myself it was probably for the best.

Chapter 46

NO LONGER STABLE

THE SECURITY OFFICER who manned the front desk at Addison handed me an envelope. I assumed it was the swatches for the Maestro dinner that Ziggy said he was couriering over, but instead, inside was a black velvet box. When I opened it, a dazzling pair of earrings, each in the shape of a flower, stared back at me. The petals formed an enchanting medley of brilliant diamonds, and in the center was a beautiful ruby. Ordinary diamonds were transformed into a work of art.

His note was anything but ordinary, too: *Dear Lady in Red, Forget-me-not. I miss you. You will look stunning in these.*

The earrings glistened when I held them up by my window. Putting them back in the box, I saw "Harry Winston" written inside. JJ's magnanimous gift catapulted me out of denial. I was in too deep, and panicked.

"Thank you for the beautiful earrings," I texted to him. I didn't know what I should or shouldn't say. A rush of guilt spiraled through me, as I thought of Mark—he would definitely notice new earrings, let alone from the House of Harry. I could lie and say that I borrowed them from Elise, but he might thank her for the loan if he saw her. Or I could say that I bought them on QVC late one night for ninety-nine dollars. Great cubic zirconia, aren't they, Mark?

My heart wouldn't stop skittering while I tried to stay focused at work. But my mind was elsewhere. At home, with Mark, I tried to pretend that nothing was going on inside my head. He continued to be in a better mood these days, which helped to keep things calm while I figured out the whole JJ business.

A week after I received the earrings, JJ sent a text:

> I'm back. Can you meet me at Cariblanco tomorrow for lunch at noon?

Now would be an excellent time to say no.

> Yes, at noon.

A new wave of panic hit. I knew I was playing with fire.

It was a warm June day. My white linen dress with fringes, baroque pearls, and gold flats looked fresh and pure.

"Elise, listen. Don't call the office. You're my excuse. I just need some time to myself, and told the office I was going to your home to talk." I knew I could trust her.

"No problem. Is everything alright?" Elise asked.

"Yes, all's well." What a lie.

"Call me if you need anything."

With the alibi in motion, the ride to Cariblanco was a blur, just like the last time. When I parked, I checked the rearview mirror to make sure my lipstick and hair were flawless. I boldly headed into his office, where I found him giving Cecilia a huge hug. What, he missed Cariblanco's manager too? Was I *jealous*? I had no right to be. He wasn't mine. He could hug whoever he damn pleased. Seeing me out of the corner of his eye, he released Cecilia, and swaggered over to me. Our eyes locked, and it was my turn for a hug. His delicious lemony scent filled my nostrils, Cecilia all but forgotten.

Once seated in the dining room, JJ described the dinner at the embassy.

"I delivered a speech about US-Argentina relations. Claudia helped prepare it."

I was so up close and personal with him, that sometimes I forgot what a man of international consequence he was. The breadth, scope, and scale of all things JJ was staggering. "How was Augusto?" I politely inquired about his son.

"Alright." Augusto worked in JJ's business, but from what I gathered, had none of his drive or passion; something that I sensed caused low-grade stress for JJ. Nadia, his daughter, was married to a successful lawyer in DC who pulled his own weight. Not that it made any difference from a financial perspective, given who her parents were. From what JJ told me, Nadia was like her mother; a player on the Washington social charity circuit.

"Augusto's a good kid," JJ said, somewhat defensively.

"My daughter-in-law Sofia, though. You should see her. Such a princess. But she's good to the three grandkids, and that's all I care about. Shopping, and accumulating jewelry is her thing. That make-up she wears. She sleeps in it. Sofia and her friends are always beautifying themselves." He looked at me. "Well, you're not like that. And you're Jewish." His stereotypical comment aimed at Jewish American Princesses normally would have elicited a negative reaction. In this context, the fact that I wasn't like Sophia was taken as a compliment.

"My ancestors emigrated generations back. From England." That would partially explain how the Mendozas passed the snooty Sealine admission standards.

"Well, my ancestors happen to be a little father east. Belarus and Galitcia. So we're all from somewhere else," I said, in an attempt to knock his English heritage down a peg.

"You're always challenging me," he said with a seductive smile.

After lunch we strolled toward the stables.

"Here's Conquistador. He's back from training. Isn't he magnificent?" he said. We marveled at his beloved horse as a groom bathed him.

"Conquistador. Of course," I said under my breath.

"Come, let me show you his house." JJ led me into a room loaded with hay, and closed the door. There were two small windows, which allowed the light to pass through, but otherwise it was dark. The air was filled with a slightly sweet odor. He grabbed me in his arms and hugged me tight, his body pressed up against mine. It felt amazing to be enveloped in his warm, strong arms. He let go slightly enough to give me a dark stare. He pulled me closer again, and kissed me. Not a soft, quick velvet kiss on the lips, but a full-blown, sexy French kiss. Part of me wanted to return the kiss; the other part warned against it. Instead of surrendering to the moment, my back stiffened.

"Relax, Estrella," he said in a soft, calming tone, still holding me close. I was speechless, unable to reply, all the while feeling embarrassed about my sub-par kissing performance. I wish I could explain to him that I really was a good kisser, but couldn't show my stuff under the circumstances.

"I love you. I missed you so much," he said. Blindsided by his words, the blood drained from my body. The kiss was a scene that I'd willingly walked into, but his words were unexpected.

"Do you love me?" he asked. He put his hands on my hips, and stared into my eyes. I averted my gaze and didn't answer.

"Please tell me you love me," he repeated.

At that moment his phone rang, piercing the silence. Saved by the bell. I eyed the exit while he rattled off to Claudia in Spanish, and hung up.

"No worries, I'm used to it." *Was I ever.*

"Now, where were we?"

I stared at him in disbelief. *He forgot that he just told me he loved me?*

"I'm kidding, Estrella. You can't deny there's love between us. I love you and want you." He moved closer, but I stepped back.

"Why do you think I came here today? I can't resist you. But it's different for me than you," I said.

"How so?"

"Of course I enjoy this time with you, but it just doesn't feel right." *I have a moral code; or thought I had one.* "Please, I need fresh air."

He backed away, and to my relief he opened the barn door. The bright sun beamed down on us, our eyes squinting to adjust. I felt like I could breathe again. We started to walk around the stable.

"Does Claudia ever sleep? Do you ever sleep?" I asked. Claudia must be pretty special to gain his total trust. She catered to his every business whim, twenty-four seven. Unless . . . I wondered. Was I jealous of her, too, in *that* way? Cat, Cecilia, Claudia. The C word . . . Cruel tricks. That's what my mind was playing.

Breaking my temporary trance, he replied, "No. She doesn't miss anything. Ever. Neither do I." His mouth curled into a half-smile, acknowledging the arrogance of what he'd said; it added to his sexiness. JJ walked me back to my car, and kissed me goodbye on my cheek. It was a friendly kiss. Everything was back to normal, even though nothing felt normal. I thought about Webster and Chandler, and how easy it seemed for them to shimmy in and out of their marriages, enjoying other relationships. It seemed just as easy for JJ, too.

Lumping all these powerful men together, as if they all had the same feelings, I wondered if they were so sure of themselves that it didn't bother them that they were cheating on their wives. Or was it as simple as the patriarchal order entitling wealthy alpha males to enjoy their hearts' desires? But . . . this was different. *He said he loved me!* Based on his words, I wouldn't be just a proverbial roll in the hay.

Flattered, confused and overwhelmed, I doubted there

was a woman on earth who could resist JJ. I had willingly pursued the relationship, but now that there was a physical element, along with his professed feelings of love, it had "catastrophe" written all over it. Like a bomb—with the potential to explode and ignite cascading consequences. Yet the thrill, the adrenaline boost made it utterly enticing. Heady stuff to be desired by a high-octane, high-caliber, high-everything guy who made me feel like the most special woman on earth, and who told me he loved me with sincerity.

But . . . what if Mark knew? What if Cat found out? It would surely hurt my ability to fundraise in her prestigious social circles, let alone destroy my marriage.

What started out as a small adventure had evolved into an exciting but benign flirtation, but now it had progressed into a dangerous game. One in which I was a ready, willing and able participant. Wearing the earrings from the House of Harry proved my complicity. By the time the car made it back to the Addison Center parking lot, I was an unstable mess. But spilling my guts to anyone meant I'd open myself up to judgment and harsh criticism.

I didn't want to talk to Nina right now, and Valerie was her partner, which made everything feel too close to home. I thought Elise might understand. Thank God, she answered her phone.

"I knew something was wrong, honey. You said you needed time alone. That didn't sound like you." Parked in the Addison Center parking lot, I started sobbing into the phone and told her everything.

"Julia. I understand."

"You do? If you're going to tell me that you had a boyfriend and David had no idea, all while he may have been having a fling with that pretty secretary of his, I don't want to hear about it. It'll just make everything worse. It's good for Chrissy, too. And Maya, with Artie. Everyone in Royal Coconut Beach." What the hell was I saying? Did I just accuse Elise of having an affair? I was spinning out of control.

"Calm down, take a deep breath," she said. My sobbing slowed just long enough to listen to her. "Look, I'm going to share something with you. First, I'm sorry to disappoint you, but I didn't have an affair. Becca, my sister did, though. She was with a married man for six years. I lived through the whole ordeal with her. Believe me, it tormented her, until finally she ended it. Cold turkey, too. That was the most torturous part."

"Was this when Becca was single?" I said in between sobs.

"Yes, she was. It puts a different spin on things, but still. Stuff like this goes on all the time. Think about our Lunch Club, and our conversations. We've heard so many stories. I'm only telling you about Becca because I don't want you to think you're alone; it's not easy. Your feelings are totally normal." My sobbing subsided as I listened. "To have captured the heart of such a charismatic man is a beautiful thing, in spite of it all. Just like Becca. I'm not saying you should act on it. You know how I feel about Mark; he's rare. He loves and adores you."

"He does?"

"You have to ask? Marriage isn't perfect, you know that. From what I know, yours is a special one, and he's a keeper."

Deep down, I knew that was true. I didn't want to lose him, either.

"Look, you need to look closer at what you do have,

and then figure out what you want. Do what's right for you. That's what matters. It's your decision, but make sure you're being sensible. Either way, you should be flattered. Just don't do anything rash. Promise me you'll stay calm, and do not tell any of this to Mark."

"Not a word. I think I'll take a walk. I have sneakers in my trunk."

"Good idea," Elise said. "Try to be a little kind to yourself. I'm in Penny's house right now, by the way, figuring out the mess. There are accessories all over the place."

"Good luck. Thank you again. Love you."

"Love you too. Hang in there, and call me later if you need me."

Walking the garage levels while trying to focus on my breath calmed my nerves. No question, JJ outranked me in terms of privilege, power, wealth and ancestry. I felt small in comparison, and totally vulnerable. Hearing about Becca's story normalized things a little. Caught up in my emotions, I wasn't consciously aware that I actually had a choice until now. Elise pointing this out was a great consolation. It was very empowering. My older, wise friend, who was ahead of her time, was more of a modern woman than I had ever imagined.

The sixth floor of the Addison Center garage was the only one that was not enclosed by another level. The fresh air, despite the humidity, would help me clear my foggy head. There were no cars, except at the very end, where there was a white Mercedes coupe. I assumed someone must have parked there overnight, tucked away so the security detail wouldn't care.

Elise was right. How wonderful and thrilling to have

the attentions of a passionate man like JJ. And perhaps that should be enough? An exciting memory to hold onto. Appreciating and enjoying this realization got moved to the asset column. The debit side was a whole other deal. My nerves were shot, and I couldn't shake the utter confusion. Such a mixed bag of emotions. *You'll be fine,* I reassured myself. Still in my own head, I wasn't paying much attention as I turned the bend where the car was parked. But what I saw stopped me in my tracks.

Chapter 47

FAIR GAME

IT WAS STRAIGHT OUT of the scene in the Wizard of Oz when Dorothy's house was dropped on the Wicked Witch. Just two legs were sticking out. But instead of wearing ruby slippers, the person was wearing stilettos. As I turned the corner, the whole body became visible. I gasped and put my hand over my mouth. My scream wouldn't come out. She was lying in a pool of blood, a gun next to her head and small dot under her chin. Maya's eyes were wide open, as if staring at the sun.

I sprinted in the other direction to the door, down the stairs, some triple at a time while I clutched the railing. Miraculously I reached the security desk without falling. I squeaked out, "Someone's dead. Someone's *dead!*" My legs gave way while I watched the man call for help.

Screeching sirens from police and fire engines descended on the Addison Center within minutes. I sat on the floor, and leaned against the wall.

"Are you okay, Mrs. Wild?" the security officer asked.

"I'm not sure. I need to just sit," I mumbled. My outstretched legs were trembling, and I urged myself to focus on my breath and nothing else. The security officer brought me some water, and I drank it slowly. I kept taking deep breaths, and he checked on me a few times. An hour had gone by when he bent down and told me I was needed in Paul's office. He helped me to my feet, and made sure I was steady before he escorted me there.

Several people were in Paul's office. "First, are you alright?" Paul asked when he saw me.

"I think so," I whispered. There was a carafe of coffee and mugs on the table. Paul pointed to it, and I helped myself to a cup, trying to ignore my shaking hand.

He introduced me to Detective Sara Jenkins, who I learned had found a suicide note in Maya's car. Since it happened at the Addison Center, it was under the jurisdiction of the local police department. FBI agent John English joined the meeting a few minutes later, since Artie was still under investigation for a federal crime, and Maya worked for Artie. Detective Jenkins read the note out loud:

> I never intended things to get so out of hand.
> I crossed the line and do not want to face the
> consequences. I don't want to go to prison. I'm
> taking my own life. No one had anything to do
> with this decision. Please forgive me everyone.
>
> Maya

All I could think of was Maya's beautiful face staring at the blue sky. Convinced that my deposition may have played a small role in her demise, I felt guilty. No question, the smart, techno-savvy Maya was capable of implementing a cyber-scheme drummed up by Artie. A collaboration of two twisted souls. The big difference was that the rich and powerful Artie had the resources and connections to cover up his guilt, and *only* his. He could have forced Maya's hand, made her write the note and take her own life. Equally heinous, Artie could have hired someone to murder Maya and make it look like a suicide. Anything seemed possible when it came to Artie Brass.

Agent English and Detective Jenkins's friendly banter was grating on my already shot nerves. Unlike crime television, the tension that typically existed between the feds and the locals fighting over jurisdiction was nonexistent.

"Julia. How long did you know Artie for?" Detective Jenkins asked.

"He and his wife, Penny, have been involved with the Addison Center before I began. I've only known them . . . let's see, not even a year," I said.

"They are very generous financially, but also encourage others to give," Paul added. *Whose side was he on?*

"That's true," I jumped in. "But there was trouble in paradise between Artie and Penny. Not to undermine you, I know you're doing your homework," I said making eye contact with both law policemen. "They were going to get divorced, but. . . ." I swallowed. "They decided to work things out. Too much at stake. Money, that is." They nodded, and I continued.

"Anyway, Maya was Artie's right arm. She was one sharp cookie. Then I found out that she was actually working on the side for Artie while still here at Addison." I shot Paul a look; his face had a blank expression. "I'm sorry. I realize I'm talking about Maya, and you asked us about Artie. Hard to talk about one without the other."

"Go on, please," Detective Jenkins said, her voice monotone.

"Like I said, as smart as Artie was, so was Maya. She was technologically brilliant, but Artie was a willing participant. Penny used to complain that Maya would call at the wee hours to discuss business. 'Can't live with her, can't live without her'. That's exactly what Penny once told me. Given their super-close relationship, it's almost impossible not to believe that Artie wasn't knee-deep in cyber-land with Maya."

The adrenaline—combined with the extra cup of coffee I'd had no business chugging, given my mental state—had me charging full speed ahead. But it was all based on sheer intuition, my brain exploding with accusations and conclusions.

I looked at Paul for affirmation, but he remained silent, his expression vacant. It drove me nuts. I couldn't imagine what he must be thinking of me now. I was sure I'd be fired after this. Unwilling to rein myself in, I said, "By the way, have you looked into Knights of the Golden Circle? Dollars to donuts, all those titans profited from these inside trading tips. That's how those guys operate."

"Yes, we know about the Knights," Agent English said, very matter-of-factly.

"And Maya was fair game," I continued. "In spite of her skills, she couldn't possibly hold a candle against these guys." At some level, as much as I loathed Maya, my comments were intended to even the score for my deposition that attacked her credibility. Hopefully my words would give the law enforcement team something more to chew on. The last thing I wanted was to have played a small part in her death.

"Paul tells us that you and Maya didn't get along. Is that true?" Detective Jenkins asked. I frowned at Paul. I couldn't believe he'd tell them that!

"Yes. Wait a sec . . . you don't think I had something to do with . . . ?" The blood must have drained from my face.

"We want to get to the bottom of it, Ms. Wild, that's all," the detective said. She rose, and I watched her deliberately move around Paul's office. Silence prevailed for perhaps fifteen seconds.

"Okay. The truth is, Maya was out to get me," I finally said. "She pulled all kinds of shenanigans to make me look bad, and I complained about this to my friend Nina. Artie's lawyer, Girard, is also Nina's boyfriend. Nina took the liberty of telling Girard what I shared with her about Maya. That's why Girard asked me to provide an affidavit. I haven't changed my mind about Maya's character one bit. But this doesn't mean that she couldn't have been a victim of Artie's machinations."

Agent Jenkins was taking notes. "Anything else, Mrs. Wild?"

"Yes, there is. You should know that Paul told me that donor checks have gone missing, and that there are other 'big things' as well. I'm not sure what he meant, but it's worth looking into." I had nothing to lose at this point, and was annoyed with him for not saying anything. "I'm sure Maya was involved. She kept blank Addison checks in her drawer."

Agent English and Detective Jenkins exchanged know-ing looks. "We'll be in touch if we need anything else. You're excused," Agent English said. I left, utterly relieved to have been dismissed.

I sat at my desk and cradled my head between my hands. I felt scared and sick. I was already an emotional mess *be-fore* I even discovered Maya's body. The gravitas of such an awful situation made me feel much worse.

Poppy barged in, breaking my train of thought.

"I just heard the news. Is it true?" Her eyes widened.

"It is, I'm sorry to say."

She exhaled. "I hoped it was a rumor. I mean, Maya was . . . well, *you* know." She shook her head slightly. "She had problems, but . . . to take her own life?"

There was a long silence. I already said too much in Paul's office.

"Shouldn't you go home? You've been through so much," she said.

"Nah, I'm better off here." The last thing I wanted to do was sit in my house alone.

THE HEADLINE in the *Society Script* the next day read, "Too Smart for her Own Good."

Maya Raffa sadly took her own life. She worked for the Addison Center. She was also associated with Top Brass Investments, owned by local philanthropist and capital venture guru Artie Brass. Mr. Brass' firm is being investigated for fraud, but all fingers point to Maya, his right arm.

Reading the article made me shudder. *What if Artie really did have Maya murdered and made it look like a suicide?*

Later that day, I feverishly pulled together notes for a development committee meeting. Andy felt we should meet over the summer, for anyone on his committee who was in town. I could barely concentrate. JJ would be in attendance, and my conflicting thoughts were spinning furiously. I wanted him, but couldn't have him. Unless I wanted to be his Other Woman. That was the reality that I finally woke up to. So far, I only had the earrings. Ones that I couldn't wear around my husband. Shame on me for disrespecting myself and my marriage.

My mind jumped to Cat, again thinking what she might do if she found out. I was sure she'd protect her family and status like a momma bear. She had done that once already, according to Savannah. No way would she want to get rid of JJ at this point. Or share. In all likelihood, Cat kept a watchful eye on JJ.

When did I become such fair game? Was it in between Mark's ranting and raving about being on austerity, while his eyes lit up every time Olivia called? Or the silence in the house, when both Mark and I turned into workaholics? It could be I really was in la-la land, expecting that things should be one big incredible fantasy.

How convenient, because in galloped a billionaire knight in shining armor on a horse named Conquistador, to whisk me away. He would take care of me, tell me every day I was his beautiful Estrella, and that he was madly in love with me. He'd validate my every word, and we could live happily ever after. Every woman's fantasy come true. Except at the end of the day, the splendid fairy tale couldn't possibly turn into reality.

———

THE NEXT DAY, Andy began the meeting with a moment of silence for Maya. He then moved rapidly through the agenda. I needed to pay attention, despite getting little sleep. We were close to reaching our fundraising goal, and everyone applauded. A beautiful cake with dollar signs that Poppy had picked up at the bakery was on the table.

When the meeting ended, and the cake was eaten, JJ followed me to my office. I closed the door behind me. Without sitting, he said, "I don't want to lose you."

I needed to stay the course. "Lose me? There you are, jetting all over the globe, going to galas, dining at your million and one clubs with Cat, and your friends, and . . . that's who you are. I'm not blaming you; it's what you do. You and Cat, that is. Three cheers. She's yours; your hers. And that's your wonderful life."

"It's not so wonderful." His eyebrows gathered in.

His comment surprised me, but I wouldn't lose my momentum. "It doesn't mean I care for you any less. I just don't want to be the Other Woman, the one you see when you can. And when I can. I'm *married*, for God's sake."

"You won't be the Other Woman. You aren't," JJ said.

"Really? Then what am I to you?" I was glad I pushed him on this, although he didn't answer. "What really gets me is that you take up all the room in my head, and I'm left in a tizzy. How can you so easily compartmentalize? I can't, I just can't. . . ." I started to cry, thankful that my back was turned away from the door. Having an office that was like a fishbowl was not a plus. "Why do you love me anyway?" I managed to whisper.

"I told you. I can't get you out of my mind. You're so pretty,

Estrella. Why won't you let me love you? Come here." He touched my shoulder, so I turned to him. Embracing was off-limits, since we were in the open. "You're so complicated."

"So are you."

JJ was experienced and masterful at this seduction game. I needed to stand my ground, prepared for an ambush. This was a man used to getting his way.

Quickly I ran through the scenario of leading him into the private wardrobe room backstage, to which I had a set of keys, where we'd kiss passionately; it would turn into our making love. Then what? I'd go home, back to my real life, and possibly have sex with Mark tonight? And JJ would merrily go back to his home on Royal Ocean Way, to Cat and the frigid Ice Palace. Was that how these things worked?

I had no idea how to do this: be with him, and be married. How on earth was he able to? Was it as easy as it seemed for him, or was he struggling with it as well?

I managed to compose myself and asked, "Why have you stayed married all these years?"

He cleared his throat. "Time passed, I built an empire, and then there was our family to consider. Grandkids came along," he said, his voice trailing off.

As oh-so-delicious as the idea of the wardrobe room was, I refused to have my body betray me. I opened the door and walked him outside to the valet. JJ looked directly into my eyes and kissed me on the cheek.

"I'm leaving tomorrow," he said, back to his usual self-assured tone. "Off to London. I'll be in touch. You are a strong woman, Julia. Stay strong, stay focused." This time, I vowed to use his words as fuel to not cave in to him.

Chapter 48

OF SOUND MIND

As expected, Piper and Paige contested Dori's will on the grounds of undue influence. For the second time that year, I was deposed. I told Mark about it that night at dinner. He had texted me earlier and asked if I wanted to grab a bite at The Upper Crust Café after work; a pleasant surprise. The last time I was there was when I spied on him and Olivia.

"How long did I know Dori, how often did I see her, what did we do when we were together, did I see her when she was ill—those were some of the questions I answered. Under oath," I told Mark.

"Sounds easy enough," Mark said. "All you had to do was state facts."

"Well, yeah. Except they tried to cast it as if Dori and

I were best friends. We weren't *that* close. I looked up to her and admired her. Fiercely determined, so sure of herself."

"So the good part was that on cross-examination, you got to tell the truth," Mark said. "You clarified that Dori never discussed her gift to the Addison Center."

"Yes. Here's the thing, though. I was the one who called her; I was the one who visited her in the rehab place. Because I wanted to—not to get a donation, but because I cared about Dori. Where were Paige and Piper, other than missing in action? They only came to the Wilkinson reception for appearance's sake. Like showing up was proof they cared. It's fair that they got nothing."

"Ah, finally something seems fair to you," he said, with gentle humor.

"Ha. Anyway, Ira, the attorney, was terrific. You remember I told you about him?"

"Yes, Jools," he said. It was refreshing to hear him call me that. I summarized Ira's defense.

"What a story," Mark said.

"Just another day at Addison. 'Other duties as assigned.' That should be my job description."

Mark gave a wide grin.

CHARGING FORWARD, I focused on my job. Poppy and I were discussing sponsors for the upcoming season, when Paul knocked furiously on my door, entering at the same time, waving papers. I held my breath.

"A verdict was reached in the Wilkinson estate case," he said. Swallowing hard, I braced myself. Although it would be a real challenge for counsel to successfully convince the court to set aside Dori's will on the basis of undue influence, there was always doubt. Never mind that calling a tough old bird like Dori on her mental capacity bordered on a frivolous action. But anything was fair game in the legal system.

"The court declared the will strictly legitimate and legal," Paul continued. "There was no evidence of coercion, no evidence of undue influence. We're home free."

"Best news I've heard all day," I said.

"Congratulations!" Poppy said. "We'll finish up later."

"The $100 million that Dori left to us is to be used for when we build a new building," Paul said. "Now that it's been determined that Dori was of sound mind, we can hit the ground running with the capital project. She'd like it to bear her name. You did good, Julia, handling this the way you did."

"Thank you, Paul. Dori was special." I placed my hand on my heart.

He looked at the vacant chair that faced my desk. "May I?" he asked.

"Of course, please have a seat." I hoped whatever he was about to say wouldn't ruin my excitement over the verdict.

"Okay, I'll lay it all out for you. Remember I told you that Mrs. McIntosh's check was stolen, and that other 'big things' had happened?"

"Yes. I've been worried sick. You told me it fell under my department."

"I had to position it that way. I never doubted your integrity, but the authorities thought that under pressure you might inadvertently disclose something that might be helpful."

Nerves humming, I needed to listen carefully to Paul to fully grasp what he was saying.

"You led us to Maya by sharing your suspicions, which

we acted on. Our sleuthing proved that Maya embezzled funds. She figured out a way to gain on-line access to our accounts and move donor checks into an account she opened in a deceased donor's name, in an offshore account. We conveniently allowed her to steal blank Addison Center checks and a stamp signature. She took our bait."

My whole body relaxed, but I remained poised. "I can't tell you what a huge relief this all is!" I said, hoping my heart would eventually stop racing. Despite the horror of Maya's death, I was grateful to know that I wouldn't be held accountable for any missing funds, or other illegal activity.

"Who's us and we?" I asked.

"Law enforcement, attorneys, forensic accountants. Andy McCormack because he's our board treasurer—we've all been collaborating. We've managed to keep it a secret, to avoid any damage to Addison's reputation. Agent Jenkins and Detective English were part of it too since federal laws were violated. By the way, they discovered that Maya even blackmailed Chrissy way back, so that no one would find out about her and Chandler. Of course, that relationship is public knowledge now."

I recalled the twenty-five thousand dollar check from Chandler to Maya way back.

"Interesting. This explains why you didn't respond when I spoke with the authorities. I assumed you might have thought I was nuts!"

Paul let out a loud belly laugh, and smiled. "On the contrary, you're completely sane."

"So what happened?" I asked.

"We gathered the evidence we needed, and were about to make an arrest. Then Maya committed suicide. There still isn't proof that Artie was involved in any foul play.

But there's never been such a dark moment in the history of Addison. It's terrible that it took this tragic incident to bring about change. Going forward, we'll be implementing stringent financial controls. In the long run, we'll be a much stronger organization, with the right checks and balances in place. And no criminal charges were filed, which meant Addison would have to sue to get the stolen money returned. That meant it could attract the press, and probably scare off donors. The last place they'd want to contribute to is an organization where money gets stolen. Choosing to litigate had the potential to bring us down."

"Obviously, you didn't go that route."

"Nope. Andy got a few of our board members to quietly refill our coffers. Our lawyers tell us we'll have to disclose this on our annual tax-exempt form, but no one should care. Anyway, I hope I didn't cause you too much worry. My apologies again."

"Apology accepted. I love it here. I admit I was very fearful for my job, let alone Addison. I'm so glad it's been favorably resolved." It took restraint not to jump and down, but as usual I maintained professionalism.

"This bodes well for Addison's future," Paul said, with a generous smile. "Our future. You're a real asset here, Julia. And with Dori's gift, we're in an amazing place."

"Thanks, Paul."

After he left I realized I'd never asked how much money was stolen. At the moment, it made no difference. It was amazing news all around: My career was on the rise, I had a newfound respect for my boss, and Dori was completely of sound mind. I wished I was, too.

Chapter 49

KISS AND TELL

IT WAS AFTER TEN in the evening, and I was in bed reading. Mark was already asleep when JJ texted me:

> Are you free for lunch tomorrow at
> Cariblanco?
>
> Sorry. I can't.

I didn't feel safe alone with him at the stable. It wasn't that I didn't trust him; I didn't trust myself.

> How about an early walk. 6:00?
>
> Sure.

Standing at the middle of the bridge, I took in the beautiful sky. The sun was slowly rising, pushing nighttime away. The illuminated clouds cast an ethereal glow. I wondered where JJ was; he was always there waiting. I looked towards the Royal Coconut Beach side, spotting him slowly jogging towards the bridge, and headed to meet him.

"Apologies," he said, in between breaths. "We had dinner at the club with a new member. Claire Dumond."

"Good morning to you, too."

"Good morning. How are you doing?"

"Doing fine." Not really.

"Claire started her own communications satellite business. She was a pioneer in the field. Once she took her company public, she made a fortune and left. She sits on its board now."

"Wait . . . are you talking about the former Ambassador to Australia?"

"Yes, that's her. She's also a serious art collector. She just loaned a portion of her collection to the National Gallery in London."

"I've been to that museum," I said, as if I needed to impress him. JJ had met his female counterpart. Sounded like they were separated at birth. My hands felt sweaty, and it had nothing to do with the morning heat.

"You really like Claire, don't you?"

He moved closer, and stopped walking. I stepped back and he gazed into my eyes. "I love you. We're one."

"I've told you, I can't handle this. It's just not how I'm built. You keep telling me that we're so much alike. But we're not . . . at least when it comes to matters of the heart."

He crossed his arms. "You're dumping me, I can tell. It's because I pushed too hard."

"No, I'm not." I hated that word "dumping." The last thing I wanted was to lose JJ, or "dump" him, which sounded harsh. If only he knew how much he meant to me. But telling him now would just make it worse.

"You are." His eyes looked downward.

"It's amazing how easy this is for you," I said, ignoring his comment.

"Easy? Who said it's easy?" he said, his voice raised. "I'm offended that you think that. I want to be with you."

Stay strong, stay focused. "This relationship—this thing between us—isn't possible for me. It doesn't work for me. It just *doesn't*," I firmly said, shaking my head. That line took every ounce of courage to say. My heart said one thing, but logic took over.

JJ didn't respond but we kept walking and went to the beach. We threw our sneakers in the sand and headed towards the water. The sand was hot, and we picked up the pace to get to the water. While the sun blazed, an unusually hard wind battered us with sand. He grabbed my hand and clenched it, as if to protect me from blowing away. I felt the familiar electricity between us; that hadn't diminished. But after a few precious seconds, I let go.

As we watched the waves lap our toes, a sense of sadness came over me. I hoped that I could stay strong. I wondered if I'd ever stop longing for him. We were both quiet for a few minutes, and I was glad when he changed the subject.

"I want WOW to be the best on-line wine distributer. If business doesn't pan out from the WOW franchises because of the internet, I'll shut them down. Build something else where all the stores are, and collect rent. Our property management division could absorb it."

"Does your brain constantly fire on all cylinders?"
I asked.

"You mean like yours?"

I smiled. I told him about Dori's case, and how it would
help Addison. We left the beach and as we continued down
a path, he pointed out a beautiful lawn with a large trellis.
On it was bougainvillea, with some other attractive climbing vines.

"This reminds me of Argentina. The vineyards," he
said, pointing at the greenery. He took my hand in his, but
I quickly let go.

Before I knew it, we were back at the middle of the
bridge. Like he'd done in the past, he gave me a quick kiss
on the forehead.

"Take care of yourself. Don't overdo it."

"Yes, sir," I said.

WORKING WITH POPPY to figure out events for next
year's season brought normalcy to my morning. We were up
to our eyeballs figuring out December, when Mark called.

"How was your run this morning? You were out earlier
than usual."

"Fine," I said, riddled with guilt.

"I'll be away next week, in New York, for meetings with
clients. Just wanted you to know my schedule. I miss you."
His remark took me off-guard. It was different from the familiar "I'll pick up the laundry, pay the taxes, what's for dinner" conversations.

"Same," I immediately said. "I'm leaving in a few minutes to have lunch with my friends."

"Enjoy."

I got stuck on a phone call, so by the time I arrived at the Waterfront Club, the Lunch Club gals were already there, sipping our signature drink.

"Oh good, we can get the party started," Nina said, after I sat in the empty chair. "Now that we're all together, I have an announcement to make." She struck her glass, capturing our attention. "Girard and I are . . . getting *married*." She beamed from ear to ear.

I let out a small scream. "When did this happen?"

"Just yesterday. I waited to tell you all in person."

"Oh my goodness!" Elise squealed. "To Nina and Girard." We clinked our glasses.

"Cheers to the one we all thought would never tie the knot," Valerie added.

"We'll be married in August at the courthouse, then off to Bora-Bora. We're planning a big celebration in the fall."

She held up her left hand to show us a stunning emerald-cut ring, and we discussed her plans.

"Enough about me," Nina finally said. "How's everything going, Julia? We haven't seen you in a while."

I planned on pushing my feelings for JJ further down, but in the company of my good friends, I felt differently.

"I'm not sure where to begin. It's just that . . . I met someone. He acts like he's crazy about me. He says he loves me. Nothing's really happened. It's more like . . . I don't know. An . . . umm entanglement? Attachment? I can't define it. It's a little romantic."

I looked at Elise. I was glad she didn't say anything, even though I'd recently told her about JJ.

"He believes I've dumped him. I just don't want to become his OW." Everyone was silent, and looked intently at me. "The Other Woman," I said. "I'm regaining my stability. It's been an emotional minefield. We're still in contact." I paused, and cleared my throat. "We took a walk on the beach this morning."

Nina looked at me and asked, "How much older is he?"

"How did you know he's older?" I asked.

"Duh."

"Um . . . about twenty years."

"Married, I assume?" Nina asked.

"Yes," I said.

"And rich. Of course."

I shot her a dirty look.

"If you don't have a seat at the table, you'll simply be on the dessert menu. Are you and Mark still like two ships passing in the night? What's going on with the two of you?" Nina was in her element, firing questions as if I was perched on the witness stand, although I wasn't sorry she pressed me.

"Nothing much. Things are better, actually."

"Shush, Nina," Elise said, glaring at her. "Therein lies your problem, Julia. You said it. Nothing's going on at home. These things happen. Trust me on this. It's easier to fall out of love, than it is to stay in love for the long haul. It requires work and effort."

"You make it sound awful, Elise. It shouldn't be a test of endurance," Nina answered.

"Really? It's not? Sorry. I didn't get that memo," Elise said. "Now that you're getting married, Nina, you need to pay attention. Look around here," she said whooshing her arms as if to cover the dining room. "Tell me whose life is perfect? Have you ever seen so many sour pusses on overly Botoxed faces? Don't let money fool you, either. You think everyone's life is wonderful? Money just complicates things even more. Besides, the perfect man is just an illusion."

"She's right," Valerie said. "All I can say is work on yourself, and your marriage."

"How? What do you mean? I still feel . . . lost. All we've done is kiss, yet. . . ." I swallowed. "Yet, I can't let go of my feelings. Just when I think I can, I'm drawn back in. The irony is that since things are better at home, it's more confusing. At least when things were bad, I had an excuse for my behavior!" I started to cry and wiped my face with my napkin.

"It's okay, honey," Elise said, rubbing my shoulder.

"I'm sorry," I said, regaining my composure quickly. "It feels good to talk about it."

"It's plain and simple: you were looking for something that's missing," Valerie said. "You think it *just happened.* Sorry, kiddo. It doesn't work that way. See this as a signpost. Maybe you're feeling lonely. After all, Mark does travel a fair amount, and has an extraordinary amount of pressure from big firm practice. He's constantly being pulled by work."

"I agree with Val," Nina said. "You've also thrown yourself into your work like nobody's business."

I sniffled. "C'mon, ladies, each one of you works like crazy. Don't your careers often serve as an escape?"

"Of course," Valerie responded. "And the independence it affords makes it worth it. On top of all that, let's face it: money *is* power. But that doesn't mean you get the luxury of ignoring the other parts of your life."

I nodded. "The going got tough, and what did I do? Run the other way."

"Don't be so hard on yourself," Valerie said. "Just don't expect this guy to fill the empty space you may feel," she said. "Unless that's what you want, and I think I know your answer. If you're looking for love, or to feel valued—like most women, whether they admit it or not—you can find that. Start at home. I'm not casting judgment, but you need to seriously think this through. Is it really right for *you?*"

"You certainly do. I mean, he's much older, and married. Not to mention, extremely wealthy," Nina said.

"You have no idea," I answered.

"What's he offering *you?*" Nina said, glaring at me. "His love? Oh, please. Give me a break."

"Well, yes, as a matter of fact."

"Sure, in dribs and drabs. Good luck with that. I'm not questioning the sincerity of his feelings. But you deserve a heck of a lot better. You're worth *so* much more than just that. You really want someone else's belongings?"

Nina's question hit home.

"Don't tell me: this guy offered to take you to Paris," Nina continued.

"South America, actually." I realized I shouldn't have told them, but it was too late. It made me paranoid that this might tip them off as to who he was.

"I hate to say it, but this can't be good, even if you believe it would work for you," Valerie chimed in. "That is, if he'd even consider changing his life. Most likely he's resigned to what he has. Even if he did, it usually wears men down at that age, anyway. The wife takes them to the cleaners, ties it up in litigation."

"I realize all this. But it doesn't diminish my feelings," I said.

"Well what about you and Mark? You crave stability," Nina said. "Your head's in the sand. Mark's head is up his ass, too or you wouldn't be feeling this way."

"Mark could've found support with Olivia." I twirled a lock of my hair.

"For now, focus on the two of you, and think about this: what you're looking for might be in your own backyard," Elise said. "Go ahead and *try* to have an affair. *With your husband!*"

We all laughed. The thought excited me.

"You're in your marriage completely by choice," Valerie said. "Not because of your history, family, or money and image, for that matter. Besides, you could easily support yourself if you wanted to. You're a modern woman."

"You're all so special to me, and you've given me a lot to think about. I feel much better. Anyway, today should be about Nina." I raised my glass, while we all did a robust clink-clink. "Here's to a happy life together," I said.

"Oh, it's not always happy. But it can be wonderful, and we wish you all the best," Elise added.

Lunch ended sooner than I wanted. The Lunch Club ladies' advice resonated. The timing was right, too. I was in a much better place than a month ago, and receptive to their suggestions. I was optimistic that Mark and I could put our marriage back on solid footing; perhaps even have a second honeymoon.

But first I needed to find out was going on with Olivia. I couldn't confront Mark; it always backfired. I had an idea.

Chapter 50

MATTERS OF THE HEART

I PRESSED THE GAS PEDAL, my body tense, as I headed to Olivia's office to confront her. Nerves humming, I rehearsed how I'd approach her. *Don't point blame. Stay calm. Deal with facts, ask what happened. Observe her reactions.* I parked in the building's lot and took a deep breath. *You can do this.*

"Good afternoon, Mrs. Wild," the receptionist said. "Mark left for New York this morning." What, she didn't think I knew my husband was traveling?

"Yes. But I have something for Olivia Woods. May I see her?"

"Please, have a seat." She pointed to the sitting area. I grabbed a magazine and pretended to read. A few minutes later, an assistant came out.

"Olivia's tied up," she said.

"I'll wait. Mark asked me to explain this to her." I held up my file, thankful I was prepared.

She disappeared, returning a few minutes later. "Follow me," she motioned with her hand.

She led me down a long corridor to Olivia's office. As we passed Mark's office, I thought about how angry he'd be if he knew I was there.

Olivia was seated behind her desk.

The assistant left, closing the door behind her. I felt trapped but there was no turning back. Olivia extended a hand to me. Her dark large eyes avoided my gaze, her fingers cold. We were about the same height. A neat ponytail held her silky black hair in place, and she had a heart-shaped face and smooth skin. I knew she possessed youth, beauty, and intelligence, and seeing her up close, I felt intimidated. But I'd never let her know.

Stay cool. "It's nice to meet you in person," I said, glancing at the wall behind her. "Wow, Harvard Law School. Editor-in-Chief of its Law Review. Now I see why you've been such a big help. To Mark, that is."

She gave a blank stare. "Thanks. He's smart, and a great lawyer."

No kidding. "May I?" I asked, looking at the empty chair.

"Please," she said, as we both sat.

"So how do you like working here?" I casually brushed the edge of her desk with my fingers.

"It's been good. It'll help with my career."

I bet. "I'm sure Mark will provide a glowing reference one day." I raised my eyebrows.

She nodded, but with a tight expression. "Excuse me, you had something for me?"

Seeing a hot pink heart-shaped post-it pad on her desk I recalled the same ones on Mark's papers.

"Cute hearts," I said, with a fake smile.

She looked at me warily, with narrowed eyes. "Why are you here?"

Good. I've unnerved her. "I wanted to meet you in person."

"Why?"

"To find out what's up with you and *my* husband."

She quickly looked away. "Why don't you ask him?"

"Because I asked you." There was an uncomfortable silence. Determined to wait it out, I fiddled with my wedding band.

"Nothing. But everything. *I'm really sorry.*" Her voice was soft and shaky.

"Go on, please."

"I've been in love with him. But he's not in love with me. He loves you very much." Her eyes welled up, and she grabbed a tissue and dabbed them.

"So what happened between you?"

"We're close," she said.

"Define 'close'." I leaned in.

She bit her lower lip and closed her eyes. "I felt alive, like a fire was lit under me. He made me believe in myself, that I'd be the best lawyer. My career means everything. That's why I fell for him. He's exceptional, and well. . . ." She sniffled.

"Yes?" I sat forward in my seat.

"But he's so in love with you, it doesn't matter. We didn't have an affair, if that's what you think. I hope you know you're so lucky. Maybe, one day, I'll meet someone like him who will love me back."

Relief sank into my bones. "I hope you find what you're looking for. But leave Mark alone."

I got in my car and exhaled deeply, releasing all my pent-up angst. My instincts told me she told the truth. Ironically, I felt empathy at how she ached to be with someone she knew she couldn't have.

I left Mark a message:

I miss you already and love you very much.

MARK AND I had dinner reservations that Saturday at La Petite Soleil, a new hot spot. I wore a black wrap dress with ruffles around its low neckline, knowing it was sexy. I looked in the full-length mirror and swapped the ballet flats for black heels. Mark was in the bathroom combing his hair, so I stood behind him, and hugged his waist. He was wearing his favorite slim-fitting black and white houndstooth blazer, and a white collared shirt.

"I'm looking forward to our date tonight," I said.

"Me too, Jools. Shall we?"

We ordered wine as soon as we got to the restaurant.

"I'd like to propose a toast," I said, raising my glass. "I want you to know how thankful I am that you're my husband. I appreciate you from the bottom of my heart."

I placed a hand on my heart. He looked at me, nodding, but remained silent, so I continued.

"I know you aren't big on matters of the heart, but that doesn't mean you don't love me. It's your actions that speak volumes, not what you say. It's one of the things that drew me to you in the first place. And your charming, devilish ways."

We exchanged a knowing glance. "You're right," he said. "I know we get lost in our everyday lives, especially work. Both of us. Sometimes we're all talked out, and just too tired to make the effort. I'm guilty of that." His smile went into his eyes.

"I am too," I admitted. "I lose sight of the simple things you do for me. Like going shopping with me to pick out clothes. Not to mention the coffee by my bed table. I guess these actions are one of the things that make our lives work and mean so much; they show how much you care, and that you support me." I paused for a moment. "Well? Aren't you going to say *anything?*"

He leaned in. "I do love you. Being there day in and day out, when things are good, and when things are bad. We walk hand in hand in life. I'm grateful that I get to do it with you."

Wow, did he just say that? That's a first.

"I love you too." I reached out my hand and he grabbed it, gripping it tightly. I felt the powerful energy between us, something that had been missing for too long.

"I love you more than you know," he said. Our eyes locked for a few seconds. That special in-love vibe was there. I took a big inhale. Behind those words was the man who stood by them. I wouldn't push for more of anything; I didn't need to. This was our reality, and it was good. No, it was great. And I chose to be there. Not because of money, a marriage contract, or status. In my heart, I knew I wanted to be Mark's leading lady—more than anything else.

"Well, aren't you profound," I said.

"I can be, occasionally." We both laughed at the same time.

I thought of JJ, and how much I thought he understood

me. But this was only in tiny sound bites, and in the best possible light. We didn't share problems or issues. Nor did I come home exhausted, only to ignore him—or be unnoticed by an overworked husband in a terrible funk. That didn't mean Mark didn't understand me any less.

We made passionate love that night, and fell asleep in each other's arms. When we woke up the next morning, we stayed in bed and talked. We went into the kitchen, and Mark fixed yogurt parfaits. He sat there in his robe reading the paper. I glanced at my phone. There was a text from JJ. I did my best to avoid looking surprised.

> Cat is away for the next few days. Are you free? How about dinner?

I froze. "What are you talking about?" I wrote back.

> So sorry, Estrella. That text was intended for my friend Claire. The former ambassador to Australia. We need to talk business. I'll explain. I hope you're taking it easy.

I was taking it easy and enjoying my husband, until now. "AND YOU THINK I'M COMPLICATED?" I wrote back.

JJ's accidental text to me was one more way to test my strength. A major bout of jealousy kicked in, right when things were going great for me. Thoughts aimlessly bounced from Cat, to Claudia, to Claire, making me feel envious and anxious. But this quickly turned into anger. Nina was right: I deserved better. I thought about all the other things my wise friends had said to me, too.

It also occurred to me that Claire was probably not the only woman that JJ was seeing behind Cat's back. For all I knew, he might have had several women on a string. I felt a little foolish for believing all of his lines, and for falling so hard for him. And as jealous as I had been about Cat, I felt compassion for her. Like other women whose lives I'd become privy to, it was pretty apparent that she put up with a lot to get a lot.

Mark was the person who made me feel loved. Not this other man. I had finally returned to my senses.

Chapter 51

AND JUSTICE
FOR ALL

I DIDN'T HEAR FROM JJ AGAIN. I checked my phone
from time to time, hoping my impulse to do this would
eventually fade. I missed talking to him, seeing him, and
how special he made me feel, but reminded myself that I'd
told him I couldn't handle the relationship.

It also occurred to me that whatever might be going
on between Claire and JJ had intensified. I was in a better
place, and I wouldn't reach out to him and unravel all the
good that I'd worked hard to regain.

One warm September evening, Mark and I were sitting
outside watching the sun go down from our patio. We chatted about our day, and then there was silence. It was tran-
quil, and our gardenia hedge was blooming for the second

time this year, giving off a delicious odor. We'd made a habit of relaxing outside with a glass of wine.

"Olivia's accepted an offer at another big firm in New York," Mark said, breaking the silence. "She'll be moving in a few weeks." He said it so casually that I wondered if he deliberately chose not to draw attention to it.

"I'm sorry for you. That's a big loss," I said, concealing my joy that she'd be leaving.

"Yes, she contributed a lot. I already have the recruiting team looking for a replacement.

That was the end of our discussion.

The next morning, Mark left for work, and I went to pay a bill on his laptop. The subject line "Thanks for Everything" wouldn't have phased me, except it was from Olivia. She'd sent it a few days ago. Taking a deep breath, I opened it.

Olivia told Mark what an incredible mentor he was, and how much she'd learned working side by side with him. She was grateful for the opportunity, and cited a few cases they'd worked on together. So far, it was professionally written.

But then she went on to tell him that it was too difficult to work with someone with whom she knew she couldn't be involved with. She said that she'd fallen hard for him, and deep down she'd believed he had feelings for her. She knew where he stood, and that when he told her what a special woman his wife was, she knew that it must be true. Olivia went on to say that she hoped one day she'd meet a wonderful man like Mark, who'd be able to return her love.

I sat there for a while. Mark had ultimately drawn a line in the sand when it came to me. Reading that he'd told Olivia how special I was, gave me goosebumps. I got dressed for work, forgetting all about paying bills.

Andy called me that morning.

"I wanted to make sure you heard the news," Andy said. "It's about Artie."

"What happened now?" I asked.

"He was just taken into custody this morning."

"Finally, they got him for Maya's death," I said.

"Way off, Sherlock. Actually, this has nothing to do with Maya, but everything to do with her. As you know, the Feds and the police had been sniffing around for quite a while, trying to find evidence about Maya's alleged suicide. Nothing turned up. Due to their investigation, they were led down a different path."

"Please tell!" I shouted into the phone.

"Turns out, Artie is a chief client of Margaux's Madams. You've heard of her?"

"Yup. It's a very high-end escort service that caters to the wealthy. What does this have to do with Maya?"

"Well, the FBI still suspected foul play when it came to Maya's death, so they trailed Artie. No evidence about her turned up, but they discovered that Artie was a client of Margaux's Madams. Rumor has it that Artie also crossed state lines on his private plane with Margaux's girls. And get this: some were underage. It was the perfect unintended sting."

"You mean they stumbled into it," I said.

"More like stepped in shit, pardon my French."

"So justice will be done at some level. Artie may not be charged with murder, but prostitution," I said.

"Yes. Not exactly the same consequences, but it's justice. Let's see how this unfolds.

"Anyone of our other peeps involved?"

"Time will tell. I wouldn't be surprised, though."

"Thanks for the scoop. Please keep me posted."

"Will do."

Artie's mugshot that was in the paper a week later wasn't much different from how he usually looked. The same big fat face, loosely hanging jowls, scowling face. Forget his appearance; what shone through was an unhappy, miserable person. All the money in the world couldn't change him.

Artie's troubles were the talk of Royal Coconut Beach, and everyone followed the legal drama that ensued. The Lunch Club crew and I got together for lunch and dissected it, each of us weighing in. We all felt sorry for Penny, but we also knew that she'd made her choice.

Chapter 52

EQUANIMITY

NINA AND GIRARD lucked out with the weather. The veranda of the Grand Oceanfront Hotel was gorgeous on that moonlit evening. The event was a Who's Who in the legal community, and also in Royal Coconut Beach society. When Mark and I arrived, he went to fetch us drinks at the bar. I spotted Nina, and made a beeline for her, waiting until the guests she was greeting moved on.

"You look absolutely stunning!" I said. "Glamorous would be an understatement. The gown is even more beautiful in person." We hugged.

"We didn't get a chance to speak, with all the party hoopla. I have so much to tell you. For one thing, Girard is joining our firm. It all happened quickly; Valerie and I had just signed the papers. The best part is that Kramer, Fields

& Bissett will represent the underage women that Artie and Margaux transported in his plane. We'll do it pro bono. Girard will recuse himself, since he represented Artie, once upon a time. But still, we're all excited about it."

I was surprised to learn about Girard; Nina's ideals must have rubbed off on him. "You, Valerie and Girard are a triple threat. I have a feeling justice will prevail. You're finally doing exactly what you want. I'm so happy for you. I love your Louboutins, by the way," I said, looking down at her shoes. "Good thing Girard is so tall."

"For sure. By the way, Penny is over there," Nina said. "I have to give her credit: she's out and about, instead of hiding under a rock. A lot of the other guests were invited for one professional reason or another. They aren't my real friends, but you are."

"I know that." We hugged before she flitted off. I no longer resented having to give the deposition; Nina was simply bound by professional duty. We were both lucky to be each other's true friend.

"Come with me and say hi to Penny," I said when Mark returned with our drinks. We edged our way over, stopping and saying hello to some other guests.

"Wonderful to see you both," Penny said.

"You look beautiful. Love your earrings," Mark said, knowing exactly the right compliment to give her. We made small talk before others interrupted us.

"Those are 'screw you Artie' earrings," I whispered in Mark's ear as we sauntered away. He nodded and smiled.

Skipping the first course, fearful that Bibb lettuce and citrus lobster would wind up in my teeth, I headed to the stage as the band leader announced me. I began my toast:

"Nina and Girard are very lucky to have met each other.

We all know what fine lawyers they are, always striving for justice and fairness. But when it comes to marriage, all bets about being fair are off. Unlike the goals of the law, placing each other's happiness before oneself sometimes takes precedence over fairness and winning. Besides, life isn't always fair."

I held my glass up, and continued speaking.

"This special quality is called equanimity—quite different from equality—and that is what true love is all about. At my bridal shower many years ago, someone told me that marriage is never 50/50. It's 100/100. Huh, I thought. Still high on the fairy tale of being 'in love,' those percentages meant nothing. I thought marriage was a day at the beach. But that's not reality. What happens when your spouse is not giving 100 percent? Maybe she or he is ticked off with something at work. It's these times when it's more important than ever to dismiss your own ego, along with your notion that you aren't being treated fairly. Hear that, lawyers? Most of you don't have egos, anyway, so it's okay."

I allowed the rumble of laughter to fade, and continued.

"Striving for fairness, and at the same time being happily married, are not compatible. Eventually, they will lock horns. On this note, I invite you all to raise your glasses. Nina and Girard, as you navigate your marriage, remember to remove your legal hats, and replace them with ones of equanimity. May this serve you well throughout your wonderful life together. To Nina and Girard!" The crowd sipped champagne, followed by applause.

As I went back to the table, Valerie and Elise approached. Out of earshot of Mark, Valerie sighed, "Well done. You've come a long way. I'm so proud of you."

Elise nodded.

"I have you ladies to thank. Nina, too," I said in a low voice. "Without all of you, I'm not sure if I would have found my way back to my old self. Come to think of it, not my old self, but my new self. So thank you. To the ladies of the Royal Coconut Beach Lunch Club!" We clinked glasses.

Mark tapped my shoulder, and I turned to face him. "Very profound speech, Jools."

"Thanks, sweetheart."

I hadn't expected a compliment from him. I'd finally stopped fretting over what he didn't say, because he showed his love through what he did for me—not by what he said. My sense of feeling emotionally disconnected, misunderstood, or resenting his lack of attention, had vanished.

Mark's willingness to listen to me chatter away about anything was priceless. And when he didn't speak, he must have a good reason. Or when he didn't indulge me with flattery the way JJ did, I was perfectly fine. A silent rule evolved between us; one that guaranteed I wouldn't push him to be more effusive. I knew that he went above and beyond for me, every day, and I was grateful.

"Thank you for everything," I whispered, leaning over to him. Mark kissed me on the lips. It wasn't only Nina and Girard that had something to celebrate. It was our time to revel in all that worked well between us. He was mine, and I was his, till death do us part. The cement that bound us was true love.

Later that evening, after watching us dance together, Valerie said "You've got gumption, kid."

"Thanks, Valerie. I tried very hard to say something to Nina straight from my heart."

"I wasn't referring to just your remarks."

I knew exactly what she meant.

Epilogue

A FEW MONTHS LATER, Mark and I received an invitation. The presence of our company was requested by Mrs. Webster Schuyler Ashton IV at the Royal International Polo Center. Webster was turning 90, and his wife, Frances, was throwing a huge birthday bash. Anyone who was anyone in Royal Coconut Beach would be there—meaning *him*. JJ. Frances' assistant asked us to cross-check our Addison list against hers, to be certain no one important was left off the Ashtons' guest list.

Sure enough, as I reviewed her list, the bold letters jumped out at me: AMBASSADOR AND MRS. JULIAN JORGE MENDOZA. These intense feelings that once were mine returned. *Stay strong, stay focused.*

I tried on five outfits, clothes flung all over. Each had its own distinct vibe. I decided to wear a pretty lace number, sweet and a little sexy. I knew there was a strong possibility that JJ would be there. We hadn't been in touch. I was afraid that seeing him might stir up old feelings. As I rehashed our lunch dates and walks together, I reminded myself that those were the fun times. But in an effort not to feel vulnerable, I also remembered that this wasn't the full scope of what a relationship really was.

Webster's party was indeed the A-list of all A-lists. Mark and I knew many people and chatted, sipped champagne, dined on foie gras, duck confit and petit fours. Looking around the room every now and then, I saw no sign of JJ.

Midway through the party, he arrived, with Cat by his side. Right away, they were surrounded by other guests. As I observed them, I locked my arm tightly in Mark's, grateful that he was there with me. My stomach fluttered from both nerves and excitement. From a distance, JJ was even more handsome than how I'd pictured him in my mind the past few months. His hair was slicked back, and his face glowed from a tan. His ivory sport jacket added to his debonair appearance.

After we finished conversing with another couple, Cat and JJ approached us. I felt a knot in my stomach. I started to do a quick mental comparison between Mark and JJ, but stopped myself; it was unfair. Mark was my lifelong partner, which included the good, the bad, and everything in-between. JJ and I exchanged cheek-kisses, and we introduced our spouses.

"JJ's on our development committee, Mark. He's been helpful introducing us to new donors. We really appreciate it, JJ," I said. "Thank you so much, Cat, for becoming a donor." I looked directly at her. "Yours and JJ's support of the Addison Center helped us meet our goals this year."

Cat was much prettier and slimmer in person than on the internet. Her ivory wrap dress contrasted well with her olive skin, and showed off her curves. She was wearing a lot of gold and diamond jewelry, and had jet-black hair. Her dark eye make-up was expertly applied.

"The Addison Center is a fabulous place for the community, and we're thrilled to support it," she said, in a warm, deep voice, her accent heavier than JJ's. "JJ mentioned you to me," she continued. "He's very impressed with the work you do there. I'm glad to meet you in person."

He talked to *her* about *me?*

"Thank you. That's very kind of you to say."

"It's nice to meet you both," Mark said. At that moment, someone tapped JJ on the shoulder, and he turned around.

"A pleasure to make your acquaintance," Cat said, as she turned away to see who wanted her husband's attention, leaving Mark and me alone.

"Another Prosecco for you?" he asked.

"You must have read my mind." We headed to the bar together.

The anticipation and angst of seeing JJ at the party did not match how uneventful it actually was, once I stood face to face with him. Seeing him, especially with his wife by his side, confirmed everything. There was no doubt that I had made the right decision. I was so much better off with Mark.

I knew it was fine to hold a special place in my heart for JJ. He was a spectacular man on so many levels. I would always be grateful for the role he'd played in my life, and most of all, how he opened my eyes to what was truly important to me, and what I valued most.

I finally understood what Elise meant when she said that it was a beautiful thing that a very special man had loved me. I wanted Mark to love me that way—and I discovered that he did. Mark and I had managed to find our way back to each other. The craving for a connection with JJ, along with all the ambiguity and emotional turbulence, was gone. That was because I treasured Mark and our marriage. Never again would I take for granted the incredible life that we had built together.

As Mark and I sipped champagne and mingled, I felt a sense of joy. There were so many things to be grateful for: Mark, my career—and last but not least, my great friends of the Royal Coconut Beach Lunch Club.

Acknowledgments

I owe an entire volume of gratitude to so many people, especially to Peter, my husband, who's remarkable on so many levels. I'm sorry that I sometimes ignored you during our walks around Palm Beach. I was too busy having real conversations with my imaginary characters or rambling incessantly about the latest plot knot. I'm beyond fortunate to have your love and unwavering support to get to the finish line. Your quick-witted humor is a big bonus. So are all the little things, such as lugging my laptop around several continents.

To my delightful daughters Rachel and Erica, two strong, independent women, who cheered me on as a writer. Ditto for Jeffrey and Christopher. Your precious little ones are the apple of my eye and make everything worthwhile.

To Mom and Dad, who, among their many wonderful qualities, understood the importance of a liberal arts education. I didn't fully appreciate this concept until I started writing this novel.

To darling Mark, Leslie and the guides who took us on exciting adventures in faraway locales. Thank you for listening to the ideas, scenes and chapters unfold, and encouraging me to keep going.

To Meridian Editions for giving this novel its wings, and to the incredible Meryl Moss Media Group team, with special gratitude to Meryl Moss and Gerri Silver. Your professionalism, creativity, dedication, and business acumen are second to none. You're truly a joy to work with.

To the Raymond F. Kravis Center for the Performing Arts for providing me with a magnificent career and serving as an inspiration for creative fiction writing.

To The Writers' Academy at the Kravis Center, its outstanding Pulitzer Prize-nominated instructor Julie Gilbert, and, my fellow authors for helping me discover my own writing voice.

To Leslie Wells, who pointed my plot in a solid direction, and helped finesse a sense of setting while keeping my characters in line. Special thanks to Joan Brookbank and Lisa Kitei for their early support of this novel. The same goes for Steve Matlin who insisted I had writing chops and reminded me to stay strong. I also appreciate Lois Cahall and the Palm Beach Book Festival for recognizing my work.

To my fairy godmother of the literary world, Susan Shapiro Barash, who believes women authors must support one another, and was indispensable in getting this novel published.

To my beta readers, and all those who were interested in hearing about this novel, I thank you for your feedback and insights. Your enthusiasm has been a great motivator.

A very special thanks to my friends. I am grateful that you constantly asked how my writing was going and often read my drafts. Your friendship during this journey and in life means more than you'll know. Don't be surprised to see elements of yourselves in the fabulous women who make up the Lunch Club.

DIANE BERGNER is vice president of Development at the Raymond F. Kravis Center for the Performing Arts in West Palm Beach, Florida. Before joining the Kravis Center, Bergner was an attorney in her native New York City, and the Director of Public Sector Career Services at Hofstra University School of Law, where she earned her Juris Doctor degree. As a Chartered Advisor in Philanthropy® she has served in leadership roles on several not-for-profit boards in Palm Beach County. She is a member of The Writers' Academy at the Kravis Center and was the runner-up in the Best Writer in Palm Beach County, hosted by the Palm Beach Book Festival. *Royal Coconut Beach Lunch Club* is her first novel.